My Name is Death

Alan Cass

authorHOUSE

AuthorHouse™ UK Ltd.
500 Avebury Boulevard
Central Milton Keynes, MK9 2BE
www.authorhouse.co.uk
Phone: 08001974150

© 2010 Alan Cass. All rights reserved.

No part of this book may be reproduced, stored in a retrieval system, or transmitted by any means without the written permission of the author.

First published by AuthorHouse   9/9/2010

ISBN: 978-1-4520-6762-9 (sc)

This book is printed on acid-free paper.

With loving memory, this work is dedicated in it's entirety to Sonja and Mary. Quite simply, two of the finest human beings to have ever lived. With clay you sculpt…with love you create. Thank you both for years of sacrifice and selflessness. I am everything I am because of you…

For Brian Carson and a life not lived…as strongly as ever before your memory remains…with love and respect, always…

Time travel's a myth?

So you have never heard a song that didn't instantly rewind the fabric of your mind by ten years? A song on your car radio that just happens to be the first song you made 'our' song with your precious departed wife? A song so deeply rooted in your heart that life simply wouldn't be the same without it. Just close your eyes and you're there, the warm afternoon sun shining on your face, the butterflies in your stomach as you uttered those immortal words. . . . Will you marry me? How beautiful she looked as you held her hands in yours, and seconds seemed like hours as she drew breath and said 'yes.'

Do you really believe time travel's a myth?

Chapter One

Sunday 1st November. 02 : 40

The roads of Washburn Springs were pretty much deserted now, it was cold, wet and late. The streetlights bounced their reflections off the wet roads like sunlight off a skyscraper.

'…please respond. Over.'

The radio hissed quietly as Officer Ray Kennedy cruised down Richmond Avenue, en route to Springwood Drive.

'Repeat, any units for disturbance at, one oh nine eight, please respond.'

He wished he *could* attend that disturbance, *anything* had to be better than this. Only the dry screech of the wiper blades reminded him it had finally stopped raining. He turned his cruiser slowly into Springwood Drive, and upon seeing many of the dwellings were each illuminated by either porch or flood lights of their own, he made the decision there and then to kill the headlights.

"Of all the nights," He whispered. "Halloween."

He glanced at a dwelling to his left to establish which side was odds, his guess was successful so he figured number sixty five, would be a little further down on his side.

"Here we go, Ray." He readied himself mentally and switched off the ignition, except for the gentle hum of his tyres on the wet road, he coasted the car in silence until his destination was beside him. A strange feeling engulfed him, not quite fear, not quite dread but considerably more than anticipation. His heart pounded as he gently pushed the brake and brought the car to rest. Sitting in silence for a moment, his attention was summoned without reason to the porch light above the front door, he was unsure why, but the courtesy light of sixty - five Springwood Drive had certainly spiked his interest. Checking his reflection in the rear view mirror, he ruffled his hand through his neatly trimmed fade, and stroked his ebony skin. "You're getting older, Ray." He whispered, fretting at the creases. "But at least you get the *chance*."

He gathered his thoughts before stepping out in to the cold night air, closing the car door gently with a *click*, rather than shut with a *slam*. Although the neighbouring houses were all beautifully well kept, and Washburn Springs was itself a middle to upper class suburb, he thought the large ornate gates were a little pretentious even for this road. The drive way was large and led to a double garage at the side of the house, although that was much further down and probably nearer the back garden. He noticed a patch of engine oil which, when illuminated by the porch light, created its own spectrum of vivid colours. His heart beat double time as he walked towards the door, and the light. He could almost *feel* the electrical surge powering through his body as he rang the doorbell, and waited anxiously. Sighing heavily, he watched as his breath misted over the patterned glass of the front door. *Mist is better than blood.* He thought. *Mist fades with the rising sun, blood remains forever, and stains…everything.* The hallway light came on, effectively ending his dalliance with the past, as once again he gathered his thoughts and watched as a shadowy figure began its descent down the curving staircase. The door swung open, immediately revealing a lady in a white night gown who, not five minutes previous, had obviously been fast asleep. He detected an angry mood about her which seemed to soften with every passing second between them.

"I'm sorry," She said. "I thought you were - doesn't matter." She pulled her gown tighter and instinctively folded her arms across her chest.

"Mrs Rose?" He removed his cap as he spoke and held it like a begging dish. "I'm officer Kennedy of Washburn State Police."

"Mmm hmm." She nodded nervously, the cruiser at the base of her driveway having now caught her eye.

"I wonder if I might step inside please?"

"Of course." She whispered, stepping back she allowed him into the hallway.

"Thank you." He closed the door behind himself, and turned to see her already positioned at the bottom of the stairs, she was clearly uneasy. He watched as she swept her greying hair from her eyes, and tucked it behind her ears.

"Mrs Rose, I have -"

"No." She said firmly, before running up the stairs and in to the darkness. "Wait."

"Ok." He said, carefully tuning his ears to the muffled voices above. "I hate this." He whispered, listening as a male's voice exclaimed '*The Police?*' He took a quick look around the large hallway and tried to get his bearings. There was a writing desk between doors, over which hung a framed portrait of two very handsome boys, twins in fact. The door to it's left appeared to lead to the sitting room, the other to the kitchen. They both quickly re emerged from the darkness.

"This is John," She said, leaning over the banister to address him. "My husband." She gestured to him as if he would be doing the talking from here on in.

"Is there a problem officer?" He asked, swooping down the stairs as if on tracks, whilst fastening his gown.

"Mr Rose could I -"

"Call me John."

Ray felt increasingly up tight and anxious with all the stalling. "John, could the three of us go somewhere to sit down please?" He pointed towards the lounge door, and did his best to ignore the portrait as he drew near to it. Ray allowed John to take the lead as they stepped into the lounge, and for Ray; the *unknown*. For Ray, this was the part he dreaded most, not only would a room full of happy smiling pictures *usually* stare right back at him, but so too would the wives, the husbands, or the parents he'd just dragged from their beds. This however, was not the case this time, the portrait he'd passed on the way in seemed to be it. The room was large and tasteful, with a white marble fire surround assuming centre stage, over which two large samurai swords were mounted on the wall. There was a dining table at the far side of the room, and six chairs surrounding it, no further pictures were required, the picture was firmly set in Ray's mind of the type of family he was about to destroy. John was stood expectantly beside the fire place, Mrs Rose was sitting on the couch, already using her gown's fleecy sleeve to catch her tears.

"I'm sorry." Ray said. "There's been an accident."

Saturday 31st October. 22 : 55. Halloween .

"Washburn state police. Lucy speaking."
"I'd like to report a car wreck, probably fatal."
"What's the location please Sir?"
"The Washburn link, under the bridge – it's gone right over."
"A car? Do you mean a car's gone over?"
"Yeah, straight through the fuckin' trees."
"Your name, please Sir."
Click.
"Hello, Sir?"

The Washburn link road, or *Valley Of Death* to the locals, due to the amount of fatal crashes on this particular stretch. Separating Washburn Springs from neighbouring Hail Wood springs, it is very dark and surrounded by woods on either side, there are no street lights – just 20 miles of trees and tarmac. The moonlight was pale and weak as it shone down, clipping the tops of the trees, but barely reaching the road below, which tonight had its *own* illumination, of the two tone strobe type. The mangled wreck of a Dodge Charger lay at the bottom of a steep embankment, with all manner of emergency services hurriedly surrounding it. With smoke still smouldering from its distorted black chassis, the stricken vehicle lay upside down with its hood submerged in a flowing stream, its wheels gently turning as the energy and life ebbed to nothing.

The shattered but somehow intact wind screen was pasted heavily with blood, as was the steering wheel and dash board. There were two male occupants inside, the driver's shoulder length dark hair was soaked through with his own blood, he remained harnessed in his bucket seat, and hung upside down, lifeless and still. He was dead.

The passenger seemed to have less visible injuries, he lay slumped on the ground, having made it halfway through the window space with fingers still embedded in the muddy bank.

Detective Joseph Vincelli, a large man with slicked back dark hair and a pot belly, stood at the foot of the bank side. He smoked what was left of his cigarette and discarded the butt to the cold night breeze. He looked down the embankment to see medics dragging free the body of the driver.

"This aint no accident." He said. His partner of only one month, Martin, stood beside him and listened. "They were rammed for sure."

"Why so sure?" Martin asked, running his hands through his shoulder length fair hair. He too figured this wasn't an accident, but simply wanted to find out the mechanics of Vincelli's mind. Vincelli looked at him, whilst throwing another cigarette in his mouth. "I just am!"

Martin was the younger of the two, mid thirties, and still considered new to this field, and while he had the highest level of respect for his new partner, he didn't care much for him, and it was clearly mutual.

"Make yourself useful kid," Vincelli said. "Go get me the flashlight from the car." He walked a few paces further up the road, moving away from the chaos that had begun behind the Police barriers, and left Martin to catch him up.

"Reporters have turned up!" Martin shouted after him, tailing him like a sulking child, flashlight in hand.

"That's fine." He whispered, accepting the flashlight from Martin. "It was only a matter of time." He spat his cigarette to the floor. "Anyway, you see these tyre tracks here kid?"

"Yeah."

"Then you know what we're dealing with." He walked up the road, carefully shining the beam down at the tarmac. "These tyre tracks here represent the point of impact, think of an aeroplane landing on a runway, the squeal of its tyres as it touches down. Now they gotta work pretty damn hard to catch up with its momentum." He quizzed him with his eyes just be sure he was taking it in. "Now that car down there, similar thing really. It's been coming down here doing what? Let's say sixty or seventy miles per hour, an then with a huge jolt from behind it's accelerated to seventy or eighty, the rear wheels have raised from the ground for a split second, and when they've hit the tarmac again, it's floundered and spun out of control."

Vincelli walked further away, leaving Martin to study the scorched tyre tracks.

"Now my guess is," He shouted back to Martin, his sentences becoming shorter as he struggled for breath. "The pursuers were driving something big." He walked a few paces further and then stopped. Martin watched him crouch down and pick something from the road; he held it close while shining the light on it. "They were driving something big alright."

"What have you found?"

"It's a G.M.C. badge," He replied. "Most likely from a pick up truck or large van." He glanced down the embankment at the mangled wreckage. "That aint no G.M.C down there, is it?"

"No."

"I wanna know who these kids are." He whispered, concealing the emblem in his rain coat. "I'll get it traced."

"You do that." He said. "And get that information to me." He waved him off and contemplated his descent. "That means now."

He scaled the treacherous bank side carefully, mindful of the many individuals present, were he to fall. Finally reaching the bottom he made his way to the upturned Charger, and brushed the mud from his hands. He looked at the young female medic as she knelt beside the vehicle's window space, she was holding the hand of it's one remaining occupant, who was clearly unconscious.

"Have we got any names yet?" He asked. "Has he spoke?"

"No." She answered. "But I think they're twins." She turned to look at him. "Oh…"

"Sorry to disappoint." He smiled.

"You're interested in this then?"

"Oh yes." He replied sharply. "How is he?"

"Not good." She answered. "They're getting ready to move him in a moment."

"And the other one?"

"They cut him free first," She whispered. "He's gone."

"It's a long way down." He said, glancing to the road high above them. "He's lucky."

"Lucky?" She asked, clearly wishing he'd leave. "He is *not* lucky."

"Touchy." He sniggered. "You know him or something?"

"I do now." She replied, turning away from him.

He strolled away from the car, glancing just once at the half dead occupant as he left. He selected his steps carefully as he retrieved his ringing cell phone from his pocket.

"What have you got?" He asked, glancing up to see Martin at the edge of the road.

"Twins," He answered. "Identical twins aged twenty - seven."

"Names?"

"Chad and Brandon Rose."

"They're local right?"

"Washburn Springs."

"Do they live alone or with their parents?"

"It's a fairly affluent area." He replied. "I'd guess with their parents."

"There's no point delaying things." He said, sighing hard. "Get a car out to them."

Sunday 1st November. 03:00.

"I'm so sorry." Ray said. "I promise you we will endeavour to find whoever is responsible." He sat silently and looked at them both, breaking his glance to occasionally look at the floor. In the twenty minutes he'd known them, twenty years he'd aged them. Pain carved around their features like broken china, as John sat with a very firm grip around his wife. She closed her eyes tightly as her shoulders heaved up and down.

"Not my boys," She whispered. "Not my boys."

Ray peered around the room, he stared at the two samurai swords mounted over the fire place, and found himself wondering why they would choose to have them there, were they purely ornate? Or were they live? In their lacquered black sheaths, they were beautiful. Of that he was certain.

"I know this a terrible time for you both," He said. "We still need somebody to identify the deceased."

John stared across the room at him. "Why do you say that?" He asked. "Deceased?"

Ray felt a rush of panic, words had failed him before but this would be a first, in this situation.

"I'm sorry, I truly am." He answered. "I didn't mean to sound clinical, it's just that -"

"It's not how you said it." He pulled his arm from around her shoulder and stood up. He walked over to the fire place and rested against it.

"Officer we know who is dead." He snapped. "It's not what you might call a conundrum."

Ray stared up at him, wanting to but resisting the urge to tug at his collar. He guessed what John was about to say. With all the confusion of the night's events, not one of the many uniforms or detectives had had the foresight to check.

"Only Brandon could drive."

"I'm sorry."

"Don't be," He answered. "You weren't to know." He walked back to the sofa and sat down next to his wife. "We raised them and sometimes we didn't know one from the other." He clasped his hands together and rubbed them as if cold. "Do you think you could understand that?" He asked. "Not to know one of your sons from the other, both of them tall and well built, similarly to you in fact, with not a single identifying feature to tell them apart."

Ray stared back, meeting Johns gaze head on. "Yeah, I think I could." He smiled. His eyes began to wonder the room before settling on the dining table, he was reminded of the times he had owned such a table. That was all before Nancy, his wife of nine years had left him, left him for a better place. That at least was what he told himself on a daily basis, though all the words in the world couldn't take away the pain he'd felt since that day. *Wrong time, wrong place.*

"We want to go and see Chad now." John said.

"Of course," Ray answered. "I'll arrange it right away."

Chapter Two

<u>Monday 2nd November.</u>

The door opened and came to a well timed stop against a spring on the wall, the faded light of the room almost reached in to the corridor outside. The lights flickered on under protest, maybe five or ten seconds passed before they finally illuminated the dingy interview room. The room was bland, with plain grey walls and a small barred window that was too high to see out of, and too small to get out of. There was a steel table with a bench on either side of it, all were bolted to the floor. A stale presence floated in the air that almost begged the question:

"Do you smoke?" Vincelli asked, throwing a bundle of files down on the table.

"Yeah."

"I'll get you an ashtray. You want a coffee or something?" He threw his rain coat down on the bench and spread it out.

"Ok."

"Take a seat young man," He said, lowering himself slowly on to the bench. "Martin can you take care of that please?"

"Of course." He replied, quickly exiting the room.

"He wont be long." Vincelli whispered, listening to the door creak shut. He proceeded to leaf through his various files, not once glancing across the table to his nervous companion.

"It aint no bar stool is it son?" He asked, annoyed by his fidgeting.

"No, Sir." He laughed. "It's hard!"

"Do you mind?" He asked, producing a large cigar from his breast pocket.

"No, hey you're the cop." He answered, observing the passion with which he peeled it open. "Sir, I wouldn't slide off a pair of panties the way you're undressing that."

Vincelli allowed himself a rare smile as he chewed the tip and lit it. "You shouldn't be putting them on in the first place."

He pulled two audio cassettes from his jacket pocket. "Now Danny," He said, finally looking at him. "You're here of your own free will, you're *not* under arrest - but I have to tell you that our conversation will be recorded, is that clear?"

Danny nodded.

"Three coffees!" Martin said, nudging the door open with his foot. He placed a small tray on the table between them, containing the coffees, and a small foil ashtray.

"Thanks, Martin." Vincelli said, taking the cups from it and placing them around the table. "Shall we begin?" He asked, sliding the cassettes into the deck.

"Just one minute please," Martin said opening the door once more and disappearing through it. Vincelli tossed a packet of cigarettes across the table to Danny.

"Help yourself, kid."

"Sorry." Martin shouted, quickly re emerging with a small, classroom style chair. "I'll use this," He said, placing it down beside the table. "I can't sit on that." He sat down and crossed his legs.

"Are we ready?" Vincelli asked, noticing Martin's white socks.

"Go ahead."

"Thank you." He whispered, placing his glasses on.

Vincelli started the recorder and glanced at his watch, then looked over his shoulder to the clock above the door.

"Ok, Monday the second of November, the time is Twelve P.M." He savored his cigar. "Persons present, myself – detective Joseph Vincelli and detective Martin Lewis." He blew a trail of smoke across the table and looked at Danny over the rims of his glasses.

"State your name for the purpose of the tape please."

"Danny Golding," He replied, leaning in to the machine. "Aged twenty six." He looked at Vincelli, nervously seeking his approval.

"Danny, your name is all we need right now," He said smiling.

14

"And please for heavens sake sit back in your chair, the machine will pick you up just fine from there."

Opening his notebook, Martin perched it carefully on his knee and jotted down the time, before nodding for Vincelli to commence.

"May I address you as Danny?"

"Yeah that's fine." He answered, stretching his long legs underneath the table.

"Ok then *Danny*, this isn't interrogation so any time you wish to take a break, it'll be ok." He leaned back on the bench and stretched out his arm along it. "Ok then, tell us in your own words, *exactly* what took place on the night of Saturday the thirty - first of October, or Halloween if you'd prefer."

Danny sat silent for a moment, not sure who to look at since they were both looking in his direction.

"Well it all just went nuts," He said, turning his attention to Vincelli, now that Martin had begun writing in his pad. "It was supposed to be wild, that's what we do, but things just really got out of hand."

"In what way?" Vincelli asked.

Danny leaned forward and pressed his ample torso against the table, for a moment there is silence, interrupted only by the gentle hum of the extractor fan.

"Carry on, Danny." Martin urged, tapping his arm. Vincelli sat quietly, unmoved.

"There were a few of us there, at my folks place."

"How many would you call a few Danny?" Vincelli asked, spinning a silver pen between his fingers.

"I don't know really," He answered. "More than twenty but less than thirty I guess." He took a sip from his coffee and set it back down with a visibly shaking hand. "Look," He said, pulling at his blonde hair. "I think I'm gonna need some representation. If I'm gonna give you the facts about what happened, I may -"

"Danny," Vincelli said. "Danny…Danny. I wondered how far we'd get before you said that."

"What?"

"Representation." He answered. "Why do you suddenly want representation?"

"Because I -"

"That wasn't meant as a question Danny, so don't you interrupt me again."

Danny sat with his head bowed and his arms folded tightly across his chest.

"Hey!" Vincelli shouted. "You came to me, not the other way around."

"Yeah, so." He answered, still looking to the floor.

"So why don't you give yourself a break here?" He paused for a moment, staring at him. "You'll have all the time you need for representation, if I arrest you!"

"What?" He asked, looking at Vincelli. "But I haven't done anything!"

Vincelli sat silently, sifting through the files laid out neatly in front of him.

"What's that?" Danny asked.

He selected the file placed on top and tossed it across the table. Danny looked at the file in front of him.

"What's this?" He asked.

"This is history repeating itself." Vincelli answered, grinning. He watched as Danny turned the first page.

"My brother." He said quietly. He closed the file shut and tossed it back to Vincelli.

"Yes, Danny." Vincelli replied. "Your brother." He opened the file for himself, squinting through his glasses. "Geoff Golding, two years your senior." He quickly glanced up at Danny. "That's right isn't it?"

"Yeah."

"It says here, he was a football player, something of a star." He flipped to the back of the file and carefully removed a photograph of him. "A good looking guy too! A real hit with the ladies, I'll bet." He showed the picture to Martin. "Good looking kid, wouldn't you say?"

"He's a pretty boy." Martin whispered. "Not good." He shook his head.

Vincelli passed the picture to Danny. "Of course Danny, those good looks won't be doing him any favours now he's behind bars. Will they?"

"I guess not." He answered.

"You guess not?" He asked, laughing. "Have you any idea what happens to pretty boys in prison?" His face turned serious. "They bitch up or get *fucked* up."

"What does that mean?" He asked, reading the graffiti etched into the table.

"I'll leave it to your imagination." He replied, closing the file gently. " But tell me, what was your brother sent to prison for?"

"Drug dealing." He spoke quietly as his eyes began to lubricate.

"Do *you* want to go to prison?"

"No." He answered, wiping a tear from his face. "Course I don't."

"Were *you* dealing drugs at your party?"

"No."

"Did *you* murder, rape or beat anyone to within an inch of their lives at your party?"

"No."

"Then why are *you* so keen to get representation?".

"I'm scared." He muttered, selecting a cigarette from the pack and lighting it.

"This is a murder investigation Danny," He said. "So I suggest you stop wasting my time, and tell me why you're here."

"My brother didn't even take drugs," Danny said. "Ok, he played around with steroids, but just enough to enhance his body for the game y' know, they all do," He looked at Vincelli. "But he didn't touch all that other shit." He rested the cigarette in the ashtray.

"I know about your brother, Danny." He replied. "I've read his file and I remember the case."

"No, you don't know!" He said, slamming his palms on the table. "You know what you want to know. My brother was a victim."

"What does that mean?" Vincelli asked.

"It means he was innocent."

"Danny I know the system pretty well," He said, loosening his tie a little. "Guilty men, nine times from ten, will plead not guilty, they got nothing to lose, but your brother admitted guilt! Now why the hell would he do that if he were in fact, innocent?"

"I'm sorry." A stream of tears rushed down his pale complexion. "I'm scared. They're gonna get me, it's only a matter of time before they realise what I did."

"Who are you scared of?" Vincelli asked. He leaned back again, placing his pen on the table. He looked at him, although a grown man in his own right, Danny was no more than a kid in his eyes, his mood softened.

"Who are you scared of Danny?" He asked. "You came here for a reason so what is it?" Danny didn't reply, he just sat staring at the tape machine.

"Danny." He whispered, leaning over the table to him. He sighed heavily and delivered a cursory glance to Martin, before again looking at his watch. "Interview terminated at…Twelve – Fifteen." He leaned his heavy frame across the table to reach the machine and with a reassuring 'click' the interview was *officially* over.

"Ok, Danny," He said, getting somewhere near comfortable again on the bench. "The *interview* is terminated, however - it's my belief that you came here for a reason and I would still like to know what that is." Martin looked at Vincelli, glancing at him indirectly from the corner of his mothers blue eyes. He threw his notebook and pen on to the table, guessing that whatever transpired now was strictly off the record.

Danny looked around the small room, and felt smaller with every passing minute as if the very walls were closing in around him.

"Ok, I don't want my name linked to this conversation."

"The interview is *over* Danny." Vincelli said, pointing his pen at the recorder.

"There's this boss man, no one knows who this guy is, and I mean *no one*. He goes by the name of Miles, no last name or nick name, just Miles." He paused. "Have you heard of him?" He asked, though judging by their expressions, he knew they hadn't.

"No." Vincelli said finally. "Carry on."

"Who is he Danny?" Martin asked. "Tell us."

"He's your local Doctor Feelgood! He sells everything!"

"Like what?" Vincelli asked.

"Drugs, guns, cigarettes." Danny replied. "Anything you want, even sex, all for the right price of course."

"Ok."

"He has guys working for him, lots of guys."

"I thought you said no one had seen him."

"You ever heard of the miracle called, a *phone*?" Danny asked, smiling. "You never see or speak to him directly, it's like a chain of command. There are only two, maybe three guys who see him directly, and then you got his enforcers, these are the guys that do the dirty work."

"For instance?" Vincelli asked.

"Everything from collecting his debts, to putting the frighteners on you."

Vincelli stood up and walked over to the door, leaning on it for a moment he stretched his legs. "So what do you mean when you say '*the frighteners*'?"

"What do you think I mean?"

"Tell me."

"They come and find you, and if you don't give them what they want they -"

"kill you?"

"No, they don't come and kill you. That's probably why you guys haven't heard of them. They come and shoot you up man." He lit another cigarette and took a sip from his coffee.

Both Vincelli and Martin looked to one another.

"Explain please." Vincelli said, sitting down again. "With detail."

"Well it's like this," Danny said. "If you weren't a junkie before, you are now, and now you're theirs."

"And then?"

"This is top grade heroin," Danny replied. "Heroin *extreme*, there aint no coming off this stuff, so you gotta have it. Do you understand?" He asked. "You *gotta* have it and you'll do anything to get it, and as far as I know there's only one place you're gonna get it."

"So they end up paying their debts by purchasing this stuff right?" Martin asked.

"Not quite." He answered. "You see money alone won't get you this stuff, they make you work for it, do their dirty deeds if you get me."

"So in effect," Vincelli said. "They're recruiting you."

"Correct." He answered. "And they…are the *enforcers*. They'll do, quite literally anything they're told to do…as long as they get heroin *extreme* in their veins."

"So they're basically an army of zombies." Vincelli said. "What's to stop one of them deciding they want out?"

"They don't decide *anything*." He replied, smoking his cigarette tenderly. "But if any *did* decide they wanted out…they'd be murdered."

"By one of their own, presumably?"

"Yes."

"I'm confused." Vincelli said. "You said they don't kill anyone?"

"They administer a lethal dose," He replied. "It doesn't take full effect for a few hours so they're normally at home in their beds by then." Danny leaned forward to Vincelli, staring him straight in the eye. "How many cases of accidental death have you had?" He whispered. "Or misadventure? Or whatever you guys are calling it now."

"Ok." He said, almost impressed with Danny's observation. "Suppose you're right?"

"Well that's where my brother comes in," He said. "He didn't realise who these guys were, he was just buying his steroids from them for his own personal use, but then he saw a chance to make a fast buck."

"Selling them to his team mates?" Vincelli asked. "Or *dealing* as it's commonly referred."

"Yeah." He answered. "But only for a little while."

"Why?" Vincelli asked. "What soured the relationship?"

"He wasn't seeing any of the money, so he told them he was calling it a day."

"They didn't like that I assume?"

"What do you think?" He asked. "He was taking maximum risk for minimal return! It must've been his lucky day though, coz you guys had been doing a sting on the football team –" He paused. "Unfortunately for him though, he was caught in possession of not just steroids, but their heroin too." He laughed. "So not *that* lucky."

"So we gave him his way out." Vincelli said.

"Yeah, at least going to prison kept him alive."

"Ok, Danny." He said, observing the time. "Your brother will walk free one day, so what's to prevent them getting him then?"

"My brother is trying to get *me* to sell drugs now." He said. "I've said no to him, but now these guys are coming round to my house. They won't leave me alone. I'm scared, not just for me, I'm scared for Geoff too."

"What's changed then Danny?" Vincelli asked. "Why now?"

"Well I think you know as well as I do, that he's just as vulnerable in prison, if not more so. Somebody is making him do it, and now they've got their hooks in me." He sat crying, the tracks of his tears glistened under the fluorescent lights above like a slug trail in the sunshine.

"What can we do from our end then Danny?" Vincelli asked. "I'm gonna need names, dates and locations if we're gonna put something together."

"I don't know." He shook his head slowly and scrubbed his tears away as fast as they fell.

"There must be something?"

"You can't help me," He whispered. "They'll know I've been here."

"Nobody knows you're here." Vincelli said. "What are you saying?"

"As soon as that door opens, who knows?" The three of them sat silently for a moment.

"I hear what you're saying." He said, studying his trembling form like a pundit. "That's why I have to do this." He pressed the *record* button, and the three of them watched as those spools began to turn. "Tell me about the events of Halloween last."

Danny relented and took a deep breath.

"We were stood on my porch having a smoke, Chad, Brandon and myself that is. My folks were outta town and man, the place was a mess. There was shit all over, but hey! You can clean mess up right? That's pretty much my only rule, smoke outside, oh and don't be fucking on my mothers bed! The house keeper can worry about all the other shit."

"Naturally." Vincelli said shrugging.

"Anyway," He added. "A truck came up the driveway, a pick up truck y'know?"

"I know."

"It's a gravel driveway so we could hear it coming before we saw it; it was kicking up all sorts of shit behind it. It had deer stalker lights fitted to it, you know the type?"

"Tell us anyway Danny?" Vincelli said, pointing to the machine.

"Four moveable lights mounted on top of the cab."

"Go on."

"I knew who it was," He said. "I had an idea they'd be coming. There were two guys in the front, and three guys riding in the back holding on to the roll cage." He paused. "I thought that was strange you know, coz it was an extended cab and yet they were riding in the back when they could've been inside." He nodded knowingly. "Of course it wouldn't be long until I realised why." He smiled. "Anyway, they looked kinda funny from a distance but I couldn't make out why. As the truck got nearer, I could see the lights on the cab swivelling in *my* direction, even though the *headlights* were shining into the trees."

"Ok." Vincelli whispered, staring at him intently with his hands clasped together.

"Then I heard my name being shouted, Danny! Danny! Danny! Come 'ere Danny! Brandon asked me who they were and what they wanted. I guess he knew they were trouble. I was about to walk over but he slammed his arm across my chest, it felt like I was walking through a fucking turnstile man. He was a strong guy, his training I guess."

"What did he do?" Vincelli asked.

"What did he do?" Danny repeated, laughing. "Jesus, what didn't he fucking do. He was in to some serious Bruce Lee shit, I don't know what he called it to be honest, Jeet - something or other." He wiped a tear from his eye. "He kept himself fit for his two other hobbies, women and skydiving."

"Women and skydiving?" Vincelli laughed aloud. "Both deadly pursuits if you ask me."

"He used to say he couldn't make up his mind which he preferred, jumping out of one, or *into* the other." He smiled.

Vincelli noticed Danny's enthusiasm, as he counted on his fingers all of Brandon's pass times and past times.

"He told me to wait for them to come to me, but I didn't want him or Chad having any part in it, I had gotten myself into it, so I had to get myself out of it. Right?"

"That's very noble of you Danny." Vincelli said. "If my memory serves me correctly, your brother is the one who got you in to the mess you're in."

Danny nodded.

"Yeah. Well they both had some make up on, y' know? I don't mean like fucking transvestites or some shit, I mean white face paint. *Hello!* it was Halloween, but dude I gotta tell you, I was whiter than they were by then, my knees were knocking together for Christ's sake. I told them to wait there and that I wouldn't be long."

"So you walked to the truck alone?" He asked. "leaving the twins on your porch?"

"Yeah." He answered, lifting his cup but finding it empty. "When I got there I could tell why they looked weird, it was because they all had masks on - clear masks. I think they're used after operations on burns or something. They weren't *Halloween* masks anyway, that much I know."

"Ok."

"When I got to the truck, the driver - who had this big dick grin on his face, asked me if I'd thought any more about the boss's offer."

"To do what?" Vincelli asked, again pointing to the recorder.

"To deal drugs for them."

"Continue."

"Anyway, he flicked what was left of a cigarette at my face; they all found that funny but when the driver guy turned serious, so did they. I told him the answer was no," Danny leaned in to the recorder, whilst grinning at Vincelli. "*I wont deal drugs for you.*"

Vincelli shook his head and rolled his eyes to the ceiling.

"The three guys in the back jumped out, one of them had a crow bar and since there were no doors that needed forcing, I drew my own conclusions on what it was for. Then before I know what's happening the driver guy has grabbed my collar and pulled me half way through his fucking window. He says, 'You're gonna wish you hadn't said that, Danny.' Then I felt a blinding pain as the bar slammed in to the back of my thighs." He paused. "It hurt. I got bruises to show for it."

"Show me." Vincelli said, placing his pen silently on the table.

"Now?" Danny asked, looking to them both nervously.

"Now."

Danny stood up from behind the table and walked to the far wall; he pulled down his jeans and allowed them to fall to his ankles.

"Can you come a bit closer please?" Vincelli asked. "We're not gonna touch you, don't worry!"

Danny shuffled backwards a few steps, until close enough for comfort.

"I feel like a fucking lap dancer!" He said. "Are we done yet?"

Vincelli stared at the bruising on Danny's thighs, which had almost blackened completely in some areas.

"Well you don't look like any lap dancer I ever saw young man." Vincelli answered. "Ok pull your pants up please."

Danny pulled his jeans up, smiling nervously as he buttoned them.

"Bet the last time you saw skinny legs like these they were hanging from a nest, right?" He slid back behind the table and toyed with his empty cup.

"So I'm on the floor, my legs just gave way under me, partly from the pain and partly because I was terrified. I'm looking up at the guy and he's got the bar in the air like he's ready to smash me. I closed my eyes, but that blow never landed." He wiped a tear from his eye with his sleeve. "I opened my eyes, I thought maybe he was *waiting* for me to look, but he wasn't standing *over* me any more, he was lying *next* to me, face down in the gravel with blood pouring from his mouth. I didn't even know what had happened."

"Well, Danny," Vincelli said. "Hindsight is a beautiful thing, so what *had* happened?"

"It was Brandon." He answered, stubbing out a cigarette he didn't remember lighting. "He and Chad had come over to help, but it was Brandon who decked the guy."

"How do you know that?" Vincelli asked. "You were on the floor with your eyes closed right?"

"I *know*." He answered. "Chad was no wimp, but he was nothing compared to Brandon. A couple of the others had turned their attention to him now, but that didn't bother him, they couldn't get near him, couldn't even land a shot on him, but he was picking them off one by one. I've never seen that kind of confidence before, he *knew* they couldn't hurt him."

"They *killed* him Danny." Vincelli said. "That's true isn't it?"

"I heard a car revving heavily," He said, ignoring the question. "It was coming from the side of my house, that's where all the cars were parked. I could even hear the gravel spitting up from its spinning tyres. There was shouting and screaming going on by the house; my other friends had come out to see what the commotion was about."

"Did they get involved at all?"

"No way!" He said, laughing. "They're worse than I am. Other than my parties, the only socialising they do is in chat rooms."

"Ok, Danny. Keep going please."

"Well the car I could hear was Brandon's." He said. "Chad was revving it up. I was trying to get up, I just wanted to get out of there but my legs were numb, I just couldn't do it."

"What then?"

"Chad was coming in the car," He answered. "Really fucking fast too! He drove the car at a couple of them, headlights blazing and he would've hit them too but they jumped out of the way. The engine was so loud, it was just *roaring*, the tyres were spinning constantly with gravel just flying all over. The driver's side door flew open, and I looked up to see Chad was climbing over into the passenger seat, then I saw Brandon jump in and drive the car in my direction. I think they wanted me to get in but there wasn't time, they had to go."

"Why wasn't there time for you to get in?" Vincelli asked.

"I was being a pussy, instead of getting up and getting in, I stayed on the floor. One of the guys had ran to the car; he smashed one of the headlights with the crow bar, and if he'd smashed the other one - they wouldn't have got fifty feet on the Washburn. They had to go."

Danny stared blankly across the room. "I thought it was over then, for me, I thought they would go after the twins. I thought wrong. That prick grabs me by my fucking hair and drags me in to the cab. He says: 'This is what happens to people who fuck with us.' Or something along those lines. Anyway, they started after them, *we* started after them, and I don't know what they had in that thing but it could move. When we made it out I didn't even expect to see the twin's taillights in the distance, I mean, a car like theirs on a long road? Forget it! They should've been gone, but they were only a little further down the road, swerving all over, even braking at times."

"Do you think they were giving you a chance to catch them?" Vincelli asked.

"I don't think so." He replied. "Once we caught up with them it was going fine. They wanted to get away believe me, but they couldn't now, not even in *that* car. We were right behind them now, and the guys in the back were shining those lights down at them and throwing missiles at the car, I think they were beer cans, but we were going way too fast by then for me to be sure."

"How fast were you going?" Vincelli asked.

"Nearly one hundred and ten miles per hour," He answered. Like his face, his voice was sullen as he recounted the final moments of Brandon's life. "I looked at the dial. I thought that was the idea you see, scare them, dazzle them, and just frighten them! But the truck, even at that speed suddenly lurched forward and rammed the back of their car; I could hear their tyres screeching on the tarmac each time we hit. I could see Brandon in the driver's seat, he looked scared, real scared. The lights were shining straight in his face; he put his hands over his eyes to shield them." He paused for a moment. "Then we saw the bridge, it was coming up fast." He laughed. "There's a sign that says 'Please drive slowly.' Ha! There's irony if you want it. We passed that at a ton, we'd slowed down a little but only because the twins did, I thought if they could just make it over that bridge they'd be ok as we'd be in Washburn. We were driving next to them on the left, we were in the on coming lane but luckily nothing was coming, or unluckily - however you choose to view it. The embankment was on their right, and it's really fucking steep by the bridge."

Danny seemed agitated, leaning forward on the table and staring through the wall behind Vincelli.

"We were right next to Brandon, on the drivers' side. I looked at him and more than anything I just wanted to say sorry, but he wouldn't look at me, well he *couldn't* look at me, too busy driving, right? Concentrating on the road ahead, what was left of it anyway. The two lanes were merging in to one and somebody was gonna have to back off, or punch it big time to go over the bridge, I thought Brandon would back off, but he didn't and I knew this maniac next to me wouldn't."

Danny fell silent; he shook his head and stared through tired eyes. "I saw Brandon, he turned to look at me just seconds before impact, he looked different."

"Different?" Vincelli asked. "How so?"

"Scary."

Both Vincelli and Martin glanced to one another, before looking back to Danny, although he continued to stare across the room, like a startled deer trapped in the headlights about to end its life.

"Do you mean, *scared*?" Vincelli asked.

"No" He spoke in a whisper. "I mean, *scary*." Tears trickled down his flushed features. "Then all at once we struck the car," He said. "That's how fast it happened. The silence was the worst part, as the car went over the embankment, it just lifted off on a cushion of air and disappeared from view."

"What was the reaction from these guys then?"

"Silence," He replied. "Even the guys in the back, they were all silent."

Theirs eyes met across the table as an unspoken conversation raged on between them.

You shittin' me kid?
No, I swear it's the truth!
You expect me to believe this?
I swear it's the truth!
You better not be wasting my time.
I swear – it's the truth.

"So after that, what happened then?" Vincelli asked.

"They stopped the truck," He answered. "They dragged me out

the cab and walked me over to the edge, and we all just stood there looking at the car. The front end was on fire, it was upside down and all I could do was watch the wheels turning. They all just walked back to their truck, but the driver turns to me and says, 'You just remember that, Danny. *We*, did that."

"What do you think he meant by that?"

"I know exactly what he meant; he meant I was just as guilty as any one of them, guilty by association right? I didn't know what to do; after they left I ran across the bridge to a pay phone and called you guys. That's it."

Vincelli concluded the interview and turned off the cassette recorder. He leaned forward as the bulk of his wide shoulders strained within the ill fitting, cheap three piece he wore.

"Well thank you for your time, Danny," He spoke slowly, as he folded his glasses and slid them in to his pocket. "That…*tale*, was most enlightening. However I can promise you, that is certainly not…*it*." He stood up and walked to the door, he gestured Danny to follow him as he opened it.

"Don't go too far." He said. "I'll be calling on you very soon."

"You know where I'll be." He said, sliding through the door.

"And where's that?"

"Home sweet home." He said, winking. "Home sweet home." He turned and walked down the hallway leaving Vincelli at the door.

Chapter Three

<u>Sunday 20th December.</u>

Twenty – one, Donald's way; Ray's house. Small and in need of desperate *modernisation*, its front lawn was overgrown and listing lifelessly to one side. The paint was chipped and peeling from the glass panelled black front door, while the brass knocker was discoloured and pale like an ageing antique. His living room contained little by way of furniture, he sat alone in a reclining armchair in just a T – shirt and pants, holding a beer in one hand and a half smoked cigarette in the other. He stared blankly at the television, upon which sat Ray's only festive reminder, a five inch plastic Christmas tree in a small red pot, the sound was turned down low as the end credits of an old Doris Day movie rolled by. There was a small wooden table next to his armchair, so fragile in state that anything more than a small table lamp could certainly finish it off. On the floor next to it there sat a tall glass vase containing roses and lillie's, looking wilted and lifeless in discoloured water.

His beloved German Sheppard, King, sat curled beside his feet and twitched with every move, voluntary or involuntary, that Ray made.

"Come here." He shouted suddenly, tapping his thigh. "Come on." He smiled as without hesitation the dog was upon him, licking his face.

"You want a cigarette?" He asked, smiling. "You're too young big guy!" He ruffled his hand up and down the dog's back, before sending him down once more.

His attention was drawn to a picture hanging above the fire place, a wedding picture - his own wedding picture. The version of himself in the picture, was not terribly dissimilar to the version sat in the arm chair, not considering it was taken almost a decade past. He was thinner now...but Nancy.

"Who dies on their wedding anniversary?" He asked himself, forcing back tears.

He closed his eyes tightly, and was taken immediately and without question, to a time not so long ago when things were... different.

It had been a wonderful day, the best of both worlds in fact. Graced with glowing rays of sunshine and a crisp December breeze. It had been their fifth wedding anniversary, and due to a broken alternator and the usual cash flow issues, a cosy day and *night* by the fire had been planned. As the day drew nearer, he'd thought of everything to give her the *perfect* day. White wine, chocolates, and of course there were flowers; lilies, and a newly released copy of Calamity Jane. He'd thought it the perfect gift.

"*I'll quit tomorrow!*" She'd said, dashing through and slamming their glass front door.

"*Back in a minute...*"

It had been Noon, and although December, the sun couldn't have been brighter. Once alone he'd used what he thought would be five minutes wisely, he arranged her lilies in a tall glass vase, her new video sat ready and waiting in the machine, and the velvet tones of Frank Sinatra filled the air. A sudden yet frantic knock on the door had brought him running faster than normal.

"*You forget your keys?*" The words had passed his lips by the time he'd noticed it wasn't Nancy hitting the glass, it was a police officer. Approaching the door he noticed what looked like smears of blood on the frosted glass panel, and as the officer knocked again he saw the bloody hands, and heard his muffled cries.

"*Ray!*" He shouted, crying freely as he banged on the glass. "*I'm so sorry, Ray!*"

Opening the door in a trance like state, he recognised the officer instantly as one he'd worked with recently, Steve Perkins had blood on his hands.

"*Where is she, Steve?*" He asked, already out of the door and running down his drive.

"*What did you do, Steve?*" He shouted, running as fast as he could to the end of their road, already commotion was visible as he turned the corner on to the adjacent main road.

Steve trailed far behind, eventually stopping and collapsing to his knees as he watched Ray turn the corner at the end of the road, he would see for himself now, what he had done.

"*She just ran out Ray, she just ran out.*"

Four years later and alone with his memories, alone with his beer and cigarettes, and alone with despair. He only began smoking after her burial, short of putting a gun to his head it was one sure fire way of seeing her again, *sooner*. It occurred to him then that bad news is just a part of every day life, like a stealth bomber under cover of darkness, there's no way of knowing when or where that bomb will drop, but rest assured it surely will.

"You would've liked it baby." He said, watching as the credits ceased. "God only knows why. But I sure wish you'd got to see it." He tossed a cigarette in his mouth. *Another three minutes closer to the checkout counter*, he thought. Ray's colleagues believed he was back on board, coping a little better these days with his loss, and with no *true* friends to speak of, who would know otherwise? They didn't notice his severed limbs. *Officer down* had only one meaning, not two.

"If only I'd just," He whispered. *Oh, I'm sorry now.* He thought.

Monday 21st December.

He was awoken suddenly and precisely at 8:00 am, he had three bedrooms upstairs but hadn't spent a night in any of them, especially the one they had shared. The marital bed's white sheets remained as ruffled and unmade as the day she died, instead he whiles away the lonely nights in his tatty recliner, with his beer and cigarettes, and of course, King. His bones creaked like an old rusty hinge as he dragged himself up. The radio greeted him in much the same way it did every morning, the cheery sound of C.W.S breakfast hour. 'First on the scene come rain or shine, bringing *you* the news bang on time.'

Monday mornings always brought out the worst, for without exception they were dedicated to the upkeep of Nancy's grave. He turned up the radio as he desperately tried to drown out his own thoughts. *Don't go today. You've made it long enough, no one would blame you. Fuck…they might not even make the connection! Hey, why did Ray kill himself? Don't know, he seemed fine to me! Fuck them all! Just fuck them all! They don't care about you.*

"No work today," He muttered, padding slowly through what once had been a dining room. "Just me and you big guy." The sun was hazy but strong as it shone through the patio doors and warmed the carpet beneath his bare feet. He opened the door wide to enjoy the fresh breeze. "Go on," He said, looking down as the dog returned his gaze. "Go pee." He watched as the dog leapt excitedly through the open space, before looking to the sky. There were storm clouds gathering high above, reluctant to take shape like an unfinished portrait. Ray watched with a smile as King charged wildly around the garden, through the long grass, behind the collapsed shed and over an old engine block, stopping occasionally to place his own unique stamp where the rain may have weakened it, a distant rumble of thunder sent the dog running back through the doors.

"It's supposed to be nice today." Ray said, pulling the door shut. "Then again…" His mind travelled back to that fateful afternoon; in a cruel twist of circumstance he saw the connection all at once as the clouds moved in for the kill, like silent assassins cloaked in darkness. *'Aint no sunshine,'* played on the radio as the rain began to fall. Stepping into the kitchen he quickly noticed the floor beneath his feet was distinctly sticky, and strangely yellow in colour.

"Son of a bitch!" He shouted, but decided to cut the animal some slack as he'd not bothered with the evening walk for the last couple of nights. From a scattering of empty beer bottles he managed to pluck a mug to safety from the chaos that was his drainer. They were not deposit bottles, nor were they being saved, and they certainly were not headed for a bottle bank, he had his own right outside.

"You gotta sort this shit out Ray!" He told himself. "Neighbours are gonna talk if you don't." With a cup of tea in hand, he sat back down to ponder the day ahead, wondering how he might minimise the living souls he'd have to interact with, the flowers, beer and cigarettes could all be purchased under the one roof, so all going to plan – the checkout assistant should be it.

'…found dead yesterday.'

He hadn't heard the morning news begin, but listened to the end with growing interest.
'Detectives had wished to question him further, in relation to an incident which took place several weeks ago, leaving one local man dead and another in critical condition. Police have refused to name the deceased at this stage, now sports…'
Ray turned down the volume, hoping his mind would fill the relevant gaps. He was aware of only one witness coming forward after the crash, a young kid. He'd heard his name mentioned a few times at the station.
"Danny." He said. "Is it you?" The question floated buoyantly in the air for a moment, he didn't know him, but hoped it wasn't him all the same.
"Another one," He said. "Just *another* open and shut case, I'll bet." Lighting a cigarette, he once more walked to the patio doors and sat down on the warm carpet.
"Junkies, crack – heads and speed freaks." He said. "The same as it ever was, but why am I the only guy who finds it all a bit too easy?"

First Brandon, He thought. *Chad's right there behind him, and now this kid? And that's besides the five or six drugs related deaths in the last year.*
"Open and shut cases." He whispered.

'And finally, the weather. You better baton down the hatches folks, coz ah tell ya…there's a storm – a – *coming*!'

Chapter Four

10 : 00 am

Ray sat alone in his old beat up Chrysler. It had faded black front wings, which he'd purchased from a local breakers yard and fitted himself, and what remained of the original panelling was a rusty shade of gold. The rain beat rhythmically on the tin roof like a steel drum as he clutched his flowers and smoked a cigarette. He observed the quiet serenity before him with delight, eight foot angels stood high over some plots, staring down in silent prayer, while others looked to the sky with open arms. Some were distinctly gothic, beautiful, with that special *something* emanating from them, like concrete charisma. They each told their own story of mans obsession with vanity, and status, the purest of sins. The urge to out class thy brother, even in death. The crisp, folding green – if nothing else assured material wealth, and *status*. His mind travelled as the cigarette burned to the stub.

Am I a lesser man because my money jingles and yours folds? Is this really all it comes down to at checkout time?

"You're the lucky ones," He whispered. "*Now*, you're equal."
His thoughts were interrupted by a car pulling up next to him, the gravel shifted under its weight as it came to rest. It was a gleaming black Mercedes saloon, with blacked out windows, chrome wheel arches and eighteen inch alloy wheels. He jammed the stub into his ashtray and stepped out into the rain, he shielded the flowers from the wind as he struggled to lock it, although he wasn't sure why he

bothered anymore. He glanced again at the Mercedes and watched as it's door swung open, to his surprise it wasn't a pimp that alighted, but a young man in a rain coat, which he hastily pulled high against his face.

"Afternoon," Ray said. "That's a mighty nice -"

"Is it?" He answered sharply. Three audible arming tones drowned out any further conversation between them, he took of at speed into the cemetery, not once looking back.

"New money!" Ray said. "New money for sure!" He began his own journey into the grave yard, though still unable to take his eyes off the man. He was no longer covering his blonde hair under the rain coat, and yet it rained still, neither was he carrying any flowers, just that Mercedes key fob. Ray slowly walked after him, up to now at least they were travelling in the same direction, which was good, in a few more seconds Ray knew he would have him made, if he could only see the grave he stopped at. He made a small bet with himself that it would be a grand one, his father's grave, his mother's grave – both perhaps. He'd used his inheritance to buy a nice stone, do the right thing.

Thanks for making me rich you guys, you had to die sometime right? Well thank god it was sooner rather than later, I mean what good is money when you're old. Anyway, ciao baby!

He laughed to himself and watched carefully through squinted eyes as the man branched off from the footpath, moments later he saw he wasn't wrong. The man stood awkwardly next to a large black marble head stone, more concerned with everything around him than the grave before him. Ray saw what appeared to be the picture of an elderly man within an oval window attached to the grave. He continued on, tilting his body in to the wind.

"Afternoon." The man shouted. Ray turned to see him casually waving at him, he gave a quick wave in response, noticing a sharp suit under that rain coat, a bit baggy though; looked like it could've held two of him in there. Ray thought his behaviour odd, like he was just waiting for a moment alone. However, Nancy's grave would be in sight soon enough, and he figured she deserved his fullest attention.

"Forget it Ray." He told himself. "Day off today, just forget it." But he couldn't forget it; his suspicions raged on, the cop in him didn't want the day off, even if *he* did.

He turned to see the man crouching over a smaller grave, the one opposite his own. He was pulling flowers from the urn, bunching up the ones he wanted and tossing the ones he didn't. Ray watched as he threw a greeting card in the air, the wind taking it quickly out of sight. He wanted to shout to the man, give him a piece of his mind, but couldn't find the words, instead he took the final few feet to Nancy's grave. Her grave was simple, a black marble head stone with gold lettering and four urns. He crouched down in front of her and assembled the flowers evenly in to the urns, sometimes he would spread them upon the grave but figured that given the wind they wouldn't last long on this occasion.

"Hey, Nancy," He said, gently kissing his wedding band. "Happy anniversary. That's nine years and counting." Tears ran invisibly down his rain soaked face. "Nine years…five years with you and four without." He stared over the mass of head stones that surrounded him, he peered up over Nancy's to see further down the hill towards the car park. The other guy was leaving, seemed to be in a hurry too, tripping over himself to get a footing in the saturated earth.

"You'll never believe what I saw coming up here babes," He said, his eyes still transfixed on the man. "This guy down here, he stole flowers from another grave and placed them on his own." He smiled. "Can you believe that shit?" His attention was caught by a third – party presence, somebody *else* was down there, a man, in the tree lined edging – just watching. Ray strained his eyes trying to pull focus in the rain, but could at least see his black hair was long, and tied back in a pony tail. Ray watched as he walked to the black marble grave and reached down for the flowers.

"I don't believe this," He muttered. "Does any one but me actually buy their flowers?" Hiding himself behind Nancy's grave, he watched on as the stranger walked with the flowers and returned them to their original plot. He knelt down before the grave and carefully arranged them back into the urn.

"You saw him," He whispered. "You saw the son of a bitch."

He felt somewhat intrusive, watching as the long haired stranger appeared to stroke the lettering on the stone. He looked tired and weak as he stared up to the blackening sky, and for one foolish moment, Ray thought it looked right back as it exploded with light like a flickering neon sign.

"Listen baby," He said hastily. "I gotta go, I'll be back soon I promise." He planted a kiss on his palm before pressing it firmly against her stone, allowing his final parting words to pass undisturbed through his mind.

"Happy anniversary." He said, pulling himself to his feet. He walked to the gravel pathway and began his return to the car, not once looking over his shoulder but glancing occasionally in to the tree lining to where *he* had stood in wait, although he now appeared to have gone. As he drew nearer the grave in question, his attention switched suddenly to a fluttering sound above him, blowing wildly – yet purposely towards him, was a greeting card.

Follow me, Ray, He thought to himself. *You have to see this, please believe me.*

The ground beneath his feet was soft once more, the card lowered gradually until within easy reach. "Gotcha!" He shouted, pinching it firmly like a fifty – dollar bill.

"Brandon," He whispered, reading from it. "My *god.*" He smiled in disbelief.

I told you, now finish what you started and come with me, you'll see.

He set his sights firmly on the grave the man had stolen from, and began his uneasy walk toward it, he stared at the blurry gold lettering until the inscription was clear.

"Our son, Brandon Rose." He said, reading from it. "Shit!" He laughed, feeling dumb struck, he looked again at the card that had brought him "Of all the damn graves," He shook his head. "And this card?"

I told you. He thought.

"I was just thinking about you this morning, kid." He whispered. He looked around nervously, though was quite satisfied he was alone. He held the card out for inspection, before placing it within the flowers. "I think this belongs to you," He said, reading the verse. "It's from your parents and I think they'd want you to keep it."

"Thank you." The voice was weak, almost out done by the gusts whipping up from the ground, but it was there.

Ray turned to see a young man, mid twenties – he guessed, stood under a large elm that over shadowed Brandon's grave. He wore black combat trousers and a sweat shirt which was also black. His hair was long and dark, pulled back tightly into a pony tail.

"Chad?" Ray asked, slightly surprised. "Is that you?" No answer came, he just stood shivering, his muscular arms were folded tightly against his lean frame.

"When did you even get out?" He took a slow step towards him, his right hand out stretched. "Sorry kid." He said. "I'm Ray."

"Please don't touch me." He whispered. "I'm broken."

"You're -"

"I fell to earth," He said. "Battered and *broken*, but not dead." He gazed down at the grave marked Brandon Rose. "That's when I discovered what I am." He said. With trembling hands he reached out to Ray.

"You need saving." He whispered, grabbing Ray's arms lightly, before letting go once more and stumbling backwards to the elm. "And one lesson at a time, you *will* be."

"How do you know my -"

"I am *Salvation*." He said. "*Your* salvation…And I'll fix you."

"I'm sorry." Ray answered, backing off a little. "You know, I don't think you should be out here." He observed the young man with growing concern. "You're so pale."

"I couldn't find the greeting card." He said. "Thank you for returning it."

Ray glanced down at the flowers and to the card within them.

"Don't mention it." He shook his head and laughed nervously, feeling the conversation had reached a natural conclusion he looked for the exit. "Listen I gotta -"

"It begins today." The dark haired stranger said, speaking much clearer now. "Nikki Farrell's gonna make the headlines tomorrow. Find another way home."

Unsure of a suitable response to such a seemingly random remark, Ray glanced over his shoulder and saw his Chrysler in the car park, he turned back to exchange a parting gesture but needn't have worried, *he* was no longer there.

On the short drive home the roads were clear, clearer than normal in fact, so the tail backs that greeted him on Route 5 westbound, took him some what by surprise. Unable to back up and turn around he quickly found himself hemmed in from all angles. There was a rail road crossing much further down the road, sometimes a moderate queue would form when an express was passing through, maybe that was it, Ray thought. Guessing he'd have to sit this one out he lit a cigarette and turned up the radio. A strong thud against his window lifted him from a day dream he didn't realise he was in, he opened his eyes wide and quickly brushed ash from his lap with one hand, whilst winding down the window with his other.

"We're trying to back some cars up!" The voice shouted "There's been an incident at the crossing so you won't be going that way any time soon." It was Vincelli.

"Hey, Joe!" He shouted, bringing him running back. "What's going on up there?"

"Ray," He shouted, trying desperately to hold his slicked back hair in place. "Didn't realise it was you." He leaned through the window. "We got a car down there, it's been shunted into the path of a train. It's a real fuckin' mess."

"I'll bet it is!"

"The girl in the car responsible says her brakes failed." He laughed. "Personally I think that's a pile of shit, first thing I noticed was her make up all over the place in the passenger foot well." He quickly lit a cigarette whilst still half way through Ray's window. "Dumb fuckin blonde if you ask me." He pulled out of the window and stood straight once more.

"You got any witnesses then?" He asked, attempting to peer around the car in front.

"Yeah." He replied. "A whole bunch, but none of them can tell us anything that doesn't start with, 'Well I heard this bang -'" He winced in pain and held his hands against his lower back. "The train driver said he could see the Mercedes, said it was stationary at the barrier, then without attempting to brake or alter course her Volvo comes flying down, rear ends the poor fucker, he never stood a chance."

"Wait." Ray pulled off his seat belt and opened the car door. "Mercedes?" He asked, stepping outside.

"Yes, Ray." He replied. "Big black one to be precise." He watched as Ray started down the queue, he closed his door for him.

He passed many cars, the occupants of some were arguing, some were shouting, all were getting restless but he heard or saw nothing, except the rear end of *that* Mercedes. It was the guy from the graveyard and he knew it, seeing him would merely be confirmation. As he stood next to it, what was left of it, it did indeed confirm what he already knew. It was him.

"Holy shit, friend." He said. It didn't look right somehow, the whole front end had been completely sheared off by the train, so much so that the base of the windscreen was at rest directly against the might of the huge steel wheels. He looked again into the cabin, the occupant was pale, *extremely* pale. As a Police officer he had seen many roadside fatalities, but none like this. Half an hour ago this guy had the tan of a Californian life guard, now he looked like he'd been dead for a week.

Peering down into the foot well he quickly realised why the man lacked so much colour, his legs were sliced off. With only two bloody stumps remaining below the waist line, he began to imagine how the man would've responded to seeing a vehicle approaching him at speed, knowing full well it was gonna push him into the path of a fast moving train. Stamp on the brakes, or brace himself for impact, either way, his legs would've been outstretched as the train sliced through the vehicle like tin foil.

"Oh Jesus." He said, covering his mouth. He guessed the man's legs were probably somewhere along the tracks with the rest of the debris. In the distance he heard the approaching sirens, the medics were finally arriving.

"About ten pints too late for you." He said, looking into the mans eyes, they were frozen wide open with panic and his face was twisted with fear. He turned to walk away but something caught his eye, something that just shouldn't have been there, it was a greeting card placed under the lapel of the mans jacket. He reached in and removed it, glancing around as he did so, Vincelli was on his way over now accompanied by the two medics, but they were in no hurry.

"You have got to be fuckin' kidding me." He said. Feeling his own legs weaken under him, he turned and rested his body weight against the car; seeing Vincelli was almost upon him now, he nervously concealed the card inside his own pocket.

"Thanks Ray." Vincelli said, shouting over the chaos. "I hope you found what you were looking for?"

"I just thought I knew the guy that's all." He said. "Which reminds me, when did that kid come out of his coma?"

"What kid?"

"The twin, Chad is it?" He waved his finger at Vincelli. "The other one died."

He looked blankly at Ray, amazed at the question and the credibility of his source.

"No Ray," He said. "The kid's still in the coma, he's pretty much dead except for those machines keeping him alive." He studied Ray's response. "I can tell by your face that's not the answer you were hoping for." He laughed. "Who told you he'd come up?"

"No body." He replied. "I just thought I'd heard someone say it that's all."

Vincelli nodded

"One other thing," Ray said. "Was that Danny I heard about on the radio this morning?"

"Yeah." He answered. "You know I really wanted to help that kid?"

"I'm sure you did everything you could Joe." He looked again at the lifeless form slumped in the drivers seat. "It strikes me that some people are just way past redemption."

"Maybe."

"Anyway, looks like your back up is arriving." He patted him on the shoulder and turned away. "I'll see you tomorrow, Joe. I'm gonna sit this one out."

Colorado General 13:45.

Otherwise known as St Augustine's accident and emergency, day or night it sees no real respite. Martha Ridge was the plump receptionist sat barking orders from behind the desk and her philosophy was a simple one, 'Nature of the beast.' Or, depending on who she was addressing, 'Nature of the beast, *sugar!*'

"It's down the hall, left after the first corridor!" She shouted. "The signs go on from there."

"I'm sorry to bother you," Ray whispered, already a little intimidated by her presence.

"I'll be right with you." She replied. "I said left!" She indicated left. "I swear to god, a grown man who doesn't even know which way left is!" She dusted down her dark blue blouse and straightened her skirt.

"Ok, so who's next?" She asked, looking at Ray. "What can I do for you *sugar?*" She smiled and once again straightened her blouse, pulling it down a little to reveal a more than ample cleavage.

"Do you wanna get that?" Ray asked, pointing to the ringing telephone.

"Persons here present." She replied. "What can I do for you?"

"Mrs Ridge, I'm a Police officer -"

"Miss."

"Excuse me?"

"*Miss* Ridge." She smiled and looked him up and down. "Anyway, Martha will do, I've been called worse."

"Martha," He whispered. "Would it be possible for me to see a patient by the name of Chad Rose?" He smiled nervously. "He was admitted nearly three weeks ago."

"I don't see that being a problem," She replied, still looking him over whilst rattling away on her keyboard. "Is he a friend?"

"No Ma'am"

"I'm guessing he's not a relative?" She laughed. "What with him being white an all!"

Ray laughed, he could feel himself relaxing in her presence. "No, he's not a relative either."

"I'm so sorry sugar," She said, still laughing. "I should be more careful, not everyone has your sense of humour."

"Our sense of humour." He said. "You're the first person to make me laugh this week."

"Well that's what I'm here for." She glanced at her screen. "Ok sweet cheeks, he's in intensive care, could I just trouble you for some identification?"

"Of course." He reached into his pocket and pulled out his wallet, but before he could open it she had reached across the desk and taken it from him.

"Ray Kennedy," She said, examining every minor detail.

"That's me."

"Well your wife is one lucky woman!" She gave him back the wallet.

"Oh I'm not -" He stopped himself; staring at the wedding ring he still wore. "Yes." He whispered. "Yes…she is."

"Aint you the modest one?" She asked, leaning over the desk towards him, her cleavage about ready to burst from her blouse. "Well you are one fine chocolate covered man, so I don't blame you!" They both laughed. "Go down the hall, *all the way*, take the elevator to floor nine and there's another reception desk you'll have to check in at."

"Thank you Martha." He put his wallet away and began down the long corridor, while Martha watched his progress.

"Damn fine ass, that one." She whispered, again, straightening her blouse and dusting down her skirt. "Ok, who's next?"

The elevator ride to floor nine was a slow one, he stood alone and watched beads of light appear then disappear through the gap in the doors. Seven, eight and finally the doors opened giving way to a large reception area, much nicer than the last one, almost homely. On his left he saw, as promised by Martha, a reception desk. Behind it stood a petite girl, probably no more than twenty – five. Her hair was dark and tied back,

"Ray?" She asked, laughing.

"Either your security is the best in the business or -"

"Martha." She said. "I think you have a fan."

He looked at the clock hung on the wall behind her desk, it was now almost two in the afternoon.

"Chad has a visitor in with him right now, Ray" She said. "It's his girlfriend, Julianne, but she's never here long on Mondays."

"No problem." He answered. He looked down the corridor to his right, there were several doors on each side, all closed.

"Which one is he in?"

"Room six." She answered.

"Do many people come by to see him?" He glanced briefly at her name tag, although he now knew her name was Emma, he chose not to use it. There was just something false about using a person's name just because it's displayed in front of you, a little too familiar perhaps, maybe next time he thought.

"It's getting less and less by the week," She replied, hopping on her stool. "It's just his parents and girlfriend really."

Ray turned to the sofa in the furthest corner away from view. "I'll be over there." He said. "If you could just give me the signal when she's coming that'd be great."

She nodded and smiled. "No problem."

It was three o' clock and Ray had almost talked himself into leaving, when finally he heard the creak of a door opening, he couldn't see *which* door, but right on cue the young receptionist good to her word gave him the signal, she coughed heavily twice. The footsteps drew nearer as he tried to remain unnoticed, by grabbing the first magazine he could lay his hands on. As Julianne passed by, she didn't fail to notice the strapping black guy with hands like shovels, reading today's woman. He held it high and proud, casting her the smallest glance over the page. She was waiting for the elevator. She wore faded ripped jeans and a lemon T - shirt, her long red hair was tied neatly into a pony tail. Ray observed she was far too thin for her height, but then that was understandable he figured. He heard her whisper goodbye to Emma as she stepped in to the elevator, he watched as the doors closed behind her.

"You can go through now." Emma said. "Only if you're finished reading, *obviously*."

"Thanks." He waved the magazine at her. "I just mastered the perfect lemon sponge."

As he walked down the corridor his footsteps echoed like gun shots in the distance.

Nobody walks into gun fire, Ray. He thought.

"What are you doing?" He asked himself. "Just turn back, what'll it solve?" He wanted to turn back, but he *needed* to keep going. He saw door number six, it was the next one on the left.

come on in. He thought. *Step right up. You'll want to see this, you need to see this. Come to me.*

He reached for the handle and turned it, the latch clicked as he pushed the door slowly open.

"Please let there be a difference." He said. "Please god." He stepped in and closed the door behind him. Upon turning around his attention was firstly drawn to vast array of machinery, all doing their own unique task to keep this young man alive and monitor his vital signs.

"So you're Chad." He whispered, although he still hadn't actually looked at his face. There were flowers on both sides of the bed, they caught his eye. They were a beautiful assortment though he had no idea what they were, except the lilies. He stood motionless at the foot of the bed, allowing his eyes to travel slowly up the man that lay within it, he struggled with the memory of his chance meeting in the cemetery. Chad's chest was bare except for the electro magnetic pads attached to him.

"Please let there be a difference." He closed his eyes tightly and readied himself. He took hold of the bed frame and clutched it tightly as he opened his eyes.

"Oh my god." He said. "How did you do that?" He closed his eyes again and clutched even tighter. It was him, the muscular frame, those good looks which were the same now as in the stormy cemetery, he even had the same long dark hair only now it flowed neatly against his pillow as opposed to being tied back. He walked to the seat at the side of Chad's bed and slumped down into it. He sat silently and gazed upon Chad's seemingly lifeless being.

"You're not a ghost." He said. "So how in gods name did you do that?" He spoke quietly, much like he did at Nancy's graveside. There was always a part of him that worried someone might hear him, hear the personal thoughts he had to speak whilst kneeling before her headstone. His thoughts were interrupted by a gentle tap on the door; he turned around to see a man standing in the doorway.

"Hi." He said. "I can leave you alone for a short while but visiting hours are over."

"No, it's ok." Ray replied. "I was curious as to how he was coming along."

"Are you a police officer?"

"Yes." He replied. "I'm Ray." He walked to the door to greet the man.

"Do you mind if I come in, Ray?"

"No," He smiled, offering his hand. "Don't be silly.

"I'm Mark." He shook Ray's hand firmly and closed the door. He was bespectacled and young, probably a little under thirty with a kind face and short spiked fair hair.

"Are you a doctor, Mark?"

"Not yet." He answered, moving towards Chad's bedside. "Nurse." He smiled and returned Ray's stare. "I know what you're thinking, I get that a lot."

"No, not at all." He lied, a rush of embarrassment swept through him. "I just wasn't sure if you were training or already qualified." He stood clear to allow Mark free and easy access around his patient.

"Just doing a couple of checks," He removed the clipboard from Chad's bed and plucked a pen from his trouser pocket and signed the bottom of it. "Then, I'll be - on - my - way." He hung it back in place. "Hey, you know we had some excitement here earlier."

"Really?" He feigned interest, in the hope that Mark wouldn't ask the question he was currently asking himself. 'Why am I here?'

"Yeah." He stopped writing. "Increased brain activity." He looked about the room nervously, especially at Chad. "Shit, that's a fucking understatement if you ask me." He moved closer to Ray who by now was not so much *appearing* interested as *actually* interested. "It went off the chart, Ray."

"So what does that mean?"

He leaned in closer as if sharing some nasty secret. "It means this one's awake." He glanced again at Chad. "Everything you say, *he* can hear." They both stood at the foot of Chad's bed, each taking their turn to look at him. "I mean, they always say talk to coma patients coz there's a good chance they can hear you." He pointed his pen to Chad. "But this one, this one's listening for sure."

"Why so sure?" Ray asked. "Did he move or anything?"

"Nothing neck down." He answered. "There were some R. E. M's, but that's not uncommon."

"R. E. M's?"

"Rapid eye movement, Ray." He cradled the clipboard tightly to his chest like a father would his newborn. "When we enter a dream state it's usually accompanied by these involuntary eye movements, we all do it. It depends largely on how powerful your dream is I guess."

"So you think he was dreaming?" He asked, unsure whether to be unnerved or relieved.

"Oh yes." He laughed gently. "Without doubt."

Ray divided his attention carefully between Mark and Chad, unable to discharge the foolish notion that not only could Chad probably hear them, but that he was somehow watching them too. "What time was that, Mark?"

"Noon time I guess." He held out his hand once more and Ray instinctively shook it. "It was nice to meet you, Ray." He headed for the door, opened it and was almost through it.

"One last thing," Ray enquired. "What do you think he was dreaming?" He walked to the door on his tip toes. "I mean, do you think he was having a flash back? Reliving the trauma of his accident or something?"

"That's any body's guess." He answered. "Digging up bones for all I know."

"Yeah." Ray laughed nervously at the thought. "Digging up bones."

"Take care." Mark closed the door behind himself.

Digging up bones, he thought. "You may not have been at the graveyard, kid, but somebody sure as hell was. He walked to the foot of Chad's bed and picked up the clipboard for inspection, none of it meant a dime to him but he hoped to find Mark's signature on the relevant page, he couldn't so returned it to his bed. He walked slowly around the bed and sat down next to him, committing his face as best he could to memory. He wanted to speak to him but couldn't figure how, and knowing he was listening made it all the more difficult. It was one thing knowing that most of his colleagues thought him a sorry excuse of a man, but for a complete stranger, who happened to be in a *coma* to pick up on it, was another.

"Well you're no ghost." He said, finally. "You're flesh and blood just like me." He held his head in his hands and gazed at Chad. "*Can you hear me?*" He asked. "But more importantly, can I hear *you?*" He stood up and walked for the door. "You take care kid."

I knew you'd like it Ray. We'll see each other very soon. He thought.

Chapter Five

<u>Wednesday 6th January.</u>

The telephone had rang continuously for nearly five minutes, Vincelli made a point of ignoring it though with limited success.

Fucking asshole, he thought. "If I haven't answered in one minute, then I'm busy." He muttered to himself. "If I haven't answered in five - then I'm *still* fucking busy!" His voice ascended in temper and he longed to pick it up and share his thoughts with him or her. He sat at his desk which was organised chaos at the best of times, but now the chaos had been pushed to edges to make way for a decent working surface. Spread evenly in the newly created space were seven files, laid out neatly with the next overlapping the previous. They were unsolved murders, with the most recent at the top. Next to these were a further seven files, these were suicides, or *apparent* suicides as he referred to them since all the victims were remarkably similar in life, and death. His interview with Danny and his subsequent demise had brought them to the forefront of his attention, especially as Danny was now number seven.

It was approaching ten in the morning when a gentle tap on the door broke his concentration. Ray stood in the doorway, carrying with him as usual his battered holdall.

"Joe." He announced cheerfully. "You got any news on the Volvo yet?"

"Come in, Ray." He waved him in. "Take a seat a minute."

"You gonna answer that?" Ray asked, slumping down in the plastic chair opposite him.

"No." He looked across the table at Ray, his hands clasped together tightly in muted frustration. "You remember some of these people, right?" He pushed the pile of suicides towards Ray, and opened a couple of them to reveal mug shot pictures.

"Yeah," He answered, glancing briefly at them. "They look familiar."

Vincelli leaned back in his seat, took off his glasses and rubbed at his temples. "I'm gonna have another look at these." He sighed. "Something just doesn't compute."

"Well they were all users weren't they?"

"Almost all, yes."

"Case closed." He looked at the phone then back to Vincelli. "Have you got something in mind?"

"Do you know how many houses are for sale in my street, Ray?" He asked. "Seven." He rested his hands on the files. "Do you know why?" He tapped gently on them. "Murder." He pointed to the suicides. " And lets not forget them, suicides or not, they're indicative of a bigger problem."

"Drugs." Ray said.

"Seven houses represents seven families who no longer feel safe." He ran his fingers lightly over the files. "Do you know how many there are here?" He asked. "Seven." he smiled and pushed them aside. "That represents seven people who didn't feel safe either, well they're dead now."

"You can't save everybody, Joe." He said, and for the first time in as long as he'd known him, he saw a flicker of emotion in his eyes. "Some people just can't be saved."

"Well that kid would've been a good start."

"Danny?" Ray asked.

"Yeah." He replied. "Danny."

"Danny killed himself, Joe." He seemed a little frustrated. "People die. Some people get hit by cars, some get cancer." He stared harshly at him. "Others choose to tie ropes around their necks and jump."

"Just because he had a rope around his neck *doesn't* make it suicide." He gathered all his files together to form one pile in front of him. He lit a cigarette and offered the pack to Ray.

"No thanks."

"So," He said, inhaling deep enough he took the word with him. "The Volvo was clean. No defects, at least not pre impact anyway." He laughed. "That girl was ugly as shit, I mean she *needed* make up, probably not while gunning it at eighty - six, though."

"Eighty - six?"

"Yeah." He answered. " The needle stuck on impact."

Ray shook his head and smirked. "You gotta love Volvo's."

"Oh," He said. "This is the best part." He rested his cigarette in the ashtray. "She saved this for the interview, but apparently, someone was in the car with her, and this *someone*, did not start the journey with her."

"She said that?" Ray asked, not certain of his meaning.

"Yeah." He nodded. "She said he appeared in the back seat, gazing at her in her rear view mirror, and told her to buckle up."

"Buckle up?" He asked, his mind raced with the possibilities. "Anything else?"

"Yeah," Vincelli answered, he gazed at the burning tip of his cigarette. "She said something that I thought was a little strange, but she wouldn't be pressed on it, she just kept saying she didn't know what it meant."

"Which was?"

"She said, that he had leaned through the space between the two front seats, and in her words, 'gently pulled back my hair and whispered in my ear.'" He paused to have the final long draw, before stubbing out the cigarette. "He whispered to her that he was her *salvation*."

"What the hell does that mean?" Ray asked. He glanced out of the window to his right, he couldn't see much from his chair but could hear the street noise from down below.

"I'm not sure," Vincelli replied. "She was hysterical, she said herself that she wasn't sure what she'd seen, only that she thought he had long, dark hair, and that he was soaking wet."

"That's really -" An unexpected day dream stopped his speech in it's tracks. *Find another way home.* He recalled

"Ray," Vincelli urged. "You ok?"

Ray shook his head and opened his eyes wide. " -weird."

"You want weird?" Vincelli asked. "I'll give you weird. The rear, drivers side passenger door on her car, was wide open." He smiled.

"Some witnesses on the scene confirmed that it flung open on impact, but no one was there."

Ray nodded. "Do you believe in outside influences?" He asked, still staring outside.

"Not really," He answered. "But my wife does, she listens to them all the time."

Ray lifted himself from his chair and picked up his holdall. "You better answer that phone, Joe." He said. "Might be important." He turned and walked out of the office, listening as the door closed slowly behind him. The phone finally stopped ringing, he could hear Vincelli's voice trailing off into the distance as he walked.

He headed up a flight of stairs, the walls were panelled with dark oak cladding all the way up. On the wall every four steps or so were portraits of officers, young and old, killed in the line of duty. There were six in all, accompanied by a polished brass plaque that read simply - 'Never Forget.' Through the door at the top was a locker area with three wooden benches in the middle of the room. He threw his holdall on a bench and sat down next to it, he opened it up and was about to search for his travel mug when he heard steps approaching, he wasn't surprised to see Vincelli standing in the doorway.

"You're coming with me." He said, smiling. Ray knew that smile, some good news perhaps, he wondered.

"I just got off the phone with Danny's Mother, she said she's found an envelope with my name on it." He held out his hand palm up and raised it. "Let's go get it."

The two of them sat in silence, with Ray driving and Vincelli staring into the distance. They drove up the Washburn link road, and even from some way off the floral tributes were clearly visible, it was a mass of flowers and notes in document wallets pinned to the trees. Eerily, the skid marks were also *still* visible on the tarmac, they scorched their way off the road and through where the flowers lay. As they drove past it both of them glanced at the bouquets left behind.

"I think we're gonna lose some sleep on this one." Ray said, he stared in his rear view and watched as it faded into the distance.

"You, maybe." He answered. "I don't sleep any how, my back sees to that."

"Well if you lost some weight," He pointed to his ample gut. "You wouldn't have so much of it to support."

"Just a little further up on the right, Ray." He said, ignoring him completely and pointing to a clearing in the trees. "Just here, that's the entrance."

Ray signalled in and turned the car on to what became a gravel driveway, lined by what looked like forests on either side.

"How the other half live." Ray whispered, slowing down so as not to kick up the gravel from under the tyres. Vincelli lit what was his third cigarette since leaving the station, he sat deep in his own thoughts and once again ignored him completely. Ray stopped the car suddenly in true gravel crunching fashion, although they weren't yet half way into the grounds.

"Why have you stopped?"

"What was that man's name?" Ray asked, reaching into his pocket for his notebook. "The man in the Mercedes."

"Nikki Farrell." He replied. "Why?"

"So, *do* you believe in outside influences?" As he spoke he pulled an elastic band from around his tatty notebook.

"What the fuck is it with you, Ray?" He asked, clearly agitated. "If you got something on your mind then say it."

He slowly opened it up, careful not to let it's loose pages fall free. "I saw that man in the cemetery, probably a half hour before died. He was visiting a grave not to far away from Nancy's and I happened to see him remove flowers from one grave, and place them on the one he was visiting."

Vincelli nodded. "So in your quest for karma you had him killed." He laughed. "Case closed, I'd have done the same thing."

"Just listen, Joe." He said.

"Then get to the point will you?" He pointed down towards the house. "I've got a possible lead waiting for me in there."

"He left in a hurry, I mean a *real* hurry." He closed his notebook after retrieving a small card from within it. "Something or some*one* scared him, he took off running and I saw someone just standing there - by the grave, just watching him run."

"Someone saw him take the flowers?"

"Yeah." He whispered. "I just thought it was some kid, I watched him clear as day place the flowers back on the rightful plot. The weather turned pretty quick after that so I thought to hell with this I'm getting out of here." He spoke so quietly that Vincelli had to lean in to hear him clearly. "I think it was Brandon." He said, cringing as the words passed his lips. "I *thought* it was Chad at first, but then… well you know." He paused momentarily sensing Vincelli's concern. "Look I know it wasn't." He said quickly, raising his hand between them as though he were swearing on a bible. "I just *thought* it was."

"Right," Vincelli said. "Well just be careful what you're *thinking* Ray, coz thoughts like that'll land you in the nut house."

"Thing is," Ray added. "There was a card in the flowers, the guy had taken it out and tossed it away. I thought no more about it until I was passing by on my way out." He held the card blank side up, rubbing it between his fingers as he spoke. "It was fluttering in the wind, I didn't see it right away but I heard it, I looked up and there it was, above me." He shook his head. "That's weird, right?" He asked, looking at Vincelli, who in turn sat looking at the card in Ray's hand.

"I just reached up and grabbed it." Ray waved the card, though still hadn't revealed it.

"Just show me the card, Ray." He pleaded.

"This card is from Brandon's grave." He passed it to Vincelli. "The *flowers* were from Brandon's grave." He laughed to himself. "Joe, he was there," He gritted his teeth. "I don't know how that's even possible, but he was there."

"No." Vincelli answered, surveying the card with little or no interest.

"I didn't even know what he looked like, I had to go to the hospital to see his twin just to be sure!"

He calmly handed the card back to Ray, though his actions disguised his demeanor with limited success.

"You knew what he looked like, Ray." He said, staring straight ahead toward the house. "You've seen his face on T.V, or in the local paper, hell you even went to their house the night he died."

"Yeah but -"

"No buts, Ray!" He shouted. "Now cut the shit, this aint funny." His face burned red like cartoon rage. "Why have you even got that thing anyway?" He asked, pointing to the card. "Why didn't you just leave it where you found it?"

"I *did* leave it there." He muttered. "I found it *again*, under Nikki Farrell's lapel."

"What?"

"You heard me." He paused, "This is a calling card."

"It's a greeting card, Ray." He said flatly. "I've had about enough of this, drive the car please I've a busy day ahead."

Ray did as instructed and slid the car into gear, and the tyres once more devoured the gravel like a mechanical beast with an insatiable appetite.

"Suppose… that *was* left in his car," Vincelli said, "You can't just go taking it, the scene of the crime, or accident for that matter, must be preserved." He did his best to appeal to Ray's better judgement. "You know that."

"It wasn't *left* at the scene." Ray whispered, "It was already there."

"I don't understand."

"Me neither." He pulled up outside the main entrance. "I've been hearing things too," He continued. "They're my thoughts, but *not* - if you get me, kinda like I'm singing someone else's song."

Vincelli laughed. "Come on, Ray." He said.

Ray looked at the front door, it was black and lacquered to a shiny finish, most likely - he guessed, steel plated on the rear. It was way beyond average size but then the house demanded it, concrete pillars adorned it on both sides.

"Funny how it works, wouldn't you say?" Ray said. He applied the parking brake, not once taking his eyes off the front door.

"What's that?"

"All that money," He answered. "And what's it brought them? One kid in the slammer, and one in the ground." He folded his arms and relaxed in his seat. "What does wealth actually bring anyone?" He asked.

Vincelli shrugged his shoulders while he too gave the house his envious approval.

"My mother always used to say that each of life's gains have to be paid for with an equal amount of loss, if not more." He shrugged again. "Be careful what you wish for, for you just may get it."

They both stepped out of the car, the sun was hazy but bright as it shone through the gaps in the trees. Ray glanced skyward, catching just a glimpse of what looked like a cable running from tree to tree, he'd seen several street lamps lining the driveway so concluded it must be a power source feeding them, not the classiest workmanship he'd ever seen but the thought vanished.

"Morning gentlemen." The voice said, it came from the gap in the doorway, gentle but troubled. Both men walked up the steps to reach the door.

"Mrs Golding?" Vincelli asked.

"I'm awfully sorry," She said. "But you see the press have been hanging around trying to get a story." She remained hidden from view.

As they neared the door it opened fully to them, she ushered them in quickly and slammed the door behind them.

"Once again, I'm sorry for these ridiculous measures." She smiled. "Follow me." She began walking at once, with an air of authority about her that couldn't be ignored, they followed behind like staff being inducted for a new job. She wore an elegant black dress that hugged her figure as though charged with static, her hair was blonde and hung down over her shoulders.

"So you have something for me?" Vincelli asked, trying to sound sympathetic, but coming off excited.

"That's why you're here." She answered, her voice was jovial but forced, Ray sensed her distaste for Vincelli instantly, but remained quiet - choosing instead to listen and observe.

Both men were led up a winding staircase until level with the huge chandelier that hung over the lobby, they were then ushered left down a narrow corridor.

"His room is as he left it," Her voice trailed off. "It's not been touched." She smiled nervously over her shoulder making eye contact just briefly with Ray. "It's a mess is what I'm trying to say."

"You wanna see my place," Vincelli joked, trying to ease her nerves. Ray had the same thought, only these days it was true. The door opened to reveal a musicians paradise, a Les Paul guitar took pride of place, hooked up to a large Marshall amplifier in the corner of the room. Ray glanced around the room, there had to be hundreds of C.D's lining the wall to the right of the door, the walls were covered with posters of bands and guitarists, Marilyn Manson and Slash were clearly favourites.

"I found it under his pillow." She said, walking to the bed. "It's still there." She lifted the pillow to reveal a brown envelope.

"May I?" Vincelli asked.

"Again, that's why you're here."

Ray winced, surely even Vincelli would pick up on that one he figured, though once again it seemed to have slipped by unnoticed.

"Thank you." He picked it up, his name was scrawled across it in what looked like a hurried last minute thought. Ray glanced at Mrs Golding who by now was stood staring from the window with her arms folded. He knew she wanted them out of her house five minutes ago, he also knew Vincelli didn't work quickly, in fact he was still yet to *open* the envelope.

"Mrs Golding," Ray said, hoping to distract her momentarily. "Have you ever considered improved security for the house? Maybe C.C.T.V perhaps?"

"It's a bit late for that." She said harshly, still staring through the window. "What have we left to protect? Material possessions?"

"I didn't mean –"

"Danny asked about that once." She turned to look at him. "We decided against it, his Father and I that is, if I could turn back the clock then yes I'd make some changes but now, it's like bolting the gate after the bull's escaped."

"I'm sorry." He said. "It's just when I was outside I noticed –"

"If that's everything." She said, striding towards the door. "Then I have things to be doing." Ray chose to ignore his urge to follow her, instead he walked to where she had been standing and took in the view she would've had. He felt a breeze seeping through the window and saw that it was not fully closed, the cable he'd seen outside was in fact being fed to something within the room, he saw it running though the window and joining up with the cables from

Danny's electrical appliances. He followed the internal side of the cable discreetly with his eyes, he saw it end at the back of Danny's wardrobe on the right hand side of the room.

"Thank you for your time," Vincelli said, standing in the doorway. "My colleague and I will be on our way now."

"No problem." Her expression was sour, the carefully constructed façade was beginning to slip.

"I'll be in touch with regards to the contents." He placed the envelope in his breast pocket. "Lets go now, Ray." He turned and walked slowly down the corridor, not once looking behind but listening for the bedroom door to close before he increased pace. They were again ushered down the staircase, across the lobby and through the door. She closed the door behind them as quickly as they could get through it, she did not bid farewell.

The two men stood beneath the open porch outside the door, they looked at each other. Vincelli threw a cigarette in his mouth. "Don't think she liked me too much." He said.

"What makes you say that?" Ray asked, smiling.

"She didn't look at me once, the whole time we were in there."

Ray frowned, he had his own theory on why it was she didn't like him, but would never be so cruel as to confirm it to him. He knew it was a natural reaction for a parent to try and apportion blame on someone else, he'd seen it many times, they both had.

"She thinks it's my fault, I'll bet."

"She's hurting, Joe." Ray took in a lungful of air, he breathed deeply and looked up, the courtesy light above him was flickering into life, it hadn't been on before or at least he hadn't noticed it. It began to burn brightly, far more than it should've been, it glowed. The surge of electricity buzzed through him, he tried to decide if he was merely hearing it or *feeling* it too, his was mindful of the porch light at the twin's house. Vincelli looked up also, they both stood mesmerised for a moment, unable to avert their gaze from it until seconds later it blew, showering them both with shards of hot glass.

"Jesus -" Vincelli shouted, cutting himself off mid sentence. He dusted at himself lightly and bowed down whilst shaking his head. " - Christ."

Ray stood motionless, still gazing at what remained of the bulb in its socket, a small trickle of blood ran from his forehead until he felt it travel over the bridge of his nose.

"You ok, Ray?"

"Yeah," He closed his eyes tightly and rubbed at them. "I can still see it," He muttered. "It's scorched my fucking eyes!"

"Don't be so dramatic." Vincelli said, stepping from the porch. "You got nicked on your forehead though, might wanna wipe that."

"Thanks." He too stepped on to the gravel and they both walked to the car. He opened the door but stopped to glance at the trees again. He followed the cable with his eyes and saw that it travelled to the ground, before climbing the trellis and up through what he now knew was Danny's window.

"What do you suppose the cable is for?" He asked, pointing to it to help Vincelli zero in.

"Don't know." He replied, his tone as non committal as ever. "Don't care really." They both got in the car.

"You gonna open that?"

"Yeah, but not here." Vincelli said. "Move the car."

He started the engine and wound the window down. He drove the car slowly, turning it around but getting as close to the trees as possible for a better look, he frowned - but once again the thought passed. As they reached the edge of the driveway they stopped on Vincelli's command, it was a private lay by that still formed a part of their estate, just before it joined the main Washburn link road, more of an acceleration lane.

"We should be ok here." Vincelli said, taking the envelope from inside his jacket. Ray hadn't heard a word, instead he was staring at the cable, that *too* had travelled parallel with them for the length of the lane they sat on, only now it was much lower, he could see it was clearly on an incline downwards. He thought about the trellis against the house, and wondered why he'd go to the trouble of lowering it to the ground only to climb the trellis to his window? *Could've gone straight from the tree to your window.* He thought.

"He's gone out of his way to hide this cable." He said. "The only reason it's now visible is because the leaves are all gone."

"Good, Ray." He muttered, engrossed in the note.

"Which means it's new." He added, excitedly. "It only been erected in the last few moths, or weeks even." He followed the cable with his eyes again, it was dropping fast as it neared the end of the lane. He could see a mail box further down, positioned right at the boundary of their property.

"This fuckin' kid!" Vincelli shouted. "He's dead and yet *still* he's fucking with me."

Ray released the parking brake and the car rolled slowly down towards the mail box, it was on Ray's side as they neared it.

"What's it say?" He asked.

"It says," He paused for breath, waving the note aggressively like a magic eight ball, though he knew the contents wouldn't change once settled. "And I quote, 'I can't tell you what, but on the night of Brandon's death - there was a witness, this one *will* stand up in court and help you where I failed. Yours, Danny."

"That's it?"

"Yeah," He replied. "But who the fuck is he talking about."

"Not *who*." Ray smiled. "But *what*."

He read the note again, still perplexed.

"A witness so strong and irrefutable," Ray whispered, staring into the shrubs behind the mail box. "That no lawyer in the land will be able to dispute it." He lit a cigarette while Vincelli read, then re - read the note.

"Come on man, you're the detective." Ray urged.

"What am I missing, Ray?"

"Besides brains?" He laughed, pointing with the two fingers that held his cigarette, he drew Vincelli's attention to the shrubs. "You got C.C.T.V my friend."

Vincelli gazed, his mouth hung open for a moment as he realised Ray was correct, a small camera was in fact mounted within the greenery.

"He's got the equipment in his wardrobe," Ray said. "The cable starts in his room and ends here, if you'd listened to a word I'd said to you you'd be reading from the same page already." He felt smug for a moment, he liked the feeling and chose to enjoy it since it didn't come around too often.

"That *there* camera," Ray said. "Is positioned just right to see any vehicles that pull into this lane, whether they go to the house or not."

"We have to get back in that house, Ray." He said. "We have to get that tape before anyone else does."

"Granted." Ray answered. "But we can't go now, we've only just left - she'll get suspicious."

"Mmm."

Ray flicked his cigarette out of the window then gripped the steering wheel tightly, he looked ahead while mulling over the next best move.

"It's probably not my business," He said finally. "But she said she doesn't go in there much, so it's best to leave it today, go back tomorrow and play it down; tell her the note indicates there's another clue."

"Which it does." Vincelli added.

"Just be cool." He said, releasing the parking brake. "Lets get back."

Chapter Six

Thursday 7th January.

 The clock on the wall told her it was now almost eleven, though time was rarely a factor in Julianne's life anymore, like a broken watch her mechanism had ceased to operate since she'd been informed of the incident, she refused to use the term *accident*, to herself or others. Her once shapely and athletic figure was now emaciated and frail, her face was gaunt and her eyes bloodshot and shadowed. Her life now consisted of broken sleep, and being at Chad's bedside, the two usually overlapped since being next to him was the only time she *could* sleep, the gentle rhythmic sound of the respirator usually shut her down as much as it kept him going, breathing life persistently to his lungs.

 "Are you dreaming?" She asked, stroking his hand as she sat next to him. "What do you see?" Of course the answer never came, though she always pictured a winding dirt road with lush green fields on either side, with the sun high in the sky both annoying and blessed as it shone brightly on his face. In her mind he was travelling, his face etched with determination and his eyes blazing with the resolve to keep moving, she just didn't know *where*.

 "Does room six have a visitor?" The voice asked
 Emma didn't need to check her day book.
 "It does." She replied, placing her magazine down she looked at the man in front of her, he was mid - twenties and staring back at her from under the rim of his baseball cap.
 "You are?"

"Matt." He answered. "I'm a friend of his, I've been out of town."

"Ok." She pushed the visitors ledger to him. "Just sign in please, I'm sure you'll be able to go and see him shortly." She watched him closely as he signed his name on the page beneath Julianne's, noticing as she did so that his cap was pulled down low, and since his eyes were only just visible to her she figured the camera mounted behind her would have no chance.

"Thank you." He said, sliding it back to her.

"Just take a seat over there," She forced a smile whilst pointing over his shoulder. "You wont be long." She watched him turn and walk away, he wore jeans and a white T - shirt, and while they were clean enough she saw his trainers were tatty and torn up. He also walked with a pronounced limp.

She dialled quietly.

"Security?" She asked

"Yes, everything ok?"

"Yeah," She tried to sound sincere. "It may just be me, but there's a guy just arrived to visit one of our long term patients here in intensive, something about him just isn't right."

"What's the name?"

"The guy's name is Matt." She looked over at him. "He's here to visit Chad Rose."

"Ok……well he's checked in as Matt down here also -"

"He was searched, right?" She asked.

"Yeah, did it myself. Nothing more sinister than a change of clothes for college."

"Ok." She said. "Sorry to have bothered you something just didn't feel, y - know."

"No problem."

She placed the receiver back and returned to her magazine.

A few minutes later the waif like figure of Julianne emerged into the hallway, she closed the door gently and made her way towards the reception area.

"Bye, Emma." She whispered, summoning the elevator.

"See you soon." Emma smiled to her, and since the elevator was still on the ground floor she seized the moment. "How are you holding up?"

"I'm ok." She replied, nodding. Her pallid skin did little to reinforce her lie.

"I see you so often and yet hardly speak to you." She stepped from behind her station and moved closer to her. "You must think me rude." They both laughed a little.

"Don't be silly." She answered nervously.

"You know where I am if you need me." She pointed to her desk. "Literally!"

"Thank you, Emma." She hadn't noticed Matt, she stood with her back to where he was seated, though Emma was stood perfectly positioned to see him in the background as she spoke with her. She could see that although Matt had his head bowed down, his eyes were still scanning the room from beneath the rim of his cap. Emma had hoped to *introduce* Julianne to him, she was certain they were *not* acquainted in any way and most likely never had been, though she wondered what it would prove and chose not to. The elevator opened and Julianne stepped in.

"Bye Emma." She said, again.

As the doors closed Emma turned her attention to Matt, who in turn was gazing directly at her, awaiting his cue.

"You can go through now." She said.

"Thank you." He got up and walked slowly down the hall to room six, when he got there he looked back to see Emma was stood watching him, she quickly busied herself as he did so. He opened the door and slipped quietly in, closing it behind him he looked immediately to Chad, who lay motionless, and *defenceless* in his sleep.

"I'm sorry about this, Chad." He said with a smile. He walked over to his bed and pulled a syringe from up his sleeve. "Now this is nothing personal, just business you understand." The syringe was pre loaded as he pulled its tip from a cork casing.

"You see, you're gonna cause them too much trouble if and when you wake up, so this has got to be done." He glanced nervously at Chad's face and placed the syringe on his bedside unit.

"That's the purest and most sought after heroin on the streets right now, Chad; and you're gonna ride for free." He laughed as he pulled his belt quickly through the loops of his jeans and held it in his hands. It was leather and had extra holes pierced through it, the holes were almost directly next to the buckle. He slid it under Chad's right arm and began to pull it through the buckle, he then positioned it at the base of his bicep before pulling it tight and using the pierced holes to lock it into position as a makeshift tourniquet.

"It's kinda funny really," He said. "Downstairs in E.R, there's kids coming in on gurneys because of this shit. You on the other hand, you're gonna be leaving because of it - if you get me." He cast one more glance into the closed eyes of his intended victim, as he reached for the syringe, he watched as Chad's veins began to protrude.

"Now that's irony for you." He lined the syringe into position and readied himself to plunge. "Sweet dreams, kid."

"I wouldn't -" The voice was weak, like dying breath only in reverse, as it got stronger with every syllable uttered. " - *do that*, if I were you."

Matt froze, his hands began to tremble instantly as he looked quickly to the door, nothing - still closed, then slowly back to what had now become staring eyes. They were themselves emotionless and still like calm waters, though Chad's face was contorted with hatred and rage.

"You'll die for what you did to us." He said, calmly removing the tourniquet while Matt simply froze in position. The belt fell to the floor as Chad took tightly hold of Matt's syringe bearing hand, he raised himself to a seating position, his dark greasy hair fell around his face as they gazed eye to eye.

"You were one of them," He smiled. "Yet today you're a messenger. *My* messenger will deal with you, and *he* will not fail, that much I promise you."

"This isn't real." Matt said, he wanted to scream, but he also wanted to get out. "This is some fucking dream."

"What is life, but a dream within a dream?" He stared hard into Matt's disbelieving eyes. "They wanted me to kill you." He muttered. "I didn't want to do it."

"Kill me?" He asked, laughing at the thought. "They came pretty close, but not close enough, and I don't mean forcing us off the road -

I mean killing my brother, that *almost* killed me." He reached around Matt's neck with his right hand and pulled him close, Matt didn't resist him. "Do you think, *you* could kill me?" He pressed his pale face hard into Matt's.

"No." He spoke softly, he was crying. "I'm sorry, I'm so sorry."

"The act is over now, isn't it?" He asked. "Or has it just begun?"

"It's over, I swear it's fuckin' over." He shouted. "Just let me walk away, you'll never see me again."

" Your life or death will depend largely on what you were about to inject into me."

"It's heroin."

"Heroin and what?"

"It's just heroin." He squirmed, trying to release himself from Chad's grip. "I swear."

"Are you a user?"

"Yeah." He answered.

"Your arms are clean? So either you're newly addicted or you inject between your toes, which is it?" He asked. "I saw you limping."

"Both." He wiped his eyes. "They don't let us jab our arms."

"So if you're a junkie, why would they give you a syringe full of the chemical you crave the most?" He shook his head. "What's to stop you just taking it yourself? Or at least taking some of it?"

"They're paying me with five times this much, just to inject this into you."

"You're lying." He said flatly. "No junkie would miss the opportunity, you and I both know it. Tell me the truth."

"Ok," He tried to turn away from Chad's deathly stare, but he couldn't, he was locked on to his eyes.

"The syringe, it's -" He paused momentarily to wipe his eyes. "It's infected with H.I.V."

"Indeed it is." Chad whispered, pulling him closer and gripping the back of his neck with all the force he could muster.

"I'm so sorry."

"No you're not, you're afraid." He spoke calmly, despite the fact his grip on the nape of Matt's neck was so severe, that blood had began to trickle from where his nails had pierced his skin. "As well you should be."

Matt winced in pain, as the syringe he didn't realise he'd let go of plunged deep into his neck. Chad pulled him directly onto it until no part of the needle was visible, then plunged its entire contents into his body.

"What have you done?" Matt asked, reaching to his neck and grasping at the syringe, his legs gave way under him and he dropped to the floor, he clawed at it to try and put some space between himself and Chad, all the while staring up to him.

"Relax," Chad whispered. "You'll be dead long before symptoms develop." He stared down to him, he'd almost reached the door. "AIDS wont take your life." He whispered with a smile. "Not so much AIDS as *blades*." He fell back into his original position on the bed, his eyes were closed and in the blink of an eye it was like he'd never moved.

"Chad?" He asked, scrambling for the door handle but still staring across the room at him. "Hey!" He shouted. "What did you do?" He felt the heroin surging through his veins, the warmth embraced him like a cheating ex girlfriend, he knew she was bad, he knew she was dangerous but god she was toxic.

"Help me, please!" He shouted, managing to pull the handle and open the door. "Somebody, help me!"

16:00.

Vincelli and Ray once more found themselves travelling up the Washburn link road to what had been Danny's house. The sky was a thick black cloak of darkness, a heavy storm was imminent but had held off so far. Ray stared blankly out of the window as Vincelli drove, seemingly unaware of anyone or anything around him, least of all the dividing lines in the middle of the road that he'd been straddling for the past five minutes. The rhythmic beat of the cats eyes under the tyres had almost sent Ray into a peaceful escape when he noticed the accident site looming on his left. As the car drew nearer he saw a figure standing in the shadows, a familiar figure, stood motionless peering over the bank side.

"Hey," He muttered, sitting up and looking closer. "Slow down, Joe."

"What?"

"Slow down." He repeated. "Slow down now." He stared at the figure as the car slowed down. "Don't you see that?" He asked, shifting quickly in his seat. "It's him, it's fucking him!"

"No, Ray." He replied, pressing the accelerator again. "I thought it was something important."

"It is import -"

"I also thought we were done with this shit!" He shouted. "This is *real - fucking - life*, not the twilight zone."

"Sorry, I guess I just thought -" He paused and bit down hard on his lip, unsure of what he actually thought anymore.

"I guess I was just half asleep, that's all." He smiled. "You know if you'd get off those fucking cats eyes I might stay awake."

They didn't speak again until they pulled into the gravel driveway of the Golding residence.

"Ok, here goes." Vincelli whispered. " We need to get in that house today, first attempt - *right now*. Get me?"

"Don't worry, we will."

"Let's go."

They both stepped from the car and whilst Vincelli contemplated the task of gaining entry to the house, Ray stared into the trees and was pleased to see the wire still resting within them.

"How could she not see that?" Ray asked. "Coming and going every day, and not look up and see that."

"Don't know really," Vincelli shrugged. "People like this don't really concern themselves with things like that, when they come and go they're coming with a new diamond ring or going for a new Mercedes, there's always something they're preoccupied with I guess." He laughed. "Fact is," He paused to touch his nose. "They don't look further than *that*."

"Maybe." Ray considered his theory.

"What do I know, Ray?" He asked. "Anyway, keep your voice down in case they hear." He rang the bell. "Actually, this kind of proves my point." He whispered. " They still haven't fixed their fucking porch light."

Ray stood silent, though his thoughts ran wild. *Was that really Brandon? Is it even possible? Why then have I never seen Nancy? With so many things left to say surely that's a reason to visit.*

"Good afternoon, Gentlemen." An elderly man stood before them, he tried hard to keep his neat silver hair in place as the strong winds whipped through it.

"May I be of some assistance" His accent was refined, almost British sounding, though his voice was strained and scratchy like a well played record. He shuffled slightly nearer to them and turned his head to the left, literally lending them his ear.

"Good day to you, Sir." Ray said, he tilted his cap as he did so before removing it completely. "We're -"

"Detective Joseph Vincelli," He interrupted, holding his credentials out for inspection. "And this is officer Kennedy." He folded his I.D and placed it in the inner breast pocket of his raincoat.

"Mrs Golding told me you may stop by." He said with a smile.

"Is the lady in question home?"

"Not presently, no."

"When will she be, *present* ?" He asked, grinning.

"I'm not at all sure but she gave me instructions to -"

"Could we wait inside for her to return?"

Ray could see the man was becoming visibly agitated at Vincelli's lack of manners or respect towards him.

"Well you'd be stood in the hallway for a further two days," He smiled and cast his eyes over Vincelli's podgy torso. "And quite frankly I don't believe you have the stamina, *Sir*. So maybe you should consider returning."

Ray couldn't believe how arrogant Vincelli was being towards the man, he burned more bridges on a daily basis than a demolition team.

"Sir," Ray said, obtaining the mans full attention before continuing. " We were wondering if it would be at all possible to visit Danny's room." He held his stare firmly. "We wont take up more than an hour of your day." He smiled. "You wont even know we're here."

"Like I said I was given instructions -"

"I understand you want to do the right thing, Sir. However we believe we may have missed something vital when we visited last, it really is extremely important to our investigations." He smiled. "We have to do the right thing too, you're doing your job but we have to do ours, and just an hour will allow us to do that."

He opened the door and welcomed them in. "One hour you say? Officer *Kennedy*, was it?"

"That's correct, Sir." He shook his hand. "Thank you."

"I'm George." He said. "Merely the housekeeper you understand."

"There's no merely in it." He replied. "It's a fabulous house, it must take a lot of looking after."

Vincelli passed them by and headed straight up the stairs, while Ray remained with George as he slid a heavy dead bolt across the door.

"Listen," Ray said, nudging him on the arm. "Don't mind him, he's a dick all the time, it's not like he saves it for special occasions." They both laughed. George turned and walked back through the lobby as Ray headed up the stairs, he could hear George's footsteps trailing off in to the distance on the marble tiles. "Oh, if I were twenty years younger…" He muttered. Ray imagined him holding his fists out in the manner of bare knuckle pugilists of days gone by and couldn't help but laugh.

Ray opened the bedroom door to find Vincelli rummaging through a chest of drawers.

"What you doing?"

"Well before I bust that door open, I figured there might be a key knocking around here someplace." He slammed one drawer and moved quickly on to the next. "So we need to find it fast and get in that wardrobe."

Ray stood and glanced around the room, he felt eighteen again just being in there, Danny had been mid twenties, but this was a teenagers room for sure. He wanted to pick up that guitar and strum it, badly - but strum it. He looked at the posters on the wall, there were many, rock bands and pretty ladies.

"Have you even heard of Motley Crue?" He asked. "Or, Nine Inch Nails?"

"Can't say I have." He replied, whilst sliding the clothes within the drawers back and forth, just listening for the sound of a key contained within. "I'm more of a Chicago, type of guy myself."

"I Guess." He said.

"Here it is!" He shouted. "Holy fuck, it was in his fucking sock drawer." He laughed. "Can you fucking believe that?" He turned to see Ray Scanning through Danny's C.D's. "Ray." He shouted. "Are you gonna join me on this or you wanna listen to some music and talk about girls?"

They both looked at the wardrobe and approached it slowly, Vincelli held the key in his hand.

"Ok lets do this, Ray." He unlocked the doors, threw them open and there it was; a small and simple C.C.T.V unit with one monitor and a video recorder. There were video tapes stacked on the floor within the wardrobe numbered one to thirty.

"It's missing." Vincelli said. "Where's thirty - one?"

"He's hidden it."

"Why hide it? He asked. "It was already locked in here so why separate it from the others."

"It's here someplace." He scanned the room, looking at those posters again. "There's a clue here someplace, we need to figure out what that clue is."

"No, Ray." He replied, slamming the door in temper. "It would be in *here*. He's fucking with us."

Ray sighed and glanced at the thirty cassettes they *could* account for. "Look, I'll take a look at one of these and make sure the date on the recording coincides with the number on the label. You search the room." He felt a rush of authority in his own voice that he didn't recognise, it felt good, and for a moment he felt in charge, that felt good too. He smiled and pressed play to see what cassette was already in.

"The interview, Joe." He said, clicking his fingers. "Did he say anything odd, something he wanted to stick in your head?"

"The whole interview was odd." He answered, already searching the room. "And you want me to remember one thing?"

"A clue, something that didn't fit."

"I don't know, Ray. Not without going over it again."

"It synchs up." Ray said. "The system is showing today's date and the time is correct. Saturday the nineteenth of December is the cassette that's in, it's not been changed since."

"I should hope not, Ray." Vincelli whispered whilst taking a quick look at it. "That's the day he hung himself."

"The only problem is," Ray whispered, rewinding the cassette a little. "This one stops at eight - fifteen in the evening." He looked at Vincelli. "Yet there's plenty of tape left, why did he stop it?"

"Maybe there is something on *that* tape," Vincelli said. "Something he wants us to see that would've been lost if it's recording on a twenty - four hour setting, it would just record over itself if not changed."

"Or," Ray said. "Maybe *Danny* didn't stop the recording." He thought hard. "Maybe someone else stopped it."

"Are you suggesting someone was in here with him?" Vincelli asked.

"Perhaps?" Ray shrugged. "It's possible."

Vincelli considered the theory. "Ok," He said. "Press play at the point that it stops recording, then cue it backwards to see if the time jumps suddenly, if every minute is accounted for then it's just been stopped, probably by Danny, as opposed to stopped - rewound a little - then erased with a new recording."

Ray did as requested and cued it backwards at speed, he watched the minutes tick backwards in perfect synchronisation.

"If anyone *was* here," Vincelli added. "They would've just removed the cassette and took it? Surely?"

"Only if they knew it was here." Ray said. All at once he saw the bottom fall out of his argument.

"Exactly." Vincelli said, seizing on Ray's slip up. "If someone was in *this* room, and they stopped *that* cassette, then of course they *knew* it was there." He laughed. "Just seize it," He said. "We'll go over it. Right now though, we need the *missing* tape."

"It's all here," Ray said. "There's no jump, it's consistent. The quality's good too." He turned to see Vincelli on his hands and knees, searching under the bed.

"No." He shouted. "Don't you get it, man? This tape is for *your* eyes, it's not gonna be under his fucking bed or anywhere else where the house maid, or his mother can find it." He rapped his knuckles against his forehead. " Outside the box."

"Maybe that's it." Vincelli said, clambering to his feet and clutching his back. "Maybe he's got a lock box or a safe."

Ray looked again at the posters on the walls. "Or, a wall safe." He felt that surge of authority once more. "God, I could get used to this." He whispered.

"What was that?"

"Doesn't matter." He replied, joining him next to the bed. "Take a look at these posters, Joe, does anything compute?"

"Oh, shit." He whispered. His attention was drawn to a gate - fold album that Danny had opened up like a book and pinned to the wall. "Home sweet home, he said that at the end of the interview, just as he was leaving."

"Home sweet home?" Ray asked, perplexed. "In what context?"

"He said he was going home," He paused. "Home sweet home."

"Then that's it." Ray said with a smile.

Vincelli walked to it and ripped it down. "Oh yeah." He said. "A wall safe." His face lit up at the sight of it, it was no more than letterbox size, it did however have a digital combination lock. "Great, Ray. Just great." He punched it lightly in a display of resignation. "Now all we need, is to guess his security code."

"One - Nine - Nine - one." Ray said, leaning past Vincelli to type it in, and four audible depressions later, a tiny lever behind the fascia panel released.

"How the fuck did you do that?" Vincelli asked. "You don't just guess entry codes like that, how did you know?" He opened the door before it locked again.

"Home Sweet Home." Ray answered, pointing to the album on the floor. "Nineteen - Ninety - One remix. It's right there on the cover." They both laughed. "Thank *you*, Motley *Crue*!" Ray said.

They both stood for a moment and stared at the contents, the missing video cassette was present as they'd hoped, but there was also a digital camera.

"Now this could be interesting." Vincelli said, reaching in for the items. "This could be *very* interesting." He gave the video cassette straight to Ray and began searching for the power switch on the camera.

"What do you think you're gonna find on that?"

"Something good, Ray." He answered. "Something good." He cradled the camera gently in his hands, it had a fold down screen which he opened up to reveal a small yellow label, it contained a message that read, 'Switch on and press play.' He did so. The footage began shaky, it was clear it had been filmed in the bedroom they were stood in, although it was still pointed at the floor and someone's bare feet as they walked, it was Danny.

'One minute!' Danny shouted. 'Just let me set this down and we'll begin.' The room came into view as the camera was raised and placed next to a small lamp on the bedside table. The camera was pointed at the bed, although Danny's window sill, and a small vanity mirror on it were also visible, another vanity mirror was positioned behind him on a shelf over his bed. The lamp, along with the ceiling light were switched on.

"Look at the time, Joe." Ray whispered, referring to the footage. "It's just gone half seven."

Vincelli nodded.

"Forty - five minutes later, his C.C.T.V is switched off." Ray smiled. "Someone's with him, I just know it."

"Well," Vincelli said slowly. "If someone is in the room with him, they will no doubt show up, however *blurred*, on their way in." He smiled back. "If your right about someone else turning it off, wouldn't they have erased their own entry to the premises?"

Both men watched as Danny appeared on screen wearing a white bath towel and nothing else, he lay down on his left side and peered closely in to the lens.

'Remember me?' He asked with a smile. 'Well you found it, I doubt very much if you were unaided but hey, you found it. You might actually have a chance here.'

Vincelli smiled.

'Now I'm gonna give you an opportunity to press the pause button so you can set the camera down on the bedside table, and come join me on the bed. Pause now.'

Vincelli paused it as instructed and placed it on the bedside table.

"It's strange isn't it? Vincelli whispered. "He seems so happy, yet hours later he was gone."

"He's found his solution." Ray Answered. "It may not be ideal, but he's found his way out."

They both sat down on the bed and Vincelli once again pressed play.

On screen, Danny looked silently at them both for a moment. 'Ok,' He said. 'Lets begin. We'll start with the most obvious point, when you see this I'll be gone, I got myself into this mess so I gotta get myself out of it. Death is my only escape now. You see, either I do it, or *they* do it.'

Both Ray and Vincelli registered a significant drop in the room temperature, listening to Danny talk of his coming death had chilled them both to the bone.

'My own FUCKING SELFISH NEEDS!' He shouted, saliva spraying from his mouth. 'That's why Brandon's dead, that's why Chad's as good as dead, it's all my fucking fault.'

"I knew this kid was lying." Vincelli said. "I knew he was holding out on something."

'The twins had made themselves some powerful enemies, but their enemies underestimated who exactly it was that *they* were dealing with, that's where I came in, I fucking sold them out good and proper. I sold them out to this gang, basically they're a bunch of drug dealers and smugglers, they all work for some guy who runs the club scene, he operates the whole thing but trust me, you wont find his name on the lease so don't bother looking. Now I don't know *why*, but I do know the twins were causing some trouble for his operations, I told them that in exchange for leaving my brother alone I could name them, no better than that - I could hand them over on a fucking plate.'

Ray leaned forward and hit the pause button. "Something's not right there." He said.

"Why?"

"Danny *already* knew the twins were causing this guy trouble, which is why he was able to offer them up for a deal." He paused to think it over.

"So who told him?" Vincelli asked. "It's unlikely the gang told him, and since he was friends with the twins -"

"We must assume it was *they* who told him." Ray said. "But they wouldn't tell him that without also telling him *why*, would they?"

Vincelli shrugged. "Maybe we should keep watching." He pressed play.

' So I had my party and invited them as planned, the night was going well and we were all having a good time, then later on - *also* as planned, these guys show up. I was outside with them both, we were smoking and having a drink, and then they show up in their truck, I saw how many there were and changed my mind - they weren't gonna hurt them, they were gonna *kill* them - I didn't sign up for that.' He was crying as he relayed his story beyond both the veil and the grave. 'They were my friends, I didn't want them dead - I just figured they get a beating or something. Anyway I approached the truck and told them that the twins hadn't showed, that's when I got whacked with the bar.' He shook his head angrily.

'Next thing, Brandon comes over to help me out - that in itself wasn't a problem, but when they saw Chad revving up the car - that was it. They came looking for twins, and now they had them.' He paused long enough to stop his voice shaking and stared directly through the screen to them both. 'The rest is just like I told you. I swear, I have no reason to lie anymore.' He reached forward to switch off the camera but stopped short of doing so.

'One more thing,' He whispered, dividing his attention between the lens and what would've been his bedroom window, he leaned in close as if to tell a secret. 'The twins, they share something special - much more than D.N.A, it's like they've got a permanent phone line between them, but they don't need no phone if you get me. If one needs the other, all it takes is a call, it's unbreakable - even by death.' Ray felt a chill as Danny spoke those words, he found them very prophetic since he was already leaning to the realm of the supernatural.

'Nothing will stop what they'll do now, not you - not anybody.' Danny once more peered out of his bedroom window into the darkness, although only his own reflection would've been visible.

'Then of course there's the Gang,' He went on, turning his attention to the camera once more. 'And gangs like them, but it's you and me, and people just like you and me, who'll get caught in the crossfire.' He was about to speak on, when without warning the bulb in his lamp flickered brightly before exploding, he reacted with a jump and glanced up and over the lens before him.

'What was that?' He uttered nervously, his eyes remained fixed at the same level for several seconds before returning to the camera.

Ray paused the footage and looked at Vincelli.

"Someone is in here with him," He said. "That proves it!" He pointed to the small screen which contained Danny's shadowed face. "He looked at somebody when that bulb blew!"

"I think you're right." Vincelli replied, rewinding the footage a little. "He does seem too." They both viewed it again.

'…And people just like you and me, who'll get caught in the crossfire. -' Vincelli paused the footage.

"Ok," He said. "He's looking into the lens now," He mentally measured Danny's line of sight from the bed to the camera, before pressing play once more. The bulb again flickered and exploded on cue.

"His line of sight changes," Vincelli whispered. "He's looking at something."

"Or *someone*." Ray added.

"Ok," Vincelli said. "The C.C.T.V cassette should help clear that one up." He leaned forward and pressed play.

'A war is coming to town,' Danny whispered. 'You can't stop it, all you gotta do is pick a side.' He reached for the camera, then the screen went blank.

"Well," Ray said. " If what he says is true, then it looks like we've got -"

" Come on now, Ray. Let's not get excited." He stood up clutching the small of his back.

"How long are you gonna put up with that?" Ray asked.

"Till the day I die, I guess."

"Well why don't you at least get some support for it?"

Vincelli stared at Ray, quizzing him with his eyes as only a detective can. "What?" He asked, musing the suggestion further. "Like a help line, or group thing? They do that?"

Ray laughed at him and stood up. "You're kidding me, right?"

"Of course." He answered quickly, he wasn't and they both knew it.

"I was talking about a girdle, or a corset or something." His laughter continued as he passed Vincelli,

"You're out of your mind." He said. Although at his own expense, he laughed with Ray. "I thought you meant -" His voice trailed off.

"I know what you thought." Ray shook his head in disbelief. "So," He said, stifling his laughter any further. "Are you gonna watch the tape?" He held it out to him.

"*We* are gonna watch the tape." He answered, taking it from him and opening up the wardrobe doors. He noticed the cassette was roughly in the middle of its run with equal amounts of tape visible in each window. "Hopefully he cued it up to the relevant part." He said, inserting it in the machine.

"What do you suppose he meant by 'all it takes is a call'" Ray asked, joining him at the wardrobe.

"Don't know." He replied. "What do *you* think he meant by it, Ray?"

"I honestly don't know." He stared at the blank screen and thought, *If one needs the other, then all it takes is a call, their connection is unbreakable - even by death. Is it possible that -*

"Ok, here we go." Vincelli said. "You ready?"

The two of them stood shoulder to shoulder, huddled between the two open doors of Danny's wardrobe. They watched as the picture jumped and crashed around for a few seconds, before giving a sharp view of the illuminated driveway.

"Ten - thirty six." Vincelli said, tapping his pen against the small monitor. "He did cue it for us." Their wait for someone or something to appear on screen was short lived, beams of light appeared from the right of the screen.

"This is a vehicle driving *on* to the property, isn't it?" Ray asked.

Vincelli nodded, he didn't take his eyes from the screen. "Hopefully it's our party crashers." He whispered., watching as the beams of light became a *source*.

"They weren't crashers," Ray said, also concentrating on the screen. "They had invitations from the host, remember?"

A pick up truck, just as Danny had described passed the camera, it had four search lights mounted on the cab and numerous bodies riding in the back holding on to the roll bars. Vincelli hit the Pause button and moved the picture on frame by frame, until the truck came into full view.

"That's our truck, right there." He said.

"It's a G.M.C, isn't it?"

"Yeah."

"Look at them," Ray said, pointing to the rear of the truck. "Three in the back, and two in the front." He shook his head, he felt tense just viewing the footage. "When that many guys show up for a fight you know they mean business. Doesn't really matter who you are or what you can do, you're gonna get hurt - *or worse*."

"Yeah," Vincelli agreed. He too felt tense looking at them all. He couldn't see their faces but could tell they were wearing the clear surgical masks Danny had talked of, the courtesy lights along the driveway reflected off them. "Five against two." He whispered. "Real tough guys here, Ray."

"They figured on resistance." Ray said.

"No, I don't think so. They just wanted a decisive victory." Vincelli smiled a little, it caught Ray's eye as maybe inappropriate.

"What?" Ray asked. "What's funny?"

"According to Danny," Vincelli answered. "They still couldn't get near Brandon, in fact he laid one of those bastards out cold." His smile vanished as he remembered that less than fifteen minutes later, he would pay for it with his life. "Good on you kid." He hit play and the truck passed from view.

As the cassette played on and the minutes went by, they both figured that if Danny's version of events were accurate, then he would be having his conversation with them by now.

"Wait now." Vincelli said. "There's something coming up the driveway." He pointed to the dark shape moving slowly towards the camera.

"It's another car." Ray said, staring just inches from the screen. "But it's not got any lights on."

They looked on as the car, a large dark saloon, slowly approached the camera before coming to a standstill just before it.

"Well we know it's not a late guest to the party." Vincelli said. "Otherwise they wouldn't be trying so hard not to be seen."

"They're watching." Ray whispered. "I'll be damned to hell and back, they're watching to make sure it's done." The vehicle began moving again, having stayed in the shadows so far, it passed slowly under one of the ornate lamp posts, crawling within it's pale halo, until the light washed over its dark chassis like moonlight across the ocean.

"I don't believe it." Ray said. "It's the car, it's the same car." He looked at Vincelli. "It's the Mercedes, don't you recognise it?"

Vincelli sat silent for a moment, he stroked his face as he gazed at the vehicle on the monitor. "It's a Mercedes, Ray." He stated calmly. "However, we don't know it's the Mercedes *you're* thinking of."

"Oh come on." Ray shouted. "It's the same car, Joe, and you know it." He walked away from the monitor and paced the room. "It makes sense now," He muttered. "He didn't kill him for stealing fucking flowers, that didn't compute. But this -"

"Stop it, Ray." Vincelli said. "It's not the same car, I mean there's a small chance of course, but have you any idea how many of these things there are on the roads?"

"Well not that one," Ray answered. "That's one less for a start."

"Just stop now." He walked to him and placed his hand on his shoulder. "Ray, Brandon is dead, it's a one way journey with no return ticket, now let it go."

"But how do you explain -"

"Ray, stop now." He ordered.

"Well whichever it is, it's leaving now." Ray said.

They both stood silently and watched as the Mercedes backed slowly down the driveway, until it was no longer visible.

"They must be coming now." Vincelli said. "The picture is vibrating, can you see that?"

The first vehicle raced past the camera, it was jet black and only gave off light from the front left headlight, Vincelli remembered what Danny had said about that in the interview so he knew they were looking at Brandon's Charger. "That's the twins." He whispered.

It was moving fast and appeared to skid as it negotiated the gravel driveway, dust was kicked up from behind and hung thick in the air even after it had gone.

"That car was moving pretty quick," Ray said, almost amazed at the speed it had passed the camera at.

"They should've been long gone." Vincelli muttered. "That car was like harnessed lightening, and a long stretch of road like the Washburn should've been the perfect setting to let it's three hundred horses run wild."

Almost thirty seconds later the footage began to vibrate again, this time it was the pick up truck racing past, in pursuit of the twins. Vincelli stopped the cassette, ejected it and placed it within it's cardboard sleeve.

"There's no way that pick up would've been able to catch that car." He said. "That's a fact."

"That *was* a mystery," Ray said. "But now we know why, don't we?"

"The Mercedes."

"Danny did say that when they made it to the Washburn, they could see the tail and brake lights of the Charger."

"That's right." Vincelli answered. "And, it was swerving across both lanes."

"So clearly it was being slowed down by something in its way."

"The Mercedes." He said again. "But he didn't mention seeing any other cars, surely he would've seen it."

"Not necessarily." Ray said. "Danny was terrified, maybe even fearing for his life at that point, so he may not have seen it from a distance, and once the pick up had caught them up, the Mercedes pulled out the way so they could speed up, which is what they wanted the twins to do -"

"So they could ram them off the road."

"That's it." Ray said.

"It makes sense." Vincelli walked to the window and stared out into the large garden, he gazed at the old oak tree at the bottom. "He hung himself from that tree." He whispered.

"I know." Ray joined him at the window. "Some people don't want help,"

Vincelli stood with his fists clenched, he tapped them gently against the window sill and pressed his forehead against the glass. "Why would anyone take their own life?" He asked. They both stood silently, neither had an answer. Vincelli stepped back from the window and looked at the scattered items on Danny's bedside table.

"Well," He whispered. "We've got what we came for, let's go."

Ray sat at home that evening with the days events playing heavily on his mind, so much so that home didn't feel like home at all. His watch told him it was almost nine o - clock, though it didn't feel like it. The nights drew by slowly of late, but tonight just seemed eternally morose. Wearing only boxer shorts and a white vest he lay slouched in his armchair and stared at the television, the thought to switch it on had arrived and passed more than once. His dog, King, lay asleep at his feet, or over his feet to be exact - so when Ray moved, King moved. A half eaten microwave burger was on the floor also, its very presence bore testament to a terrible burger, or fussy dog. The room was silent except for a ticking clock, and the grunts and groans only a sleeping dog can make. Ray lifted himself to his feet and after instructing King not to follow, he made his way to the patio doors, flung them open and lit a cigarette. The clear night sky was like an ocean of diamonds as it sparkled above, he'd always felt an affinity with it - ever since childhood. His Grandmother had told him that when the stars were out in all their glory, it was like a spy glass to heaven, any dream was possible and any wish within reach, all you had to do was ask your loved ones who had passed on, *'From your lips - to their ears.'* She would say.

"All it takes is a call." He whispered, watching his smoke trail float skyward. "What does that mean?" He hugged himself as he stood in the doorway, the night air was cold and so he decided to cut short his cigarette, he tossed it into the garden and slid the door shut behind him. "I'd sure like to know how to make that call," He muttered to himself as he returned to his chair. "I know who I'd call."

Ray awoke suddenly and in complete darkness, moonlight shone through his windows as shadows danced elegantly across his walls, he vaguely remembered turning off the lamp on the table next to him though couldn't remember why. His slumber had been unnatural and had left him without reason, he was afraid.

"Here we go." He muttered, kicking the recliner to an upright position. As fear tightened its clammy grip over him he tightened his on the armrests and trembled, it would normally run its course within a couple of minutes but sometimes took longer. In a conscious state he knew the warning signs of an impending anxiety attack, and knew how to control them through positive self reassurance, and if needed, concentrated heavy breathing, but those that came in the moments preceding a fully conscious state, came like stealthy warriors on a mission to destroy. Since Nancy's death he'd waged an often unsuccessful war against his nerves, but refused medication on the grounds that they may dull his senses, or maybe his *memory*. He closed his eyes tightly and tensed every muscle in his body.

"Go away now," He whispered. "Go on, leave me alone, I just wanna be." He relaxed his body, tears trickled down his face when he opened his eyes. "I just wanna be." He said again. After a few moments his grip on the armrests eased off, and his anxiety drew away from him - though his fear did not. His heart pounded in his chest, perhaps a lasting legacy of a terrible dream, he wondered. But of one thing he was certain, unlike his anxiety attacks, this was no *irrational* fear. King, who up until then had slept peacefully, began to growl - staring at the shadows that danced across the walls.

Ray stared from the corner of his eyes, concentrating on the shadows and the darkness they occupied, his fear mounted as he worked through them, as he realised one wasn't dancing at all. A figure was stood in the shadows, a silhouette stood perfectly still like a mime in a carnival, staring straight back at him. He slid his hand slowly over the table, no heroics, he thought to himself, not once looking away from his uninvited guest, just turn on the light.

"Don't do that."

Ray hesitated, there was something comforting in the words, it wasn't a command - it was a request.

"*Please*." He added.

"Who are you?" Ray asked, his voice shaking. "Are you gonna hurt me?"

"No." He said. "In this life…your killers come with smiles, they'll disarm you with charm and charisma." He smiled. "The backstabbers Ray, they're the *real* threat."

"I know." He whispered, shocked. "I know people like that."

"You *think* you know." He replied. "Watch them *smile*. Watch them *pretend*."

"I'm not sure I -"

"I'm sorry, Ray." He stepped forward from the shadows into a shard of moonlight.

Ray recognised instantly the shoulder length dark hair, those pale features were highly accentuated in the moonlight, he looked like a - *ghost*.

"It's you." He whispered. "It really is you." He wanted to stand up and approach him, but feared he may simply vanish if threatened in any way. "Can I touch you?" He longed to move to him.

"No." He answered flatly. "Don't spoil the illusion."

"Of course," He nodded obediently. "You're right, I'm sorry." He couldn't help his excitement.

"You have nothing to be sorry about." He replied, "You're a good man, that's why I'm here."

Ray stared in awe, stood before him, was quite possibly the answer to his prayers - there *was* another side, there was indeed a realm to be crossed and a fourth dimension to an otherwise two dimensional world.

"Brandon." He whispered. "You died."

"Sick people die, Ray." He answered. "I was murdered. You know that."

"So how -" He stalled. "How exactly do you, come back?"

"There are no boundaries in this life," He said, kneeling down in front of Ray's recliner. "They exist only in the mind."

Ray looked him over, his eyes had accustomed to the faded light now and although still terribly dark he could at least see that his guest, was attired differently to how he'd looked in the cemetery. He was still clad all in black, though his trousers appeared to be leather since the moonlight reflected off them, and they gave off that distinctive sound when stretched, he also wore a tight fitting long sleeved T - shirt. Most noticeable even in the dark, was that he appeared to be strapped in to a full body harness, with tensioning points at the chest and waist, and he couldn't see what exactly, but something was also strapped to his back as it was visible over his shoulders.

"Are you a ghost?" He asked, finally.

"Before you know what I am, you first need to know what *you* are."

"And what's that?"

"Well you asked earlier, how do you make a call?"

"You heard that?" He asked, amazed. "So they really can hear what's said?"

"Well I can't speak for *them*," He replied with a laugh. "But I was stood right next to you as you had your cigarette, all you had to do was look left - and there I was with my back to the wall, hoping you wouldn't see me."

King, was no longer growling and had emerged from Ray's side to perform his own brand of questioning, Ray resisted the urge to stop him and watched on as the stranger offered his hand to the animal, his heart warmed at the sight.

"My brother is in danger, Ray." He said, his pale features turned rather more sinister. "You must protect him, I need *you* to help me now." He went on, still kneeling before Ray with King licking from his hands. "In turn I offer you *my* protection, although I fear I need you far more than you need me." He spoke with an almost childlike vulnerability, Ray picked up on this immediately.

"But, why do you need me at all?" He asked. "What can I do that *you* can't?"

The visitor raised to his feet, laughing as he did so. "*Everything.*" He replied, turning his back to Ray and walking towards the patio doors, he was illuminated fully as he stood near them and looked into the night. Ray could see now exactly what it was he had strapped to his back. Two large samurai swords. They were encased in protective sheaths that were secured to his torso with straps. The harness was rather more visible too, he could see what looked like steel clasps, there were four of them - one by each shoulder and two at the waist that ran parallel.

"Protect him, Ray." He whispered, then walked once more to the shadows from which he'd emerged.

"Wait a minute!" Ray said, jumping from his chair. "How do I call you if I need you?"

"You don't." He answered. "If you need me I'll know it."

"Ok," He answered smiling. "Then, *what* do I call you?"

"I'm a reaper, Ray." He replied.

"A reaper?"

"Yes," He whispered. "I'm here to collect souls, of that you should have no doubt. Their last words will be spoken to me and their last breaths will fall upon me, I am the cancer in their bones. My name is *Death*."

"I thought you were -"

"You assumed."

- *Brandon*. He finished, in his mind.

"What's with those things?" He pointed to the swords. He stood with his back to Ray, his hands were pressed up against the wall like he was about to push it down.

"My equalisers." He replied, he did not turn around but Ray knew he was grinning. "Beautiful aren't they?" He asked.

"Yes," Ray answered nervously. "Yes they are."

He peered over his right shoulder and looked at Ray, although his features remained very much hidden from scrutiny behind his long black hair.

"You know, they say the value of these things sky rockets once they've taken a life." He smiled. "These will be worth a *fortune*." He drew his finger to his lips. "Sshh." He returned to the patio doors, pulled them open and stepped out into the cold night air. "They're watching you, Ray." He said. "Don't give them a reason to hurt you." He slammed the doors shut and stepped from view.

Ray ran to the doors and opened them again, he peered in all directions but he was nowhere to be seen, without a trace it would seem, he'd vanished. Ray closed the doors once more and turned on the light.

"Did that just happen?" He muttered to himself. King, who was sat by the recliner, stared blankly back at him. Ray was unable to stop the smile that crept across his face, for he knew the answer was yes - he also knew that, whoever *he* was - wasn't a figment of his own imagination, and more importantly that he wasn't losing his mind. He glanced at his watch, it was ten minutes past midnight. He lit a cigarette and slumped in to his chair, for the first time in a long time his body felt *happily* tired, as opposed to sick and tired. As so many questions raced through his mind, the truth was, he didn't care - he knew the answers would find him, and for once - find him *well*.

Chapter Seven

<u>Friday 5th March.</u>

The sun shone brightly although it was deceptively cold. Ray drove his Police cruiser through Washburn Springs at speed, the sirens cleared a path for him as the early morning traffic parted ways to allow him through. His thoughts were many as he raced to the Washburn link road, although he wouldn't allow them any hang time while he drove. It had been two months since *his* visit, but that didn't matter anymore - the call was in. Other units had sealed off the filling station on the link road since the early hours, though he'd only heard about it on the morning news and the details had been vague to say the least, but the buzz in the station had been firm - a decapitation had taken place last night.

Ray arrived at the filling station and was greeted by a small media circus, a couple of news crews had set up and a live broadcast was taking place just outside the cordon. The filling station was quite remote in its setting, just off the Washburn link road with only fields surrounding it as far as the eye could see. As far as *Ray* could see, it was the perfect setting to lay in wait, there were no fences around the premises and the fields ran straight up to the forecourt at both the sides and rear. He wasn't surprised to see the scene of the crime was at the pumps furthest from the road, at the rear and just feet from the fields, he noticed some trees and bushes too.

"He didn't stand a chance." He muttered with a smile. He parked the cruiser as close to the rear of the forecourt that the cordon would allow, he quickly got out and slammed the door behind him. He stood by the car and observed his surroundings fully, although it was furthest from the road and near the fields, it was quite close to the payment window where the attendant would've been, this struck him as risky although he guessed Brandon would've watched the attendant as much as he did his quarry. He saw also the C.C.T.V cameras, every pump was covered by one, but having reviewed so many evidence tapes over the years he knew full well that in most cases, time lapse footage was a waste of time, Brandon was home and dry.

"Ray!" The voice shouted, he recognised it instantly as Vincelli. "Over here."

He acknowledged him with a wave and made his way over. He ducked beneath the tape and looked at the gathered onlookers he'd passed. He smiled, laughed actually.

"What's wrong with these people, Joe?" He asked, tossing his thumb over his shoulder. "They've driven here for no other reason -"

"Well this is their town, Ray." He answered. "People are going to be scared when this gets out, and we aint doing shit to reassure them, are we?"

They both approached pumps seven and eight, the ones nearest the field. They were cordoned of within the cordon, as Ray neared he saw white sheets laying on the ground, they were covering the body, it was no more than five feet from the edge of the forecourt.

"He was attacked while he gassed up that car." He pointed to a sky blue Chrysler Neon. "It's a stolen car, so that's problem number one." Vincelli knelt down next to the bloodied sheets. "Problem number two, if you're ready for it?"

Ray nodded.

"Ok." He pulled the sheets back a little.

"Oh, Jesus." Ray whispered, muffling his own words as he spoke since his hand was planted firmly across his mouth. He knelt down next to Vincelli, his legs were weak.

"It isn't pretty is it?" Vincelli asked, watching Ray's facial expressions.

"Blood," He said. "There's so much blood." He felt sick.

"Well my friend, that's a side effect of having your head sliced from your shoulders." He smiled. "But that isn't the only problem"

Ray's hands were shaking noticeably, his *own* body felt drained of blood as he gazed down. *They* had done this, *The equalisers,* as Brandon had called them - those beautiful swords, so elegant and mystical yet so deadly in purpose.

Vincelli pulled the sheets further down to expose more of the mutilated body that lay before them, again he studied Ray's every reaction big or small.

"His hands," Ray said. "His hands are gone."

"As is his head, Ray. Gone." He covered up the body once more and they both raised to their feet. "This happened at three - thirty this morning, now the cashier didn't witness the actual attack but what she did see has left her pretty shook up."

"No doubt." Ray answered, again looking at the payment window.

"She saw him in the car."

"Who?" Ray asked, "This guy?"

"No." He answered. "She saw *him*." He looked around, gazing out into the fields, to the many possible escape routes he may have taken. "Whoever he is, he's extremely calculated, almost professional in his approach."

"What was he doing in the car?"

"Wiping it down." Vincelli answered. "The steering wheel, the gear shift and then the handles." Despite standing next to gasoline pumps, he threw a cigarette in his mouth and lit it.

"Forensics have been here all morning," He said. "There's not a single print."

"It wasn't his own prints he was removing, was it?" Ray asked.

"No." He sighed. "He's making it as hard as possible for us to identify the body, that's why he's taken the head, and the hands, with him." He sighed as he cupped his cigarette secretly within his palm. "He got to him *before* he'd even removed the pump from the tank." He laughed a little. "At least if he'd have made it to the payment window…we'd have a good shot of his face and be able to identify the poor bastard."

"You're giving him too much credit, Joe." Ray whispered. "It's a stolen car, do you really think he'd pay to gas it up?" He stared out into the fields, they ran for several miles so he knew sealing them off wasn't an option. "Do you think he's dumped them out there somewhere?" He asked. "His head and hands?"

"No chance." Vincelli replied. "Why remove them just to dump them? There's dog handlers combing the fields in sections but I know they'll draw a blank."

He agreed completely with Vincelli's theory, he knew there was no way Brandon would've just dumped them in the fields, what he didn't understand was why he's taken them in the first place.

"What's the C.C.T.V like?" He asked, staring up at the cameras.

"Well it's been seized." He replied. "It'll be analysed *naturally*, but I'm not expecting miracles." He smiled at Ray. "But at least it's not time lapse."

"It's not?"

"No." He said. "It's live…they get a lot of drive outs here."

"So did she get a look at his face?"

"No." He answered. "She said he had long dark hair, and that he kept his head tilted down so it covered his face."

Ray felt relieved, almost proud that Brandon had pulled it off with such ease, he was true to his word. *This boy is special*, he thought. *Very special, and very dangerous - and my friend.* He felt powerful.

"But I'll tell you what she did see," Vincelli said, walking past Ray and out onto the grassy verge. "She saw him walking calmly out into these fields, with the guys head in his right hand, she said he had a fist full of the guys hair wrapped around his hand and carried it like a hammer, and he had his hands in his left." He stood and tried to imagine his path, carrying such macabre trophies. "You know what?" He asked. "For all we know, he may as well have took off into the sky."

"Yeah." Ray agreed with a casual tilt of his head. "Did she describe his clothing?"

"He was dressed head to toe in black," He answered. "And he had two samurai swords strapped to his back." He laughed. "I guess there's no point searching for the murder weapon either."

Ray followed him to the edge of the forecourt and he too gazed out into the fields, he kept Vincelli in his foreground as he closed his eyes and took a deep breath, he said nothing.

"The funniest thing," Vincelli said, almost as an afterthought. "When I pressed her for any details she may have forgotten, even the smallest thing - do you know what she said?"

"No."

"She said that as he walked away into these fields, she could see he was wearing what looked like a harness of some kind, like he was going mountain climbing or something." He laughed and turned to face Ray, "Do you see any mountains around here?"

"No, Joe." He answered. "I do have one question though."

"What is it?"

"You said he doesn't want us identifying the body," He looked down at the sheets, blood had soaked through them at the edges. "So why leave us anything? Why do it here?"

"He wants us to know he's out there, Ray." He said. "Or he wants *someone* to know he's out there."

15 : 00

"Good afternoon, Julianne." Mark said, peering into Chad's room. "How are you today?" He spoke in a whisper, almost respectful of Chad's slumber.

"I'm ok." She answered, she didn't mean it, the tone of her voice told him all he *really* needed to know. She brushed her hair from her eyes as she looked at him, and forced a smile.

"Can I come in?" He asked.

"Of course." She answered, rising from her chair. Mark entered the room and closed the door quietly behind him, his hand brushed across her waist as he circled past her.

"I'm sure you've been told of the fluctuations that happened this morning?"

"Yes." She answered. "But that's happened before so I'm not running away with myself on this one."

"It's our most promising signal yet," He said. "It happened at half three this morning, he just spiked out, which is strange because between two and six in the morning is when the human body is at it's lowest ebb, many terminally ill patients give up between those times." He stood at the base of Chad's bed and looked him up and down. "He's got a lot of brain activity going on, you should remain optimistic, Julianne."

"I'm trying." She whispered, *but giving up*, she thought.

"You're looking much better these days." He said, adjusting his glasses a little on his face. "You've put some weight back on too." He smiled, though it quickly faded as he realised what he'd said.

"What girl doesn't want to hear that?" She laughed.

"I'm sorry." He looked a little embarrassed with himself. "That just came out *so* wrong."

"It's ok." She slid back into her chair and glanced nervously at Chad.

"You don't need me annoying you with all you're going through." He took off his glasses, folded them and placed them in his overall pocket.

"I know you meant well, Mark." She darted her eyes from Chad, to Mark and back again.

"Erm," He muttered, unsure of himself as he looked to the floor.

"What's wrong?" She asked, trying to find his eyes with her own. "Tell me." She urged.

"Oh god," He said, running his hands through his spiked hair. "I didn't think it would be this hard."

"We know each other, Mark." She smiled. "You know me at least, Do I know you?"

"You do." He answered.

"Well, it can't be that bad can it?"

"Well there's a carnival coming to town," His voice shook as he spoke, he tried not to look at Chad as he struggled to find the words. "I was wondering if you'd like to go?" He breathed a sigh of relief as he looked at her and saw she was smiling. "We could get a beer, or a *coffee* even, hell - we could get a hot dog if you liked." He relaxed a little as she nodded her approval. "If you don't like beer, coffee or hot dogs, there's rides too!" He seemed excited.

"Mark you're a really nice guy." She said. "Did anyone ever tell you that?" She stood up and walked to where he was stood. "I think you and I could be very good *friends*." She took his hands in hers. "So yes, I'd love to." She patted herself on the back, figuratively speaking for avoiding an awkward moment.

"I do too." He replied. "It's about time you had a little fun." He rubbed her hands in his own. "I guessed you could do with a friend." A moments silence engulfed the pair, they just stood and looked at each other for what seemed like an age. "You *could* do with a friend, right?" He pressed her gently to answer.

"Like you wouldn't believe." She bowed her head against his chest and stepped a little closer to him.

"Why have you not got a girlfriend?" She asked.

"I just don't have the time." He shrugged his shoulders. "I'm here all the time, the hours are long - the pay is awful." He laughed. "I guess my on - line profile writes itself."

Julianne laughed, her head was still against his chest. "I'll buy the hot dogs, Mark." She said with a giggle.

Chapter Eight

<u>**Saturday 20th March.**</u>

The floral tributes at the crash site, which up until recently had still been pouring in, lay wilting or dead, the hand written verses had blown free from the trees they were pinned to, and the candles in the jars were no longer being renewed. For the many who passed, it was noticed by few, not anymore. The traffic moved slowly but steadily through the dense fog that had engulfed the Washburn Link road, by late evening it would normally be deserted, but not when the carnival was in town, it drew the masses from Colorado and Washburn Springs. It was opening night at Lily May's Travelling Fun Fair, a night referred to by many as, *Danger Night.*

Julianne did her best to ignore the wind chill, it was freezing. She also did her best to ignore those tributes, or lack thereof that she had passed a short while ago. She walked slowly with her arms folded, seemingly unaware of the company beside her. Heavy bass pumped through the speakers like rolling thunder in the blackest skies, it grew louder as each ride she passed competed with the previous. The lights flashed and pulsed in rhythm with the music and screams filled the cold night air, screams of laughter and screams of terror as the rides spun at break - neck speeds. Never would she set foot on any one of them, to her they looked like a horrific way to lose your money, or lunch. But she did like hot dogs, and did need a break. The ground underfoot was sludgy and uncertain, she felt pleased she hadn't dressed up as once again her foot sank into a puddle of mud, though she had spent most of the afternoon thinking about it, the jeans and sweater she had carefully chosen didn't say *'date,'* but showed a willingness to look nice for her chaperone. Mark reached out and took her arm as she struggled for balance.

"Is this why you brought me here?" She asked, pulling her foot free. "To watch me fall flat on my face?" She smiled, her eyes reflected the many lights shining in them.

"I just wanted an excuse to touch you." He laughed nervously before letting go of her arm.

"You're a bad man, Mark." She pushed him lightly as she gazed at the stalls around her. *Maybe this will be a good night*, she thought to herself. Mark noticed a smile that finally seemed to be genuine.

"It's about time." He told her.

"I hope you realise we're not going anywhere until you've won me a prize."

"Name it!" He said firmly. "A bear? A fish? What do you fancy?"

"Well that's a different question isn't it?" She looked into his eyes for a moment. *Jeans and sweater, Julianne*. She reminded herself.

"Why don't we start with a bear?" She said. One stall in particular had caught her attention, it was nestled neatly between a helter skelter and a games arcade. It had a red and white striped vinyl roof whilst the door was blue with white stars on it, she strained her tired eyes a little to read it.

"Star Spangled Anna." She said. "Cute." She laughed. Underneath her name it read 'Your future, here!' She felt intrigued by this little tent, something about it was pulling her, drawing her in. In a few days time the tent, along with everything else around her would be packed into trailers and gone, with nothing more than holes in the ground where the pegs were driven. She had toyed with the idea of seeing a palmist, or having her cards dealt for a long time.

She hadn't heard Mark speaking to her so was a little surprised to feel him grasping her arm and pulling her in another direction, away from the tent. He was pointing into a mass of people though she didn't know why, nor did she care. She still couldn't hear him, the music was just so loud, deafening in fact - sense numbing. He was striding into the crowd and pulling harder, she looked down at her wrist to see his hand clamped around it, she lost her balance a little but even that failed to slow him. She felt like a child being dragged from a playground, weather being saved from a bully or abducted from safety, she now felt fearful. All around her she saw excited children running around. *Would anyone hear me scream?* She wondered. The lights too seemed more intense than ever, burning brightly, flashing - pulsing - surging, before finally exploding - one after the other, shards of glass reigned down but no one seemed to notice, least of all care. She looked behind her and was relieved to see the tent was still in her line of sight, despite the hoards of people between her and it. She screamed for help but the words didn't come out, nothing came out except her warm breath against the cold mist, no one was looking, no one could see her as she struggled against his grasp. As more lights exploded overhead she shielded her face with her available hand, she felt the glass slice through her skin and was instantly aware of her own flowing blood, she uncovered her face to see how deep the laceration was, and then she saw *him* - standing there. She felt her body go limp, as logical thoughts escaped her, she knew it was Brandon. She couldn't move and struggled to deal with the image that burned through her mind like a thousand fires.

"It can't be you." She whispered, pulling hard she felt Mark's grip tighten. *Is it Chad?* She wondered, *has he recovered? Is he looking for me?* She shook her head and reminded herself that not six hours ago, he was unable to breathe without assistance, least of all dress, walk and look *that good*. Brandon had more chance of returning from the dead, than Chad had of recovering so fast, it was *him*, she felt *him* - she *always* had. She studied him, he was attired completely in black and his hair was flowing beautifully around his chiselled features. Chad was identical in every physical way, but there was never any question of dominance between them or anybody around them, Brandon's power was absolute and he was acutely aware of it. He was stood on the entrance platform of the Waltzers, leaning casually on the guard rail. People moved slowly in the foreground that separated them, but their connection remained, he stared into her eyes and she stared back - stalemate. He pointed to the tent she'd seen, she knew instantly what he wanted and dragged her hand from Mark's grasp.

"I'll go." She whispered.

He stood straight and passed effortlessly through the turnstile to enter the ride, the flashing lights around him cut into his muscular physique, then he was gone.

"Hey!" Mark shouted. "Do you think I'm fucking stupid?"

She turned to find him shouting directly in her face, she rubbed at her wrist and tried to make sense of the last few minutes, she looked again at the Waltzers but Brandon was no longer anywhere to be seen.

"Mark, I -"

"If you want to go running off with someone then be my guest."

"What?" She asked. "I just thought I saw someone I knew, that's all."

"Some friends of mine are over there," He pointed into the crowd. "But if this is how you're going to be then forget it."

She stood silently whilst still rubbing at her wrist and peered into the crowd, she was aware of her vulnerability and realised she didn't know him at all.

"Why don't you just fuck off!" He said, moving into her and forcing her to retreat a little.

She felt threatened but couldn't move, she saw three men emerging from the crowd, they were laughing at her while they counted some money between them.

"I thought we were friends, Mark?" She looked down at the muddy ground beneath her and tried to focus through her tears.

"Friends?" He asked, moving closer to her. "You want to be friends? That's it?" He crouched a little to level his eyes with hers. "You don't want more than that?"

"No."

"Not even a little?"

"No, Mark." She shook her head and found the courage to look into his eyes. "I can't, I thought you understood that."

"I understand, Julianne." He said, smiling. "I understand you're a cock teasing bitch." He stepped back and glared into her eyes, he had a wild smile on his face. "You're just like the rest of them aren't you?" He laughed at her.

She stood and watched as his three friends circled around him, all four of them stared back and took their turns in screaming obscenities at her. She could no longer determine what exactly was being said as the music had taken over, everything else was muted, but the music was clearer and louder than ever. For a moment she wondered if it was closing time as the lights began to fade around her, it was a moment *later* when she realised *everything* was fading around her, fading to black.

Laying on her back she opened her eyes to see people gathered around her, they peered down and were clearly concerned. Mark was knelt beside her, he was talking to her but she couldn't hear him, though she could feel him stroking her hand. It was different to how it *had* been, very different. The music was lower, although still extremely loud. She noticed she could at least construct a thought despite it, the lights were brighter than she remembered. Mark pulled her to a sitting position, he was gentle with her and stroked her back. They looked at one another and she saw instantly in his eyes how worried he clearly was. To her relief the gathered onlookers began to disperse as Mark gave assurances she was going to be fine, one by one they nodded sympathetically at her then thanked Mark. She was embarrassed.

"Oh my god." She stared at Mark, who was still crouched beside her supporting her. "Did I faint?" She asked.

"You sure did." He replied. "You had me worried there, you went down hard." He looked closely at her. "Are you feeling ok?" He asked.

"I'm so ashamed," She laughed at herself and clambered to her feet, Mark clung tightly to her arm as she did so.

"Don't be silly," He said, patting her down. "I'm just glad you're ok, you know I'm off duty tonight, right?" They both laughed.

"Am I dirty?" She asked, pulling the back of her jumper as much into view as it would allow.

"A little." He answered. He removed his leather jacket and now stood in just jeans and a white T - shirt. "You can wear this if you like?" He placed the jacket over her shoulders.

"Thank you."

"Now listen here young lady," He took hold of the jacket around her shoulders and pulled her towards him. "I'll have no excuses from you, we are going to enjoy ourselves - and that's an order." He laughed at her.

"Ok," She answered, inspecting the jacked as she fed her arms through the sleeves. "Are you going to be ok in just that?" She pointed to his T - shirt.

"I'll be fine." He assured her and placed his arms around her shoulders, she didn't object - she was just relieved he was Mark again.

"Have you ever wanted to have your fortune read?" She asked.

"Oh no," He laughed a little. "You want to go in there don't you?" He nodded to the tent. "I saw you looking at it."

"Can I?" She asked. "I wont be long, I've always wanted to."

"Of course you can."

They both walked slowly towards the tent, Julianne's attention was divided between it and the Waltzers they were about to pass, she knew not to bother looking for *him*, though she still nervously scanned the crowd gathered about the entrance platform.

"Oh hey!" Mark said. "There's some friends of mine." He pointed to a group gathered outside the toll booth of the ride. She felt her stomach churn and her legs trembled once more.

"We could do this another time if you wanted to see them?" She asked, hoping he would agree.

"Are you kidding?" He asked, nudging her in the arm. "I'll just go and say hi while I wait for you?" He saw doubt in her eyes and wondered if maybe she wasn't ready for an evening out after all. "Is this what you want?"

"I do," She hesitated for a moment. "It's just, if you wanted to see your friends instead, that would be ok with me."

He sighed heavily and studied her, it was clear to him she was nervous.

"Are you ok?" He asked, rubbing her arm slightly. "You're acting kinda funny."

She clapped her hands together slowly as she chose her words, she still didn't understand what had happened during her blackout and although she accepted it was just a dream of some kind, the fact his friends were now present was just a little too ominous for her to ignore.

"I'm just not ready to meet them, Mark." She said. "I'm just feeling scared, I don't even know why, I just think they'll laugh at me." She divided her weight from one leg to the other and stared down at the grass beneath her feet. "I think maybe *you'll* laugh at me too." She felt silly, saying it made her feel pathetic.

"Julianne," He said. "You really are a piece of work, do you know that?" He reached out to her face and lifted her chin up, her eyes found his after a moment. "Why would you even let such an idea enter your head? That's just crazy." He kept his fingers under her chin as he knew she would look down again given an opportunity to. "I brought you here to give you a nice evening out, you deserve it. But also, because I happen to *like* being with you."

"Thank you, Mark." She said. "I'm sorry, I know I'm hard work." She knew he was trying.

"Ok." He removed his hand from her face and pushed her gently. "Now go waste your money over there. The sooner you go the sooner you're back."

She resisted the urge to hug him and nodded her approval instead. "Ok." She smiled and headed for the tent.

She waited outside it for a moment and pretended to search for her purse, although she knew exactly where it was. Instead she was buying time so as to catch a glimpse of Mark once he'd joined his friends by the Waltzers. She glanced nervously over her shoulder to see him, he was laughing and joking with them, she saw him light a cigarette and throw the lighter at one of his friends. To her eyes he *did* seem different with them, *but he was bound to be, wasn't he?* She wondered.

"Are you coming in?" The voice asked. She was caught unaware and spun round to see who it belonged to, dropping her purse as she did so.

"Are you -?"

"I'm Anna," She replied with a smile.

"You must be good," Julianne said, kneeling down to retrieve her purse. "Already you're finishing my sentences." As she rose to her feet she observed Anna with growing enthusiasm, there was nothing stereotypical about her. She was a petite young girl with flowing blonde hair, she wore a long blue dress that hugged her figure like it was statically charged, with a red headscarf hanging loosely around her neck.

"My *real* name is Lisa," She said with a grin. "But it's a damn catchy slogan, wouldn't you agree?" She held the flap back for her guest and beckoned her through.

Julianne smiled and walked in behind her, as the flap fell back into place she felt the warmth hit her immediately and unzipped Marks jacket. The tent was, as she'd expected, small and cramped but incredibly cosy and welcoming. It had only a small round wooden table with two chairs opposite one another, there was a gas heater in one corner and a coat stand in the other. Her attention was drawn to the wooden chest in the space that separated them, she guessed it was Anna's box of tricks since the table was empty.

"You're not how I imagined you'd be." Julianne said. "I thought you'd be old with a wart on your nose or something." They both laughed.

"What's your name?" Lisa asked, sitting down in one of the chairs. "That'll be the only thing you tell *me*." She directed her open palm at the vacant chair.

"I'm Julianne." She slid out of Mark's jacket and put it over the back of the chair, before sitting down.

"What would you like Julianne?" She asked. "Tarot cards, Crystal ball or a palm reading?"

"I don't know," She replied, "I didn't even consider there would be choices like that." She felt flustered, unaware that her every move and nervous chatter were being expertly read by Lisa - or *Anna*, and providing all the clues necessary to build a profile that would form the basis of her reading.

"Which would you recommend?" Julianne asked.

"I think for you," Lisa paused, looking her directly in the eye. "The crystal ball would be most beneficial." She smiled.

Mark stood beside the entrance booth for the Waltzers with three of his friends, Jake Gibson and brothers Tommy and Jason 'Jet' Turner, his inner circle from a much larger group they ran with. He cupped carefully in his hand what remained of his cigarette, not once putting it to his lips without first glancing at the tent.

"Why don't you just fucking relax?" Jake asked. "You're making me nervous, she's not your girlfriend just smoke it." Jake was in his early thirties and was a bouncer from one of the clubs in town, a tall stocky man with a shaven head and a bad temper, if he wasn't in the gym he was in the tanning studio next to it, he wore a long leather jacket with ripped jeans and a black shirt.

"Well she doesn't know I smoke and I want to keep it that way." Mark said.

"She doesn't know a lot of things," He leaned closer to mark and nudged him in the ribs. "Does she?"

"She doesn't know anything just relax."

"You sure about that, Mark?" He asked. "I think you're sweet on this little thing." Tommy and Jet laughed beside them.

"I'm not fucking sweet." He replied. "Would I like to fuck her? Yes. Will I fuck her? Yes. Does she suspect anything? No." He laughed.

"Well you can fuck the shit out of her for all I care," He pointed angrily towards the tent. "But don't let that bitch find anything out."

"I could tell her anything right now," Mark said. "She trusts me. So should you." He glanced again at the tent and smoked the last of his cigarette before stamping it into the grass.

Having produced a crystal ball from her box of tricks, Lisa placed it in the centre of the table and draped a purple silk scarf over it, which she immediately pulled off again in a slow purposeful motion.

"It resets the energies." She whispered. Julianne sat quietly, almost too excited to speak, she watched as Lisa moved her palms slowly over the smooth surface of the ball, her bracelets rattling as she did so. Lisa closed her eyes and took a deep breath.

"There's a presence here," She whispered. "A young man, dead but not gone - he's trapped between our world and the next." Julianne sat completely stunned. *How can you possibly know that?* She wondered. She wanted to ask but was now too *scared* to speak.

"His is a forced exile," She added. "He is here for you and wont make the transition until you are safe, until he has made it *possible* for you to be safe." She pulled her hands away from the ball and sat back in her chair, she appeared scared. "I'm sorry," She whispered. "This never happens."

"What never happens?"

"This."

"Can you get more?" She asked. "Safe from what? I need more."

"I'll try again." She placed her hands upon the ball and closed her eyes.

"We're going on," Tommy shouted, tilting his head at the Waltzers next to them. "Are you guys coming or what?"

Mark shook his head and observed the tent. "I'm going soon, just waiting for her."

"You two go." Jake said. "I'll wait here with Mark."

"Why don't you come on with us?" Tommy asked, "Are you scared you might get seen smiling or something?" He laughed. Tommy was tall and skinny with spindly legs and long dark hair, it was always scruffy and unkempt, he was in his early twenties while Jet was, by far the youngest in their wider group of friends at just seventeen. Tommy pulled his wallet from the inside pocket of his red and black lumberjack shirt.

"Just taking care of business." Jake replied. "Not here to have a good time, Tommy." He looked him up and down and tensed his muscles within his jacket. "I've got a rep to think about, screaming like a girl on those things wont help it, will it."

"Have it your way." Tommy said, running past them to catch his brother up at the turnstile. Both Jake and Mark watched as their two friends excitedly treaded the wooden platform for an empty carriage. A tall thin, heavily bearded man in a dirty white vest stood next to one and gestured them over to it. He pulled the safety bar outwards and held the circular carriage still while they fell into it. "Six dollars!" He shouted, competing with the sound system that surrounded him on the ride, his dirty hand remained outstretched while his eyes scanned the remaining empty carriages. A large group of teenage girls boarded the wooden rotating platform, the ride operator had it moving very slowly so he could observe how many were still vacant as they passed his booth. Tommy noticed the man's filthy fingernails as the money changed hands, they were blackened with engine oil, he could smell it. He threw the money into a leather pouch around his waist and kicked the safety bar into place over their legs, though he didn't lock it. "Enjoy!" He shouted, moving on to the next carriage.

"He didn't lock it, dude." Jet said, pointing to the safety bar. "Can you reach it to lock it?"

Tommy laughed. "Just fucking relax, man." He answered. "You don't need to lock it, just hold the fucking bar if you're scared."

"I'm not scared!" He answered quickly. "I was just saying." He shrugged his broad shoulders and leaned forward to observe the money collector, he relaxed a little when he saw the man wasn't locking any of the safety bars, Tommy continued to laugh and patted him in the arm. "Just fucking chill, Bro."

Julianne's gaze was focused hard on Lisa across the table, she held her breath as she waited for her to speak.

"You're in some degree of danger," She whispered. "You must be sure of your company as they're whispering now."

"Who's -" She stopped herself with a very childlike, hand over the mouth gesture. "Sorry." she whispered.

"He's insisting you *must* be sure of the company you keep, as your fate lies in their hands, you are most definitely in danger here, he's insistent of that. He wants to tell you something but wont communicate it through me, but the clues are in the photographs." She shook her head and intensified her grip on the ball. "What?" She asked, her eyes were closed tightly and she seemed to be in some pain, beads of sweat trickled down her forehead as she slumped back in her seat and without warning, her eyes were wide open and staring at Julianne.

"Leave this place, Julianne." She whispered, in a voice unlike her own. "Before it's too late, leave now." She stared blankly across the table to Julianne, before shaking her head and appearing to awake from a dream state.

"Oh my god," She screamed, springing from her seat and running for refuge behind Julianne, tears streamed down her face and Julianne felt her *magic* hands trembling on her shoulders.

"I don't know what just fucking happened," She shouted. "But I want you out of my tent right now."

"What?" Julianne asked, twisting around to see her. "What did I do?"

"You brought something with you." She was crying hysterically. "You gotta go right now."

"You know what?" Julianne asked, pushing her chair out and standing up. "I don't know where you get off doing that, but you can just go and fuck yourself." She grabbed Mark's jacket from the back of the chair and threw it over her arm.

"This is supposed to be for fun, I'm sure whoever employs you doesn't pay you to ruin people's evenings." She took a twenty from her purse and slammed it down on the table "Keep the fucking change." She stepped from the tent and stood with her back to it, before taking a moment to catch her breath.

"She's out, lover boy," Jake said, tilting his head towards her. "You better run along now." Mark laughed and made his way slowly over to her, he kept his hands in his pockets as he did so. "You ok?" He asked. "Look like you've seen a ghost or something."

"I want to go home, Mark." She said. "I'm sorry, I'm just not ready for this." Lisa appeared from within her tent holding the twenty, she looked over Julianne's shoulder and stared at Mark.

"I can't take this off you, Julianne." She said, still staring at Mark. Without turning to look at her, Julianne ran off in the direction of the park's exit, barging past Mark as she did so. He watched her run away then turned to face Lisa who was stood motionless, just staring into his eyes.

"What kind of shit have you been telling her?" He asked. "She was fine!"

"I told her what I saw." She replied. "If it upset her then I'm sorry."

"What you saw was twenty dollars," He pointed to her hand. "You'll do anything for money you fucking whore."

"Is that so?" She asked, "Then why was I trying to give it back to her?"

"Give it to me." He held out his hand for the money.

She took his hand in her own and held the twenty at eye level, like a magician performing a trick.

"You can have this if you give her a message for me." She spoke slowly, deliberately stalling for time as she held his hand, she smiled at him and slammed the twenty into his palm. "Tell her to keep running."

As the Waltzers began their clockwise journey around the wooden platform, the carriages turned limply one way and then the other, until the *spinners* appeared. Jet had noticed there were two men treading the boards doing the spinning, the tall thin man they'd paid and another man, much larger in build wearing a bland tatty grey sweater and jeans. He was the ride operator too, as Jet had watched him jump off the rotating platform and return to the booth to increase the speed, the jolt could be felt each time he did so, though it mattered little if the carriages were being left idle.

"Hey!" Tommy shouted, trying to stand up. "What about this one right here?"

Neither of the men seemed to hear, as they were too busy spinning the carriages with the girls in.

"If we had tits you'd be over here!" He shouted again but realised it was futile as the music was just too loud.

"This is a waste of fucking time, bro." He said, falling back into his seat. "It's like a fucking merry - go - round, we should be holding hands or some shit." Without warning they both felt their carriage jolt, it no longer limped from side to side, it had fallen under someone's direct control. Tommy looked over his shoulder to see a pair of hands were holding it still from behind, clean hands. Using the safety bar as leverage, Tommy pulled his body weight forward in an attempt to see above the head rest, he saw a man standing behind them holding the carriage tightly, he had long dark hair which covered his face almost entirely.

"Come on!" Tommy shouted. "Get us going before it's too late!" The lights over head began flickering and losing sync with the music, they surged and one by one they began exploding over head. Screams rang out from some of the other carriages as shards of glass rained down on unsuspecting revellers. Tommy watched with growing curiosity as the man leaned down to the side of the carriage, he reached for the locking mechanism and engaged it. As he did so, Tommy was able to catch a glimpse of the face within the hair. Jet tested the bar and found it to be securely fastened across their legs. "He's gonna give us a fuckin ride to remember, Bro." He shouted excitedly. Tommy did not reply.

He turned his head slowly and greeted both Jet and Tommy with a smile.

"So you want a hot ride, do you?" He asked, staring exclusively at Tommy. "Then you shall." A noticeable jolt from beneath the ride sent the rotating platform into overdrive, it whirred around faster and faster. Screams of terror competed with the deafening music as strobe lights over head flashed white light down on the three of them, Tommy tried to retreat further away from him but quickly realised there was nowhere to go.

"What are you doing?" Jet shouted. "Stay there." He tried to force Tommy back again but couldn't, his torso was rigid with fear and simply wouldn't be moved. Tommy turned to face his tormentor.

"When did you get better?" He asked nervously. "I mean, I thought you were -" His words trailed to nothing as he realised there would be no answer. He flinched as the man leaned down into the carriage, all attempts to remain calm were now gone. Tears streamed down his face as he felt the man's breath in his ear.

"Do you regret what you did to me?" He asked calmly, which despite the loud music Tommy heard.

"Do you even know *what* you did to me?" He moved slowly away from the side of Tommy's face and watched him react.

"Yes!" He shouted. "I didn't want to be involved, Man. I fucking swear on my brother's life!" Tommy wiped frantically at the tears on his face. "I'd never have hurt you." A blow he hadn't seen coming landed squarely across his jaw.

"Liar!" He shouted, jumping on to the carriage and squatting down in front of Tommy, he clung tightly to the safety bar as the carriage once again began swaying back and forth. He grabbed Tommy by the throat and pinned him securely against the head rest, with his face just an inch from Tommy's, his eyes bored deeply and silently into his terrified victim. "When fate stands before you as I do," He shouted, his saliva spraying into Tommy's face. "Do you really want to tempt it?" He asked. "Do you even comprehend what my being here means for you?"

"Please don't hurt me." He whispered, staring into his eyes. "I'm sorry, I didn't want to -"

"Sshh." He placed his finger across Tommy's lips and turned to look at Jet. He sat motionless, stunned into silence by the mysterious figure clad head to toe in black, who was literally terrorising his brother to death, a brother who until now he had believed was fearless. He didn't recognise this face, this face was devoid of all emotion, this face was pale, this face was dead, his flowing dark hair and the strobe lights overhead accentuated this in frightening detail. "Who are you?" Jet asked, himself rigid with fear.

"Ask your foolish Brother." He replied, pulling his hair from his face he revealed fully his features to Jet.

"Now," He whispered, turning once again to Tommy. "Do I have your full attention?"

"Yes." He answered, he was now crying hysterically. "I'm sorry, Jet." He shouted. "I'm so sorry."

"Do you love your brother?" He asked, holding him still by the throat.

"I do." He replied, "I do, I do - I fucking -" He was almost blinded by the tears in his eyes as he tugged wildly at the safety bar. "Don't hurt him, I'm fucking begging you." He screamed, but no answer came. "Chad, he wasn't there, man." He said. "Leave him out of it, please."

"Do you *love* your brother?" He asked again. Although the carriage was spinning wildly on the rotating platform, he held on with ease. His long hair flew up like a luxurious mane on a charging stallion.

"Yeah." Tommy replied. "You know I do, Chad."

He leaned into the carriage once again, and gripped Tommy tightly with both hands.

"I loved mine, Tommy." He said, speaking directly in to his ear but keeping Jet in his sights. "And like I lost mine, you shall lose yours."

Tommy gripped the bar tightly. "Chad, please don't hurt him - he wasn't there." He looked into the black eyes before him. "I'm sorry, it wasn't meant to go that far."

Their eyes locked for a moment. "I'll be sure to tell Chad." He replied.

Tommy looked again into those eyes, those *black* eyes. "What?" He asked, closing his eyes tightly. He felt his skin tingle as the breathing in his ear moved downwards to his neck.

"Karma just takes too long, Tommy." He whispered. "You need *Salvation*."

Pain burned through him as he prayed for his escape, his grip fell from the bar and his head lolled limply against the head rest, Jet looked on in horror, though was blindsided to the fact his brother was bleeding to death beside him.

"Hey!" Jet shouted. "Who the fuck are you?" He saw the stranger's mouth was smeared with blood, around his chin and dripping from his lips, though he stared calmly and unperturbed back at Jet.

"Who are you, motherfucker?" He watched on as his visitor seemed to have weakened, from his squatted position on the other side of the safety bar his grip loosened a little causing him to stumble, though he remained on the carriage. He appeared to be dazed.

"That's what you get, motherfucker!" Jet screamed, laughing wildly. "We'll fuck up the rest of your face when this ride stops!" He pushed Tommy. "I knew you were fucking with me!" He leaned in to him. "You head butted that prick!" He spoke with pride, until that is Tommy's body slumped back towards him and fell across his lap, he saw the river of blood pumping from his neck, his flesh was pierced and torn at the jugular. Jet looked again at what was now *his* tormentor, the disorientation he'd suffered moments prior had now vanished, he once again gripped the bar and balanced himself with ease, the carriage spun with such force he may as well have been hanging on to the aileron of a jumbo jet. His pale features mirrored Jet's to perfection as he smiled at Tommy's lifeless body.

"Why?" Jet asked, cradling Tommy's head in his lap. "Why did you kill my brother?" He screamed hysterically, holding Tommy's body protectively. "Why did you kill my fucking brother?"

He stared back at Jet, watching him cradle Tommy with tears running down his face reminded him of the innocence of childhood, the most basic of human instincts, to nurture. He imagined Jet and Tommy as children playing games as he had, as a child, opening their Christmas presents as he had, as a child. He knew fully his reason for ending Tommy's life, he also knew he was now as bad - if not worse than him, his smile faded as his evil deeds lay bleeding and crying before him.

"I'm sorry." He said, staring Jet directly in the eye. "One day you may come for me as I came for him, you may feel there is a debt to settle, but I'll *never* come for you." He released his grip on the bar and with breathtaking velocity launched from the carriage into the darkness, in a millisecond he was gone. The rotating platform slowed to a standstill as Jet gripped the bar tightly and stared down at his dead brother. The applied G - forces had caused Tommy's blood let to travel upwards over his face, his sleeping features looked pale and almost demonic under the strobe lights which flashed relentlessly upon them both.

Mark arrived back at his car, breathless and pale having chased her down, her scent hung thick in the air around her.

"Are you ok?" He asked. "I was worried, you just took off running." He leaned next to her against the car and caught his breath.

"I'm sorry." She whispered. "I'm just not supposed to be happy anymore." She pulled her fringe away from her eyes, they were red and puffy from crying. "Can you even imagine what some people will do for money?" She asked, her voice broke mid sentence. "The things she said, Mark. I don't know how she could've known the things she *knew*." She folded her arms across her chest and looked out into the cold night sky, her tears glistened as they trickled free. She leaned on Mark as the pair stood silently, they listened to the music and screams in the distance as they rode the night breeze to them. "I guess that kinda sucked." She said, trying to smile. "We didn't even get a drink in the end."

"Well now," He said. "That's not altogether true." He walked around the car to the driver's door and unlocked it, he reached inside and pulled a rucksack from the back seat. "*This is the end*," He said with a grin. "Here and now." He placed the rucksack on the floor and produced two bottles of Coke from within it. "We're not leaving until we've had a drink." He unscrewed the cap and handed the bottle over to her. "Here."

"You *do* come prepared, don't you?" She placed it to her lips and drank long and hard from it.

"It's just as well I do," He said, taking a sip from his own. "You look like you need it."

"I guess so." She held the bottle up against the lights in the foreground. "I've already had half!"

"Good." He smiled and placed his arm carefully around her shoulders, he was spurred on since she didn't immediately retreat. "Listen, don't let that crazy woman ruin our evening, the night is still young."

"I'm ok." She answered, squirming a little within his embrace. "She's not upset me, at least not now anyway." She slipped herself free of his grip. "But I still want to go home, if that's ok."

"Yeah," He answered flatly. "Ok, no problem."

"We can try again another night if you'd like?" She found herself following him as he walked away from her. "I hope you will, Mark."

"I will." Without so much as looking over his shoulder at her, he walked to the driver's side of the car, leaving her trailing. "Drink up, let's get you home."

She walked back to the passenger door, but instead of opening it and climbing in next to him, she chose instead to lean against the door and look out across the car strewn field to the fun fair. She sipped at her Coke and in her solitude noticed the music had stopped, but screams were still ringing out in the cold night air.

"Do you think something's wrong?" She asked, tapping gently on the window.

"What?" He asked, lowering the window on her side.

"Something's wrong." She said, looking across at the rides that were high enough to be visible from her vantage point. "The music has stopped and I can't see any rides moving."

"Maybe they lost power or something." He said, starting the engine.

"All the lights are still on." She tossed the empty bottle on to the floor, opened the door and climbed inside.

"Let's hit the road." He said, revving the engine to warm it a little. "Looks like it's closing early anyway."

Jake threw down his cigarette and crushed it underfoot, he glanced at The Waltzers behind him and noticed the ride was in total darkness, a group of teenage girls ran screaming down the steel steps. He looked at the other rides around him and saw that they too were being shut down, turnstiles were being flung open and revellers were being hastily evacuated in every direction he cared to look.

"What the hell?" He muttered. A large man came running towards him, wild eyed and screaming as he clanged down the platform in Jake's direction. Without warning Jake smashed his forearm into the man's throat as he passed him and knocked him clean off his feet, he landed heavily at Jake's feet, still screaming and struggling.

"You're one of the operators aren't you?" Jake shouted, kneeling on his chest. "Why are you running?" He gripped him around his neck tightly. "Tell me right now you fat fuck or I'll snap your neck here and now."

"Murder," He shouted, struggling to get Jake's hand from his throat. "There's a killer up there."

"What?" Jake shouted. "What the fuck are you saying?"

"Someone's been murdered on the ride." He said. "Get off me and get out of here."

Jake released his grip and watched as the man clambered to his feet and ran, he didn't even look back as he did so. Jake stood motionless for a moment - taking in what was happening all around him, it felt like a dream. The carnival was now almost deserted, and an eerie silence had swept through like the wind. He cut a lonely figure as he walked slowly up the steel steps, which until twenty minutes ago had been a hive of activity, but were now completely vacant. He listened carefully for any signs of life but heard only his own footfalls, they banged like drums on the sheet metal. He recognised this wasn't the most opportune route to take if he wished to remain unnoticed, but he didn't - he wanted to announce his presence in the hope of bringing out whoever was there with him. As he reached the summit and stepped onto the wooden platform his courage failed him, he stood still and tried to see movement from the corner of his eyes.

"Tommy!" He whispered loudly. "Are you still here?" He listened for something and clung tightly to the guard rail that circled the ride.

He noticed a rucksack on the floor next to his feet and found that old habits died hard, he knelt down and emptied the contents onto the wooden boards beside him. He rifled through them whilst looking around, his eyes had accustomed slightly to darkness and his confidence had returned since he had seen nor heard nothing. He selected a packet of cigarettes and quickly pocketed them before fanning out the remaining items, non of which held any interest for him except for a set of car keys with a mini flashlight on the key fob. He stood up and dusted down his leather coat, then aimed his newly acquired flashlight at the carriages before him, he couldn't see in them all since they rested at varying angles and inclines on the motorised platform, he could see however that they were all stationary. The operators booth to his right caused him the most concern due to its all round tinted windows, he knew someone could be staring right at him from behind the glass and he would be none the wiser, with that in mind he kept as much distance between him and the booth as possible.

"Jet!" He shouted. "Tommy?" He called again. "Are either of you still here?" He aimed his ear into the breeze once more, though he was reasonably content he was alone. "Fuckers." Keeping the booth in his sights he retreated slowly back down the steps, still listening for anything that broke the silence. A shudder came from underfoot as the platforms, both steel and wooden began to vibrate. Without turning to see the carriages he knew the machinery was powering up, he knew also that someone *was* in the booth. He turned to see the carriages had now recommenced their journey around the inner platform, a jolt from beneath the ride kicked them up a gear as Jake moved slowly back towards them. They all spun freely as they travelled around and passed him at speed, since they were vacant they were virtually weightless and spun relentlessly once their momentum had grown, all except one. His flashlight lacked the power to illuminate it from where he was stood, he knew he'd have to get a lot closer to the carriage in order to see into it. Jumping onto the rotating platform was not an option since that would mean passing the operator's booth, and disorientation. He chose instead to play a waiting game, sooner or later he was going to get a glimpse inside that carriage.

"What the fuck is this shit?" He whispered. "Who's in there?" He shouted at the booth. "Who are you?" He paced back and forth, and although he was still on the opposite side of the platform to the booth, he was gearing up to fight its occupant. "What are you still doing here?" His stare at the booth was unbroken despite the carriages thundering past him just inches from his body. "Fuck this." He shouted and headed for the booth. "You better want this coz I'm gonna fuckin' destroy you!" Glass crunched beneath his boots as he made his way around, he focused and swallowed hard as he reached for the handle.

"Jake!" The voice screamed.

Any thoughts of opening the door were forgotten as he spun around to locate its source. "Don't open the door!"

"Jet?" He shouted. "Is that you?" He was uncertain as the voice was so high pitched it could've belonged to a pre pubescent girl, but he knew deep down it was him. "Where are you?" He asked, scanning the carriages wildly as they passed him, he waited for the only one *not* spinning wildly to come around. A powerful strobe light above the ride flickered into life and poured a dazzling white light down on them. Jake's vision blurred as everything appeared in slow motion under the rapid flashes, he strained his eyes trying to focus on the carriages as they rocketed past him, he knew he'd have to jump onto the moving platform to get to Jet.

"Get me out of here," Jet moaned. "Please get me out of here before he comes back." His voice was taught with fear as he whimpered to himself. "Don't go, Jake." He pleaded with his friend as best his faculties would now allow. Although already dizzy from watching the carriages rotate under the flickering light, Jake chose his moment carefully and leapt onto the platform as the docile carriage approached, Jet screamed with fear as Jake took control of the carriage from behind. He looked down to see Jet pinned to the seat by a mangled safety bar, he saw Tommy slumped in his seat facing away from Jet.

"It's ok." He said, reaching down to touch Jet on his head. "I'm gonna get you out of here." He looked down at Tommy, he knew already his friend was dead but pulled him from the corner to get a look at him to make sure.

"Jake, no." Jet said.

Jake saw the terror in Jet's eyes build as he pulled Tommy closer to him.

"He's dead, Jake." He said, "I Can't look at him again, please leave him there." He spoke calmly although shivering uncontrollably, his eyes were bloodshot and swollen from crying. "We will be next, Jake." He whispered. "Get this bar open fast."

Jake walked around to the front of the carriage, he kept hold of it at all times until at the other side where he squatted down to inspect the safety bar. He struggled to hold the carriage still while he fumbled with the locking mechanism. As a powerful jolt from beneath the platform once again sent the carriages in to high gear, Jake knew he could now only look at the safety bar and Jet, if he tried to focus on anything else he would certainly lose his bearings and fall at speed from the ride. With the flash light between his teeth he used both hands to pull frantically at the locking device, but failed to release it in any way. With the increased speed Tommy's lifeless body slid along the seat towards Jet, who in turn tried to avert his gaze from him by pressing his own face into the padded head rest beside him.

"Jesus!" Jake shouted, having just caught a glimpse of Tommy. He stumbled away from the carriage and fell down just inches from the next as it spun relentlessly on its axis, it narrowly missed smashing into Jake's head. He clambered back and once again took hold of the safety bar, and tugged wildly on it. Nothing had prepared him for what his friend now resembled, his face was almost blue beneath the strobe light, trace lines of blood covered his once handsome baby face, veins beneath had raised to the surface to create a gory road map of pain.

"What the fuck did he do to him?" He asked. "What the fuck happened?" His words trailed off like the end of a song as his eyes moved over Tommy's body.

"He's watching us right now." Jet whispered. "Please hurry, Jake. Get this bar off me."

"How do you do this?" He asked.

"I don't know, just keep trying."

"Who is this motherfucker, anyway?" He glanced at the booth as they rocketed past it.

"I don't know who he is." He replied, trying to roll Tommy back in the opposite direction. "I heard Tommy say he was sorry, I think he called him Chad."

"Chad?" He asked. "Are you sure?" He stopped pulling at the bar and found himself unable to look at anything but the booth. "What did he look like?"

"He looked…" He paused for a moment. "…Like death."

"What?"

"Pale," He muttered. "Really pale, like death."

"And?"

"Long dark hair."

"He had long dark hair?"

"Yeah."

He gave up tugging on the bar and stood up, he held the carriage for support and watched the booth as it came around every few seconds.

"I can't release you, Jet." He said. "The bar has been forced down."

"You gotta get me out, Jake!" He tried to reach out his hands to him but couldn't reach. "Please don't go - he'll kill me."

"No he wont." He replied calmly. "You'd be dead already, it's me he wants - you were just bait." He paused. "He knew I'd come for you."

The strobe lights began flashing noticeably faster as metal boomed without warning from the sound system.

"Stop fucking with me, Chad!" He shouted. "I know it's you!" He waited for a moment, anxiously watching the side door on the booth each time they passed it by, they both felt the jolt from the beneath the central platform, it was slowing down. He let go of Jet's carriage and began walking the boards to maintain a safe, consistent distance between him and the booth. The platform finally came to a rest with Jet's carriage dead opposite the booth, with Jake stood beside it.

"Come on, Chad!" He shouted. "I'll fuckin' kill you right this time." He looked down at Jet, he was crying. "I'm sorry, Jet." He said. "This isn't your war, it's ours." He paced the boards looking for a missile to throw at the glass, but found nothing. The music ceased as quickly as it had came on, and once again there was silence - although the microphone inside the booth was now live, as were the speakers since they could both hear breathing coming over them. "Come on, Chad." He shouted again. "Let's do this."

"It's not Chad." Tommy whispered, his voice was barely audible and took them both by surprise. "It's Brandon."

"Tommy!" Jet shouted placing his arm around him. "Tommy it's ok, you'll be ok." He did his best to reassure him but the look he and Jake exchanged said otherwise. Jake leapt on to the carriage to get as close to Tommy as he could.

"Who did this to you, Tommy?" He asked, leaning in close to him, although no reply came. Jake gripped his hand tightly as Jet rocked him gently too and fro in his arms. "Tommy!" He shouted. "Who is in that booth?"

"Br -" His breath was shallow and weak, with only spit bubbles of blood leaving his mouth with each attempt to speak. "Brandon." He muttered.

"No, Tommy." He shouted. "It's not Brandon." He felt shivers run up and down his own spine. "It's not Brandon."

"Who's Brandon?" Jet asked, still holding Tommy tightly.

"It's Brandon." Tommy said, he spoke clearly and tried to raise his head a little. "Danny was right, Jake." He laughed a little, though it was clear his breath was expiring with each word he uttered. "He was fucking right." He looked Jake in the eye. "You better run, Jake." His body fell limp, they both knew he was dead. Jet stroked Tommy's hair and kissed him gently on the forehead before returning him to his previous position away from him. "Who the fuck is Brandon?" He glared angrily at Jake.

"Are those sirens I hear?" The voice boomed over the sound system, it scared both Jake and Jet.

"Brandon." Jake whispered. "Can't be."

"Sirens…Jake."

Both Jake and Jet saw the booth was now illuminated inside, through the tinted glass they could see a man's silhouette within, he was stood perfectly still looking out to them both. Jake stared hard and determined shoulder length hair but no more.

"You better run, Jake." He spoke calmly and gently although his voice coursed through Jake's body from the speaker directly behind him.

"Fuck you!" He shouted, pointing both his hands like guns towards the booth. "You don't scare me."

"I think I do, Jake." He said.

"It's you that needs to run," He shouted. "Before I come over there and fuck you up." He saw two large fire extinguishers secured to front of the booth, he moved against his instincts towards them. Laughter spilled through the speakers like poisonous gas filling the air around him. As he neared the booth he noticed the light within it diminish to nothing, the silhouette likewise as the glass reverted to normal form, revealing nothing more to him than his own reflection under the strobe light. He ripped one of the extinguishers from its mounting and stepped back with it to a perceived safe distance.

"You better run, now." The speakers vibrated wildly as his low tone powered through the subs.

"I aint running motherfucker." Jake shouted, throwing the extinguisher as hard as he could at the front pane of glass, finding its target the glass shattered before him.

"Fuck me." He whispered, his jaw hung open as he stared into the booth, the intermittent flashing lights illuminated its occupant adequately. His attention was drawn to what he thought was a rock climbing harness, secured to his torso. "I - I watched them bury you?" He stumbled backwards towards Jet's carriage.

"Is that a crucifix around your neck, Jake?" He asked, brushing glass from his body. "God played no part in your life, he wont help you now." He stared out at Jake with the blackest of eyes and clutched his own harness.

"Danny *was* right." Jake muttered.

"Run Jake." He whispered. "Run like hell."

Jake turned and ran, he charged down the steps taking them two at a time, shedding his long leather jacket as he did so since it would only slow him down.

"I aint never gonna die!" He shouted. "Least of all in some fuckin' kids carnival." He charged in the first direction he saw an opening in, confused and disoriented it soon occurred to him he'd ran further *into* the park. He reached a wooden fence that closed off adjoining farm land not rented by the carnival owners, he vaulted over it and sat on the top for a moment looking for a point of reference to work towards. Fields of wheat, some six feet high and drenched in darkness spread out before him as far as his limited vision could determine, although the Washburn link road was on the other side, he couldn't see it but could hear yet more police cruisers racing in his direction. From his vantage point on the fence he thought he could see a scarecrow in a small clearing, he guessed that would probably represent the middle of the field so decided to work towards that. Jake readied himself for the jump into the wheat, but glanced quickly over his shoulder back into the carnival, he could see *him*, stood perfectly still and watching his every move from the other end of the main straight.

"How did you come back motherfucker?" He whispered, glaring straight back at him. "You're fucking dead. I'll kill you right this time, Brandon Rose." He sliced across his own neck with his palm while staring back at him.

"You'll regret this, Brandon!" He shouted. "What the fuck are you waiting for?" To Jake's regret this seemed to act as a call to arms as he watched him step out into the open and move slowly in his direction. Jake watched as lights from various abandoned rides and stalls he passed began to explode, his very presence under them seemed to create massive energies they couldn't withstand, they shattered with every step he took, as shadows walked with him and darkness cloaked him, neither would *reveal* him. Jake had seen enough, he dropped down into the wheat and instantly began charging through it, he resisted the urge to look back deciding instead to remember the location of the scarecrow. The wheat tore into him as he raged through it, he waded as quickly as he could while adrenaline was surging through his body, it was hard work and he tired quickly. He changed his mind and decided to look back after all, figuring that if he was coming fast, he'd stop and fight him on the spot, before he had no fight left in him. He was relieved to see there was no sign of him, not even on the fence, but disheartened to see he had created a virtual footpath through the wheat for him to follow, he swallowed hard and ploughed on.

"Some fuckin' scarecrow!" He shouted, listening to what he thought were crows overhead, although it was too dark to confirm his suspicions. Finally he saw it, the scarecrow was ahead - suspended about six feet above the wheat, and since it meant he was halfway to the main road, it was a welcome sight. He was thankful for having spotted it from the fence, since under the black sky and out of the blue it was a terrifying sight to stumble across, even if the crows didn't think so, although he could no longer hear them at all - just silence.

"Halfway there, Jake." He said to himself. "Keep going, just keep going." He reached the clearing and stopped for a moment to observe the scarecrow, he breathed hard and doubled over in pain, he knew he'd have to stop for a moment and rest, despite Brandon's image being scorched in his minds eye, replaying over and over like a broken projector. Shrouded in a cloak of both darkness and fabric, the scarecrow hung in the centre of the cross with its arms outstretched across the beams. Jake stood before it and stared up, his vision was severely limited but his other senses were razor sharp, there was a pungent smell of vinegar in the air around it, a sharp contrast to the sweet smells of the carnival he'd fled. Gazing skyward to the scarecrow's head, he pulled focus on the effigy hanging before him. With all hope of an escape dashed, he dropped to his knees with tears in his eyes, shock began to take hold and his actions were no longer his own.

The scarecrows head was human, disjointed and skewered crudely on top of the upper beam, as were the hands, nailed to the cross through what remained of the wrists. Those eyes, though sunken slightly within their sockets, still registered fear, or *surprise*.

"Matt." He whispered. "I knew it was you they'd found." He raised to his feet and stumbled backwards, he looked back through the trail he'd cleared in the wheat, there was still no sign of his pursuer, he found that to be strange. He looked again at his former friend's decapitated head.

"What did you see in your final seconds?" He whispered, gazing into those sunken, haunted eyes.

"Nothing." A voice declared. "Nothing at all."

Jake recognised the voice instantly and spun on his heels to once again look into path of cleared wheat, his suspicions were quickly dashed - he was alone.

"He didn't even know I was right *beside* him." It whispered again.

He strained his eyes as he looked up again at the scarecrow, it's body was concealed within a large waterproof sheet, but he could see it's head - it's *real* head, was bowed down and tucked neatly against it's chest, it's eyes peered down from beneath the rim of a dirty old Stetson. He stumbled backwards again as the head began to move, it raised it's chin from against it's chest and stared down to Jake, *his* features were chiselled, *his* eyes glistening and focused as they caught the pale moonlight.

"Hello Jake." He whispered, tossing aside the weatherproof sheet and dropping to the ground heavily. Jake stood motionless and watched with growing terror, as this killing machine, the likes of which he knew he could never match, casually tossed the dirty hat from his head to Jake's feet, before reaching over his shoulders with both hands to retrieve what Jake could already see, were samurai swords. Jake found it difficult to determine his silhouette in the near total darkness, he could see the harness though as the steel strong points reflected the moonlight, as did the lethal blades he wielded menacingly before him.

"You didn't have those before." Jake whispered. "In the booth… you didn't have them."

"You haven't *seen* me before." He answered, scratching the tips of the blades in the dirt beside his feet.

"How did you get ahead of me, Brandon?" He asked. "You were behind me."

He laughed. "My work is almost done, Jake." He whispered. "Did you think it was natural selection, or did it occur to you that someone or *something* might be coming for you too?" He raised the swords and began crossing them back and forth over one another, forcing Jake to retreat. "When you killed me, you created me and yes, Jake -" He took a moment to pause and pointed both swords directly at Jake's face. "Danny *was* right!" He shouted. "I am the Reaper, your body will lay bleeding but your soul is coming with me." He parted the swords, and with lightening speed sliced them through Jake's neck, they passed one another at his spine. Liberated - his crucifix took flight, he knew nothing - nor felt nothing as his body hit the ground twitching.

"My name is *Death.*"

Ray awoke from a deep sleep and was momentarily surprised to find himself at the wheel of his car, with the engine still running. It was dark and it took him just a second to gather his bearings, it was a while since he'd been to Springwood Drive, it was a while since he'd gazed at *that* porch light, he wasn't entirely sure why he chose to now. He wound his window down almost fully to allow the cold night breeze to hit him and switched the ignition off. The clock on the dashboard clicked, reminding him another hour had passed, it was one in the morning. His attention was drawn to a cat stealthily crossing the road in front of his car, it's eyes were green under the streetlights. He shuffled in his seat and watched as the cat suddenly stopped in it's tracks and looked directly at him, for a moment their eyes were locked before the cat walked on. Looking around him he counted only four houses that still had lights on, excluded were the porch lights of which there several, especially *that* porch light.

"That thing should be rotating above a rocky bay." He said, slightly amused with his assessment. He stared from across the street to number sixty - five, which - porch light aside, was in total darkness.

He lit a cigarette and blew a trail of smoke from out of the open window, he thought he could hear laughing coming from outside, but careful evaluation confirmed to him that not a living soul was to be seen.

"I think it might be time to get out of here, Ray." He said to himself. He reached for the keys in the ignition but stopped short of starting the engine, he didn't know why but his attention was again summoned to the porch light of number sixty - five, it was getting brighter, it was pulsing.

"What's going on here?" He whispered. Feeling activity of some kind was imminent he slid further down his seat, until just his eyes were visible over the rim of his steering wheel. To his surprise the porch light slowly began reverting to a normal state, before going off completely.

"That's a first." He said. Since the porch light had burned so intensely it was difficult for him to re - acclimatise his eyes and focus, especially now that it had gone off. A metallic thud just outside his open window broke his concentration, something had landed just short of his car door. He wanted to start the engine and go, but something just wouldn't let him, instead he raised up a little in his seat and peered outside. A silver flip - top style lighter lay on the road just next to his car, he was certain it hadn't been there earlier. He quietly opened his door just enough to reach down and retrieve it then hid from view once more as he inspected it. He wondered if someone had thrown it, but dismissed that idea quickly as it was an expensive lighter. He mused several theories while crouched down beneath the window line, but only one persisted. He listened to what sounded like bins rattling at the side of number sixty - five, he raised again in his seat to catch a glimpse of the side of the house. It was at that moment that the porch light began to illuminate once more, and that Ray saw the apparition again, he was stood motionless at the end of the driveway next to two dustbins. Ray could see he was dressed in what looked like a long leather jacket, which he slid off, revealing in full his *equalisers,* which were strapped to his back as before.

"I wonder how much they're worth now?" Ray whispered, mentally reminding himself not to utter another word out loud. He clasped the lighter tightly in his sweaty hands and watched *him* place the jacket in the dustbin, before walking to the rear of the house and out of sight.

"Where did you get that jacket?" He asked. His theory still persisted in his mind although the possibility scared him, but he rationalised that with everything else he'd seen so far, that surely *anything* was possible. He stared at the porch light, which for the first time in all the times he'd seen it, was burning at a normal level. It didn't *pulse,* nor did it *glow* - because he was *home.* Ray leaned out of his open window and glanced skyward, the sky was clear and the stars were out. *How do I pick just one star to aim for when they all look the same?* He wondered. *If the tables were turned and I were up there looking down, wouldn't it be the same, wouldn't everything look the same?* He started the engine and pulled away, watching as a light came on in the attic of the house.

"I don't know about rotating above a rocky bay," He said to himself. "It's a fucking landing light." He laughed to himself as he drove and lit a cigarette with his newly acquired lighter, he didn't mind that it had *Jake* inscribed across it, nor did he mind keeping it - he knew Jake wouldn't be needing it any time soon.

"There's no shortage of fire where you're going, Jake." He laughed again.

Chapter Nine

<u>Sunday 21st March.</u>

The curtains were open, allowing sunlight into the cluttered yet spacious bedroom. Julianne looked at her watch and saw it was almost ten, she then rubbed at her eyes as they adjusted to the light and took in her strange surroundings for the first time. There were clothes strewn all over the floor, her heart sank as she realised that not all of them were her own, she felt naked.

"Oh god," She whispered, raising herself to a seating position whilst gripping the duvet tightly across her chest. "Why don't I remember?" These thoughts and more raced through her mind as she fully surveyed the room, there was a large mirrored wardrobe adjacent to the king size bed she was in, she tried to ignore that. There was a weightlifting bench at the foot of the bed, and to her dismay she saw her bra was thrown over the weights suspended across it.

"Fuck." She whispered. "What the hell did I do?"

"Julianne," Mark shouted, knocking gently on the closed door. "You awake?"

"Just a minute, Mark." She replied, reaching for a white T - shirt that was on the floor, it wasn't hers but she didn't care, she hastily pulled it over her head and propped herself up against the pillows.

"Come in." She said, pinching the duvet tightly around her waist, she dreaded the door opening.

"Good morning." He said, opening the door and walking in before kicking it shut behind him. He approached the bed holding two cups of coffee. "I thought you might be ready for this." He said, placing them on the floor next to her.

"Thank you." She said, struggling to remain gracious. She clasped her hands in front of her. "Mark, did you open the curtains?" She cursed herself, but knew she had to bite the bullet.

"No." He answered, smiling. "You don't remember anything then?" He sat down on the bed next to her. "Justin left them open."

"Justin?" She asked, fearful that things could actually be worse than she'd first thought. She shifted restlessly and was unable to look at Mark, she stared instead at the large mirrored wardrobe. *Oh dear god.* She thought. *Justin? I don't know any one called -*

Mark laughed. "Relax, he's my -"

"Mark, what the hell happened?" She interrupted angrily. "Who's Justin?"

"Will you just -"

"Why don't I remember what happened?" She raised her trembling hands to her face and buried herself within them.

"Probably -" Mark paused and pulled one of her hands away from her face. " - because nothing *did* happen." He parted her hair to reveal her eyes. "Justin is my *kid brother*." He whispered. "He came up to stay with me last weekend." He laughed as he watched a wave of relief wash over her. "So what exactly *do* you remember about last night?"

"I remember the fairground," She replied. "And the fortune teller, I remember her."

Mark nodded. "What else?"

"I remember us drinking coke by your car," She paused as she ran through the final events in her memory. "And us driving off, but that's it." She looked at him. "I don't remember us coming here."

Before he could answer he was distracted by the gentle hum of his cell phone, it was vibrating on the bedside table in *his* bedroom.

"Well," He said finally, once it had stopped. "You fell asleep in the car on the way home, and I do mean asleep." He reached for his coffee. "I tried to rouse you - but it wasn't happening."

"Are you serious?" She asked, intrigued at the notion. "Then how did I get undressed?"

"That was all you!" He mocked. "I put you to bed fully clothed, I swear." He smiled and held his hands high like he was at gunpoint.

"Then I must've -" She stopped talking as her thoughts took over. - *undressed myself in the night? Would I?*

"I was going to take you home," He said. "But then I saw it how your parents might've seen it."

"Wait," She said. "I remember falling down, I fainted didn't I?"

"Yes." He nodded. "I was just about to say, the knock on your head probably contributed to it.

She nodded and sipped at her coffee. *Well he knows best.* She thought. *I obviously wasn't in a normal state of consciousness.*

"So I decided to bring you here," He said. "Then at least I could keep an eye on you."

"Thank you." She said, smiling at him.

Mark listened as again the cell phone began vibrating in the next room. "Will you excuse me?" He asked, although he was already half way to the door before she could answer him, he left in a hurry without looking back at her.

"No problem." She said to herself. Mark hadn't closed the bedroom door properly as he'd left, so she daren't get up in case he came back in, she cursed as she watched the door slowly open itself fully. Mark was only in the next room but it bothered her that she couldn't picture it, or any other room in the house besides the one she was in. She sipped at her coffee and again looked around the room, only this time she paid more attention to detail. On the wall directly behind her she saw a large framed mosaic of various photographs, Mark was on most of them together with faces she didn't know, and girls - lots of girls. One picture in particular drew her attention, although she had no idea why. It was of a large blue pick - up truck, attached to the roll bars were four spot lights that peered over the cab, and despite it being a sunny day when the picture was taken, they were illuminated. Four men were leaning against the front of it, on what she could see were bull bars, they were all smiling and striking various gestures to the camera. She wasn't aware of Mark's voice in the room next to hers, but was startled when he began to shout.

"What?" He said. "Are you fucking serious?"

She placed her coffee down and quickly grabbed her jeans off the floor, if she could *hear* him then she could *place* him, she knew he was still in his bedroom so quickly pulled them on, along with her jumper.

"Then I'm not safe either!" He shouted. "Who ever it is -" His voice was abruptly cut off by his own bedroom slamming. As she quickly put her underwear in her pockets, she was again startled to see him appear once more in her doorway.

"Are you ok?" She asked, noticing immediately that he was pale and trembling.

"I think you should go now." He whispered. "I gotta go meet some friends." He left the room in a hurry.

"Is everything ok?" She asked, listening as he ran down the stairs. "I guess not."

16:00.

Vincelli planned his steps carefully, avoiding the empty beer cans and broken glass across Ray's driveway wasn't easy, but with practice… He pressed the doorbell but wasn't surprised to hear no chime. He turned his attention out into the road, he saw small children playing in the fading light of early evening. He walked to the front window but couldn't see through the dirty net curtains, he banged twice on the glass panel.

"Open up it's the police!" He shouted, laughing to himself as he returned to the front door. He listened to barking come from the living room as he waited, he knew Ray was home since his rusty Chrysler was slumped on the pavement like a tired dog on a hot day. He was about to walk away when he saw Ray approaching the door through the patterned glass.

"Finally." Vincelli whispered, taking a quick look around him and shaking his head. "Are you fucking deaf?" He asked, barging past Ray who was stood in his shorts and T shirt.

"Come in, why don't you?" Ray said, closing the door behind him.

Vincelli stood awkwardly in the hallway until Ray had passed him.

"What are you waiting for?" Ray asked. "You know the way, go through."

"I'll let you go first." He said, beckoning Ray to take the lead.

"I don't think your dog likes visitors does it?" He followed Ray through to the kitchen, stepping over the empty tins of dog food and unopened mail littering the floor.

"*He*," Ray said. "*He*, doesn't like visitors."

"Why are you in your shorts, Ray?" He asked, inspecting the filth as he went. "It's almost tea time for crying out loud."

"It's my day off." He muttered. "And besides, I was about to take a shower."

"You lazy fuck."

"What?"

"A stroke of luck!" He answered quickly. "It was a stroke of luck me finding you, as you're normally at the cemetery today aren't you?" He stepped into the kitchen and quickly wished he hadn't. There were T.V dinner trays all over the worktops, take away wrappers, dirty dishes and yet more beer cans on the floor, his shoes stuck to the torn lino with each step he took.

"I go on Mondays." He answered. "Can I get you a coffee or something?" He held a filthy mug briefly under the cold water tap then placed it next to the kettle.

"Err, no I'm good." He answered. " Have you got a can of something other than beer?" He asked.

"Coke?"

"Yeah," He answered. "It's in a can right? A sealed can?"

"Yes." Ray replied, a little surprised at the question. "Why?"

"No reason." He walked towards to the living room. "A can would be great." He said. His words trailed behind him as he headed for the door that adjoined the two rooms.

"You want a glass?" Ray asked, smirking.

"No thanks." He answered, opening the door and being set up on by King. "Down!" He ordered, wiping the dog's paws from his rain coat. "Shit!" He shouted, as the dog jumped frantically up to him. "Down for fuck's sake!" He could hear Ray laughing behind him. Once the dog had stopped mauling at him, he made it through and was disappointed to see yet more of the same. There were ashtrays all over, overflowing with cigarette butts and used tea bags, the carpet was bald in some areas and looked like it hadn't seen a hoover in years.

"I really like what you've done with the place, Ray." He said, smiling and taking it all in. "You've got a real minimalist approach going on here." He added. "To *cleaning*, anyway."

"Ok, I get it." Ray answered, passing Vincelli his can.

"I like it though, Ray." He said, taking the drink from him and smiling. "I especially like the smell, I mean - what is that? Dog piss?" He moved a stack of damp clothes from the sofa and sat down. Ray sat down on his recliner and swivelled it to face Vincelli. "I know I gotta clean," He said. "Don't rub it in." He placed his feet on the table.

"I'd like to scrape it off, Ray." He replied, laughing. "Not *rub it in*." He lit a cigarette . "Oh, and do me a favour." He said, opening his can. "Put some pants on, or put your feet down - if you get me?"

Ray jumped to his feet and strolled to the patio doors, leaving Vincelli free to look around the room. He looked at the mantle piece and was not surprised to see even that was covered in junk, opened and un opened letters were shoved behind a decorative clock and wedged between various ornaments, coffee mugs that had probably sat there for months acted as newly converted paper weights for his house hold bills.

"Why are you here, Joe?" He asked, struggling to slide open the patio door to let King outside.

"Well, you've heard about last night, no doubt." He answered, still looking around. "I mean, even though I got your machine all night, you must've heard." He watched Ray intently from the sofa.

"I heard something on the radio this morning." He replied, lighting a cigarette whilst leaning out of the open door. "To be honest I thought maybe it was some wonderful dream, but then I opened my eyes and wonderful no longer described it." He laughed, clicking open and shut his newly acquired steel lighter.

"A wonderful dream, you say?" Vincelli asked, joining Ray at the door. "What's wonderful about it?"

"What's not?"

"Why didn't you answer your phone last night, Ray?"

"I was asleep."

"Where?"

"In my chair."

"In that chair?" He pointed back at the recliner.

"Yeah!" He answered, raising his voice. "In that chair!"

"Where were you last night, Ray?" He flicked his ash through the patio door.

"I'm a suspect now?" Ray asked, barging past Vincelli and pacing the room erratically.

"Or perhaps," Vincelli whispered, "The lead role in your wonderful dream." He inhaled deeply on his cigarette and flicked again. "Where where you last night?" He followed Ray to the other end of the room.

"I was…" He paused. "I was asleep…in my chair." He walked slowly back to the patio doors and massaged his temples as he breathed deeply.

"You want a paper bag, Ray?" He asked, strolling back to join him. "Look like your panicking a little to me?"

"I'm a suspect?" He whispered. "You think I'm responsible in some way?"

Vincelli laughed. "Don't flatter yourself, Ray." He said. "I saw how you struggled to open that fucking door!" He threw his cigarette through the open door and immediately plucked another one from his pack. "Our guy is strong, *very* strong. I *know* where you were midnight 'til one. What I want to know is *why*?"

"You know?" He asked, looking a little confused. "Why didn't anyone come by to check me out?"

"In a quiet road like that people notice things." Vincelli said. "We got four calls all describing your car, but as you may recall we were a little preoccupied with a gangland executioner running amok at the carnival."

"I wonder how they saw me?" He asked, lost in thought. "There was no one around."

"There isn't a car in that road worth less than thirty grand," He laughed. "That hunk of shit you drive isn't worth thirty dollars." Vincelli laughed and tossed the cigarette in his mouth. "Now listen, I want to ask you something." He searched his pockets for his lighter but couldn't find it. "Give me a light, please."

Ray held out the lighter and flipped it open for him.

"Thank you." Vincelli said, quickly removing the cigarette from his mouth and glancing at Ray's hand as he lowered it to his side. "Nice lighter, Ray." He said. "Is it new?"

"Erm -" He paused, having just realised his mistake, having just realised his potentially *fatal* mistake. *He saw it,* He thought. *Jesus Christ - he saw it.* He stood silently for a moment. *You're fucked - you stupid motherfucker - you're fucked.*

"Paper bag, Ray?" He asked again.

He's got you - he's fucking got you - you've blown it you stupid fucking cunt! How could you be so fucking dumb?

"It's nice." He left Ray trembling and walked back to the sofa.

"Yeah -" Ray muttered. "It's new… it's nice… it's err… new." He made sure Vincelli still had his back to him, then tossed the lighter through the patio doors into the garden, then moped his brow and relaxed a little. *Destroy that fucking lighter, it almost got you fucking pinched asshole.*

"Well like I said, I wanna ask you something." He dropped into the couch heavily, the leather wheezed like a punctured tyre beneath his weight "That shit you were spouting off about," He paused a moment to laugh at himself. "You know I can't believe I'm even gonna ask you this, but here goes."

"What is it?"

"*Brandon.*" He said. "Were you for real with that?" He waited for a moment, pretending not to notice Ray's trance like state, but having failed to generate a reply he urged him on. "Ray!" He shouted. "The cemetery, did you see him or not?"

Hoping to stop the room from spinning he closed his eyes tightly. *Now isn't the time to fuck up, Ray.* He thought. *Get a grip and keep it together, he'll be on to us if you act like this.*

"Ray!" He shouted again.

"Yeah," He whispered. "I saw him." He returned to his recliner and sat down.

"Do you *really* think it's him?" Vincelli asked, already knowing the answer to his question.

"It's him."

"I just don't believe it's him," He said, observing Ray with growing concern. "But, I do believe that *you*, believe it's him."

"It really is him, Joe." He whispered, staring at the floor. "I'm not making it up, I've seen him several times -" He stopped abruptly. *No Ray, he'll think you're crazy - don't tell him anything now, it's between us and only us.*

"You've seen him several times?" Vincelli asked.

"No, just at the cemetery that day." He replied.

"But you just said -"

"I meant pictures!" He snapped. "I've seen his face in pictures, so I knew it was him."

"You're worrying me, Ray." He leaned forward.

"Do you know something, Joe?" He asked rhetorically. "Have you any idea how many nights I've sat here alone, hoping and praying to one day see Nancy again?"

Vincelli sat silently and shook his head, enjoying briefly the only eye contact Ray had offered so far.

"Well let me tell you," He went on. "Every fucking night!" He shouted. "Every fucking night!" He stared into Vincelli's eyes, with more emotion than anger brimming up within him. "Where was your concern when I was sat here deciding whether or not to kill myself? Where were you?"

"I'm -"

"Don't say sorry, Joe - I don't want to hear it." He wiped tears from his eyes. "I sit here and wait for her voice, I wait for a vision or maybe even a gentle breeze that I can tell myself is a sign that she's here, but she isn't here - she's gone. Don't you think that if I were going to imagine a ghost - I'd imagine her?"

"I'm truly sorry, Ray." He whispered. "I had no idea you felt like that, I've just been so wrapped up in -"

"Felt?" Ray asked, laughing. "It's how I *feel*, Joe." He gazed around the room. "You think I like living like this? You think I like all this chaos?" He laughed again. "Chaos is my fucking life, but what's to improve upon? Every fucking day I look myself in the mirror and tell myself I'm to blame, she's dead because of me and there's nothing I can do to change that." He stared continuously at his wedding picture above the fire place.

"Do you think meeting someone else is even an option any more? Do you think I'd want to inflict myself on someone else?" He sat motionless, and stared at the picture. "I'm halfway to the funny farm, Joe. It's all just falling apart ever since I saw him."

"He's dead, Ray." Vincelli whispered. "There are *no* ghosts. This is a manifestation of your state of mind." He clasped his hands together and sighed hard. "The person you saw at the cemetery was not Brandon, nor was he a *ghost*. He is living - breathing, flesh and blood, it's your mind that's creating this back story, Ray."

"How can you possibly know that?"

"Because today I interviewed a young man by the name of James Edward Turner," He lit another cigarette and tossed the pack to Ray. "You'll probably know him as Jet, he witnessed his brother being murdered last night, so needless to say he's extremely distressed," He took a long drag on his cigarette. "But he provided me with a damn good description, and it matched perfectly with that from the cashier at the filling station."

"Really?" Ray feigned interest.

"And while we're on that subject," He added, laughing. "This just gets better and better, our John Doe is no longer John Doe. You see, his missing extremities turned up last night - nailed to a fucking cross!" He paused for a moment as he replayed the image in his mind. "It was just a few feet from where Jake Gibson's decapitated body lay, and it was the single most terrifying thing I've ever seen, an I've seen some shit."

"So who is he?"

"Matt Johnson." He answered, grilling Ray's every move with his eyes. "A bit of a rogue but nothing too heavy."

"Yeah, I know that name." His surprise was genuine.

"Well something makes this one even more strange if that's remotely possible." He observed Ray's behaviour with growing interest. "A little over two months ago, he stumbled out of Chad's room with a syringe hanging out of his neck, he claimed *Chad* had done it to him."

"Chad?" Ray asked. "That's a good one!" He shifted restlessly in his chair.

"Well you think you're seeing his *dead* twin, Ray." He tried to make light of it. "He also claimed the syringe was infected with H.I.V, although he wouldn't tell us how he knew that, or why he had it." He stubbed out his cigarette. "He was treated for the overdose, to be honest he was lucky to survive, you or I would've been stone dead, but that's one occasion where being a junkie paid off for him. He had some level of immunity as it was a lethal amount he had in his system, the ironic part is he was waiting for the test results to determine if he was in fact H.I.V. positive. It seems he needn't have worried, *doesn't it?*"

"He's getting them all, Joe." He whispered. "One by one, he's taking them out." He seemed lost in thought once again. "They're all linked to Brandon's death, at the very least they're all linked to each other."

"*Anyway*," Vincelli said loudly. "I also interviewed the ride operator today, his description matched the cashiers also." He reached into his pocket and took out a handkerchief, he dabbed at his glistening brow. "He said there was a figure clad head to toe in black clinging to the spinning carriage like no living person possibly could. He said it simply wasn't possible for a human to possess the strength and balance to stay upright and resist the G forces they'd be subjected to as a result, least of all bite someone to death in the process."

"What?" Ray asked suddenly. "What did you just say?"

"He was bitten, Ray." Vincelli answered. "That's what Jet said, and Tommy's injuries would certainly substantiate that."

"Did Jet mention the swords?" He asked. "The samurai swords?"

"No." He replied. "There were no swords used on Tommy, both Jet and the ride operator were pressed on whether he possessed weapons of *any* description." He paused, again watching Ray's behaviour. "He had no swords, Ray."

"But Jake was decapitated?"

Vincelli laughed as he put his handkerchief back into his pocket. "Jake was most certainly murdered by the same assailant as Matt Johnson, but Tommy died at the hands of someone else entirely, I have no doubt."

Ray stood up and paced the room. "Do you believe me now?"

"*Something's* going on here," He answered. "But like I said earlier, this aint no ghost."

"Why, Joe?" Ray asked. "Why are you so closed to the possibility?" He spoke excitedly.

"Well for one thing, he's got fucking samurai swords strapped to his back!" He stood up and walked slowly towards the door to the hallway.

"This guy's human, he may live by the *sword*, but I promise you he'll die in a hail of bullets." He pushed open the door and moved slowly into the hallway, deliberately stalling. "Ray," He said, spinning around to look at him. "The names of the victims from last night haven't been released yet," He looked at Ray, who was standing awkwardly as if he had something to do the second he was alone. "I just told you their names and you didn't seem even slightly surprised, it's almost as if you, *knew*." He opened the front door, kicking the empty cans out of the way as he did so. "I never did get round to telling you," He whispered, turning to face Ray. "I myself have viewed the C.C.T.V footage from the filling station, and let me tell you this…it makes extremely disturbing viewing."

"You've seen him in action?" Ray asked, almost enthralled. "Tell me!"

"He is quite literally, the *single* most deadly man I've ever seen." He shook his head. "It's like watching a horror film." He added. "He walks slowly from the fields, and I do mean *slowly*." He took a deep breath, clearly troubled by his recollection. "His face is completely covered by that long hair, looked like he'd just got out of the shower it was that straight, but when he drew those swords…I got a shiver down my spine." He reached over his shoulders with both hands, providing Ray with a visual accompaniment to his running commentary. "It's just like that," He whispered, failing completely to capture the moment.

"Really?" Ray asked, trying his best to replace the fat man before him, in the rain coat struggling to contain him, with the lean muscular physique of Brandon.

"Yeah." He replied. "He stalks him, so slowly it was just unbelievable." Again he shook his head. "He just holds the swords out in front of him, has them pointing at the ground before him like some fucking metal detector." He stared at Ray, willing him to finish the sentence for him.

"Then?" Ray asked, excitedly.

"Then?" He asked. "I'll tell you what happens then, Ray." He stepped through Ray's front door and into the cool evening air. "Then

Matt Johnson dies." He added, shooting Ray a questionable glance as he walked down his driveway. "You take care." He waved over his shoulder as he walked to his car. He hadn't planned on looking back at Ray, but couldn't resist feeling annoyed when he heard the front door being closed on him.

Relieved and happy to be alone, Ray walked back into his living room and lit himself a cigarette, he placed it in the overflowing ashtray after tipping some of it's contents on to the table. "Sit down, King." He whispered to his dog whilst patting him on the head. "Where are you, Brandon?" He asked, pacing up and down the room. "Talk to me!" He urged. "Let me hear your voice so I know I'm not fucking crazy." He watched as King dropped to the floor panting heavily. "Just say something, communicate with me *please*."

He strolled towards the patio doors but stopped at the mirror on the wall, it was next to the doorway to the kitchen. He stared at his own reflection and smiled to himself.

I'm here, Ray. He thought to himself. *You did good, you did as I asked and kept him in the dark.*

"I told him nothing." He whispered. "He doesn't need to know what I know, he wouldn't be able to handle it anyway."

None of them would, Ray. He thought. *We'll show them all, for all the wrongs I've suffered at their hands, for the torment heaped upon me for their gratification, my tears run dry and I laugh as I bathe in their blood.* He smiled at himself. *Forget the wasted years, a new day has begun - from the shadows death shall appear, I am death, you are death - together we are death.*

"My name is death." He whispered, staring at his reflection. "My name is death," He said again, although this time he spoke with a little more conviction.

Tuesday 6th April.

Julianne sat silently, her legs were crossed and twitching wildly as she bit down hard on her nails. The chair next to Chad's bed, her vigil chair, was empty as she chose instead to sit by the window and stare down at the cars in the car park below. Across from the car park she observed the traffic and passers by, nine floors beneath her and going about their daily routines. She wished she could join them, even if joining them meant a nine story swan dive off the ledge. She looked at her watch and sighed as she realised it was almost noon. Two hours had already passed, but her words had not.

"Chad," She whispered finally, closing the blinds. "I hope you can hear me, I've -" She paused, unsure whether she *should* speak in case he *could* hear her. "I've - met someone." She spoke quietly, her words and thoughts uncertain. "It's been so long now." She began to cry as she looked at his sunken features.

"Just when I think I've seen a sign, or something worth clinging too, you just stay in limbo, and I don't think you're coming back now." She wiped at her eyes and stood up. "I'm just glad your eyes are closed for this, Chad." She grabbed her handbag of the window sill. "You're never coming back to me, you've only fought *this* hard for me. I love you so much but I've got to let you go now." She glanced around the small room that had become her world, and at the broken man that had been her world.

"If you come back to me, we'll never part." She tried to laugh but couldn't. "But we shouldn't start the year together, as we both know we're not going to finish it together." She was unable to look at him, almost blinded by her own tears as she passed his bed for the door, unable to notice as she closed the door, his left hand grasping loosely at the sheets.

Outside the sun shone brightly as she negotiated the parked cars in her dream like state. A terrible mixture of regret and relief surged through her veins, her fingertips tingled as she searched through her handbag for her keys. As she neared her car she realised a woman dressed in a long black cardigan was leaning on the car next to hers. Her features were hidden by a thick woollen hat pulled down low, but Julianne could see she had long blonde hair.

"Can I help you with something?" She asked, shielding her eyes from the sun as she tried to get a look at the woman.

"Not really," She replied, "But I can help you, Julianne."

"Really." She replied, unlocking the door and tossing her bag on the seat. "Don't let this nice car fool you," She said, aiming her words over the roof of the vehicle to the woman. "It's my dad's. So if it's money you're after you're out of luck." The woman laughed as she removed her hat and shook free her blonde hair.

"You've already paid me once," She said. "And I gave you that back, if you recall."

"Oh," Julianne whispered. "I remember you, you're that bitch from the carnival right? The carnival has left town so why are *you* still here?" She walked slowly around the car to join her on the passenger side. "Was once not enough? Have you come to finish the job off?"

"I've come to help you," She replied, retreating nervously as Julianne stalked her like a hungry lion. "If you'll let me."

"You can help me alright!" She shouted, slapping her square in the face. "You can get the fuck away from me." She regretted slapping her instantly, her guilt was compounded as she watched the woman fall to the ground after losing her balance whilst trying to avoid the blow.

"I'm sorry." Julianne whispered. "I shouldn't have done that." She watched her climb back to her feet.

"It's ok." She said, placing her hat back on. "From your point of view I completely understand your anger."

"What do you want, Lisa?" She asked. "That is your real name isn't it?"

She nodded. "Can I tell you a little something about my job?" She asked. "It's all a hoax, I'm reading your every move before you've even opened your mouth." She stepped back a little from Julianne. "It's called cold reading, and with every little thing I tell you, I watch your reactions however small, and that tells me whether or not to proceed with that *vision*."

Julianne nodded. "What's your point?"

"Something happened when you came into my tent." She said, closing the space between the two of them once more. "You brought something, or someone with you. I've never felt that before, he *made* me tell you the things I told you."

"Let's not do this again." She said. "I can't do this anymore, Lisa."

"Julianne, you're in danger." She said, clutching Julianne's hands tightly. "You must find those pictures, maybe you've seen them already I don't know, but more importantly, maybe *you* don't know."

"What pictures?" She asked. Her body was drained and she wanted to leave, but the image of Mark's picture mosaic troubled her now.

"*Photographs*, Julianne." She said. "Find them, and get away from him."

"Mark?" She asked.

"Get away from Mark." She replied nodding. "He's not who he says he is, that's all I know."

"What about Chad?" She asked. "Mark works in there." She pointed to the building behind her. "I've got to go back."

Lisa gripped her arm tightly and pulled Julianne towards her. "No." She said.

"No?" She shouted back, pulling her arm free of Lisa's grip. "What do you know?"

"I know you just said goodbye to Chad."

"How do you know that?"

"How do I know any of this?" She shrugged her shoulders. "I don't know the answer to that." She looked at the ground for a moment. "I know something else, Julianne." She whispered. "Chad has gone." She spoke quietly. "He's let go."

Julianne shook her head. "No, you're lying!" She stared at her wild eyed and desperate.

Lisa stood silently and reached out her hand for Julianne's. "They're together now." Julianne's body finally gave out under the stress and she collapsed screaming. Lisa knelt down to comfort her as best she could, she held her tightly against her body and stroked her long hair.

"Together they are strong." She whispered, planting a gentle kiss on her head. "It's meant to be."

Chapter Ten

<u>Monday 19th April.</u>

Vincelli swallowed hard and began to wish he hadn't requested the company of his captain, the less he saw of George Scott, the happier he was. He quickened his pace through the corridor as their meeting time was imminent, and he knew better than to keep George Scott waiting. *No one*, kept George Scott waiting. Vincelli's heart sank a little as he saw his office door was closed, and for a man who's motto was 'My door is always open,' he thought this a bad sign.

"Here goes." He whispered, knocking gently on the hallway's last windowless blue door.

"Come in." He shouted.

"Sir," Vincelli said, opening the door and stepping into his office. "Is this convenient?" He asked, peering in whilst wishing all at once that the reply would be negative.

"Indeed it is." He replied, from behind his desk. "Come in and close the door." He did not get up as he welcomed Vincelli into his domain, he merely pushed his chair back from his desk a little and tilted it backwards. A tall well built man with neatly combed greying hair, Captain Scott was every bit as sharp as he looked, wearing a neatly pressed blue suit, his gold cuff - links as ever peered from under the sleeves in a very under stated manner, with over stated impact. He observed as Vincelli stood awkwardly by the door.

"You're making my office look untidy, detective." He said. "Either sit down and begin or turn and leave."

"Well, as much as I hate to get all serious on you," Vincelli said, sliding gracefully for a man of his dimensions into one of two chairs, positioned opposite Captain Scott's un amused but smiling face.

"You have some concerns regarding Ray?" He asked.

"Yes, Sir." He answered in a surprised tone. "Yes I do." He tugged at his tie a little and unfastened the top button on his shirt. "Sir, I've not told that to anyone, how did you know?"

"A Good sense of humour is all I *do* lack, Vincelli." He replied. Leaning forward on his desk he clasped his hands together and lowered his voice. "I've been hearing things, evidently - so has Ray." He disarmed Vincelli with a smile. "I know you two are friends, I sensed concern rather than complaint in your voice when we spoke on the phone."

"Sir," He said, gripping the arms of the chair tightly. "I don't quite know how to say this, but my concerns for Ray have surpassed his general well being." He paused to consider his words. "He's *seeing* things, as well as hearing things."

"What things?" He asked.

Vincelli rolled his eyes and braced himself for words he was about to say. "Brandon Rose, Sir." He said with a sigh. "He believes the ghost of Brandon Rose is haunting him."

Scott took just a moment to digest Vincelli's claims, and chose his response carefully.

"If that were the case," He said softly. "Then of course that would be of serious concern to me." His hands remained clasped tightly on the desk. "How do you know?" He asked. "Has he told you or do you suspect?"

"He's told me." Vincelli replied, glancing at the rear of two photo frames on Scott's desk. "He believes that completely, I've tried to rationalize with him but…" He stopped suddenly.

"But?"

"I'm afraid there's more."

Scott sighed heavily and released his hands, they began wandering over his desk looking for tasks to complete, pens to place in the small steel pot, a cell phone's home screen to check for messages or calls, or paper work to file. Of course none of these things required his attention as he'd long since completed them, although his idle hands hadn't received that memo yet and longed for work.

"I'm afraid to ask, Vincelli." He said. "Do enlighten me."

Vincelli stared nervously around the office, there were several steel file cabinets lined against the wall on his left and a table next to the door with several plants on it. He began to wonder what it was about sitting in front of a desk, rather than behind it, in an office that contained filing cabinets, that had always seemed to spell trouble for him.

"He believes -" He stopped to laugh a little and began rubbing his hands on his knees. "He believes that Brandon is responsible for the killings, Sir."

"Brandon Rose." Scott whispered. "Brandon is our swordsman?" He asked. "That's very interesting, Vincelli."

"Sir?"

"Our killer is a *ghost* then?" He asked, nodding his head as if to answer his own question. "Back from the grave to murder those who, *presumably,* murdered him." He smiled. "Not entirely original, but appealing all the same."

"A ghost that can wield samurai swords, Sir." Vincelli added. "That's the part I like."

"Get him to write that one down, Vincelli. I like it." He smiled as the tension lifted from his shoulders, he felt all at once that any concern for Ray's well being was *probably* unfounded, convincing himself instead that Ray was in fact, *probably* - amusing himself at Vincelli's expense.

"I guess it's in the way you tell it, Sir." He said, mopping at his brow. "And he's pretty damn convincing." Their eyes met for a moment as Scott surveyed him carefully.

"Well I suppose to some extent it makes sense!" He feigned excitement as he pushed his chair backwards and stood up. "Let's take a look at the individuals who have lost their lives, since *Brandon* lost his."

"The murder victims?" Vincelli asked.

"No." Scott answered flatly. "Let's pay close attention to a certain demographic here, details are easily lost in translation if attention isn't paid to them." He began pacing the small area behind his desk then stopped to look out the window. "First we had the young man who died horrifically in the Mercedes, Nikki Farrell was it?"

"I believe so."

"That's one." He said, holding up his index finger. "Mathew

Johnson was next I believe, he was beheaded at the filling station," He laughed as he extended his forefinger. "His head, as you know, turned up at the murder scene of Jake Gibson and Thomas Turner, so we know without hesitation they're certainly linked to one another." He stood with four fingers outstretched and held them out for Vincelli's approval.

"Yes, Sir." He said.

"All those young men are linked, Detective." His expression was angered as he looked at Vincelli, who in turn sat squirming in his seat.

"Firstly - they're linked by their age range." Once more his fingers kept count for him. "Secondly - they're linked by a criminal past, mostly drug possession if you're still searching for a pattern here."

Vincelli nodded. "I know, Sir."

"Thirdly - they're all friends, they've often been dealt with as co - accused so we know they run in the same gang, they're guilty by association - quite literally." His voice had raised to a quiet telling off. "The witnesses we *do* have, which includes Tommy's brother James, have given the same description of the assailant." He moved around to the other side of his desk and sat on its edge. "Tall, pale and with long dark hair." He folded his arms across his chest. "I'm not saying for one moment that Brandon Rose is back from the dead, but he may as well be a ghost for all the leads we have!" He frowned down heavily at Vincelli. "His very *name* is littered with irony!" He laughed. "Rose!" He said, framing the word with his hands. "What happens when you crush a rose?" He asked, Vincelli remained silent and shrugged his shoulders a little. "When you crush a rose, you get pricked by a thorn! We need to find that thorn." He shouted. "The public are scared shitless right now as we're no closer to finding this maniac!" They both sat silently for a moment and listened to the ringing phones and printers that echoed through the corridor beyond the door.

"I want you to picture this, Detective." Scott said. "Families having a well deserved night out, boyfriends - girlfriends, husbands and wives - not necessarily their own but I digress!" He smiled. "Mothers - fathers, sons and daughters, all running for the exit, running for their lives in fact, did any one of them see *anything*?"

Vincelli shook his head. "It would appear not, Sir."

"No." Scott whispered. "No they didn't." He shuffled until comfortable on the edge of his desk. "But we *know* he was there, don't we?" He asked. "He hadn't finished yet, Jake was next and Jake knew it, there's nothing random about it."

"Sir." Vincelli added with a casual nod of his head.

"The question is, how does he move silently amongst them, cause such devastation, and then disappear?"

"Well," Vincelli said. "Suicide bombers do a pretty good job of that." He smiled a little.

"Suicide bombers, Detective." Scott said. "As the title might imply, die in their own devastation, they don't blend back in to the crowd after the attack." He paused. "But *he* does, he enters the shadows and he's not seen again. What they *do* see, is widespread panic and terror, which at that point was caused by what one man had witnessed, the ride operator." He spoke quietly and gazed around his office as the sentences formed themselves in his mind. "It was *he*, who raised the alarm and caused everyone to flee, we know James witnessed it also, but he was trapped in the carriage so he played no part in the panic that ensued. What that man saw shook him to his core, Detective. A hydrogen bomb exploded on that ride when our killer struck." He arced his hands in the air to emphasise his point. "The panic that followed was the mushroom cloud spreading outwards from the epicentre." Leaning casually on the desk, he smoothed over his trousers as Vincelli looked on silently. "It's a special kind of maniac that kills twice and leaves three bodies, Detective." He sighed. "Wouldn't you agree?"

"What are you saying, Sir?" Vincelli asked.

"Whoever he is, he's out there laughing his ass off at our incompetence." He smiled through his misery. "For all intents and purposes, Detective, he *is* a fucking ghost."

"We'll catch him, Sir." Vincelli whispered, he leaned forward a little in his chair as if to reinforce his words with positive action. "He'll slip up, they always do."

"Not all of them do," Scott replied. "They don't *all* slip up."

"Alright, *he* will."

Scott laughed. "Did you see the guy outside?" He asked.

Vincelli nodded as they shared a glance.

"He was wearing an A - frame," Scott whispered. "It said 'As we walk through the valley of the shadow of death, fuck the police - Jesus saves.'"

"It's just some weirdo." Vincelli replied with a shrug. "Don't worry about that."

"He's a fucking priest!" Scott retorted. "Just some weirdo we could deal with, but a respected priest is a terrible sign. Either we get this fucker, or we'll face a public backlash."

"Sir -"

"It's not what *he's* doing right," Scott interrupted. "That keeps him at large, it's what *we're* doing wrong." He sat quietly for a moment, his head resting on his right fist. "Danny's suicide, Nikki's altercation with the train, they're just a little random wouldn't you say? Maybe a little *too* random, a bigger picture has so far evaded us but I think it's time to look at these individuals as a piece in the puzzle, just because they weren't murdered doesn't mean they're not part of the bigger picture, their deaths are just too *timely* for my liking."

"I'm not sure I -"

"But James," Scott added. "He wasn't touched, not so much a hair on his head. That begs a pretty big question in my mind, with only one possible answer."

"Why wasn't he murdered too?" Vincelli asked. "Why leave a witness? Or for that matter why kill Tommy *in front* of a witness when he could've killed him privately like he did Jake?"

"He wanted to kill Tommy publicly," Scott whispered. "He wanted to send a powerful message, that he can get them *anytime* and, quite literally *anywhere*. But Jet, he had no misgivings with Jet, which is why he let him live."

"What are you thinking?" Vincelli asked.

"Well," Scott answered. "For one thing, he's much younger than the others, but that's not it." He puzzled it over for a moment as Vincelli waited for his cue. "He's never been caught in possession so we could possibly assume he's not involved with drugs? Yet."

"No, Sir." He replied. "To my knowledge, drugs aren't his thing - he does cars."

"But that's not enough," He went on. "Something separates

him from the others," He held his arms outstretched. "Something monumental." He paused. "He wasn't in the truck that rammed the twins' Charger off the road."

"Sir," Vincelli said nervously. "With all due respect, that's a pretty big assumption to make, they were never in the frame for that."

"That's all it is, Detective." He said quietly. "An assumption, but for me - it's the only one we should now be focusing on, and as you can probably understand, it shall remain an *unofficial* line of enquiry." He smirked proudly. "And with reference to what you said about them *not being in the frame*, they would've been had they *not* lost their heads."

"I just -"

"Our swordsman," He shouted, "Is knocking off Brandon and Chad's killers one by one, and in spectacular fashion." He raised off his desk and began to pace the room, he gazed at various framed photographs on the walls, though he wasn't really looking at them. "A killer of killers if you will." He felt the hairs on the nape of his neck raise up as he said the words. "You can't really believe, that four random *victims* - would all have that same shit in their veins, can you?"

"Well to be honest -"

"No." Scott said. "The drug problem isn't that widespread." He walked angrily, back to the other side of his desk. "You find whoever remains of their circle of friends," He ordered. "The circle within the circle," He added. "So far we have three *victims*, if we include Nikki Farrell, we have four *victims*." He sat down and leaned heavily on his desk.

"Sir, he died in a car accident." He spoke with a hint of frustration.

"So did the twins." Scott replied. "But their deaths were orchestrated by a third party, so go with it."

Vincelli shook his head, and although clearly annoyed he decided to leave it alone. He waved his hands a little then began fumbling with his tie.

"Danny said that five people, besides himself, were in that truck, Detective." Scott said. "If one more remains, then you better find him fast, before *he* does,"

"Enquiries are still on going on that one, Sir." He answered. "Without the truck, we've got nothing."

"Well let me tell you something," Scott said, pointing at him. "Whoever this guy is, he knows *exactly* who they are, so if there are any that remain from their circle, we need them because this guy wont stop until he's dead, played correctly we could lure him in." Both men stared across the desk to one another. "He'll come, detective." Scott said. "He's not finished, believe me." He smiled. "Let's find ourselves some bait, let's bring this motherfucker out into the open one more time, on an even playing field." He laughed a little as he spun his chair around and glanced out of his window, once more he pushed it back on its axis. "Only this time *we'll* know the location of his next target."

Vincelli slumped back in his chair. "It's risky." He said. "*Our* heads will roll if it goes wrong." He sighed. "If there is indeed one more, wouldn't he have turned himself in?" He asked. "You know, to stay alive."

Scott shook his head. "No, these kids couldn't run the operation, they've got a boss just like the rest of us. Someone else is pulling the strings, someone who has an equally fearsome hold over them."

"Who do you fear more." Vincelli replied. "It's possible, yes."

Scott smiled as he gazed through his window at the clouds above. "We'll find out soon enough, Detective." He said. "One thing's for certain in my eyes, he'll go for the boss last." He paused. "If indeed such a man exists, it's all conjecture at this point." He placed his feet on the desk and relaxed into his reclined chair. "But if there *is*, a boss," He added. "Then I will guarantee he is on this guy's list. If he's working his way through the soldiers, it's only to reach their commander." He laughed. "In that sense, he's doing us a big fucking favour."

Slouched awkwardly in a chair that was probably too small for a man of his size, Vincelli gazed at Scott and watched him draw a deep breath.

"If I may, Sir?" He asked. "Since we're throwing theories around like confetti, I've got one of my own." His tone, like his face - was uncertain. Scott dropped his feet from the desk and turned his chair to face Vincelli. "Go on." He said, giving him his fullest attention.

"It's more of a hunch, really." He said. "I've not acted on it yet because it's a dangerous line of enquiry." Seeing that he did indeed have Scott's full attention, he readied himself. "What if the twins were killing drug users," He said. "I mean, I know it's an extreme scenario I'm putting to you, but what if?"

"Why?" Scott asked. "Why that? Why now?"

"Danny said that the gang were killing their own, once they had served their purpose," He gauged Scott's reaction to his idea as he spoke. "That just didn't compute with me," He went on. "A man who will do virtually anything you ask in return for drugs, never becomes of *no* use in my opinion."

"Unless he becomes a liability, Detective." Scott countered, swamped in the possibilities.

"What if, for arguments sake," Vincelli argued. "The twins had access to the same shit that those clowns did, is it at all possible that *they* were administering the lethal doses, killing them - but making it look like they had overdosed." He hauled himself to the edge of his seat. "Danny said the twins had some powerful enemies, now that would make me mad as hell if they were *my* customers, or *my* employees being murdered." They stared silently across the desk. "If I discovered the culprits…I might even order their deaths." He smiled. "In his own words, Danny sold them out, he thought he was siding with the winning team, he was terrified." Vincelli pulled his chair closer to the desk. "*Something*, convinced him to shift his loyalties back to the twins that night, which is why he tried to protect them, but it was too late." He smiled proudly. "He made enemies of the twins that night, they knew he'd set them up. He also made enemies in the gang that night, for changing his mind - but they dragged him along for the ride anyway."

Scott sat silent, he stared through Vincelli as he considered what he'd heard.

"Who do you fear more?" Vincelli asked.

"Ok," He said, nibbling nervously at his already none existent nails. "It is *indeed* a dangerous line of enquiry." He whispered. "Their parents have suffered enough, who have you told about your hunch?"

"No one."

"Not even Ray?"

Vincelli laughed. "God no!" He said. "Right now I wouldn't share a coffee with him!"

Scott nodded as he stared reluctantly into Vincelli's eyes. "Let's keep it that way."

"Like I said, Sir." Vincelli whispered, once again slouching back into the chair. "Ray believes that Brandon *himself*, is responsible for the killings." He laughed. "He's fucking convinced."

"Brandon *himself*." Scott whispered. "It's interesting that you put it like that, it's somewhat of a play on words." He tilted his chair back once more. "Brandon *himself*." He whispered.

"I'm not sure I'm with you, Sir." Vincelli answered.

"Well," He said. "It's not possible that Brandon *himself* is at the helm of the good ship payback, is it?" He paused for a moment. "But what *is* possible, is that someone who looks an awful lot like him, is."

"The only person who's actually seen this guy up close, *and lived*, is Jet." Vincelli added. "What we do know," He went on. "Is that he has long dark hair, and dark shadowy eyes."

"And pale." Scott whispered, picturing his words on an imaginary blackboard before him.

"And pale, Yes." Vincelli agreed. "Almost *unnaturally*, pale."

"Like a face paint of some sort," Scott said. "All readily available, especially at Halloween."

"Yes, Sir." He agreed again.

Scott once more raised to his feet and emerged from behind his desk, he walked slowly to his office door, opened it and quickly peered out before darting back inside and closing it behind him.

"Whoever this man is," Scott said quietly. "He feels a sense of injustice," He paced around the office slowly. "He feels let down by the system, of that I'm certain. He's righting many wrongs in his eyes with his actions, and almost certainly harbours a grudge against the Police."

"Because of the twins' death?" Vincelli asked.

"No, not the twins." He replied. "Their deaths were a catalyst certainly, but something precedes them, something personal to him."

Vincelli nodded and smiled wryly. "The victim nobody helped."

"Maybe." Scott sighed heavily as he stood with his back to Vincelli, he gazed once again at the pictures, and plaques on his wall. "But these things *are* certain, he has no respect or fear for the police force hunting him." Folding his arms he revealed a muscular physique beneath his blue suit as it clung tightly to him. "No doubt he's left a few subtle diversions along the way, just in case he's taken to task on it."

"Like?"

"Like on the worst night of violence this town has ever seen."

"The amusement park?" Vincelli asked, knowing the answer.

Scott nodded, he turned to look at Vincelli. "The night good ship payback sailed into town, and downed anchor." He stood in silence for a moment, his arms were still folded tightly against him. "Where was Ray?" He whispered.

"Ray?" Vincelli asked. "I don't know, Sir." He shook his head at the question and rubbed gently at his face.

"Yes you do, Detective." Scott said. "Think."

Vincelli nodded and closed his eyes tightly. "He was outside their house." He said.

Scott nodded in agreement. "He, or should we say, his *car*, was parked outside their house 'til way after midnight." He began pacing again. "Mrs Rose must've called at least five times!"

Vincelli sat silently, he desperately wanted to light a cigar but knew better than to even ask.

"Do you think it's possible," Scott asked. "That Ray has become so intoxicated with this ghost notion, that he has assumed the identity of Brandon Rose?"

"No, Sir." Vincelli replied with a deliberate shake of his head. "No way."

"Literally, becoming Brandon, *himself?*" He asked. "And ultimately, killing as Brandon, *himself?*"

"No!" He shouted, squirming awkwardly. "No I don't!" He met Scott's stare dead on. "This is Ray!" He added. "Ray! Not some sword wielding maniac! Sir, with all due respect, I've watched him struggle with a can opener!" He slumped into the depths of his chair. "If you want to talk about individuals who've been through the mill, then yeah, Ray's right up there, but murder? No. No way."

Scott studied him carefully for a moment, watching every move he made. "A paradox." He said finally and with mild amusement. "You contradicted yourself beautifully there."

"Can we keep this down here? Please?" Vincelli asked, feeling increasingly frustrated.

"There is no question he's suffered enough." Scott said. "But he *may* hold a grudge."

"Bullshit."

Scott shook his head as he peered down at Vincelli. "Correct me if I'm wrong," He said. "But the reason you came to see me, was to inform me of your concerns about him!" He awaited Vincelli's answer but was growing rapidly short on patience. "So he's ok now?"

"No." He spoke quietly and stared at the tiled floor. "But Sir, I'm not sitting here saying he's Jack the ripper."

"But the fact remains unchanged," Scott whispered, sympathetically. "He could be harbouring a grudge."

Vincelli didn't reply, he chose instead to avert his gaze to the ceiling and tap his fingers repeatedly on the arm rests.

"Detective?"

"I'm sorry," Vincelli whispered. "I'm not buying it."

Scott sighed and again perched himself on the edge of his desk, he crossed his legs as he stretched them out in front of him. He admired his newly polished black brogues, but couldn't help comparing them to Vincelli's dirty, tanned leather shoes.

"You remember Ray's wife, don't you?" Scott asked. "Nancy, you remember her?"

"Of course I remember her." He answered flatly, briefly meeting Scott's gaze on his way from the ceiling to the floor.

"Then you'll recall her being struck and killed by a Police cruiser," He said. "A little over four years ago." Scott searched for a response, it didn't arrive. "Now I know you haven't forgotten *that*, you were after all, in the car that killed her."

"Thank you." Vincelli said. He raised his head a little to stare at Scott from beneath his brows. "It was an accident." He whispered. "I don't need reminding of that."

Scott nodded. "So says the inquest." He said sharply.

"We were answering a call, Sir." He said. "End of story."

"For you, maybe."

"Ray doesn't know I was in the car," Vincelli said. "He didn't know me back then, I was in uniform and weighed at least two stones less!"

He searched the room with his eyes. "He'd only just transferred in and quite frankly, I don't think he'd remember too much of anything from that day except for what happened to his wife."

"And now?"

"And now we're friends!" He shouted. "Good friends, he mentions her all the time to me, he doesn't know, Sir. I haven't the heart to tell him, it would only open up old wounds."

Scott nodded. "I agree." He said. "But if he does know, if that information is locked away in a tiny reserve somewhere in his mind, then technically - he could recall it at any time. That inquest was, after all - extremely inconclusive."

An uncomfortable moment forced both men to retreat a little, neither spoke for a moment.

"I'm sorry." Scott said. "That was uncalled for."

Vincelli mopped his brow with a white handkerchief he'd plucked from his jacket pocket, his trembling hands didn't go unnoticed.

"Well," Vincelli said. "If Ray *had* been at the amusement park that night, he wouldn't be too worried about anyone responding to Mrs Rose's calls, he would've known where our efforts were being focused."

"Like dealing," Scott whispered. "With the worst night of violence, that this town has ever seen." Neither had he failed to notice Vincelli's increased perspiration during the last few minutes, he watched with growing concern as Vincelli slackened his tie further and popped open another button, with barely functioning hands he seemed to have little, if any control over.

"Is there something you wish to add?" Scott asked.

"I visited his house the day after the killings," He replied. "The amusement park killings."

"And?"

"He had a lighter, and for a minute I thought I saw -" He paused to gaze around the room before meeting Scott's stare evenly. "It was one of those flip - top petrol lighters, and I thought I saw an inscription on it." He stopped again and began cursing beneath his breath. He beat his hands down hard on the arms of the chair and shook his head so violently that his slicked back hair fell down across his face. He quickly scooped it back from his eyes and over his head.

"What did it say?" Scott asked. "Or at least, what do you *think* it said?"

"Jake." He replied, tears formed in his eyes as he went on. "I'm certain it did, I watched him throw it in the garden when I turned away from him, I saw his reflection in the television. It's probably still there now."

"Yes," Scott added, travelling quickly back behind his desk. "We've had it confirmed that Jake was wearing a long leather jacket that night, it wasn't present with his body or anywhere else for that matter." He picked up the phone and dialled urgently. "The lighter was most likely in the pocket," He went on. "They always keep trophies, Detective."

"What are you doing?" Vincelli asked.

"I'm arranging a warrant to enter his house." He answered. "He goes to the cemetery on a Monday doesn't he?" He asked, shifting his attention between Vincelli and the receiver against his ear. "The time is now, we go in today."

"Excuse me, Sir." Vincelli said, as he raised to his feet. "I've a quick call of my own to make."

"Don't go far." Scott answered, waving him out.

Vincelli walked quickly to the door and wasted no time in getting on the other side of it, he closed the door carefully as he didn't wish to confirm his urgency to Scott. He dialled frantically with hands that still trembled, seemingly independent of what their neuronal impulses were delivering. He placed the phone to his ear and stepped quietly away from Scott's office door.

"It's time," He said, peering down the corridor. "He ended up convincing, *me*." He added with a grin. "Get him in right now, it'll be swarming soon so be quick." He ended the call and slid the phone back into his pocket.

Chapter Eleven

Kneeling down, he placed the flowers next to Nancy's grave and enjoyed the sound of the rain landing on the plastic wrapping, it was constant and rhythmic, almost hypnotic. He stared at the gold lettering on her headstone, before reaching out to stroke the curvature of the black marble.

"I don't care how much it rains today," He said, undoing the pink ribbon and breaking into song. "Because, *aint no sunshine when she's gone.*" The plastic wrapping fell open and rustled gently in the wind, he arranged his white lilies and roses before the headstone.

"Every time I turn on the radio, that song seems to be on." He pondered. "I think." Still kneeling down he unzipped his tan leather jacket to reveal his otherwise bare chest, beads of sweat were quickly washed away by the falling rain. He glanced furtively around the graveyard and, satisfied he was alone, held his arms outstretched like a rock star soaking up a stadium full of adoration. He closed his eyes tightly and leaned back as the rain nourished him like wisdom.

"I can feel you touching me, Nancy." He whispered as he straightened up again. He looked down at the flowers he'd laid and removed two red roses from them. "These one's are for someone else, baby." He whispered, clutching them loosely. "Not for a woman, you understand." He added quickly as he zipped up his jacket. "These are for a couple of young guys I met." He laughed to himself. "That sounded even worse didn't it?" He looked up at the blackened sky and imagined her laughing with him, he remembered how she used to cover her mouth whenever the giggles struck, to be *lady like*, she'd always say.

"That's where I'm going now, you see." He stood up and looked down the hill towards what was now Brandon and *Chad's* grave. "They were little more than kids, and they're dead now." He stood silently and watched for any activity, although all he could see were crows circling overhead. "I just felt I should do the right thing." He swallowed hard and was aware of an overpowering sense of guilt and foreboding. "You used to say I spent too much time fighting other peoples battles, listening to their problems and rooting for the underdog," He paused, the guilt suddenly felt intense. "And yet, I didn't fight yours."

What have I done? He wondered to himself. *I've let you down, Nancy - I just can't - remember.* He stood motionless. *What did I do, what did I do?* He reached out for her headstone and closed his eyes.

"Watch out for these boys, baby." He whispered. "You'll know them when you see them, trust me." He began his descent while waving the roses gently over his shoulder. "My love."

He felt fearful as he sloped down the hill, his eyes were already transfixed on the Rose's gravestone, the elm near it caught his eye. A gentle breeze urged him down the hill, like an invisible yet tender reassurance not to be afraid, an unnatural warmth coursed through his veins as he progressed. A red petal from each of the roses he carried broke free in the wind, rising before his eyes they fluttered with life, animate and free, they remained unburdened by the driving rain.

Follow us, Ray. He thought.

The ground beneath his feet was soft and uneven, having left the certainty of the gravel pathway he treaded carefully, and began negotiating his way between the grimy headstones. As the grass grew longer, so too the headstones appeared *older*, he saw statues of angels with their wings cracked and crumbling, laying smashed at their feet. Leaves began descending all around him and he quickly found himself very disoriented, he hadn't realised it before but saw all at once that the two floating rose petals had led him into an area he'd never seen before. He watched as the petals landed with purpose in a puddle, they floated buoyantly as the black water reflected an even blacker sky. There was a clearing behind some tall swaying trees, his attention was summoned there although he wasn't sure why. He clung tightly to his two roses as the wind ripped impatiently at them, he walked towards the trees, noticing as he did so that the trees appeared to circle a small plot of land.

As he approached it he could see it contained seven graves, two of which were still vacant and were mere holes in the ground. As he stepped between the trees and entered the circle he became aware of a vicious temperature drop, although now the wind had ceased completely. The five makeshift graves were fresh, lined neatly before him with mounds of freshly dug topsoil to cover them, they each had a wooden cross driven into them, they all contained names. He shook his head as his eyes struggled to focus in the heavy rain. "Danny?" He muttered, reading the first. "Nikki, Matt." He dropped the flowers to the ground. "Tommy and Jake." He thought for a moment and realised apart from the grave marked *Nikki*, they were arranged chronologically in order of death, with the two empty graves following them. "Who's Nikki?" He asked aloud. He paced slowly from grave to grave. "It just doesn't make any sense," He whispered, hugging himself tightly in the freezing cold. "Why is Danny's grave amongst *their* graves?" He asked. "*They* were your conspirators, *he* was your friend." The sky overhead was damn near black, day had become night in a fleeting instant as he squatted down next to the grave marked *Nikki*.

"Who are you?" He asked, begging his memory to provide the answer as he sifted a handful of dirt through his fingers. "What's your part in this?" He reached for another mound of his grave and felt a small metallic object just beneath the surface, dusting the top soil from it he carefully extracted what he could now see was a Mercedes emblem.

"Oh my god." He whispered. "You stole his flowers." He tossed the emblem on to the mound of earth, dusted his hands and stood up. "Another piece of the puzzle falls into place," He said. "You were driving the Mercedes that got shunted." He laughed as he gazed at the trees surrounding him. "But more importantly, you were *probably* driving the Mercedes on the night Brandon died, weren't you?" He paced up and down as he thought hard and pieced together what he knew and what he suspected. "You're the reason they hadn't disappeared from view in their Charger, when the pick - up joined the Washburn link road," He smiled and shook his head in disbelief. "Danny said the Charger was swerving across both lanes of the road, even braking - well it would be *if* it was trying to pass a car that was deliberately halting it's progress." He looked again at the black sky, he could barely see anything now it was so dark, he smiled as the rain fell on him. "But Danny never mentioned seeing you at all, so if you moved over once the pick - up had caught up, what was to stop the Charger's three hundred horses obliterating the pick - up?" He pondered the question for a moment. "Either, Danny *did* see you and lied to us, or that's one hell of a powerful pick - up." He laughed once more. "I *knew* he didn't kill you over flowers." He walked to the foot of Danny's grave and stared at the small wooden cross that bore his name. "You, I just don't understand."

"He was one of them, Ray." The voice came from behind, although Ray didn't feel the need to turn and confirm who it belonged to.

"I wondered when you'd turn up." He replied, still staring at the grave. "But I knew you would, after all - this is for my benefit, right?"

"Very perceptive."

Ray turned to look at him, except for his deathly pale face he remained almost invisible within the tree line. Ray was mildly relieved to see he wasn't armed, he smiled genuinely at Ray, like he was greeting an old friend.

"Brandon?" He asked. "Or do I call you *Death*?"

"It's not always easy to tell is it, Ray?" He stood perfectly still, with his flowing black hair shielding his face almost entirely. Ray saw all at once why he was a virtually indestructible force to be reckoned with, he could blend like no other and be at one with the shadows. "I'm sorry about Chad." Ray said. "I really am, I hope he's at peace."

"Thank you," He whispered. "I'm certainly not at peace, but let's hope *he* is."

Ray smiled back nervously. "Have you got yourself a lair around here or something?"

"Why do you ask that?"

"I'm just curious where your equalisers are," He answered. "I'm guessing you keep them close to hand since you never know when you're going to need them."

He laughed a little. "Don't be naïve, Ray." He whispered. "I know *exactly* when I need them." He stepped out from the tree line and walked slowly towards Ray, and the graves. "You were *so* close, Ray." He said, pointing at the grave marked *Nikki*. "So close, but not close enough."

"Then feel free to enlighten me," Ray replied. "Because no one seems to know anything."

"That's right, Ray." He said, smiling down on the graves like a mother putting her children to sleep. "No one knows anything."

"Then tell me."

"Well he wasn't driving the Mercedes that night," His expression turned sinister as he spoke. "He was in the pick - up, just like the rest of them." He guided his open palm over all five graves. "In fact, he was the one who took the crowbar to the headlight of our car."

"So how come he was driving it on the day he died?"

"Bait." He answered flatly. "For the police, not me."

"Bait?"

"The car had been in storage since its involvement in the chase, but it's a nice car - so the boss decides that a month is enough, and the time had come to send it out for a road test to see if it would generate any interest from the police." He looked at Ray for a moment but averted his gaze quickly back to the ground. "You see, he couldn't be certain it hadn't been seen by someone that night, so he used our friend Nikki as bait, told him to dress nice so he looked like he owned it," He laughed. "After all, he didn't want the car getting pulled because the driver looked like he'd stolen it, did he?"

"Ok," Ray whispered, thirsty for knowledge but fearful of angering him.

"Nikki just didn't count on going from bait, to a crash test dummy in one afternoon."

"So why did he come here?" Ray asked. "Why take your flowers?"

"He was told to bring the car here, nothing's coincidental."

"Why?"

"I was murdered, Ray." He answered. "Keep up." He shook his head. "The boss wondered if the grave was under observation, so decided to wave the car in their faces, if it hadn't acquired a tail after a couple of days, then it was clean."

Ray nodded. *Makes sense.* He thought.

"But Danny most certainly *did* see it, it remained in our path the entire time."

"So why didn't he -"

"He was afraid." He answered. "He lied."

"And you killed him for *that*?"

"No, Ray." He replied, almost insulted at the question. "I didn't end his life."

"But his grave, it's here with your victims."

"I may not have killed him," He whispered. "But he was on my list, and he *knew* I was coming for him when darkness fell."

"Why?"

"Because he betrayed us in the worst possible way." He glared down at Danny's grave. "He had to die for what he did to us, he was always going to be first."

"I thought he was your friend," Ray whispered. "Jesus Christ, him as well."

"Not to my knowledge," He replied with a smirk, glancing skyward. "But if I find out he was involved, I'll go after *him* as well." He laughed and stepped closer to Ray. "Danny ratted us out," He said. "Stabbed us in the back, sold us down the river - choose your metaphor."

"To whom?" Ray asked. "About what?"

"Here's a good one," He said, circling Ray in the darkness. "You might say we gave him just enough rope -"

"Which is ultimately what you killed him with." Ray interrupted.

"You know," He said quietly. "Someone once said, that in life you should always pick a side, never *ever* sit on the fence."

"Why?"

"Who's going to help you if you haven't shown loyalty?"

"And Danny?" He asked. "Who's side was *he* on?"

"Both." He answered flatly. "He upset both sides, it was only a matter of who got to him first."

Ray walked slowly to Danny's grave and knelt before it. "Pick a side." He whispered, lost in thought. "You said 'pick a side,' on your tape."

"On his *confessions* tape, you mean?" He asked. "Not so much *confession* as *dictation* I'm afraid."

"What does that mean?" Ray asked, climbing back to his feet and dusting his knees.

"I suggest you watch it again, Ray." He said. "Clearly you've missed something."

"I have?"

He nodded. "Pay close attention Ray," He whispered. "A good detective would *never* have missed it."

"Well I'm not a detective." Ray replied. "I've been doing the best I can with what I've got."

"No!" He shouted. "With what you've got, you could've done a whole lot more!"

"What the fuck is that supposed to mean?" He shouted back, impressed with his nerve and resolve. "I've been putting my neck on the block for you!" He saw the irony all at once. "I probably shouldn't say that around you, should I?"

"You don't have too many friends in this town, Ray." He said, standing inanimate in the darkness. "I'm one you need."

"I shouldn't have said that." Ray whispered, holding himself tightly. "I'm sorry."

"Don't be." He answered, moving slowly to Ray. "Did you ever get so scared of death, that you became afraid of life?"

"I Guess -"

"You've been waiting for death, haven't you?"

"Yes." He replied, averting his gaze to the ground.

"Well here stands death before your very eyes, Ray." He reached out his hand and placed it gently under Ray's chin and lifted his head. "There's no answers beneath your feet, just earth." He said. "And since you're not buried within it just yet, wake up."

Ray fought hard to contain the tears he knew were about to flow from his eyes, but he couldn't stop them. "I just want to die." He whispered. "How about placing me in one of those empty graves?" He asked, they both knew he was only *half* joking.

"*Oh no.*" He spoke with conviction and shook his head. "They may be vacant but they're very much taken."

"Who?" Ray asked.

"The final conspirator, Ray." He replied. "The last one responsible for our demise, and the man who ordered it." He held two fingers aloft and stared at Ray. "Just two more to take down," He smiled menacingly. "And of course, *anyone* who tries to protect them."

"Then what?" He asked. "What happens then?"

"All this will soon be over, Ray." He said, staring hard into Ray's eyes. "Don't be in the wrong place at the wrong time, because terrible things happen when you get caught in the *wrong place* at the *wrong time*." He paused for a moment. "Don't they, Ray?"

"What?" He asked. "I don't understand."

"There must be certain days in your life, when all you do is wish?" He began circling Ray once more, stoking his shoulders as he passed slowly behind him. "Wish you still had Nancy?" He whispered. "Wish you'd gone to the store instead of her?"

"I do." Ray whispered, shivering violently and numb with cold. "I do."

"Or maybe you wish you'd given her the pack of cigarettes you'd bought for her?"

"What?" Ray asked, stunned with disbelief. "How do you -"

"You thought of everything that day," He whispered, standing directly before Ray. "Everything! You knew she was running low, which is why you bought her some when you got the wine."

"I just…I was planning to…it just didn't -"

"Why didn't you give her them?" He asked, his black eyes mirrored Ray's to perfection in the darkness as they locked. "They were right there in the sideboard."

"I needed her to go out," He mumbled, his legs were struggling to support his weight as he stumbled back a little. "I had to lay out her gifts for when she returned."

"I know that." He said, taking hold of Ray's arms to stabilise him. "I know it, because you know it."

"Why are you doing this to me?" Ray asked.

"It's not mere coincidence that you see me," He whispered. "Or hear me, or speak with me."

"Then tell me."

"Nancy's death was no accident, Ray." He allowed Ray to pull away and fall flat on his face, he landed on the mound of fresh earth upon Danny's grave.

"I know it, because you know it." He whispered whilst watching Ray clamber desperately to his feet. "You know the answers, Ray."

"No!" He shouted. "You're not fit to say her name!" He closed his eyes tightly as his body trembled with fear and remembrance. "You're not fit, you're a murderer." He shook his head. "It was an accident."

"It was a cover up." He answered, grabbing at Ray's throat suddenly and violently. "What kind of pathetic wimp are you?" He shouted. "You listened as your colleagues made a joke of your wife's death, you listened as they plotted to absolve themselves of blame, you listened as they racially abused her, as she lay dead in your arms." He squeezed tightly at Ray's throat. "All you had to do was look at them, you ought to be ashamed of yourself." He threw Ray to the ground and stood menacingly above him. "You should've killed yourself a long time ago, Ray." He laughed. "You're as dead as I am anyway, night after night you sit in that fucking chair coz you're too chicken shit to kill yourself, let alone anyone else." He knelt down next to Ray. "When all you have is taken from you, *anyone* would kill those responsible if justice failed, but any system is only as good as those who represent it." He pointed his finger directly into Ray's face. "I wouldn't place any faith in you, you're fucking useless."

He lay in the dirt and stared up at him, he had no response, just silent acceptance. With not a word in his own defence forth coming, Ray reached out his hand and hoped he still placed enough faith in him to help him.

"It's about time, Ray." He said, pulling him to his feet.

"She was hit by a black and white," Ray said, his voice breaking mid sentence. "It was answering a call and she ran out in front of it, it's that simple." He massaged at his temples as he thought back. "I don't understand, I really don't."

"Black and white?" He asked. "The irony just smacks you in the face, doesn't it?"

"I don't under -"

"Nothing is that simple, when it comes to *black and white*." He said, his dark shadowy eyes probed for a response. "But I don't have to tell you that, do I?"

"No."

"You must feel it, Ray. It's all around if you care to look." He smiled and paced slowly in front of the graves, his arms were folded casually behind his back. "Some people would argue that racism is a thing of the past, but racism exists as strongly to this day as it ever has, it's a terminal disease at the very heart of society, it has *no* cure. Once upon a time they wore white sheets, now they wear white *shirts* with their ties on, sitting behind their desks or driving their trucks, and still they judge you on the colour of your skin and elevate themselves above you because you're *black* and they're *white*." He laughed as he kicked dirt from the graves as he passed them, one by one. "To this day, there are those who would see you swing from a tall tree in the midst of a burning cross that reflects in your eyes, as bright as the hate that burns in theirs."

Ray stared blankly, he remembered the crowd of gathered onlookers around her. "Nobody was helping her." He whispered. "They just stood watching."

"That's shock," He replied. "Not racism." He walked to Ray. "The question here, is *why* did she run out? If it was in fact answering a call, then wouldn't she have heard the siren?"

"Maybe she -"

"Shouldn't *you*, have heard the siren?" He asked. "You live close enough to have heard it, and that's what they're for, built up areas - right?"

"Nobody was helping her," Ray said again. "They just stood around her."

"She ran out," He whispered. "Because she didn't hear it," He held Ray's stare firmly. "She didn't hear it, because the siren wasn't on,"

"And it wasn't on because," Ray whispered, pausing mid sentence as the gravity of his own words finally hit home. "It wasn't answering a call."

"You know what you saw," He said, gripping Ray's arms tightly. "You know what you heard, it's all in there." He tapped his finger gently against Ray's forehead. "The tape is still intact, you need to restore it, digitally re master it if you will." He smiled. "Just like *Calamity Jane.*"

"Why don't I remember?" He asked. "I just can't remember."

"That sense of guilt that hit you at her grave," He said. "It's not what you've done, Ray. It's what you haven't done that keeps you in that chair, night after night, waiting for death."

"Why didn't I do something?" Ray asked, "Why did I let her down, she was my wife!" He felt the stab of guilt rip through him, desperate and short of breath, he felt a rush of nervous energy surge through his veins, he knew an attack was imminent.

"It's not panic attacks that plague you." He whispered. "It's a guilt complex that triggers in you when *something*, takes you back."

"Help me!" He begged. "Please, Brandon. *Death*, whoever the fuck you are" Ray grabbed at him tightly. "Help me, I need to know."

"I'm going to take you on a journey," He whispered. "A journey through time."

"Time travel's a myth!" Ray shouted, trembling with desperation. "You can help me!" He said. "You can tell me what to do to end all this!"

"Time Travel's a myth?" He asked, grinning wryly. "So you've never heard a song that didn't instantly rewind the fabric of your mind by ten years? A song on your car radio that just happens to be the first song you made '*our*' song, with your precious departed wife? A song so deeply rooted in your heart that life simply wouldn't be the same without it. Just close your eyes and you're there, the warm afternoon sun shining on your face, the butterflies in your stomach as you uttered those immortal words….Will you marry me? How beautiful she looked as you held her hands in yours, and seconds seemed like hours as she drew breath and said '*yes.*'" He watched on as Ray absorbed his words. "Do you *really* believe time travel's a myth?"

Ray shook his head, still lost in the telepathy of a shared thought. "No."

"Allow me to give you the trigger," He whispered, grabbing Ray's hands tightly he placed his fore and index fingertips against Ray's wrists, their pulses fused almost immediately.

"Please!" Ray shouted. "Do it!" He could feel his own pulse

surging into his host's hands, or vice versa, he wasn't sure but could feel both pulses synchronising into one.

"It's just one less fucking *nigger*." He whispered, his eyes as black as marbles in the dark.

Ray felt the grip tighten against his wrists, he was sure they must be bleeding as he could no longer feel his own hands, the pain was immense. He closed his eyes tightly as they too hurt like never before, pain seared into his brain as several electric pulses shocked his system into a trance like state, like a computer crashing.

"When you awake, everything will be different," He whispered, tapping deeply into Ray's subconscious mind. "Time has run short my friend, they're coming for you as we speak but we must allow this. Do not doubt me, I assured you my protection and I will not fail you."

Ray gasped aloud and choked for breath, pain ripped through his chest and gripped - vice like, at his heart. His arms were free, released from contact he fell backwards and seconds really did feel like hours as his body headed south. The falling sensation was sweet and idyllic as the water logged earth beneath him beckoned.

"Do you wish to know why Nancy has never visited?" He spoke softly, more than aware his words were being heard. "The living no longer visit you, why should the dead?"

Ray's body landed on the ground, he lay outstretched as though nailed to a cross. "You must choose, life or death." He stood at Ray's feet and watched him draw his last breath. "You've been dead a long time, Ray." He whispered. "You just didn't know it."

A jolt of electricity awoke him in a pent up anxious state, like a vivid dream that fails to end although awake. He opened his eyes and quickly held up his hands to block out the filtered sunlight coming through the tilted blinds, it caught him square on as he shifted uneasily in his recliner. He glanced around his living room and was aware immediately that it was different, he glanced at the clean carpet, there wasn't an empty beer can in sight, the records were stacked neatly against the music centre.

"What?" He muttered. "What's happening?" He placed a hand over his mouth and braced himself momentarily before peering over his shoulder, from within the chair he knew so well - he saw it.

"It was a dream." He whispered, tears fell freely as he spoke. A large mahogany dining suite filled the empty space he'd gotten so used to, beyond it were the patio doors and through them the sunshine was a sight to behold. He was aware of the commotion coming from the master bedroom above him, he distinctly recognised the sound of the sliding doors on their walk in wardrobe, it was being closed in a hurry.

"Nancy," He whispered. "My baby, I get to see my baby." He fought hard to control his emotions. "Don't let her see this, Ray." He said, listening as the banging upstairs began its rapid descent down them. He stood nervously and twirled his wedding band expectantly as his body trembled with fear. The idea occurred to him that what had seemed like a life time of absence in his eyes, was mere minutes in hers. He did his best to shake off the tension that clung to him like a wet overcoat. His heart beat beside itself as the living room door flew open, as genuine shock rendered him stone cold and speechless.

"No!" He said, watching on as version of *himself*, a version long since forgotten, a version inhabiting only the darkest realms of his memory, rushed hurriedly yet *happily* past him, clutching amongst other things, lilies.

"What's this?" He asked himself aloud, while watching his *other* self hastily arrange the flowers into a vase on the dining room table, "Why am I here?" He whispered, moving slowly towards the front window, trying to calm himself as he went. "There's a reason you're here, Ray." He said reassuringly to himself, whilst trying to open the blinds further, however he soon saw the futility in his actions as he couldn't influence them in any way. With fingers that had no feeling, he had no touch. "I'm Ray." He said, in a voice he knew could not be heard, generating from within a body made up of not physical matter, but memories.

"*Calamity Jane!*" The voice behind him said. Ray turned to see himself stood by the dining table removing the cassette from it's protective case, he walked with it to the video player and inserted it ready for viewing. "*Digitally re mastered?*" He said, glancing at the case before dropping it on the floor next to the television. "*I sure hope she like this,"* He went on. *"For that matter, I hope I like it since I've got to sit here and watch it with her."*

"Don't you worry," Ray whispered, attempting to twirl his wedding band. "It's a grower." He watched silently from by the window, as his other self plucked a Frank Sinatra long - player from the collection, he placed it quickly on the platter and rested the tone arm on the vinyl, ready to power it up when she walked through the door.

"Digitally re - mastered," Ray whispered, "Where have I heard -" He paused as the memory hit him. "Digitally re mastered, just like *Calamity Jane*." He shivered for a moment, fearful of the knock he knew was imminent, the backlash of which would send a wave of destruction through the time line of his life, from a ripple to the ultimate tsunami of devastation.

"I'm not dead, he sent me back - *to watch*." Dread began to swell in his mind like a cancerous tumour. *Any time now*. He thought.

"That's everything." He said, pre-empting his virtual self and clutching his wedding band tightly.

"That's everything." He said, smelling the flowers.

"Now all we need…"

"Now all we need…"

"Is Nancy."

"Is Nancy."

Like a sprinter on the starting blocks Ray stood in wait, he closed his eyes tightly as the footsteps approached, the banging on the door was every bit as sudden and frantic as he'd recalled.

"You forget your keys?" He whispered, watching on as his other self repeated with a split second time delay.

"You forget your keys?" He shouted, hitting the power switch on the music centre. As the velvety tones of old blue eyes began to fill the room, the room began to shake - violently, or rather the *picture* of the room shook violently, as another image faded gradually over it, like a recording over a recording.

Did you forget your keys, baby? The words echoed around his brain like an explosion of his senses.

"*It was all supposed to be perfect, Nancy.*" His virtual self cried. Leaning over her body he ran his fingers gently through her jet black, blood soaked hair. "*This isn't happening!*" He shouted, cradling her lifeless body against his own.

"It's happening, Ray." He whispered, staring down at himself. It troubled him that he wasn't able to look anywhere he *wanted* to look, he could only see that which he'd *seen*, and committed perfectly to memory on the day.

"*It was all supposed to be perfect.*" He said again, looking up at the cruiser. He was filled with contempt and hate for his inanimate love rival, that which had succeeded where men had failed, in taking her away from him. Steam hissed relentlessly through its smashed and distorted grille, which in a cruel twist of circumstance actually appeared to be smiling. The windshield had been smashed by an obvious spherical object and had cracks spider webbing from the bloody epicentre. He sat rocking her gently too and fro, carefully shielding her face from onlookers, his hands were bloody and sore from her gushing - glass infested scalp.

"I got you everything," He said. "*Even your cigarettes, that's why I let you go - even though you didn't need to.*" He held her close and watched the sunlight sparkle in her lifeless eyes. "*I just wanted it to be perfect, but instead I've done this to you, and I'm never going to be able to say sorry enough.*"

Ray watched on as a strange fog descended at shoulder level, it hung like clouds on a mountain top and everyone around him was faceless. He longed to reach down and touch her lips, to feel her warmth one final time before it slipped away forever, but couldn't shake the feeling of intrusion, even though it was *himself* he was observing, he wanted to allow *himself* - space.

His attention was drawn to a uniformed officer who was hurriedly cordoning off the area around Nancy with yellow police tape. He noticed that the traffic had ceased completely, so guessed the road had been closed off beyond his line of sight. His attention was drawn again to the police tape, more importantly to the wording on it. '*Police line do not cross.*'

"It almost breaks your heart." The voice said quietly. "Doesn't it?"

Ray listened closely whilst still watching himself cradle Nancy, the voice intrigued him for reasons unknown, it wasn't what he'd said, rather the tone he'd said it with.

"It does, yeah." Another voice replied, in a younger somewhat naïve sounding tone. "But why do I get the impression *you're* not being sincere?"

Ray listened with growing interest as a cigarette was lit, the sound of a metal flip - top lighter being snapped shut was unmistakeable.

"Touchy, aren't we?" His voice was the same as before only this time preceded by rapid inhalation.

"Do you think she'll be ok?"

"Ok?" He asked, sniggering at the question. "She's as cold as your mother's bed."

"So what's going to happen now?" The voice asked

"Well let's see," The reply came in a whisper. "A new fender, a grille and a windshield, and *this* will be up and running in no time."

"That's not what I meant."

"I know it's not what you meant!" He shouted back, although he quickly lowered his voice again. "It's one less fucking nigger, that's what happens now."

Ray looked again at the police tape, and again at the wording on it but especially, '*Do not cross.*'

"Wait a minute," Ray said to himself. "*This*, will be up and running in no time."

'*Do not cross.*'

"They're standing next to the cruiser." He whispered.

'*Do not cross.*'

"They were in the car," Ray said, swallowing hard and doing his best not to go down with the sickness that coursed through him. "I thought you were my..." He listened closely but heard no reply. He struggled to contain his anger at what he'd heard, but it bothered him more that he'd heard it all along and chosen not to act, his guilt finally had a reason to be. He'd known all along who was driving the cruiser that had struck and killed Nancy, he was subsequently cleared of any wrong doing, but resigned soon after the inquest with failing mental health. The testimonies of the two other officers riding in the car with him however, had always occurred to Ray as scripted and planned to the letter, but witness statements, both police and independent, had all corroborated that at least one of Ray's colleagues had battled to save her life prior to him arriving on the scene, a fact he accepted since Nancy's blood was smeared across his front door's window pane.

"We don't want them here." He said, his tone was aggressive as he stamped his cigarette into the ground.

"What about Steve?" The voice asked. "He's killed her, he's going to be in trouble, right?"

"Listen kid," He replied. "You better learn something and learn it fast, in this life - you better pick a side, and stick with it." He sniggered. "No one's going to fight your corner if you haven't shown loyalty to someone, Get it?"

"How do I know if I'm choosing the right side?"

"A simple rule of thumb, kid." He answered. "Pick the guys that you're most afraid of."

"There's a dead woman -"

"You shut the fuck up!" He replied fiercely. "You with us? Or you with the nigger?"

"I'm with you." He replied, clearly terrified. "I'm sorry."

"We had just engaged in a pursuit," He said sternly. "We hadn't called it in because it had only just begun, blue Ford Taurus with two niggers in the front - no passengers in the rear, didn't get the plates in time and most importantly -" He paused briefly. "The siren and lights were *on*. Have you got that?"

Ray heard no reply but figured a nod had occurred in response to the question.

"If they found out we were doing seventy in a built up area for no good reason, we'd all hang." He laughed. "Do you want to hang, kid?"

"No Sir," He answered meekly. "What about Steve?" He asked.

"I'll take care of Steve," He replied, lighting another cigarette. "He'll sing from the same hymn sheet or I'll fucking bury him. Period."

The mist was lowering, not fading, but engulfing him completely until nothing of what he'd just witnessed remained.

"Do you think he's ok?" The voice asked, it was different from the voices he'd heard so far, older and kinder.

"I don't know." The reply came, again from a much younger sounding companion. "I'm going to the car to phone an ambulance, stay with him."

Struggling for breath, Ray quickly opened his eyes and was immediately blinded by a burning white light, like a new born baby he was unsure of where or *what* he was. The rain had stopped and was replaced by sunshine simply too intense for him to absorb. He saw the silhouette of a man leaning over him, and after some degree of effort in the face of near blindness he could tell the man was elderly, probably mid eighties he figured. Ray could feel the man's hand had a tremor, he hoped it was a condition the man had lived with for some time, rather than the result of their chance meeting.

"Stay where you are, Ray." The man said, he spoke in a voice that like his face, was kind and reassuring. "My son has gone to get help." He pointed towards the car park.

"How do you know my name?" Ray asked, still struggling for breath.

"This was lying next to you," He answered, showing him his own wallet "I took the liberty of checking for some I.D, I hope you don't mind."

"No." He said. "No, course not." He allowed his eyes to close again. "What the hell happened? How did I get here…I don't remember."

"Well, my son and I were passing by on the footpath," He said. "We were going to see his mother, my wife - when we saw you - you just collapsed." He smiled a little. "You fell flat on your back, right were you are now."

"I was with my wife," Ray said. "She's around here somewhere." He smiled.

"She's a very pretty lady, Ray" He said, looking at the picture of her in Ray's wallet. "She must make you very happy."

"If you see her will you call her, please?" Ray asked. "Don't let her leave without me."

"What's her name, Ray?" He asked.

"Nancy," He whispered. "Her name is Nancy."

The mans smile faded a little, he noticed the headstone that Ray was laid outstretched before bore the same name.

"I'm sure she's around here somewhere," He whispered. "You just relax now."

Chapter Twelve

Colorado General. Thursday 20th May.

22:45.

"He's waking up!" The voice said. Ray heard him clearly despite his obvious efforts to whisper. He sounded alarmed, it troubled Ray also that he sounded like he was sitting right beside him.

"So what!" The reply came, this time there was no attempt at whispering. "He's not going anywhere is he?"

"He might start asking questions?"

"Just be quiet."

Ray opened his eyes and was relieved to see the room was in darkness, he struggled for a moment to pull focus on his surroundings, but knew instantly he wasn't at home, for one thing - he was in a bed rather than his recliner. He found himself wondering if he'd in fact imagined the voices, or maybe dreamt them since the room was now peaceful, but the hallway outside the door wasn't, he assumed it was a hallway as the comings and goings seemed contained and travelled past the door - rather than away from it.

"I don't like this." The voice came again. "What if he goes fucking schitzo on us?"

"Just don't engage him." The reply came. "I've done my hours. I'm not a fucking psychiatrist, how do I know which one's waking up? Could be any one of them."

"It creeps me out."

Ray tried to obtain a logical train in the conversation, but he just couldn't grasp what, or *who* they were talking about. Nor could he understand why there was a rattling chain in the room.

"Just fucking turn away if he speaks to you."

"Turn away?" The voice asked. "I'd like to walk away, but this fucking chain takes care of that idea, doesn't it?"

Chain? Ray wondered. *Why a chain?* His eyes were beginning to adjust to the darkness.

"I know he's not going to come out at this time," The voice next to him whispered. "But he said he wanted to be the first one to speak to him."

"Tough."

"Well can't they find a nurse who can put him out 'til morning?"

"Why are we in the dark?" Ray shouted, he felt a sudden jerk on his wrist and a simultaneous rattling of the chain, the meaning of which still eluded him.

"Fucking scared me, man." The voice next to him replied.

"Where am I?" He asked. "And who are you?" He gazed at the figure sitting in a chair on the right hand side of his bed, although he couldn't successfully see him he quickly recognised the uniform, he'd liaised several times during his career with the transportation or transfer of prisoners, with prison custody officers. He could see the man's white shirt was unbuttoned at the top, and his contrasting dark tie was clipped against the collar on one side. He didn't appear familiar to Ray even after concentrating on him with his peripherals in full swing, but he could tell the man had blonde wavy hair.

"Who are you?" He asked, trying but unable to move. "Why are we here? *Where* is here?"

"That's a lot of questions." He replied, with a smirk spreading across his face like acne, which Ray imagined he suffered from due to his obvious immaturity.

"It is *Ray*, right?" He asked, giggling like a school girl.

"Yes." He answered, already wishing he had the strength to wipe the grin from his smug face. "Who else would I be?"

"Don't know really," He replied, running his free hand through his hair whilst slouching in his best 'trying to be casual' pose. "Brandon, perhaps?"

"What the fuck are you talking about?" Ray shouted, strength or no strength his temper flared.

"Maybe Chad?" He continued. "You tell me, Ray." His words prompted laughter from somewhere within the room.

"You're real funny." Ray said. "You're only talking tough because you got your boy in here with you."

"Do you want funny?" He asked, leaning over Ray. "Here's funny." He raised his left arm and waved it a little, drawing Ray's attention to the chain that joined them both at the wrists. "Where ever you go, I go." He said, laughing. "You go the toilet, I go with you. You take a shit, I'm there. This chain may be just long enough to spare your blushes, but I'll make sure it takes your dignity." He laughed again. "Anyway, you should be used to chains where you come from."

"What?" He asked, redoubling his efforts to stay calm but struggling beneath the sheets. *Why can't I move?* He wondered.

"The slave ships didn't allow you lot to run around, so it's only right."

"Oh you're a funny one." Ray said. "Real funny." He struggled on beneath his covers, although he soon realised there was more at play than wasted, or disabled muscles, he could feel the restraints as he fought against them.

"Why am I fucking tied down?" He shouted. "Why am I even here?" He slammed his head down repeatedly on his pillows, it was after all the only part of his body he still had free reign over. "Why am I here? What did I do?" He shouted. "Tell me!"

"Alright, alright." The second voice said finally. "Stop it now, Peter."

Ray lifted his head to see from where the voice emanated, and for the first time was able to take in his new surroundings. There was a window directly opposite his bed, he was surprised to see it wasn't barred, but nevertheless it allowed in the moonlight which aided his orientation. There was a windowless door on the other side of the officer he was chained too, he could see light shining through the gaps all around it. The walls were plain and the room empty of furniture, except for the bed he lay in and the apparatus next to his bed, he wasn't sure of its purpose. He watched as a shadow shifted slowly across the room, he was tall, slender and dressed in dark clothes. He moved silently and with purpose.

"Brandon?" Ray whispered.

"Grant, actually." He said, switching the light on. He stood and looked down on Ray as he unbuttoned his jacket a little. "This here is Peter." He moved back to his seat opposite the door as Peter gave a casual wave in Ray's direction.

"You don't know us." Grant said, as he lowered himself into the chair. "And we don't know you. That's how it's going to stay."

As Ray's eyes adjusted to the brutal fluorescent lights directly over his bed, he saw that Grant was a Police officer, clad in a dark combat style uniform, complete with a baseball cap that he had turned to the left a little, he looked to be in his early thirties. Grant was suited - booted - and armed, he kept the weapon pointed at ground as it rested between his legs, though he held the muzzle and was clearly ready to take aim at a moments notice.

"Why are you here with me?" Ray asked, allowing his head to fall to the pillow. "If I'm in hospital, why are you here with me?"

"*We*," He said, allowing a pause to follow. "Are here for your protection, and believe me, *you* need it."

"Pro -"

"Secondly!" He said, raising his voice over Ray's. "We are here to detain you, and detain you we will." He smiled at Ray. "But the fact remains, Ray," He went on. "You've suffered four massive heart attacks since your arrest, so right now your health is too poor for you to be detained in prison, or perhaps in your case, a mental institution."

"It's over then." Ray whispered. "It's over, he got them all." He smiled and felt moderately relaxed despite his location. "They're all dead."

"For you, Ray," Grant said. "It *is* over."

"Thank you, God." Ray whispered. He closed his eyes tightly and missed the curious glances being exchanged by his guards. "He took me to the brink of insanity and back, I'll never know why he chose to show himself to me."

"Back?" Peter asked. "I didn't realise it was a return ticket?"

"So he's coming for me now, is he?" Ray asked, ignoring Peter completely.

"Who?" Grant asked, sighing heavily and looking at his watch.

"Brandon." Ray replied, opening his eyes and staring at the window. "He's coming for me now? Because I know what he is? And you're going to stop him?" He laughed, clearly amused at the idea he shook his head. "You're going to need more than that gun," He said.

"He'll blow through here like the fucking wind and reduce you to a bloody pile of flesh." He gazed at the window again, in fact it was his sole focal point away from the judgemental glances he *now* knew were being exchanged. "I'm not crazy," He whispered. "He promised me his help, he promised to protect me, he failed and so shall you."

"Just relax, Ray." Grand said. "It'll be ok."

"It wont." He answered. "He gave me a fucking heart attack, under the guise that he was helping me." Tears rolled down his face, frustratingly, he was unable to wipe them so turned his head and wiped them on his pillows. "He may as well kill me."

"No one's going to hurt you, Ray." Grant said. "Not on my watch anyway." He smirked.

Ray smiled and stared out into the blackness, through the window and beyond. "Do these restraints come off at any point?" He asked. "Or the chain?"

"The restraints will come off, yes." Grant said. "But not for a while yet, Ray."

"And the chain?"

"Until you're locked up in a government facility, the chain will remain at all times."

"At *all* times?" Ray asked.

"The only time that chain comes off," Grant said. "Is if you suffer another heart attack, then and only then will it be released." He laughed as he looked at Peter. "It's not good for whoever is on the other end to remain attached to you, when they get their paddles out and shout clear!" They both laughed at the prospect as Ray stared through the window. "And don't get any ideas about the window," Peter said. "We're twelve floors up, so forget it."

He felt his anxiety raising through his body like mercury in a thermometer, he tried to remain calm but struggled with his nerves as his body struggled with the restraints.

Why did you place me here? He wondered. *You said everything would be different when I awoke, but I never imagined you'd allow this.* He shook his head and once more closed his eyes tightly, he tried to ignore the sniggering taking place beside him. *Are you coming for me, Brandon?* He thought. "Are you coming, Brandon?" He whispered. "Are you coming?" His attention was disturbed by the fits of laughter erupting beside him.

"Are you *coming*?" Peter asked, lowering the tone of his voice. "Oh yeah, are you *coming*, Brandon?" He asked, whilst pretending to masturbate. "Oh, I'm *coming too,* Brandon." He said. "Oh, *come* for me, Brandon. *Come for me.*"

"Stop it," Grant said, trying to contain his amusement, and embarrassment.

"Sorry," Peter said, still laughing. "This guy is fucking unbelievable."

"Ray," Grant said firmly. "There is *no* Brandon." He held Ray's stare as securely as his restraints held his body. "It's been seven months since he died, Ray," He added. "The only part of that kid that remains is what's living inside you. *You*, are Brandon Rose, Ray. You and you alone." He smiled in disbelief. "You're in a world of trouble." He laughed as he gazed at Peter. "Do you know what they're calling you?"

"What?" Ray asked, remaining otherwise silent.

"The Black Widow." He said, getting up and taking the three steps to Ray's bed. "The Black Widow," He repeated, whilst walking slowly along the length of his bed. "That's not a reference to your skin colour obviously, that wouldn't be very P.C, would it?" He laughed, as did Peter. "It's a reference to the long dark hair, and the dark clothing you had on whilst prowling the shadows, dedicated to your kill." He shook his head. "But biting the flesh off that kid's neck was pretty fucked up, even for a psycho." He held the muzzle of his assault rifle and aimed it briefly at Ray's head. "No," He whispered. "We didn't realise we were looking for a *nigger*, until we uncovered your killing kit."

"What kit?" Ray asked, flinching on the wrong end of a laser scope.

"The wig," He answered. "The face paints, and of course your swords."

"No," Ray whispered. "No, he wouldn't do that!" He shouted. "Why did you do that?" He thrashed wildly in his bed as saliva sprayed from his mouth. "You motherfucker, Brandon!" He shouted. "You motherfucker, you fucked me over this time!" He forced himself against the straps and felt them straining, but he knew they'd never break, the white sheet draped over him and them, hadn't even moved or fallen from his bed. "It's a dream!" He cried. "It's a fucking dream! Wake me up, Brandon - you owe me, you motherfucker!"

"And that, Ray," Grant said, shouting over Ray's hysterics. "Is why your restraints will remain for the foreseeable future." He returned to his seat. "Whilst you're being detained in a mainstream hospital, they wont even let you scratch your nose without an armed guard."

"He'll kill you all!" Ray said, calming down a little. "He'll kill you all, anyone who stands in his way had better be wearing a steel polar neck when he arrives." He laughed wildly and raised his head to see where Grant was. "Your gun is useless," He said, pausing for laughter. "May as well shove it up *his* ass!" He tilted his head to Peter. "I think he'd enjoy it!"

"Where's the nurse?" Peter asked. "This one needs putting back under, something seems to have upset him."

"You racist mother fuckers!" Ray shouted, struggling again but only managing to move his feet. "He was right, it's always beneath the surface if you care to look for it!"

"Fuck this!" Grant shouted, leaping from his chair to Ray's bed. "Here comes the nurse, now." He said, holding the gun towards the floor with his left hand, he punched Ray twice with his right, hard and directly on the side of his jaw. "Night - night - nigger." He returned slowly to his seat, glancing at Ray as he did so, just to be certain he was out. Peter sat silently, unsure of what to say to him, but one thing was certain, he didn't expect nor enjoy the sight of Grant hitting Ray as hard as he did. He watched as a small trickle of blood and saliva ran from Ray's already swelling bottom lip. He finally looked at Grant, who by now had slumped back into his seat. He was looking at Ray, more precisely at the small pool of blood forming on his white pillow case.

"I didn't think you were going to hit him," Peter said, he averted his gaze from Grant just as soon he averted *his* from Ray. "That's not -"

"Shut up pussy!" He interrupted with a smirk. "He's a fucking murderer." His smirk turned serious as he sat up for a moment and clicked his fingers to rouse Peter's attention. "He's a fucking killer!" He reinforced his statement with a point of his finger, although it may as well have been his gun since Peter was virtually frozen on the end of his steely dark stare. Peter nodded his head, again utilising his 'trying to be casual,' pose.

Friday 21st May. 09 : 30.

'CAUGHT!' The large black lettering came slowly into focus, reminding him of the living nightmare he'd left behind ten hours earlier, sucker - punched into dreamland, his aching jaw and swollen lip filled in the blanks for him.

"The Black Widow unmasked!" The voice said, it's owner remained hidden behind the front page of the national newspaper, that was being suspended directly above his face.

"A community breathes a sigh of relief, as the samurai killer is unmasked." Ray still couldn't *see* who it was, but he *could* see the shiny cufflinks, that he'd seed many times before.

"The sword wielding executioner," He went on, slowly pulling the paper back from Ray's eyes. "Who over the past two months, has held the small town of Washburn Springs in a state of prolonged terror, is finally snared."

Ray turned his head to see the chair next to his bed was now vacant, his guards were not present, although his restraints were. The room seemed somehow different in the harsh light of day, equally as bland as he'd remembered, but as the sun sat high in the sky it projected beautifully on to his bed, reminding him of all he'd left behind.

"Good morning, Ray." Scott said, folding the paper in half and placing it on the bed. "I don't think I need to continue, do I?" He stood upright next to Ray's bed, immaculately turned out in a black - three piece. He tugged at the cuffs on his jacket until they were level with those of his crisp white shirt.

"Why me?" Ray asked, not once looking at Scott. "Why?" He gazed up at the ceiling, noticing for the first time that it was the suspended type, that consisted entirely of foam tiles. "How did this even happen?"

"That's good, Ray." Scott answered. "I'd expect nothing less." He laughed. "Diminished responsibility may save you from the harsh realities of prison, but it wont lessen your sentence, *you* should know that." He pointed to Ray. "You'll never see the light of day again which ever way you go. The fact remains, Ray, you clearly are insane even if *you* don't know it."

Ray turned his head to see the door wasn't closed, but ajar. He heard voices from behind it but couldn't see anybody through the space. "Where are the guys from last night?"

"Which ones?" Scott asked.

"In particular," He answered slowly, whilst gazing dreamily through the window. "The one who did this."

"You obviously slept through the last shift change completely," Scott said. "They're ready to change again, and will do so for as long as you're detained here, every eight hours without fail, alert and ready." He sighed and pressed his hands against the steel guard rail on Ray's bed. "I demanded a minute alone with you before the next officer cuffed himself to you, I'd like to think that some semblance of the man I once knew, remains." He looked into Ray's eyes. "Does it?"

"I'm not sure anymore." He replied, still staring at the sun.

Scott walked too and fro across the small room, he smoothed his neatly combed hair at the temples with his hands, and thought hard about Ray's situation. Sentences were reluctant to take shape like unfinished artwork and words failed him. He sat down in the chair opposite the door and stretched out his legs, crossing both them and his arms simultaneously.

"Why?" Scott said finally. "There just aren't enough words in the dictionary to explain -" He paused for a moment. "There's nothing I can say," He shrugged. "I've got nothing, Ray, but I needed this time with you. Perhaps for closure, perhaps because I feel I've let you down, I just don't know." He held himself tightly and avoided Ray's tearful eyes, which were trained directly on him. "Why?" He shouted without warning. "Why the fuck would you do that?"

The door opposite opened a little more, Ray assumed the man who's head appeared in the doorway was, just as Grant had been, the Police officer sent to guard him as he was sporting the same combat attire. Although Ray couldn't see the weapon, he *could* see the strap running diagonally across the man's chest to his waist, he figured the gun was once again pointing downwards and just out of view.

"Is everything ok?" He asked.

Ray was mildly surprised to note that the man looked at both him, and Scott as he spoke. He was tall and well built with blonde hair in a *marine* cut that peeked tidily from beneath his cap, he was younger than Grant had been, he was younger than *he* was.

"It's fine," Scott replied. "I'm sorry, you go back outside this wont take a moment."

"Sir." He said sharply, before nodding gently in both of their directions and vanishing from view.

I like this one. Ray thought. *He seems better than that other fucker, but then he would be while he's here with me, Right? Let's see how he is when it's just us.*

"Why?" Scott said again, this time taking pains to remain calm. "Where did all that rage come from?"

"It wasn't me," Ray replied. "I swear to god." He tried to catch Scott's gaze but he would only look at the closed door before him. "Sir?" Ray whispered, finally grasping his reluctant attention. "It wasn't me, it wasn't." They both looked at one another for what seemed like an age. "The guards last night said that Brandon was in my head, that's just not true, Sir."

"Well, that's about the size of it." He answered bluntly, once again staring at the door.

"I'm not Brandon," Ray whispered, finally relenting and turning his attention to the window, and all he'd left behind. "And I'm not your killer, you'll learn that soon enough though."

"Why them, Ray?" He asked, choosing to ignore his pleas. "That's what I want to know, why them? What did you know that we didn't?"

Ray stared blankly, and directly at the sun, it hurt his eyes after a few seconds, but it felt good to *feel* anything right now. "I know a lot you don't." He whispered. "I just don't know *why*."

Scott leaned forward and clasped his hands together. "You had friends, Ray." He said. "You should've spoken out, or sought help."

"I didn't do it." He replied flatly. "I've got no friends, but I'm used to that, being lonely didn't tip me over the edge. I may have teetered on the brink a couple of times, but never over it."

Scott sighed. "How do you explain the two samurai swords?" He asked. "They were found in your bedroom, along with your kit."

He turned his head slowly to look at Scott. "My bedroom?" He asked, shaking his head.

"Yes, Ray." He answered. "Where you left them."

I'm so sorry baby, He thought. *That was your room, and I couldn't even protect that for you.*

"Coming back to you now, is it?" Scott asked.

"Many things have come back to me." He said, turning his attention once again to the window. "But there's one thing that everybody else seems to be forgetting."

"Which is?"

"Last time I checked, I was *black*."

Scott laughed. "Exactly! That's the best part!" He laughed so hard he sent himself reeling backwards against the soft foam padding, before again pulling himself forward to the edge of his seat. "You're black," He said, grinning like a game show host. "You're *black*, and Jet - our only living witness who's *really* seen you, said the killer was white, with long dark hair and the blackest of eyes. Now that presented us with a problem, but then we worked on the theory of *unnaturally* pale." He pointed to Ray. "Which all fell into place when we found your wig, and face paint." He applauded. "Well played."

"Looks like I'm pretty fucked then, doesn't it?"

"Yes." He said. "When you live by the sword, I think you know the rest."

"Do you want to know something?" Ray asked. "This is *one* time I thought being a nigger, might actually help, but I guess you fuckers have got that one covered." He laughed sharply. "Face paints and wigs?" He shouted. "By the time this gets to court you'll be saying I was wearing stockings and suspenders!" He gazed up at the blue sky, lost in his own thoughts and set adrift in a sea of madness. "The swords were planted." He whispered. "I thought I had one friend, but turns out he was waiting for the right time to hurt me."

"And who's that?" Scott asked. "Vincelli?"

"I'm talking about Brandon." He replied. "It must've been him."

"Do you *really* believe that?"

"Oh - yeah," He whispered. "I *know* that. It was him who put me here yesterday, or the day before. He gave me this heart attack."

"Try, four weeks, Ray." Scott said. "You've been here four weeks."

Ray looked suddenly at Scott, his eye's begged the question his lips dare not speak.

"Oh - yeah," Scott said. "You've been in a trance like state since your arrest at hospital, don't you *remember?*" His expression mocked openly. "Or are you *pretending*, that you don't remember?"

"You really think you've got me made, Don't you?" Ray asked. He stared angrily at Scott whilst resisting against his restraints. "The truth will reveal itself soon enough, it *always* comes back to haunt you. A man doesn't have to have blood on his hands, just holding the shovel is enough - you can't bury a secret."

Scott paused just long enough to tell Ray his words had hit home, he'd struck a nerve and some common ground was under their feet.

"Am I the killer?" He asked, holding Scott's attention steadfastly. "Or am I innocent?" He smiled knowingly as Scott sat perched on the chair's edge. "Will justice be served? Or will it *once again* be covered up?" Ray laughed and broke the eye contact that had engaged them both. "Is that a shovel in your hand?" He whispered, staring through the window. Scott sat silently, watching as Ray lay helpless in his bed, he sighed and raised to his feet.

"I'm sorry, Ray." He said. "I'm truly sorry for this turn of events." He stepped for the door and grabbed it's handle.

"The more I think about things," Ray whispered, "The more I think Brandon didn't plant them, he knew they were *being* planted."

Scott stood and listened,

"He knew," He added. "That's why he put me here, to give me an alibi." His voice was slow and laboured, he closed his eyes and appeared to be close to sleep. "While I'm in here, I'm not out there, killing whoever remains on his list - and there *are* more."

"Is that so?"

"The man who began all this is a dead man," He slurred. "No one can help him, I just wish I could be there to see it."

"You shall be, Ray." Scott whispered. "Good bye." He slid gracefully through the open door and Ray's guard's immediately replaced him.

"He's all yours." Scott said. "Good day gentlemen."

"Watch the tape." He whispered. "There's something you should see."

"What?" He asked, turning quick on his heels. "What tape?"
"Danny's *suicide* tape."
"And what's the *something* I'm going to see?"
"I don't know." He replied. "But apparently…a good detective wouldn't have missed it."

14:45.

The young security officer sat behind the reception desk with little to do, his neatly trimmed brown hair had '*the new boy,*' written all over it. His oversized blue shirt, which hung loosely around his neck, and the straight - from - the - wrapper creases all over it, did little to state otherwise. He shuffled nervously at the paperwork in front of him, but the truth was he was unable to take his eyes from the pretty blonde in the patchwork dress, who was sat in the waiting area opposite. He'd smiled to her on more than one occasion but so far she'd failed to return the gesture. Having sat there with her legs crossed for nearly an hour, he followed her with his eyes as she leapt from her seat, leaving her coat behind, and charged down the hallway like a bullet from a gun. He felt compelled to challenge her as he knew he should, but she was halfway to the elevators at the bottom of the corridor before thoughts became actions.

"Excuse me!" She shouted. "Mark?"

Mark stood bewildered as he watched her run to him, he looked quickly at his watch before taking his glasses off and placing them in his pocket.

"Can I help you?" He asked.

"Yes." She answered, slowing down to a quick walk and catching her breath. Having caught up with him she stood silently for a moment and unravelled her red scarf, she waited for a moment as they were passed by a lady pushing an elderly woman in a wheelchair.

"For starters," She whispered. "I'd like to know how you sleep at night?" She looked him up and down, as he held both sides of his white overcoat and clasped them together in a clear defensive gesture. "Maybe you prescribe yourself some kind of sleeping aid?" She smiled as he squirmed nervously.

"Can you keep your voice down, please?" He asked, looking all around. "This is a hospital."

She stood silent for a moment and folded her arms. "You don't remember me, do you?" She asked, a stifled laugh escaped her lips. "Well you should, you called me a fucking whore when we last spoke." She paused. "About two months ago, at the fun fair?"

"Oh I remember you," He said. "And I stand by my judgement." He glanced over her shoulder towards the reception desk, then gazed into her eyes. "You see, Anna? was it?"

"Lisa, actually."

"Well excuse me all the way to hell!" He laughed. "I don't share your *gift*, which is why I didn't remember you, but now that you've opened your mouth I see all at once why I called you a fucking whore." He drew her attention to a cleaning cupboard beside them by way of a gentle nod, she looked to see it.

"If you'll step into my office," He said. "You can get on your knees, open your mouth again and suck my fucking cock." He grinned. "You've got such a pretty mouth, put it to some *good* use."

She stood unfazed as he awaited a response.

"Choice language for a respected member of the medical staff, Mark." She shook her head and tut - tutted. "You're not a very nice boy, are you?"

"Look," He said, again looking at his watch. "Do you want me to say sorry?" He asked, his tone was as insincere as his smile. "I'm bored now." He added.

"I'm not the one you should be sorry towards." She whispered. "It's that poor girl you should -"

"Listen to me," He said, grabbing her tightly by the arm. "You leave her out of this and fuck off back to your freak show, *wherever* they've pitched their tents is where *you* should be."

"You need to tell her!" Lisa shouted. She pulled her arm from his grasp and stepped back from him.

"I can't tell her!" He said, struggling to keep his voice down. "It's too fucking late for confessions."

She looked over her shoulder as she took several steps back from him, she was eager to put some distance between them, distance that he was happy to close as quick she gained it.

"You have no idea what, or *who* you're dealing with, Mark." She whispered. "If you feel anything for that girl, you'll come clean before they come for you." She jumped nervously as she felt the cold concrete wall behind her. "It's not right she should grieve twice, Mark. If she knew the real you she'd spit on your grave. Clean up your mess before you face them."

"Who?" He asked. "Face who?" He laughed as he put his glasses back on but his trembling hands betrayed the façade.

"They're coming for you, Mark." She whispered. "I can hear you begging for your life when I lay in bed at night. You probably deserve what's coming but I just *had* to warn you." She stood pinned to the wall as she spoke, with nowhere to run she stared at the floor as he placed his hand on the wall beside her, effectively blocking her retreat, but also turning their heated discussion into somewhat of a tête-à-tête for anyone who cared enough to be observing.

"Stay away from the Washburn link, Mark." She whispered. "They're gonna get you on the Washburn link." She smiled. "There'll be bloodshed on the Washburn link."

"Get out of here." He whispered. "Go now." He placed a kiss on her cheek and walked away, although he remained aware of her eyes burning into him.

"Remember my words, Mark." She shouted. She began to cry as she watched him leave, she stroked her fingers beneath her eyes and forced herself to regain her usual, more resilient self.

Monday 24th May.

The familiar odours of tobacco, stale sweat and cheap offensive aftershave filled the small room as Ray slept, they evoked a dream that ended for Ray as sharply as it had begun. He was riding in a car being driven by Vincelli, it was dark outside except for the brilliance of the headlights that illuminated the long, seemingly endless road before them. Ray glanced nervously at the speedometer to see the needle was resting between 90 and 95 mph. Vincelli lit a cigarette before lowering his window, the wind rushed in as his smoke was drawn out.

"Slow down," Ray whispered. "You're going too fast."

Vincelli shook his head and gripped the wheel tightly, his cigarette protruded from between his fingers on top of the steering wheel.

"No." He whispered, which Ray understood just fine despite the wind rush, which at almost 100 mph felt more like a hurricane.

"Slow down," He said again. "You'll kill us both."

"We're riding this one all the way, Ray." He replied. "*All* the way until one of us is dead!" He laughed. "One of us must die." He punched the accelerator as hard as he could.

Ray looked into the darkness with a sense of dread, and was about to close his eyes when a fire in the distance caught his attention, he stared at it as they drew nearer, the road was leading them directly to what appeared to be a mini inferno.

"One of us must die." Vincelli said again.

Ray remained silent, although he was relieved to see their speed was dropping rapidly, the needle had dropped below 50mph. He was fixated by what he could now see was a large burning cross in an otherwise empty field. Vincelli turned the wheel sharply to the left and they veered off the road, the car jolted violently as it dropped a foot or so onto the grass. It rumbled incessantly as it struggled to regain it's traction, but that mattered little as Vincelli brought the vehicle to a rest in front of the cross, the *burning* cross, which stood almost ten feet tall.

"One of us must die." Vincelli whispered. "But who will get caught -"

"In the cross fire." Ray whispered.

"It'll be you," Vincelli said. "It's never going to be me." He laughed and placed the cigarette in his mouth. "Wake up, Ray." He gripped the wheel with his smoking hand, and placed his arm over Ray's shoulder like a drive in - *movie date*. "Wake up!" He said again.

Ray opened his eyes and for a moment, he stared at the ceiling as he clung to the dying images in his mind, the dialogue had already escaped him, but the image of that burning cross remained. The smells that had probably conjured up the dream were as pungent as ever, sitting next to him in fact, clinging to the man like a jealous wife, he knew it was Vincelli before he turned to greet him.

"Well," Vincelli whispered. "It's about fucking time!" He was only half joking. "I've been waiting since ten o' clock."

"That means nothing to me." Ray replied. "What time is it *now?*"

"It's twenty - past."

Ray shook his head and smiled. "Twenty minutes?"

Vincelli tossed him his *'I'm a busy man,'* look, followed by the *'I haven't got time for your shit.'* frown.

"Anyway," Ray whispered, opening his eyes fully to the harshness of the sun. "Is that any way to greet an old friend?"

Vincelli slid his chair and pulled himself closer to Ray's bed. "All this leather, Ray," He said, referring to the restraints which had now been secured over his white sheets. "I'm not sure it's a good look for you." He laughed.

"Fuck the leather!" He shouted. "You mind telling me how the fuck I'm going to get out of here?"

"Listen, Ray." He said, leaning in close enough to whisper in his ear. "I've been accused of some shit in my time, but if you think I'm going to abet your escape, then you're as crazy as they're saying you are." He laughed aloud.

"Escape?" Ray asked. "I'm not talking about fucking escaping, I'm talking about clearing my name, not going on the run."

"Good," Vincelli replied. "Because I've got to tell you, you wouldn't make it down the street. You made the front page of nearly every paper in print!" He tapped Ray's shoulder firmly. "You got your fifteen minutes, Ray. Unfortunately for you, that made you public enemy number one." He relaxed into his chair.

"What happened to innocent until proven guilty?" Ray asked. "Where did they get my picture?"

"It's not important." Vincelli said. "What *is* important, is what happened to you."

Ray shook his head and looked out of the window. "All I know, is *someone* put those swords in my house." He paused. "Maybe Brandon, not because he's trying to hurt me - but I think he *wants* me here, I think he knows who's setting me up."

"No, Ray." He said. "Brandon's been dead for months, my friend."

"What I don't know," Ray whispered. "Is why he'd put them in the bedroom." He thought to himself. *That's her room, he wouldn't go in there I just know it - he wouldn't do that to me, I don't have to have told him, he'd just know.*

Vincelli sighed. "But how do you explain the lighter" He asked. "You were using that lighter the day after the fun fair killings."

Ray spun his head to look at him. "You mean you -"

"I *saw* that lighter," Vincelli said. "I saw the name on it, I also saw you throw it into your garden when you thought I couldn't see you."

"You wouldn't believe me if I told you." Ray said.

"That lighter was *still* in your garden," He said. "Rusted a little, but good enough. Besides the inscription on the front of it, it also bore Jake's prints on it's insides, from when he'd filled it or something. So it was easy to link it back to him, what's equally as easy is linking it to you." He stared Ray in the eyes. "So explain that one?"

Ray shook his head. "No point." He said flatly. "Just no point anymore."

"Ok, back to the swords then." Vincelli said. "What's your theory?"

"Brandon wouldn't have gone in that room, Joe." Ray said. "He just wouldn't go there."

"Well if I had to guess," Vincelli whispered. "He *knew* you wouldn't find them there, even if you got home from the cemetery before we raided your house, you wouldn't have been able to hide them, because you wouldn't have known they were even there, because you *never* go in there." He smirked.

Ray raised his head from his pillow. "You said, Brandon is dead?" Ray shot a quizzical glance to Vincelli.

"I did." He nodded in reply, switching his gaze nervously from Ray, to the shadow looming beneath the door. "He is."

"Yet, you're -" Ray paused as they looked at one another. " - Agreeing with my theory, that the swords were -"

"Planted." He added in a hushed voice. He pulled his chair closer once more, and leaned on the guard rail of Ray's bed. "You and your imaginary friend," He whispered. "You just wont leave things alone, you're asking questions that prompt questions." He smiled and stroked Ray's hair. "You're a liability, I can't have you running around shouting shit about Ghosts and fucking goblins, it had to end somewhere, and you were as good as dead anyway, Ray."

"It's you." Ray whispered. "You planted them?" He pulled his head away from Vincelli's hands. "It's you, it's always been you."

"I didn't plant them," He replied with a smile. "I've got people for that."

"Why, Joe?" He closed his eyes, that burning cross appeared as vividly as he'd remembered it. *One of us must die,* He thought. *But who will get caught in -*

"You got too close, Ray." He whispered.

"It's *all* you?"

Vincelli nodded. "Yeah," He answered. "I'm afraid so."

"I don't believe you, Joe." He cried. "Why are you telling me this?" His voice raised to a shriek.

"Who the fuck would believe a word you say?"

Ray shook his head. "Why did you start all this?" He asked. "Brandon and Chad, why

order their deaths?"

Vincelli laughed. "They're killers." He answered.

"What?" Ray asked. "Now they are," He agreed. "I mean before?"

"I'm talking about before," He whispered. "They were killing junkies, and those junkies were *my* customers."

"No." Ray shouted. "That's shit."

"Is it?" He asked, glancing nervously at the door. "Is it really?" He laughed. "All those *accidental* overdoses, suicides - and what about those individuals who were never found?" He asked. "They were all junkies, coincidental?" He raised his eyebrows. "I think not."

"And how did you know?" Ray asked, already knowing the answer. "Who told you?"

"Danny," He said. "It really is amazing, what you can get someone to tell you when you threaten to have their brother killed in prison." He smiled and pulled a packet of cigarettes from his coat pocket.

"When Danny contacted the Police," Ray whispered. "He would never have guessed he was spilling his guts to the master and commander of a criminal empire."

"Well, like I said - I have men who do the dirty work for me." He lit his cigarette and blew a smoke trail high up towards the window, he laughed a little as he savoured it.

"Now *this* is the good part," He said. "This is why I've remained so untouchable for all these years, insider trading an' all that. If anyone made any reports that might jeopardize my business, they vanished." He glanced at Ray. "*People* stop seeing things, when *people* start vanishing." He added with a smile.

"How?" Ray asked, fighting his tears. "How were they killing?"

"Well, according to Danny," He answered, quietly. "They were in fact responsible for administering the lethal doses of heroin, and a nasty rumour was taking hold that *I* - was killing my own men." He sucked hard on his cigarette. "And that's just not good for business, creates division you see. I guess they thought they were taking out the trash, which I suppose you could argue was true, but they were *my* trash - lining *my* pockets." He sighed. "Normally I trust in my boys to do a job, and do it right, but I broke from tradition in their case and went along to see it done right."

Ray laughed and shook his head. "You were in the fucking Mercedes, weren't you?" They laughed together like the old friends Ray had thought they were. "How did you avoid the camera?" He asked. "The C.C.T.V, how did you avoid it if you -"

"Didn't know it was there?" Vincelli interrupted. "What do you take me for?" He asked. "Of course I knew it was there. Come on Ray, you're smart."

Ray nodded. "Just not smart enough."

"Listen," Vincelli whispered. "I *know* you're not the killer, but I also *know* you're protecting him, you're in league with him." He winked at Ray. "And that was your first mistake, you didn't pick a *side*, you can't go through life sitting on the fence." He smiled.

"He's only got to kill again, Joe." Ray said. "And he will, but once he does, I'm vindicated."

Vincelli shook his head. "Not so," He said. "He's just your *accomplice*. It wont change *your* current situation one iota."

Ray hadn't considered this notion before, it scared him. "No." He whispered.

"I *know* who this fucker is," Vincelli added. "I'm the only one who knows he's still at large, and that's good enough for me. You see, I know something you don't - I know how to draw him out." He glanced over his shoulder at the door, then quickly back to Ray. "He may be a thorn in my side, but like a splinter in my finger, he'll come out in time with some gentle persuasion." He threw the cigarette to the ground and stamped on it.

"What do you mean you know who he is?" Ray asked. "And how can you draw him out?"

"I *know* who he is," He replied. "That's enough to draw him from the shadows, and no doubt he'll come out all guns blazing," He laughed at the idea. "But the fact is, he isn't bullet proof."

Ray laughed. "You don't know shit." He shook his head. "This is a ghost you're dealing with, a vengeful spirit that isn't going to rest until you're dead."

"Are you fucking serious?" Vincelli asked. "Jesus Christ, Ray." He added. "He's *not* a ghost, he's living - breathing - flesh and blood." He looked again at the door. "Danny told me *many* things before I," He paused for a moment. "Well, let's just say his *suicide* was very tragic."

"You -"

He nodded slowly to Ray. "Danny just knew too much." He whispered. "I couldn't allow him that much knowledge, it wasn't good for him."

"So you -"

"Yeah." He laughed. "It was all planned Ray," He whispered. "Why do you think I took you along each time I visited his room? I needed you there, I needed *you* to find the tape, I already knew where it was." He laughed again. "I let you take the lead, I played dumb and you thought you were out witting me. There I am wading through fucking bushes to avoid his camera, because I *had* to leave the tape in the machine just to make it look like he'd stopped it himself."

"So he was looking at *you* when the bulb blew?"

"Yeah." He smiled. "I told Danny he was making a mock suicide tape, if he did as I said and disappeared for a while, I would call of *my* dogs." He nodded. "It had to look genuine at least before he was dragged…*carefully* to the large tree in his garden."

"And you did that?"

Vincelli shook his head. "Once he'd recorded the tape for me, I stopped his C.C.T.V and called my boys, they were waiting at the bottom of his driveway."

Ray stared blankly through the window, he tried to imagine his friend's reaction when finally faced with the error of his ways, when faced with the truth that he knew would inevitably return to haunt him. Would the black eyes of death reflect his demise, or would the hate burning within them illuminate it, either way -

"You're a dead man, Joe." He whispered. "I can't believe you've done this to me, to *them* and to Danny." He paused. "And whoever else for that matter."

"I'll be waiting for him, Ray." He replied, speaking with a calmness that suggested he genuinely believed it to be true. "And, I'll be ready."

"He will kill you, Joe." He whispered. "You can't imagine how, but it'll be big." He smiled. "He wont make a secret of your death, you're bowing out big and public - he'll make an example of you, I swear to fucking sweet - Jesus, you motherfucker."

"Ok." He whispered as he raised to his feet. "It's been nice talking to you."

"Anyone!" Ray shouted. "That you stand before him, he'll slice to fucking pieces to get to you!"

"You know something, Ray?" Vincelli asked, reaching for the door handle. "They were going to finally remove your restraints today, but I don't think they'll deem you placid enough after this."

"After what?" Ray asked.

"You being in here," He laughed. "It's just one less fucking *nigger*." He laughed as he swung the door open and stepped through it, leaving quickly as Ray began screaming. He thrashed violently as his guards came running in.

"He killed her!" He screamed, "He was there…joking as she lay dead." His voice trailed to nothing as Vincelli strolled down the hallway, he smiled to himself as he pushed the stairwell door open.

"Fucking niggers." He whispered to himself as it closed slowly behind him.

Chapter Thirteen

<u>Wednesday 26th May.</u>

Mark sat in his car and gripped the steering wheel tightly, he was grateful for the isolation that the darkness provided, and thankful that Julianne hadn't heard him pull up outside the house, as there was some last minute thinking to be done. Her small red Kia was parked on his driveway, he smiled as he recalled how she would always refer to it as *Kitty*. The small clock on his dashboard told him it was almost eleven o' clock, the wind howled around his car and rocked it violently, although he actually found the sensation to be calming. He found himself staring at his own living room window, and although the curtains were drawn he could easily see the flickering white light of his television beyond them. His own motives eluded him as he wondered if giving her a key had been a mistake. He took a deep breath as he looked at the garage, it was directly adjacent to his house with two big wooden doors that met in the middle. *At least there's no way she can get in there.* He thought, staring at the padlock that secured them.

Leaves whipped up around him as he stepped from the car and walked slowly to his door, he was surprised to see Julianne's silhouette meeting him from the other side. She opened it but only enough for him to slide through, she remained concealed behind the door until it was closed once more. He looked her up and down as he stood awkwardly in his own hallway, he was both surprised and disappointed to find her clad only in black lacy underwear, with just stockings and a smile to complete the outfit.

"Hello, *nurse*." She whispered, while removing his black summer jacket. "I hope your day hasn't been *too* hard, I think I need an examination." She dropped his coat to the floor and ushered him towards the living room, stepping on his jacket as she went.

What's she doing? He wondered. *Why now?* His eyes were lost on her slim yet toned body, although arousal turned to embarrassment with ease as she stumbled into his living room. Following on behind her, and with thanks in part to a serious lack of eye contact, he was left with the impression that she'd spent the day rehearsing for this moment, and now that it had arrived, he guessed she didn't really *want* him, she *needed* him. Once beside his couch, she turned to face him and draped her arms across his shoulders. Taking hold of his hands, she placed one around her waist and moved the other slowly to her breasts.

"Start here," She whispered.

"No." He answered, pulling his hands away. "It's not right, Julianne." He backed away from her and moved around a small glass coffee table.

"It's just role play, Mark."

"No," He said. "You don't understand." Searching for a handle on the moment he gazed around his living room, his eyes settled finally on the intricate brick work surrounding his fireplace. "We have to talk," He went on. "I need to ask you something." He took off his glasses and threw them on the table. "That night...at the carnival," He whispered. "When you came running out of that tent, what *exactly* had that girl said to you?" His eyes begged the truth. "I *really* have to know."

Covering herself as best she could, she sat herself down on the couch and looked across to him. "I feel like such a fool," She whispered, feeling naked and rejected. "I thought you wanted this."

"You've no idea *how much* I've wanted this." He replied. "I still do, but right now...it just wouldn't be right."

"Then what's going on?" She asked. "Why are you asking about *that*?"

"Julianne," He said, his frustration beginning to show. "You *have* to tell me, I need to know what she told you!" He knelt down in front of her and held her hands in his own.

"It was nothing," She replied. "*Really*, it was just me being silly."

He shook his head. "You don't react like that over something *silly*." He squeezed her hands a little and stared into her eyes. "What did she say?"

Julianne sighed and looked at her hands in his. "She told me…" She paused and looked into his eyes, her own were beginning to fill with tears.

"She told me there was a man," She shuffled nervously. "That he was dead but not gone, and that he wished to communicate with me. She also said that people around me were whispering…" She smiled as tears ran slowly down her pale skin. "Were *you* whispering, Mark?" She asked, although she was afraid to wait for his response.

"She said his was a forced exile, and that he wasn't able to move on until I was safe…" She noticed Mark was now beginning to tremble, she felt tremors in his hands just before he removed them from hers, a guilty pleasure aroused within her, although she didn't understand why. "…That he wasn't able to move on, until he'd made it *possible* for me to be safe."

"Was there anything else?" He asked nervously, clearly hanging on to her every word. "*Anything?*" He begged. "*Anything* at all…it's very important."

She nodded as she recalled the events in her minds eye. "There was something strange," She said. "She told me to leave."

"Leave?" Mark asked. "As in…leave the *tent?*"

"No." She shook her head. "Leave the carnival…before it was too late."

"She said that?"

"I don't think so," She replied. "Someone else entirely spoke those words." She gazed at the large television in the corner of the room. "It was like *he,* whoever *he* is…possessed her momentarily to warn me…to tell me…he was coming." She stared dreamily through him.

"Do you know who *he* is?" Mark asked.

"No." She said. Her voice was certain, although her mind was not. "Not really."

Mark stared blankly at her, the colour had washed from his face almost completely as he sat shaking.

"There was one other thing." She said. She felt Mark's eyes rapidly find her own. "She mentioned photographs." She quizzed him with her eyes. "You *know* what she's talking about, don't you?"

"Yes." He whispered, his composure was beginning to slip. "I do."

"What photographs?" She asked.

"Julianne," He said. "There are things I've got to tell you."

"You can start by showing me these *photographs*."

"I can do better than that." He walked towards the hallway. "Follow me."

"Why?" She asked. "Where are you going?" She felt vulnerable all at once.

"There's something in the garage I can't hide anymore." He left her trailing in his wake.

"Hang on," She shouted. "What am I going to wear?"

He picked up his jacket and took his keys from the pocket, before tossing it to her. "Put this on." He said, already opening his front door.

"Mark, I'm in stockings…what if someone sees?"

"It's dark out," He replied. "Jut come on." He stepped quickly from view.

She put the jacket on and listened as Mark struggled with the padlock outside, she wasn't leaving the hallway until she heard one of those doors opening.

"Are you coming?" He shouted impatiently.

She glanced from behind the door, she felt happy - or at least content, that no one was about, and stepped outside. She joined him at the garage, just in time for him to open one of the heavy doors.

"I'm scared, Mark." She whispered, clutching the jacket tightly around herself.

"I'm scared too," He replied. "Scared of how you're going to react." He stroked her face.

"Don't be afraid." He said. "Just wait until I put the light on, I don't want you standing on something and hurting yourself."

"Ok." She said, and watched as he disappeared into the darkness. Even from her vantage point at the door, she was aware of something cumbersome sitting in the darkness before her, waiting for her like a wild bear in a cave. Whilst she listened to Mark climbing over objects, her eyes adjusted a little to the darkness and enabled her to see it was a vehicle of some description, although it was shrouded completely by dust sheets.

"Ok," He said. "Step forward and close the door behind you."

"Ok." She replied, stepping into the darkness as instructed and closing the door.

"Just watch your step as you come around to me." He said, turning on the light.

She now saw that it was not so much of a bear, as it was a mammoth, with only it's enormous wheels visible beneath the sheets, the space around it was limited and littered with household junk.

"Ok, I'm trying." She whispered, whilst negotiating her way around to him. "What is this thing, Mark?" She asked.

He climbed over some boxes to meet her at the front end of it.

"I think you know the answer to that." He gripped one of the dust sheets tightly and tugged it until it fell to the ground, revealing the front end of a badly damaged pick - up.

Her eyes greeted it with a mixture of surprise and shock, like meeting a long lost friend who just *looks* somehow familiar. She ran her hand along the distorted lines of the bull - bars, they were forced inwards against the smashed grille, she pulled her hands away fast as though burned, when she saw it's front end insignia was missing.

"How could I be so stupid?" She asked, stepping back a little from Mark. "I've seen this car, it's on a picture in your bedroom." She covered her mouth with her hands. "There's four men leaning against it…laughing."

Mark nodded. "I guessed you had."

"But you're not in it."

"I took the picture." He replied

"The car in the photograph," She whispered. "And this one, it's the same one." She paused as she surveyed the damage. "I think I know how this happened." She turned her attention from the vehicle to Mark, who was stood nervously beside it, holding onto the bull bars as if he was about to throw up.

"This is the truck that was used to kill my boyfriend." She said. "And Brandon."

He nodded but didn't speak.

"You're one of them, aren't you?" She said. "You're with them."

"I can't get *away* from them." He said. Letting go of the truck he stepped towards her, although she quickly matched it in reverse.

"Don't." She ordered. "Don't you fucking touch me."

"Julianne," He pleaded. "I had to!"

"What do you mean you had to?" She shouted. "You didn't *have* to do anything. You could've just left me alone, but why trick me?" Her tears came in a hurry as she struggled for balance, she hit the ground hard and fell beside the vehicle's large front tyre, leaving Mark unable to catch her.

She awoke some ten minutes later to find herself back on Mark's couch, with him kneeling down beside her dabbing at her forehead with a wet cloth.

"I carried you in," He said. "I think you fainted again, although this time of course I know why." His expression was serious.

She looked at the steaming mug of coffee on the table. "I bet you do."

"I'm so sorry," He handed her the drink. "I didn't mean for any of this."

"You're sorry?" She asked, smacking the coffee out of his hand. "You can't make it better with a hot fucking drink!" She almost felt bad as she watched it smash into the glass table, before spilling over onto the carpet. "You better tell me, Mark." She said.

He sighed. "They were my friends," He whispered. "To start with anyway." He stood up and walked to the fire place. He ignored the mug on the floor.

"Yes I was with them on the night," He said. "I was in the truck, I was involved in the fight." He tried to look at her as he spoke, but his *conscience* wouldn't allow it. "We all had these masks on…so yeah, I knew we were going to seriously hurt someone." He paused. "Ok," He added. "I knew we were going to *kill* someone, I knew that and I'm sorry."

She shook her head and began to cry.

"I'm sorry," He said again. "I had too, there was just no *choice* in it."

"There's always choice." She whispered. "Good or bad…you *choose*."

"It was too late to choose," He answered. "When you get on the ride you can't just get off. It just doesn't work that way. I didn't think it would go that far though, I didn't think we'd end up with instructions like that."

"You didn't *think* at all, Mark."

"I agreed to supply them with prescription meds, Julianne." He whispered. "I needed the extra money that it brought, and it brought a lot…believe me." He knelt down by the fire. "But they wanted more and more," He went on. "Until it got to the point that I could no longer say no to *anything*. I was better off with them than against them…that wasn't an option, they'd have killed me."

"You deserve to die." She held his jacket tightly around her. "For what you've done, you *all* deserve to die."

Mark shook his head. "You don't mean that." His eyes pleaded with her. "Please, don't say that."

"Right now," She whispered. "That's what I'd wish for."

"I'm going to die, Julianne." He said. "I'm next." His desperation was beginning to take it's toll on him. "Everybody who was in that truck," He paused for a moment having caught himself short of breath. "They're all dead." He said. "A couple of them were at the carnival that night, I was talking to them while you were in the tent. They're the ones you've been reading about in the papers, and on the news."

"*Whispering*." She said, staring him straight in the eye. "So what you're telling me, is that Chad and Brandon's murderers, are the *victims* of this sword person who's just been caught?"

He nodded.

"Well all I can say is this, It's a fucking shame he didn't get to finish his work before they caught him."

Mark buried his head in his hands and began to cry. "They haven't caught him." He whispered. "He's still out there, *somewhere*." He began mumbling incoherently to himself.

She watched the tears run down his face, while she sat in silence and digested the information.

"He's still out there," She whispered, gazing into nothing. "*Somewhere*." Never was the vision of Brandon stronger for her, passing beneath the flashing lights, cloaked in black and haunted by the laughter around him, *charging* from the joy around him.

He found me, She thought. *With those cold piercing eyes, he found me with ease. And with equal ease, so too he'll find his murderers.*

"Yeah," Mark said, calling forth her attention once again. "The guy they've charged is innocent." He laughed. "He's also a fucking cop."

"What did you just say?" She asked, staring in disbelief.

"He's a cop." He whispered.

"And you know this how?" She asked.

"Because…I helped frame him."

Julianne shook her head and jumped to her feet, she ran for the door but Mark caught her before she got to the hallway.

"I had to!" He shouted. He held her against the wall by her arms. "Please just listen to me, *please…just…stay.*" He released his grip a little as she nodded, she returned to the couch under his watchful eye.

"I was made to do it," He said, kneeling down by the fire once again. "I was told I'd be picked up early in the morning and that there was work to be done, the work in question - although I didn't know it at the time - was sitting outside this guy's house in a car."

She nodded.

"I was terrified, I had no idea what they expected me to do." He paused. "There was something on the back seat of the car we were in, it was long and wrapped up in bin bags…I thought it was a shotgun. The guy who picked me up, his phone rings and it's the boss on the other end, that much he told me, so I knew he was a big player since he had a direct link with the boss."

"So."

"So?" He asked. "Julianne, there's only two, maybe three guys who have contact with the boss, and normally *they* are just as invisible as he is, but since somebody is systematically eliminating gang members one by one, the high rollers are having to take a more pro - active role under his command."

"What did you do?" She asked.

"I was sent around the back of his house," He answered. "I was told his patio doors would be unlocked, that they were *always* unlocked, and I was told to be *quick.*" He shook his head and looked at the coffee stained carpet before him. "I had the package off the back seat with me," He said. "My instructions were to take it upstairs, take it into the master bedroom at the front of the house, and then and *only* then was I to open it and leave it on the bed."

"What was it?" She asked. She was appalled and unable to look at him, although non the less intrigued, she fiddled with the zipper on his jacket.

"I opened it up to find two large samurai swords," He said. "They were in dark red sheaths, there was also a long dark wig, and several pots of half used white face paints."

She laughed bitterly for a moment. "You're unbelievable," She said, sweeping the room with her eyes.

"I'm sorry, Julianne!" He begged, moving closer to her. "Please, help me…I want to get away from them I'm so fucking scared."

"Don't come near me you animal." She shouted, pulling her bare legs onto the couch and balling up. "Don't touch me." Her anger quickly turned to fear as she began to wonder if Mark would now turn on her to save himself.

Why is he telling me all these things? She wondered, watching as he retreated back towards the fire place. *I have to get out of this house*, She thought. *Please god, let me get out of this house in one piece…if I can just make it to kitty…if I can convince him to let me go…that I wont tell…that I love him and will stand by him…until I'm through the door…and then…*

"Please," He begged. "Help me." He walked to her again and knelt down before her. "She came to see me a few days ago," He went on. "She told me I'm next. She told me that *they*…whoever *they* are, are coming for me soon." He grabbed her hands and pulled them to his chest. "Who are *they*?" He asked. "You know, Julianne - I know you do?"

"I saw him." She whispered, longing to offer comfort but unable to. "When I fainted at the carnival, I saw Brandon as clear as day." She looked into Mark's glistening eyes. "He was beckoning me to the tent, but more importantly he showed me a vision of *you* that I didn't think was possible." She began to cry as she slipped her hands free of Mark's grip. "He was present that night, Mark." She whispered. "I knew it was him, *nobody* I've ever known possesses the presence he does, I *felt* him." She paused. "I *still* feel him."

"It's him isn't it?" Mark asked. "He's back to settle the score." He stood up and paced the room wildly as Julianne looked on from the couch.

"But who's helping him, Julianne?" He asked. "That *bitch* said *they*…were coming for me." His actions were becoming erratic and uncoordinated.

Get out of the house, Julianne thought. *Get out and run, run like hell…he's going to hurt you. Your car keys are on the bottom stair, leave now and don't look back.* She watched as Mark wandered to the other end of the living room, past the hallway entrance and into the kitchen, she flinched as he began shouting and smashing plates.

"I'm not gonna die like this!" He shouted. "I'll die my way, when *I'm* ready."

She recognised the sound of his cutlery drawer being dragged open in haste.

The knives are in that drawer, She thought. *What are you waiting for? You must leave now, get to your car. Go now!* She jumped to her feet and ran for the hallway door. *Mark will have to come back through the living room to get to you, keep running, Julianne.*

"Aint no fucking ghost gonna kill me!" He shouted.

"I'm scared." She cried. She found her keys on the bottom stair and opened the front door in a hurry.

He's realised you've gone, Julianne. She thought. *He's coming now, move faster.* She ran to her car and fumbled with the keys in the darkness.

"Julianne!" He shouted. "Don't you fucking leave me, you're gonna keep me alive."

Open the door, She thought. *Open it now, Julianne.* She slid the key in the lock and turned it, it clicked reassuringly before she flung it open and jumped inside. The wind had whipped up into what felt like gale force, it caught her by surprise and snatched the door from her grip, flinging it back on it's hinges before she reached out to reclaim it. She screamed in terror as she saw Mark charging through the front door and over to her.

Lock the door. She thought, although the action was completed before it had entered her mind.

"Open the fucking door!" He shouted. He began banging on the glass panel of the driver's door. "Open it, bitch!"

Fumbling for the ignition key, she watched in horror as Mark reared up a little and kicked at the glass panel with such force, she was certain *Kitty* would not withstand it, though thankful she did.

"Mark, please!" She screamed. She found the key and quickly rammed it home. The engine rattled to life as he lunged again with all his might - this time it smashed outright, showering Julianne with glass as she put the car in reverse and backed quickly down the driveway, dragging Mark a short distance as she did so.

"I'll fucking kill you bitch!" He shouted as he struggled for balance. He fell hard and sprawled out face down on his driveway, before jumping quickly to his feet and watching to see which direction she drove off in. He ran into his garage having remembered that his keys were still in there, attached to the padlock. He was more than aware of his own blood running freely from a scalp wound, already it had matted his short fair hair against his head, before trickling heavily down his face. He charged through the clutter to retrieve his keys from the other end of the pick - up. He quickly liberated them from the padlock and was about to set off towards his car on the street but stopped dead in his tracks.

This'll catch the bitch, He thought, tossing his keys aside and reaching for the handle of the pick - up. *As soon as she gets to the Washburn this'll fucking obliterate her.* He quickly pulled off the remaining dust sheets before jumping into the cab, he slammed the heavy door behind him.

"I'll fucking destroy you, Bitch." He shouted. He turned the key - which was already in the ignition - and was relieved though not surprised when it purred into life. It snarled like a growling beast as he revved it heavily, he quickly buckled up his seat belt before slamming it in to gear and tearing backwards down his driveway.

"You don't fucking run out on me!" He shouted, struggling to control the truck as it skidded wildly out into his quiet road. He quickly rammed the gearshift into drive and accelerated off in the direction he knew she was headed.

"I'll fucking kill her," He shouted. "I've put a lot of time into this fucking bitch." The truck thundered through the quiet residential area at speed, it narrowly avoided sideswiping several cars as it went. It's engine hammered out a low guttural tone, which suggested it still wasn't firing at the velocity that it had been race - tuned to operate at.

I'll kill her, He thought. *I've got to, it's her or me now, and it's not gonna be me - she'll fucking blow me up first chance she gets. I'll ram the bitch then torch this fucking monstrosity.*

Julianne struggled to see the road ahead through her tears, her car wasn't designed for the speed she was running it at and it struggled to retain its grip on the tarmac as the engine screamed for mercy.

"Don't let me down, baby." She cried, wiping her eyes as quickly as she could. "Just keep going…*please,* keep going." She looked ahead and saw the bridge that led to the Washburn Link road, it was wide enough for only one lane and had concrete barriers on each side of the approach that were some four feet thick. She passed over it at speed and once more her attention was summoned ahead, this time to the spot where Chad and Brandon had been murdered. She concentrated hard on the spot where the floral tributes had lain for weeks, as she neared it she was surprised to see it was glowing with the light of *many* candles.

"Oh," She gasped. "*My god.*" Her surprise was genuine as those candles had sat in their jars for many weeks, and had remained untouched by hand or element. Drawing almost level with it - she slowed Kitty to a more manageable speed of forty mph, the car seemed to breathe a sigh of relief as the burning smell that had begun to creep into the cabin subsided. She stared in amazement at the vast array of candles on the left hand side of the carriageway.

All the candles in the world, She thought. *And they're burning just for you…My love.* The thought troubled her as she wasn't herself certain as to *whom* she was referring to. They seemed to be leading to a spot adjacent to the carriageway, concealed from view by trees and shrubbery. She thought them to be reminiscent of the landing lights on any given runway, albeit *wonky* - landing lights, and slowed the car to a standstill to inspect further.

Follow the candles, Julianne. She thought, although her instincts wouldn't yet allow it. *Drive the car between the candles and follow them, right now.*

"Who are you?" She asked, gripping her steering wheel tightly.

He's coming. She thought. *You must conceal your car behind the tree line, do it now.*

"Ok, ok." She said. She drove the car as instructed between the candles, she followed them carefully and slowly, as she was more than well aware of a steep embankment being present, although in the darkness it was no more visible than the *darkness* itself. She followed the candle trail to its end and sat motionless.

Turn off your engine, She thought. *Turn off your headlights, and do not place your foot on the brake pedal.*

"Ok." She whispered.

And whatever you do, do not get out of the car.

She watched in wonderment as an *unearthly* gust of wind returned the candles to the burnt out state they had been in for weeks, stranger still was its ability to penetrate the jars protecting them. Through her smashed window she smelled the distinctive odour of freshly extinguished candles. The broken window scared her but she felt overwhelmingly safe, *guarded* in her solitude and not just by the greenery between her and the road. Both the tranquillity and her thoughts were shattered by an engine revving somewhere in the distance, it was being driven hard and approaching fast. She daren't look as it rocketed past her.

"I've got twenty miles now." Mark shouted. He glanced at the speedometer and saw the needle passing ninety mph, the turbo whined relentlessly as it competed with the harnessed lightening of it's huge engine.

"You're fucking mine, bitch." He gripped the wheel tightly as already it had topped one hundred and fifteen mph, he struggled for control while he found the switch that activated the mounted lights on top of the cab.

"There you are." He whispered. He flicked the switch and watched as they showered light down, over the cab and out across the road ahead. With both hands firmly back on the wheel he held the pick - up steady, it had topped out at one hundred and twenty - five mph.

He glanced habitually into his rear view mirror to see only darkness, before returning his attention to the road ahead.

"Where the fuck is she?" He asked. "Something's wrong." He gazed again into his rear view mirror, but this time a face awaited him, deathly pale and framed like beautiful art, by long black hair, staring back at him with a smile.

"Hello, Mark." He whispered. He leaned forward and gripped Mark's throat with both hands, pulling his head forcefully against the head rest. The pick - up swerved wildly across the dividing lines, as his attention was shattered by the fear that gripped him quite literally in a vice like choke hold.

"Observe the road." He whispered, speaking directly into his right ear. "You can outrun the law with a supercharger," He laughed a little. "But you can't outrun your destiny, and *you're* about to come face to face with yours." He released his right hand from Mark's throat, although his left remained firmly in place. He reached down to the locking mechanism of his seat belt and pressed the red release button, he allowed the belt to retract around half way before wrapping the available slack twice around Mark's neck.

He released his hand from Mark's throat and pulled at the seatbelt instead, applying just enough pressure to control Mark's movement.

"I do believe I have your full attention." He whispered. "Then let's begin." He smiled.

"What do you want from me?" Mark asked. He looked at the face in his mirror whilst tugging wildly at the belt around his neck. He had the blackest of eyes, they glistened as they calmly returned Mark's gaze in the mirror. He could see the handles of what he knew were samurai swords, protruding over his assailant's shoulders - and the steel strong points of what he guessed, was a body harness - although the harness itself was as black as his attire and not easily visible.

"It can't be you, Brandon." Mark shouted, his voice was broken and breathless. "We fucking killed you, I watched them bury you." He divided his attention between the road and his attacker, his speed had dropped to eighty mph as he struggled to concentrate.

"I knew it was you." He said, shaking his head. "I just *knew* you'd come back," He paused. "When you died, when they buried you, I just knew I'd see your face again." He wanted to turn his head and look him in the eye, but he couldn't. "As soon as I knew what you were, I knew you'd be back…I just didn't accept it."

"Murdered." He said, leaning between the two front seats to stare at him. "When I was *murdered*." He went on. He gazed at Mark's fear riddled features with a mixture of intrigue and pleasure, before running his finger gently down the tracks of his tears.. "Don't sell yourself short," He whispered, tugging hard at the seat belt. "You murdered me…of that there should be *no* doubt." He smiled. "Bravo."

"Ok…ok" Mark shouted, struggling for air. He clawed in vain at the belt, trying desperately to get his fingers between it and his neck.

"Don't touch the belt." He said. "Reach for it, I *tighten* it."

"I'm sorry," He shouted, battling for control of the pick - up. "I'm so fucking sorry."

"Danny's house is a little further up on the right," He whispered. "I want you to turn this truck around and follow my instructions to the letter." He paused. "Is that understood?"

"Yeah." He replied.

"Do it now." He said. "I've been waiting for this moment." Like a child arriving at a theme park, he stared excitedly through the windows at the sight of Danny's house. He clung tightly to the belt wrapped around Mark's neck, and to the passenger seat before him as Mark turned the pick - up around.

"What do you want me to do?" Mark asked, bringing the pick - up to a sudden halt beside the acceleration lane on the Golding estate.

"We're going to perform a little re-enactment," He replied, gazing ahead at the miles of open road before them. "Speed, Mark." He whispered, tilting his head at the speedometer. "I want speed, *break - neck* speed." He leaned forward once more. "You're not gonna drive away from *this* one I promise you."

"Brandon…" He choked a little as he tried to pull forward. "…Please, just let me live."

"My name is your imminent departure," He shouted. His face twisted violently, spraying Mark's face with saliva. "My name is your forthcoming demise." He smiled as once more he tugged at the seat belt, like he was taking control of a wild dog. "My name is *Death*." He looked out at the flood - lit tarmac. "Now *drive*."

Mark stamped hard on the accelerator and the pick - up lurched violently forward, it's turbocharger whined incessantly as it propelled the huge engine with terrifying ferocity.

"Now," He said, "Here's where the *real* fun begins." He watched as the needle climbed steadily, before coming to a rest at one hundred and twenty - five mph. "You ready ?" He asked, laughing. "You're the last one!" He shouted, slapping Mark across his head. "Why so sad?" He punched at the roof of the cab enthusiastically and winked at Mark.

Mark's concentration on the road ahead was shattered, as without warning *all* of the windows in the rear of the cab shattered. *Something*, although he didn't know what, had slammed down into the outer loading space of the pick - up with such velocity, that he was mindful of a meteor falling to earth, or *something* falling to earth, and that something was now riding *with* them.

"What was that?" Mark shrieked. "What's happening?" He felt the seat belt tighten further as he tried to move forward towards the steering wheel. "Please don't kill me!" He shouted. His face glowed red as his oxygen supply was intermittently seized, and cut off. His eyes strained at the road ahead, it approached flooded in light before disappearing, cloaked in darkness.

"You can't run from *fate*, Mark." He shouted. With his right hand he reached over his right shoulder, and gripped the sword's woven handle. "You're time has arrived." He said with a smile. Mark recognised the metallic grinding sound of the weapon being drew from it's sheath instantly, the thud that interrupted it however was *unexpected*. He turned his head a little to see his deathly messenger struggling to retrieve the weapon, it's handle had struck the roof of the cabin before it was half way clear of it's protective housing.

"These things are not made for confined spaces," He said. Keeping tightly hold of Mark's seatbelt he leaned away from him and used it as leverage. He pulled the sword clear of the sheath and relaxed back into the spacious rear seat behind Mark. With the seatbelt pulled tightly like reigns on a race horse, he pointed the sword directly into the back of Mark's seat.

"The end of the road draws near, Mark." He whispered. "Very soon we'll approach the bridge, you remember the bridge…don't you." He smiled. "Only this time, you're not going over it." He laughed. "When you burn bridges like you do, there's no going back." He smiled menacingly. "This one's no different."

"Please!" He begged. "Please don't do -" His sentence was seized by surprise and shock, as the driver's door was dragged open with such force, that it departed completely from it's hinges and smashed onto the road in a trail of sparks. Clinging to the frame of the doorway and balancing with ease on the narrow chrome kick - plate just beneath it, was a figure identical to his current passenger. He was dressed in a black - long sleeved T - shirt, and black combat trousers. He too was harnessed up but his possessed no visible strong points, unlike those of the sword wielding executioner in the rear. His hair was tied back to fully expose his pale features, although unlike *Death*, his eyes glistened like the stars above, beautifully human and brimming with emotion, albeit rage.

"Remember me, Mark?" He shouted. "*I'm* Brandon, you motherfucker!" Strapped to his right thigh was a serrated hunting knife which he reached down to retrieve before Mark could even answer.

"Beware the masquerades, Mark." He shouted. "We all hide behind masks nowadays!" He laughed as he let go of the doorway and stepped from the kick - plate, before *freefalling* next to the speeding pick - up. Mark gasped in disbelief as Brandon maintained unburdened, and sustained flight right beside him, his arms were outstretched and his legs bent at the knees, only he wasn't falling to earth at one hundred and twenty - five mph, he was gliding effortlessly along just two feet from the road below. Glistening in the moonlight were four steel strong points, attached to the *rear* of his harness.

"It's true." Mark spluttered. "You're one of *them*." He trembled uncontrollably as his hands slipped from the steering wheel. "You're a V -"

"There's no such thing." He shouted, cutting Mark off. "There's *no one* quite like me," He laughed wildly with all the adrenaline fuelled excitement that freefalling would muster. "You and your friends just didn't count on what *I am*." He turned to see how much road was left before they reached the bridge, it was visible in the very far distance as that was were the street lights began, and the final section of road was *dead* straight. Unfazed he glanced quickly into the passenger seat behind Mark, he smiled at his brother and gave him the thumbs up. *Death* returned a smile whilst tugging tightly on the seat belt, and inserted the sword to the hilt with sudden aggression, he held it in place as Mark gasped in pain, although he was unable to scream.

"Never hesitate," Brandon whispered. "When you *know* confrontation is imminent." He smiled as he moved in closer to Mark, revelling in the sight of the samurai sword that had now become as much a part of Mark's anatomy, as the lung it had just sliced through. Mark stared open mouthed, spitting bubbles of blood as Brandon reached out to him, using him as leverage he pulled himself halfway into the cab although his legs remained outstretched into the darkness.

"You had all the choice in the world, Mark." He watched as the sword was slowly retracted by his brother, retracted and *twisted*.

"You had a future, yet you deviated from it…such a silly boy." He grabbed at Mark's face forcefully. "You started *whispering*," He laughed as he quickly glanced again at the rapidly approaching bridge, and the rapidly approaching concrete crash barriers. He grabbed the large steering wheel and pushed the top half down against the dashboard, before checking it wouldn't turn either left or right as a result.

"The mask of insincerity," He said. "You wear it like a second skin, and that's the worst one of all. Just be thankful you're not an addict, you have *nothing* I want." He lunged in and stabbed the blade wildly into Mark's neck, the serrated edge tore his flesh apart with each frenzied retraction, spattering Brandon's pale face with blood. He quickly leaned down and stabbed the knife through the accelerator pedal, he pushed it through with such force that the floor pan was also pierced with ease, effectively jamming it at full tilt he pushed himself free of the pick - up truck, before once more *freefalling* without *falling*.

"Come on!" He shouted, rousing his brother into action. "You've got just seconds!" He tore off the passenger door in the same manner he had the driver's door, setting it free, it too scorched a trail of sparks behind them, before disappearing into the shrubbery. Brandon hovered with precision with his back to his brother, who by now had shuffled to the edge of the rear seat, his legs hung from the pick - up as he guided Brandon closer to him. Once close enough he began attaching the steel strong points of *his* harness, to those of *Brandon's*, one by one, until all four were secured.

"Ready?" Brandon shouted, tilting forward and easing away from the pick - up.

"Yeah!"

With his brother strapped securely to his back, Brandon launched skyward with breathtaking speed, before levelling out and once more adopting his freefall position, only this time in tandem mode and with *death* as his canopy. They both stared down as the pick - up, still travelling in excess of one hundred mph, slammed into the concrete crash barrier to the left of the bridge. They screamed excitedly as it's chassis contorted and twisted on impact, before bursting into flames.

"Burn you motherfucker!" Brandon shouted, gliding them directly yet *silently* over the crash scene, some two hundred feet above the flames. They screamed excitedly as though riding a fairground attraction, as adrenaline surged through them *both*.

Thursday 27th May. 02 : 30.

Vincelli stepped from his car and walked slowly towards the bridge, he pulled the collar on his beige overcoat as high as he could get it as the wind attacked him with force. The bridge was completely sealed off, but the efforts of those at the scene appeared to be concentrated on the other side of the bridge, the direction that those *leaving* Washburn would ultimately have to take. Three Police cruisers blocked traffic from accessing the bridge, although no traffic was attempting too as Vincelli nodded at the officers, and walked across it. He stared at the hulk of mangled steel, only some of which he could actually see since the concrete barriers blocked his line of sight to it. He sighed, knowing full well what *it* was, he braced himself for a problematic confrontation with Scott, who was already walking across the bridge to greet him.

"Nice of you to show up, Detective." He shouted. He took Vincelli's arm and guided him quickly to the smouldering pick - up.

"Now!" Scott shouted. "What do you see when you look at this?" He looked angrily at Vincelli. "What's wrong with this picture?" He asked, shouting still.

"A moment please." He whispered, attempting to survey the interior and it's partially burned occupant.

"You take *all the time* you need." Scott said. "I'll be right here." He stood next to the wreckage and smoothed over his jeans.

"Well," He said, almost too afraid to score eye contact. "It obviously didn't happen too long before the emergency services arrived on scene, as it's clearly been on fire…but put out so quick that we've got near perfect preservation of evidence."

Scott nodded.

"So my guess is we have a *witness* to this incident." Vincelli added. "Someone who called it in almost as suddenly as the wheels stopped turning."

Again Scott nodded, although he remained silent and stood with his arms folded tightly against him, the short sleeved dark polo shirt he wore strained at his biceps.

"Most notably," Vincelli said, walking around the pick - up to the driver's side. "The truck's operator is hanging from the vehicle, suspended by the very thing that should've saved his life." He cringed as he looked closely at Mark, noticing the multiple stab wounds and lacerations in his neck.

"Nor is it my belief that he did that to *himself*." He said. "He appears to have been violently attacked while still in transit." He shook his head. "Both of the doors on this side are completely gone, they're not even present with the wreckage. The impact was head on, so it's not at all consistent that they shouldn't be present." He shifted his attention to the fire truck that was parked on the other side of the road, and the fire crew milling around it.

"Did those guys use the jaws on this?" He asked, pointing to them.

"No," Scott answered, laughing a little. "As you can see he's *dead*, Detective."

"Then where are the doors?" He asked.

"One of the doors has been found," He replied. "It was found four miles away as they sealed off the road, it was lying in the middle of the carriageway." He smiled as he drew Vincelli's attention into the darkness beyond them. "As you can imagine, no searches will take place until first light for the other one, it was mere luck us discovering the one we have."

While actually driving. Vincelli thought. *You're good, you're good.*

"Do we know who he is?" Vincelli asked, gazing upon his lifeless body.

"Yes." Scott answered. "His neighbours alerted us to a disturbance, they were concerned at the commotion." He studied Vincelli. "And then of course…" He paused and looked at the murder scene on the *other* side of the road, their *Halloween,* murder scene.

"…There's our witness to consider."

"Who's the deceased?"

"Never mind that for now, Detective." Scott said, joining Vincelli on the driver's side. "There's still something you're not seeing."

"There is?" He asked, frowning a little.

"Look in the back, Detective." He whispered, tilting his head at the space where the door used to be.

"Oh, Jesus." He said, staring at the samurai sword in the rear foot well of the cabin. "I guess this helps Ray's chances." He smirked.

"Not really." Scott replied. "Anyone can acquire a samurai sword, *can't they?*"

"I suppose they can." He said, still staring at it and noticing for the first time, the incision in the back of the chair and the blood that had filtered through it. "So do you think Ray's got himself a copycat?"

"No." He answered flatly. "I think Ray's got himself an accomplice, he *always* had himself an accomplice." He sighed and stroked the mangled wreckage before him. "I told you I didn't believe the killings were random, Detective." He stared hard at Vincelli. "This proves it!"

"I disagree." He said, shaking his head. "Like you just said yourself, *anyone* can lay their hands on a sword…that's not proof enough to link this killing to the *other* killings, let alone to the twins' murderers."

"Perhaps." Scott said. "But how do you explain why he would be in the truck that was used to *kill* them?"

"This is -"

"Oh yeah!" He shouted. "This is the fucking truck!" He banged his hand down on the chrome roll bars next to the cab. "It was here all along, right under our noses." He walked away leaving Vincelli to follow behind. "His name is Mark Williams." He said, striding up the road into the darkness. "He worked in the hospital that was treating Chad Rose before his death, on top of which…he'd formed a close friendship with a young woman by the name of Julianne Leigh… on top of which, he was hoping to be." He jabbed his forefinger repeatedly into his clenched fist. "If you get me."

"He wanted her?" He asked, shrugging. "So?"

"Well," He said, stopping and turning to face Vincelli. "Julianne Leigh, just happens to be the girlfriend of Chad Rose, prior to his *death*…of course."

"Ok…" He nodded.

"So in order for the two of them to form a close friendship, they would have to be spending a considerable amount of time in each others company…would you agree?"

He nodded.

"He was Chad's fucking nurse, the clues were there all along, Detective." He shook his head angrily. "Vast amounts of medication," Scott whispered. "From morphine to methadone have been stolen from the hospital stores, over a prolonged period of time." He laughed. "Even Danny, on day one of the enquiries, said they were wearing clear masks of some kind. He said, and I quote…'I think they're used after *operations*, on burns or something.'

"I remember." He said quietly.

"He was our ace in the hole," He said, pointing back at Mark's hanging body. "He was the bait we should've been waving, we should've *known* he was involved…especially once he befriended Julianne." He observed Vincelli with growing distaste. "And given that someone had *allegedly* tried to take Chad's life in the very hospital he was being treated, and let's not forget this, *that someone*, went on to be decapitated, we soon see a link emerging. A few simple phone calls would've revealed a young man with access to almost every drug in there." He once again began walking up the Washburn Link road. "And of another thing you can be certain," He shouted back, himself struggling a little for breath. "He was in a great deal of debt, and was almost certainly lured in with offers of financial reward." He slowed finally, allowing Vincelli to draw level with him.

"Does this spot look familiar?" Scott asked. He pointed into a large artificial gap in the shrubbery. "Let's put it this way, Detective… that gap didn't exist before Halloween last."

"Of course." He replied. Throwing caution to the wind he lit a cigarette, and gazed further up the road.

"It's awfully close to where *he's* hanging *dead*, right now…isn't it?"

"It's weird is what it is." Vincelli looked back at the wrecked G.M.C, and the bridge into which it had ploughed. "It's eerie." He whispered.

"Well what's even more *eerie* than that," Scott said. "Is that this is where our witness was hiding in her car…the car is still parked just behind those trees, but I wouldn't venture to it if I were you."

"Why?"

"Because it's parked just two inches or so, from the steep plunge that killed her boyfriend, and *Brandon*." He turned to look at Vincelli. "But that's not all, look at the way the way candles are arranged."

He nodded and smiled. "They've formed a trail of some kind."

"A trail to safety," Scott said. "They were on, she claims…but I believe her, or she'd have gone down that embankment."

"Where is she now?"

"She's been taken away," Scott replied. "She was in shock." He turned back for the bridge.

"And *who* is she?"

Scott smiled and turned to look at him. "Chad's girlfriend." He started walking again, leaving Vincelli to smoke his cigarette in the darkness. "And later on today, she's all yours, Detective." He waved casually. "Find out everything she knows."

I'm gonna get you, He thought, enjoying the remainder of his cigarette and gazing at *that* space in the tree line. *You're good, but I'm good too…it's not for kicks that you've saved me for last…you know I'm gonna take you all the way, you wanted to kill them because you know you wont take me down.* He laughed aloud. *Come and get me, Brandon. I'm waiting for you now…I know you'll be coming soon.*
"Look to the skies," He whispered. "You're invited to the party, but don't forget your invite…because if your name's not down, you aint coming in."

He reached into his pocket and retrieved his cell phone, he dialled while he watched Scott arrive back at the bridge, he was heading for his car.
"He's killed Mark." He said, throwing his cigarette to the ground. He held the phone close to his ear and cupped his mouth, he gazed nervously at the trees, and the darkness engulfing them. He felt unsafe and began walking with a pace unlike his customary stroll.
"It means I'm next." He whispered, walking quickly towards the bridge and the safety of others.
"It's time to set the trap." He whispered, glancing nervously as he walked. "I've decided on the theme for next Friday night's re‑launch." He laughed. "Horror…*in the Crossfire.* Get it advertised on the radio by tomorrow afternoon, and if that alone doesn't work… well I've found the consolation prize, he'll come for this one - of that…I'm certain." He laughed again. "Apparently she's all mine." He nodded as he once more scanned his surroundings, his pace slowed as stepped within the comfort of the bridge's floodlit halo. "He'll come, it's show time…hold your nerve on this, and don't lose your head." He ended the call as he stood next to the battered pick‑up. He glanced quickly at the remaining fire crews before walking to Mark's hanging body.
"You couldn't even get that right." He whispered. "All you had to

do was keep an eye on the bitch," He leaned in, resisting the urge to strike him. "Just watch her, that was all you had to do." He rubbed at his chin. "Now she's loose, and god only knows what you've told her." He shook his head. "You just killed her, Mark."

Thursday 27th May. 16 : 40.

Vincelli sat silently in the passenger seat of his car, his glasses were perched on the end of his nose as he stared down through them, he held his notebook in one hand and a cigarette in the other. He looked at Martin and smirked, amused at the rigidity of his colleague.

"You need to relax a little." He said, observing Martin's perfect *ten to two* grasp on the steering wheel. "You're making me look common."

"Safety first." He whispered, glancing in the rear view mirror.

"We're on a straight fucking road!" Vincelli said, laughing. "It's what's in front that you should be worrying about." He shook his head in disgust. "Anyway," He said. "We want the next left." He gazed at the address he'd scribbled in his notebook. "Twenty - three Oxford Pass…" He looked out of the window as Martin duly fed the wheel through his hands, and turned the car in to Oxford Pass.

"That's it," He said, slamming the notebook closed. "Right there." He pointed to the small single storey dwelling beside them, her red Kia was parked on the driveway beside the house, it was blocked in by a large maintenance truck.

"Well done, Martin." He whispered, removing his glasses. "You got us here in a record…oh I don't know…" He concentrated on his watch for a moment. "…Forty - five minutes!" He laughed. "I can do Washburn to Hail Wood in twenty." He shook his head as Martin released his seat belt.

"You put that on in case somebody tried to pull you from the car?" He laughed as he opened the door and stepped out into the sunshine.

Glancing over the roof of the vehicle to him, Martin raised his eye brows and slammed his door shut. He chose to ignore Vincelli in his foreground, as he glanced at the row of well kept houses around him, they were all single storey houses, most with long driveways that led to a garage set further back against the rear of the property.

"You coming or what?" Vincelli asked, glancing at his watch somewhat impatiently. He watched with growing anger as Martin walked slowly towards him, glancing still at the tranquil surroundings.

"Today." Vincelli said, holding the gate for him to pass through. "Right," He whispered, letting go of the gate, it closed quickly as the spring mechanism snatched it shut behind them both. "I do the talking -"

"As ever," Martin replied. "Let's just speak to her and get back." He stepped into the porch way and rung the bell next to the solid, windowless door, before stepping back from it and waiting for his invite. He watched Vincelli throw his cigarette butt to the ground and step purposely on to it, he remained on it while they waited for the door to open.

"What a nice front garden," Martin whispered. "Look how tidy it is." He couldn't help but look down to Vincelli's feet.

"Eyes front, hot shot." Vincelli said, more than aware of his colleagues thinly veiled sarcasm.

They listened as a chain was released on the other side of the door, followed by a bolt being slid back on it self, accompanied by the turning of a key.

Vincelli raised his brow in surprise and leaned in closer to Martin. "Maybe," He whispered. "It's not as nice around here, as first impressions might suggest." He seemed pleased with his flash evaluation.

"Or maybe," Martin replied, also in a whisper. "She's scared for her life." He stared at Vincelli. "And let's face it, she has *every* reason to be." He smiled.

"Good afternoon," Vincelli said, quickly shifting his attention to the door as it was drew open to them. A well built man in his late forties stood in the doorway, he wore jeans and a red sweater.

"Good afternoon," He replied, studying them both suspiciously. "How can I help you?" He asked, running his hand through a glorious array of strawberry blonde hair, while staring them both down with ease.

"I'm Detective Joseph Vincelli," He said, producing his identification for inspection. "This is Detective Martin Lewis."

"Hello," Martin said, also holding out his identification.

"Sorry," The man said, stepping back a little. "Come in, please." He stood aside and welcomed them both into the narrow hallway, their footfalls echoed on the wooden floor beneath them.

"I'm Julianne's father, Gerrard." He said, closing the door. "Needless to say, nobody's coming through that…or any other door to get near my daughter." He smiled as he turned to face them. "Unless of course, they can show me credentials… and have a *damn good reason*, for wanting to see her."

"I understand," Vincelli whispered, sensing his brimming hostility towards them. "But we have to speak with her about what she saw," He held his hands out to him in an attempt to pacify him. "I know it doesn't feel like the time to be doing this, but believe me…now is the *best* time to do this, while it's fresh, as the details are so easily forgotten with the passing of time."

"Then I'll go get her." He replied, although still clearly not convinced. "You can go sit in the living room if you want?" He pointed to a closed door on their left.

"Thank you." Martin said, nodding appreciatively. He reached for the brass handle and pushed the door open, he treaded lightly as he noticed the floors were wooden throughout, leading the way as Vincelli followed slowly behind, notebook in hand.

"Shall we sit?" Martin asked, "Or wait for her?" Ordinarily his own decision would be made and carried out without hesitation, but Vincelli's presence always gave way to his underlying insecurities when they worked together.

He knows best, He thought. *Just do as he does*. But sometimes… Vincelli did *nothing*, and for Martin that was the hardest trait to emulate.

"Just wait," Vincelli replied. "We'll only end up having to get up, when daddies little princess is among us." He rotated his hand and bowed a little as though greeting royalty.

"Ok." He whispered. Turning his back on Vincelli he stood casually with his hands in his trouser pockets. He gazed around, looking firstly through the window at the back of the room he saw an extremely well maintained garden, his attention was drawn to two trees planted in the middle of the lawn, they were clearly infant as they had chicken wire planted around them both, to protect and allow them to flourish. A woman was kneeling at the edge of the lawn, she was tending to shrubbery and had her back to him. Under the hazy afternoon sun, her hair was golden in colour and complimented the beautiful garden perfectly, when coupled with the floral maxi dress she was attired in.

"It's *your* garden," He whispered. "Or rather, it's *their* garden." He nodded and turned away as the man they'd just conversed with, approached her.

He turned and walked back towards Vincelli, noticing that although he'd elected to sit down after all, he was perched on the edge of the tanned leather couch, still consulting his notes. In the centre of the room, there was a thick wooden coffee table most likely, he thought, styled on an era of times long forgotten - the display cabinet at the rear of the room matched it perfectly. He found the room to be tastefully presented, although caught somewhere in time. In Martin's eyes, the large plasma television in the corner struggled with its surroundings to say the least, but the net curtains on the front window eluded him completely.

"Detectives," Gerrard said, pushing open the door. "Here she is." He ushered in a frail looking Julianne, who in turn stood nervously before them.

"Hi." She offered her presence hesitantly, clasping her hands before her.

"Ah, Julianne." Vincelli replied, slamming his notebook closed. He jumped to his feet in an uncharacteristically polite manner. "I'm sorry to disturb you." He reached out to shake her hand. "I'm Detective Joseph Vincelli," He said. "This is my partner -"

"Martin Lewis." He stepped forward and shook her hand also. "I'm very sorry to have interrupted your gardening."

"Well you're introduced," Gerrard said. "I guess I'll leave the three of you alone." He looked reassuringly at his daughter as he stepped through the door, and closed it behind him.

"Julianne," Vincelli whispered. "Would you be happier sitting down?" He pointed to the couch and placed his glasses back on, before flipping the notebook open on a blank page.

"Ok." She whispered, sitting herself gently down and smoothing her dress across her knees.

"Right then…" Vincelli whispered "I have some details of what you say you saw," He sat down and turned himself to face her, he pulled open his overcoat to free himself a little as he fidgeted uncomfortably. "But what we need, is to establish *exactly* what took place *prior* to what you saw, or heard by the bridge." He held eye contact with her for a moment. "It's my intention to decipher from our conversation today, whether or not you need to be interviewed under caution at the station." He smiled, sensing her mounting fear. "I'm trying to keep this as informal as possible at this difficult stage, so it's important that you're honest with me."

She nodded.

"So," He gazed at Martin before turning his attention back to her. "Can you tell me what took place at Mark's house?"

"What do you need to know?" She asked.

"Everything."

She sighed and stared at the open fire place opposite her. "Well, he came home and I was waiting for him -"

"In his house?" He asked.

"Yes, in his house." She replied. "I had my own key."

"Ok."

"I'd planned a nice evening for us, and when he came home he was acting weird from the offset."

"Weird how?"

"He was jumpy and nervous," She answered, giving him a sideways glance. "He wasn't being himself." She began to shake as tears formed in her eyes. "But it soon became apparent why." She said, wiping them dry. "He started asking me some really random questions."

Vincelli nodded. "Like what, Julianne?" He held his pen at the ready. "Just take your time," He went on. "I know it's difficult."

She took just a moment to compose herself. "Well," She whispered. "He took me to the carnival on the night of those terrible murders."

His eyes raised suddenly from the blank page to hers. "You were there?" He asked.

She nodded. "We were."

Vincelli nodded slowly, still holding her attention fiercely. "I didn't know that." He said. "I'm sorry you had to witness something like that." He gazed at her questionably as he awaited a response.

"No," She replied, smiling a little. "I certainly didn't witness *that*." She paused and stared blankly at the fireplace. "He wouldn't have shown me such barbarity."

"Who?" Vincelli asked. "Mark?"

"Mark?" She asked, turning her head to Vincelli for verification. "Mark?" She laughed nervously. "I'm talking about Brandon." She faced front once again. "He was there."

"Julianne," He said. "I keep hearing this name…Brandon." He sighed and gazed at Martin, who was now leaning against the window sill at the back of the room, his arms were folded as he stood and quietly observed them both.

"Brandon," Vincelli said, looking at her. "Is dead." He shook his head. "I understand your grief, but we have to stick to the facts here."

"And we are." She whispered. She slipped her fingers just below the neck line of her dress, before pulling them back clasping a small steel pendant, which she held in her fist tightly, for comfort.

"I saw him." She whispered. "Lisa saw him too."

"Lisa?"

"She's a fortune teller," Julianne replied. "She had a small stall at the carnival, it was called 'Star Spangled Anna.'"

He nodded and jotted it down in his notebook, as with all his entries it was written in a barely legible scribble, intended exclusively for his own understanding.

"Ok," He stared at her attentively, notebook at the ready. "Go ahead."

"I was intrigued by her stall anyway," She said. "But then I blacked out, and whilst I was unconscious I had a vision, a vision of what Mark was to become. *He* bestowed that vision upon me, to warn me."

"Brandon?" Vincelli asked.

She nodded. "He showed me aggression, and he showed me hate…but he also showed me the way." She sat silently as she recollected the experience. "He was pointing to the tent," She added. "He *wanted* me to go to that tent as much, if not more, than I did."

"Where was he, Julianne?"

"He was stood by the entrance to the Waltzers." She replied.

"Are you sure?" He asked, again looking at Martin. "The Waltzers?"

"Positive." She answered flatly. "He stood by the guard rail, before moving straight through the turnstile…" She paused. "It didn't even move."

"Ok," He said. "Well let's not lose sight of the fact that this was a *vision*, and not reality."

"How many dead bodies do you have, Detective?" She asked. "How *real* do you want it?"

Vincelli nodded, although he remained silent at the question.

"When I came too," She said. "Mark was tending to me, after all…he was a nurse, right? I was relieved it had been a dream, although slightly concerned at it's clarity. I wanted to go home but he looked so worried and appeared so genuine, I just couldn't accept it had been anything but a vivid…vision."

"What happened then?" He asked, skimming the pen backwards and forwards on the page.

"Well I was putting it behind me," She replied. "Although by now I couldn't get Brandon out of my mind, but that was nothing new."

"Ok." He said, raising his hand between the two of them. "Julianne I'm going to stop you there." He sat silently for a moment and considered his approach. "Did you harbour romantic feelings for Brandon?"

"Oh god *yes*." She replied. "It was difficult not to." She laughed. "I was bowled over by his presence, he was magnetic…he had an aura about him that was unquestionable."

"And Chad?"

She sat silently, staring into Vincelli's eyes. "I loved him," She answered finally. "He was a wonderful human being, and he looked identical to the man I was in love with." She clutched the pendant tightly. "But he was a distant second to Brandon, *he* made me weak… *he* made me quiver."

"Were the two you ever…intimate."

"No." She answered. "Brandon would never have done that to him."

"Was it ever discussed?" He asked. "Did you tell him how you felt?"

"No." She closed her eyes tightly. "I didn't need to, he was more than aware of my feelings for him."

"Why?"

"Because he *shared* them." She answered. "He loved me, it was our mutual connection that kept us apart."

"Chad?"

"Yes."

"Ok." He said, giving her a reassuring rub on her shoulder. "So, you couldn't get Brandon out of your mind, then what?"

"I told him I wanted to visit the fortune teller -"

"Star Spangled Anna?"

She nodded. "And I was ok until things resembling my vision started happening." She sighed and glanced around the room. "He met some friends of his by the Waltzers, and in my vision he'd met his friends and then turned on me, so needless to say my concerns were growing."

"So you went?" He asked.

"I went to the tent, and he went to his friends." She said. "I watched him and right away I could see he was a different person." She smiled. "I mean, I know people act differently around different people, but he wasn't the same *person* when he was with them."

"How?"

"Well for one thing," She answered. "He was smoking, as far as I knew he didn't smoke."

Vincelli shrugged. "Some people can smoke socially," He said. "Me, I don't understand it…I wish I could." He smiled at her. "Was there anything else that caught your eye?"

"Yes." She answered. "They were, well you know…rough looking."

"Rough looking?" He asked, jotting it down. "Can you elaborate on that?"

She pursed her lips as she thought for a moment. "They looked like criminals."

Vincelli raised his eyebrows at her, once again skimming his pen over the partially filled page. "Elaborate please."

"Well one of them was really big," She said. "He had a shaved head and a long leather jacket, I would've crossed the street to avoid him, and yet here was Mark…a nurse, a professional, openly associating with him. He looked dangerous."

"Have you seen him before or since?"

"Not before." She answered. "But since? Yes."

"You have?"

"Yes, although until yesterday I hadn't realised it."

"Explain."

"He's dead." She answered. "His picture has been in the papers, and on the news." She paused as Mark's words reverberated around her mind like a pinball.

They're the ones you've been reading about in the papers, She thought. *And on the news.*

Vincelli sat silently and digested her information. "How does that make you feel?" He asked.

"Well," She glanced at him. "Ask me again when I've told you the whole story."

"Ok," He whispered. "Go on."

"At that point I went in," She said. "In fact, no…she came out to me."

"Anna?"

"Yes," She replied. "But she quickly introduced herself to me by her real name -"

"Which is?"

"Lisa."

"Any last name?" He asked, jotting it down.

"No."

"Ok, Julianne." He said, nodding to her.

"Well I went in, and she asked me what I wanted to have done." She smiled as she rubbed the pendant gently between her fingers. "I remember being surprised at the question, because I didn't count on there being several methods…I didn't know much about it really, she must've had a field day with me." She laughed at her own naivety, but her eyes, in stark contrast once more brimmed with tears. "Although I know that's actually not true," She added. "She ended up giving me my money back, what con artist does that?"

"You'd be surprised." He replied, tapping his pen impatiently on the notebook.

"I told her to choose for me," She said. "I was starting to feel foolish and to be honest I really wanted to just get out of there, but on the other hand…getting out of there meant going back to Mark and his friends, and my *vision*." She bowed her head down and sighed, before breathing deeply and raising her head again. "Lisa chose the crystal ball," She whispered. "And immediately it took a turn for the worse."

"What happened, Julianne?" He asked, his intrigue bordered on the genuine.

"She said there was a young man," Her brimming tears began to fall. "Dead but not gone, and that he was…or should I say *is*…trapped between our world and the next."

"Hang on a moment…" He whispered, scribbling furiously. "…Ok."

"She said that his was a forced exile," She paused, seemingly staring into space. "And that he wasn't able to make the transition, until he'd made it possible for me to be safe."

"She said that?" Martin asked, strolling over from the rear window.

"Yes." Julianne whispered.

"Ok," Vincelli said, pushing Martin back to the window with a hand gesture. "Let's keep moving forward." His annoyance at Martin was barely concealed rage.

"Sorry." Martin whispered, back pedalling to the window once more.

"She took a few moments to regain her connection," Julianne whispered. "She seemed shocked at what she was seeing…but I know now that she was in shock *because* she was seeing."

"What happened then?" He asked.

"She told me I was in…" She held her head in her hands, dropping the pendant from within them. Vincelli saw for the first time, that it was an inverted crucifix, it swung hypnotically from her slender neck.

"…Danger." She cried, her hands muffled her voice a little. "She said I was in some degree of danger, and that I had to be sure of my company…because they were whispering."

"Whispering?" He asked.

"She said my fate lies in their hands." She raised her head once more and quickly clutched the pendant. "She went on to mention something about photographs, she said the clues lied within them?"

"Ok" He whispered, dictating rapidly. "What clues?"

"I'm getting to that." She replied, turning to look at him. "She said that *he* wanted to communicate something to me, but that he wouldn't do it through her…then it got weird."

Weirder than this? He thought. *Unbelievable.*

"Lisa changed," She whispered. "She stared at me all wide eyed and curious." She shook her head. "It wasn't Lisa anymore," She squeezed the pendant so hard that the muscles in her forearm contracted fiercely. "It was *him*," She said. "He'd entered her, I could see his eyes within hers, not the physical matter obviously…but the passion and the rage, all at once she captivated me with her stare and I was a deer in the headlights…resigned to my fate and unable to move."

"What did…" Vincelli paused momentarily, but decided to humour her. "…*He* say?"

"*He*, told me to leave." She replied. "His exact words were, 'Leave this place, before it's too late…leave now.'"

"Ok," He replied, allowing his shorthand to catch her spoken words. "Then what?"

"Then she freaked out." She answered. "She jumped from her chair and ran behind mine, she was screaming and crying. I remember her hands were trembling as she was holding my shoulders."

"What did she say?"

"She told me to get out," She cast a furtive glance at Vincelli, observing his frantic scrawl. "She said I'd brought something with me -"

"Did you know what she meant by that?" He asked.

"No, although I had a fairly good idea obviously." She paused. "I just didn't readily accept it at the time."

"So then what?"

"Then I ran outside." She answered. "Well if I'm honest I told her to go and fuck herself."

"As you do." He said, smirking.

"I went outside and Mark came over to see what was wrong." She stared blankly once more. "He seemed so caring," She whispered. "How stupid am I?"

"Julianne," Vincelli whispered, patting her on the arm. "You're not *stupid*." He said. "You were vulnerable, and certain people have no hesitation in targeting the vulnerable." He rubbed at her arm and once more poised his pen ready for action. "Tell me more, Julianne."

"I was telling Mark I wanted to go home," She said. "When Lisa emerged from the tent behind me. She told me I could have my money back but I just ran away, I couldn't bring myself to look at her."

"And Mark?"

"I don't know." She answered. "I think he had words of some kind with her, because he was certainly acquainted with her as of last night."

Vincelli nodded and drew two thick black lines beneath his notes. "So," He whispered. "Did he take you home that night?" Or did you go back to his house?"

"Well it's funny you should ask that," She replied. "Because I remember being at the car with him, we were having some Coke…" She paused, laughing as Vincelli raised his eye brows to her.

"I mean the drink." She said, smiling. "We were having a bottle of Coke."

"Ok," He smiled a little and shifted his body weight. "Go on."

"Well that's it." She said. "I don't remember any more, I woke up in a bed in his spare room…naked."

"Really?" He asked. "That's more than a little curious."

"He assured me that nothing had happened," She explained. "He said he'd slept in his room, and that he'd put me to bed fully clothed." She thought hard about that morning. "He said maybe it was due to my fainting, but I fell asleep in the car and he couldn't rouse me…so he brought me home."

"Ok." He said. "Pardon the following question, Julianne." He sighed and scanned the room with his eyes. "Did you feel as though intercourse had taken place?"

She stared at him wide eyed. "God *no*." She replied. "I'd have been straight to the Police if I even *thought* he'd done that." She blushed a little. "I just felt scared and confused, but I believed him… despite last night, I *still* believe." She glanced at Martin across the room, he smiled back to her before averting his gaze.

"But I saw the pictures." She whispered. "They were arranged in a glass frame, all bunched together. I just didn't figure on their relevance."

"What were they?" Vincelli asked.

"The pictures," She answered slowly. "Were mostly of Mark and what I thought must've been his friends. There was one in particular of his friends, they were leaning against a large blue pick - up truck."

"I see."

"That pick - up was used to murder my boyfriend." She said. "Like I said though, I just didn't realise it at the time."

Lost in thought and staring across to the television, he flipped the page in his notebook and hovered the nib just above the blank page. "Ok." He said. "Is there anything else you wish to add before we move on to last night?"

She nodded. "Yes." She whispered. "I was visited by Lisa, it was actually just after I'd been at Chad's bedside." She paused. "I'd just told him I couldn't continue to wait, and that I'd met someone else."

"Mark?" Vincelli asked.

"Yes."

"Would it be safe to assume that the two of you had…" He paused to look her in the eye. "…Shall we say, commenced in a relationship?"

"That's what I wanted." She answered. "At least I thought I did."

"Ok." He said, adding to his already substantial inserts. "So, tell me about Lisa."

"She was waiting for me at my car, well…my Dad's car actually, so I have no idea how she knew which one it was." She shrugged. "She told me that I had to get away from Mark, and that he was not who he appeared to be." She smiled again. "This was all after I hit her, I'm sorry to say."

"In light of currents," He whispered. "I wouldn't worry too much about that."

"Thank you." She said, managing a smile. "Anyway, she went on to tell me that normally she does something called *cold reading*." She shrugged. "I had no idea what that was."

"It's all about your body language, Julianne." He smiled at her. "They're watching every action," He went on. "Or *reaction*, however small…that you make." He laughed. "You don't even know you're doing it, if it's a positive reaction…they'll proceed in that direction, if it's negative…then the *vision* will become *hazy*, allowing them time to redirect their efforts."

"Well," She whispered. "Yes." She raised her eyebrows to him. "How did you know that?"

"It's textbook." He answered. "There's no *magic*, just the *illusion* of magic."

"Well…" She laughed nervously. "That's basically what she confided in me, before telling me again about the photos." She paused. "Then she told me that I'd brought someone, or *something*… in with me. She told me that *he* had made her tell me those things, and that I was in danger."

"Anything else?"

"Oh yes." She said. "She then told me that Chad was dead."

"Dead?" Vincelli asked, surprised at the crudity of her words.

"Yes." She replied. "I reminded her that Mark worked in that hospital, and that Chad could be in danger."

"And what did she say?"

"She said that…" She stalled as once more tears formed in her bloodshot eyes. "She said that he'd let go…she said that together they were strong, and that it was meant to be."

"And when exactly was that, Julianne?" He asked. "Do you remember?"

She laughed, more in disbelief than nerves or amusement. "Tuesday the sixth of April." She whispered. "That's the date you'll find on Chad's death certificate." Her lips quivered.

"I'm sorry, Julianne." He whispered. "Truly I am."

"She wasn't wrong about a single thing," She said, holding herself tightly. "And by the looks of things, I *am* in danger." She began to cry. "Mark tried to kill me last night." She shouted. "If he'd have caught me I'd be dead…not him."

"Ok." He said softly. He reached across and placed a reassuring hand on her shoulder, gripping her firmly he felt just how emaciated and frail she had become. He saw a large picture in the alcove above the television, it was of Julianne and her father. He saw instantly the obvious changes that she'd been through since Halloween. Her figure had been full and curvaceous, most likely he thought, the envy of her peers, whereas now she was literally skin and bone, with a body resembling that of a tall teenage boy.

"Now," He whispered. "I think I have enough of a picture with regards to the relationship between you and Mark." He glanced over his notes. "I know this is difficult," He said. "But now I need to know about last night."

She visibly braced herself and took noticeably deep breaths. "Ok."

"Ok," He said, scanning his notes for the relevant insert, "So, you'd planned a nice evening for the two of you…" He used the pen's nib as a guide as he struggled to read his earlier notes. "…He came home, and started asking some random questions…" He looked at Julianne, his piercing eyes glared over his glasses ordering her to complete.

"I'm a little embarrassed to be honest," She whispered. "But I was wearing…you know, bedroom clothes shall we say?"

Vincelli nodded.

"And basically I threw myself at him." She avoided eye contact with both Vincelli and Martin, choosing instead to focus on the magazines under the coffee table. "But he rejected me outright," She added. "In fact he pushed me off him." She sighed. "I asked him if he wanted to, he said he did…more than anything, but that he had to ask me something."

"What was his question?" Vincelli asked. His voice was more than a little impatient as his pen was poised at the ready.

"He asked me about the carnival." She replied. "In particular, he wanted to know what *she* had said to me." She frowned as she struggled to recall his words. "He was adamant about me telling him," She said. "But I didn't want to."

"Why not?"

"Because to tell him meant telling myself." She answered. "I knew she was talking about Mark, I just *knew* it was him she was referring to…I just went on pretending. I wanted to believe my *own* better judgement, I didn't want to believe that some young girl, younger than me…knew more about my life than I did." She paused and glanced at Martin. "I wanted Mark to be who *I* thought he was, not who *she* thought he was."

Martin nodded to her, but said nothing.

"When he started asking me about her." She whispered. "I knew it was over…the dream I mean, it was over."

"Why?"

"Because I already knew, he was *whispering*."

Vincelli sighed. "Did you tell him?"

"I had too." She replied. "I told him firstly that she'd warned of a man, that he was dead but not gone…basically everything I just told you."

"And how did he react to that?"

"He began to tremble," She answered. "So I suppose you could say, *not too well*."

"And then?"

"And then *he* asked me if there was anything else." She sighed. "That's when I told him she'd told me to leave before it was too late." She concentrated hard on the fire place, listening as her father passed through the hallway beyond them. "He didn't understand what I meant, and expressed surprise that she would say that."

"Did you tell him what you've told us?" Vincelli asked. "That you think it was…*Brandon*."

"No." She replied. "Although I did tell him that I believed that *he*, as in…the *he* that she had referred too, had spoken those words directly to me."

"Did you tell him how…" He quickly consulted his notes. "…Lisa, had reacted to that experience?"

"No." She whispered. "He didn't ask, but he did ask me if I knew who *he* was." She quickly second guessed Vincelli's next question, watching as he inhaled to speak.

"I told him I didn't." She went on.

"Why?" He asked. "If you're so certain, why not tell him?"

"My beliefs are mine alone." She replied with a glimmer of anger.

"Did he press you?"

"No." She replied. "I told him she'd mentioned photographs, and there was something about the way he looked at me that told me everything I needed to know."

"How so?"

"He *knew* I knew." She answered. "I said to him, 'You know what she's talking about, don't you?'" She paused. "He said he did."

"You must've been more than a little curious?" Vincelli asked, scanning her carefully.

"He said there were some things he had to tell me." She returned his stare for a moment, but quickly relented under his intense concentration on her. "I told him I wanted to see the photographs." She whispered nervously. "He told me he could do better than that, and with that he jumped up and left the room…telling me to follow him."

"And did you, Julianne?" He asked. "Follow him?"

Again she tried to look at him, but couldn't. "Yes." She whispered.

"Where was he going?"

"To his garage." She replied. "I'd never been in his garage, it was always secured with a padlock, but I didn't think anything about it until that moment."

"Ok." He said. "Now I know already that you were discovered in…your *bedroom clothes*, with a mans jacket covering you…so I'll just go right ahead and assume that he tossed you his jacket after some level of protest by you, would that be accurate?"

She nodded. "Yes."

"Then what?"

"Well," She said. "I joined him outside as he opened one of those big doors, I told him that I was scared." A feeling of distrust began to swell within her, like a river about to burst it's banks.

"He told me he was scared too -" She whispered. "Scared of how *I* was going to react."

"How did that make you feel?"

"No worse," She answered. "If anything I was *comforted*, I was afraid he was going to hurt me…so I felt reassured a little."

"What happened then?"

"He went inside." She said. "He had to make his way to the opposite end to get to the light switch, and when he found it, he instructed me to step inside and close the door."

"Whilst still in darkness?" Vincelli asked.

"Yes."

"But if you were fearful for your safety," He added. "Was that wise?"

"I'd heard him struggling," She replied. "So I knew he was at the other side, I knew he wasn't waiting to pounce on me." She smiled. "Just because I couldn't see him…doesn't mean I couldn't place him."

Vincelli nodded.

"*Then*, he switched on the light." She said. "He asked me to join him at the front end of what I could see was a large vehicle…but it was hidden beneath sheets."

"Then?"

"I asked him what it was," She said. "To which he replied, 'I think you know the answer to that.' He pulled off the sheet and revealed that horrific truck." She paused, more than aware of Vincelli's eyes burning through her. She noticed his note - taking had decreased rapidly as he barely put pen to paper anymore, choosing instead to scrutinise her every move.

"He wasn't wrong." She whispered. "I knew alright."

"You knew what?" He asked.

"I *knew*," She said, meeting his gaze head on. "That I was looking at the truck that had been used to kill my boyfriend." She shivered as she had when the sheets had been pulled from the pick - up.

"I told him that I'd seen the truck before," She continued. "Minus all the front end damage of course, on a picture in the bedroom." She laughed. "I said there had been four men leaning against it, but that he wasn't in the picture…turns out he took the picture."

"He told you that?"

She nodded. "I told him I knew it was the same truck." She laughed again. "I mean, what do I know about cars? But that thing was very distinctive, and it's badge was missing." She gazed ahead blankly as she recalled Mark's reaction.

"He looked as though he was about to pass out," She whispered. "He was scared." She smiled, almost fondly. "I told him I knew how all the damage was done, and he didn't disagree."

"Did he confirm it?" Vincelli asked. "Or just…*not disagree?*"

"Yes." She replied, nodding. "I mean, he didn't physically say *hey, Julianne…this is the truck that killed your boyfriend."* She ignored Vincelli's obvious distaste at being openly mocked.

"I mean, come on!" She shouted. "He nodded, that's enough confirmation for me."

"Keep going."

"I told him he was one of them," She said. "And that he'd killed my boyfriend."

"How did he answer?"

"It wasn't a question." She said "He *was* one of them, but he said he couldn't get *away* from them. I don't know how hard he tried… but he claimed he had to do it."

"Do what?"

"Take part in their deaths."

"Then what?"

"I passed out." She answered. "I must've fainted because I woke up on his couch, and he *said* I'd fainted." She shrugged.

"You fainted again?" He asked, noting it down. "Do you faint often, Julianne?"

"No." She answered. "Not really."

Vincelli smiled and flapped his notebook between the two of them. "Well, we've been talking for what? Fifteen minutes or so? And you've described two instances of you fainting in that time alone." He stared at her. "Are you certain of these details, Julianne?" He asked.

"Yes I am." She replied sharply. "Believe me…I'm certain."

"Ok." He said. "Then please, enlighten me."

She looked him over before glancing across to Martin, he was still leaning against the window sill with his arms folded, she thought him kind looking compared to her more immediate company.

Why can't you ask the questions? She wondered, before returning her stare to Vincelli.

"I came too on the couch," She said. "He was dabbing at my forehead with a wet cloth." She pulled her golden fringe to the left, revealing a small graze just above the temple.

"I banged it on the ground I guess."

He nodded his approval and made a fresh insert into his notes.

"He tried to give me a cup of coffee," She said. "But I smashed it from his hand and yelled at him. I demanded he tell me everything."

"And…did he?" He pressed the end of his pen in to retract the nib, before tapping it nervously against the notebook.

"I can't possibly know that." She replied. "All I know is what he told me."

"Which was?"

"He began to tell me that they'd been his friends," She said. "The men in the picture I mean, and that he *had* been present in that truck when it was used to kill them and yes… he said that."

Vincelli laughed a little although his eyes clearly did not share in the amusement, instead they burned through Julianne with the intensity to which, through years of cross examination, they were now accustomed. He nodded and gazed at her pendant as she held it in her hand.

"He told me they were all wearing masks that night," She said. "And that he *knew* they were out to find and kill the twins."

"Did he tell you why?"

"The *reason* why?" She asked, glancing into his eyes she found the answer. "He mentioned *instructions*." She looked again at Martin. "I don't know *why* they were instructed though."

"Instructions?" Vincelli asked. "Do you mean they were given instructions, via a third party shall we say?"

After short deliberation she nodded her head and shrugged. "I guess so," She whispered. "He told me that in return for money, he had agreed to supply prescription drugs to them." She paused. "He said that they wanted more and more, until it got to the point that he couldn't refuse them anything, because once in the gang, you couldn't just walk away. He said he was better off with them than against them."

"Why?" Vincelli asked.

"He said they'd have killed him." She replied. "Most likely, he feared the rest of them would receive instructions to kill *him*."

"What did you say, Julianne?"

"I told him he *deserved* to die." She answered. "That they *all* deserved to die." She stared again at Martin, before settling on Vincelli.

"That was a terrible thing for me to say," She confided. "But death is a terrible subject, and one that Mark had proved he was more than well versed in. He looked so scared, so desperate...I remember just wanting him to hold me and be *old* Mark, not to be telling me all these terrible things, but things just went from bad to worse."

"How?"

"He told me that he was going to be the next to die." She whispered. "He said that everyone else who was in the truck that night, was...*is*...dead."

Vincelli watched as she cradled her pendant between both hands, she sat silently for a moment with her eyes closed tightly. He snatched the opportunity to glance over at Martin, and with his index finger made small concentric circles against his right temple. Martin nodded back slowly in order to appease him, but instead gazed at Julianne.

"He told me that a couple of them had been present that night," She said. "At the carnival. They were the ones he'd been talking to by the Waltzers." She opened her eyes and looked at Vincelli. "He said they were the ones I'd been reading about in the papers, and seeing on the news." She paused for a moment. "That's when I asked him if they were the *victims*, of this swordsman who's been captured. What are the media calling him...the Black Widow?" She smiled wryly "He said they were, and I remember saying how it was a bad thing that he hadn't got to finish his work before he was captured, or words to that effect." Her lips quivered. "I *meant* it." She said. "But then he told me something else -"

"And what was that?"

"He told me that the *real* Black Widow, is still out there... *somewhere.*"

"Really?" Vincelli asked, feigning mild amusement. "And how exactly would Mark have known that?"

"He said he'd helped frame him." She replied, shaking her head in disbelief. "I ran for the door, I wanted to get away from him but he caught me...he didn't try to hurt me, he persuaded me to stay and listen."

"And did you?"

"Yes." She whispered. "In a funny kind of way, I *wanted* to stay." She laughed at her own stupidity. "I guess you could say I was waiting for the punch line! Or I was waiting to wake up and find him stroking my hair or something."

"Ok." Vincelli said, choosing to ignore her romantic notions. "So, according to *Mark*, the guy we've got in custody is innocent…despite the evidence chain connecting him to the murders." He laughed a little. "Did Mark tell you *how* he'd managed to frame him?"

"Well, if by *evidence chain*," She said. "You mean the samurai swords, the wig and the half used tubs of white face paint? He told me he'd planted it all in his master bedroom at the front of the house, after gaining entry through his patio doors, which…incidentally he was assured were *always* unlocked…then I'd say your evidence chain has all the strength of a *daisy* chain."

"Now just a -"

"And!" She shouted, cutting Vincelli off. "He also told me the swords were in dark red sheaths…how could he know that?" She asked. "More importantly…how could I know he's a cop?"

Martin pushed himself from the window sill and strolled slowly over to them both, he looked at Julianne with growing interest as he retrieved his own notebook and flipped it open.

"Red sheaths?" He whispered, making an entry of his own. "How do you know that, Julianne?" He asked. "And why would you think he's a Police Officer?" He gazed into her eyes as she sat silently. "There's a gagging order in place," He whispered. "That's *not* something you've read in the news papers…or seen on the news for that matter."

"Because that's what he told me." She replied. "And obviously he was right." She gazed into his blue eyes and sensed a kindred soul, one who seemed to be listening without prejudice, without ulterior motives of his own.

"I don't like you." She whispered firmly, having returned her stare to Vincelli. "I've done nothing wrong, I'm not a suspect and I'm certainly not under arrest." She shook her head and looked again to Martin, who was stood directly in front of her.

"If we're going to continue *here*," She said. "Then I'll continue with him, or not at all." She jumped to her feet and opened the living room door. "If I must continue with you," She said, glaring harshly at Vincelli. "Then it's at your station, with representation."

"Ok." Vincelli whispered, climbing to his feet. "Let's just calm down."

"No." She shouted. "You've done nothing but smear and belittle me since you got here."

Vincelli climbed to his feet a defeated man. "You can continue with my colleague." He said, walking to the window sill where Martin had remained perched. "But I have to stay in the room as this is *my* investigation." He spun around to face her as he leaned casually against it. "Agreed?"

"Agreed." She replied, closing the door.

"Julianne," Martin whispered. "Take a seat for just one moment." He walked to Vincelli and leaned in close to him.

"Why are we not doing this at the station?" He asked. "This needs documenting," He added. "These are important factors in an important investigation." He stared hard into Vincelli's eyes. "I'm not following your way of thinking…clearly."

"I'm attempting to ascertain what she actually knows." He replied angrily. "I'm not interested in hearsay. Just get her to continue -"

"But what about the swords?" He asked. "Aren't you even just a *little* curious as to how she actually knows that?" He awaited a response, glancing quickly again at Julianne. "And how the fuck does she know he's a cop?"

"Oh, come on." He replied. "So she guessed correctly, or rather he guessed correctly." He shook his head and smirked. "And a guess is all it was until you went and fucking confirmed it for her." He shook his head. "Fucking gagging order! You don't tell her that, if she wants to speculate then fine but you don't concur."

"You're right." He whispered. "My apologies." He glanced over his shoulder to an increasingly impatient girl. "I'll find out what she knows."

Martin nodded and returned to Julianne, who was perched on the edge of the couch with her arms folded tightly against her.

"Sorry," He whispered, sitting down beside her. "This wont take much longer." Aligning his silver pen against the faint blue lines of his notebook, he took a deep breath, after all, Vincelli was watching and he was acutely aware of it.

"Ok." He said finally. "Then tell me a little more, regarding what he told you about *planting* these items."

"The night before he planted them," She replied. "He said he'd received a phone call from someone…he never mentioned who, but they told him he'd be picked up early the following morning as there was work to be done."

"Work?" He asked, leaning in closer to her. "Did he specify what *kind* of work? Did he tell you if he knew what the work entailed?"

"No." She replied, noticing the sharp creases in his black trousers. "He didn't know what they wanted. He said they were sitting in a parked car outside this guy's house -"

"Who's they?"

"Just him and some guy." She whispered. "He *did* say that this guy was a big player, because he got a call direct from the head of the organisation, or *the boss*."

"How did Mark know that?" He asked. His eyes moved involuntarily over her thin figure as he spoke.

"He said the guy told him." She answered, her eyes darted furtively to and from Martin's. "He said there was something on the back seat of the car." She whispered. "He said it was something long, but he didn't know what as it was wrapped in black bin bags."

"Ok." He said. He whispered to himself as he wrote it hurriedly down, although his notes were impeccably neat, a detail not lost on Julianne as she watched his note taking with interest.

"So, what then?" He asked, glancing up at her with a smile. "What happened then?"

"He was sent into the house," She replied. "Via the patio doors, which were always unlocked according to Mark." She paused. "Oh, and he was told to be quick."

"And then?"

"He was told to put them on the bed," She answered. "In the master bedroom at the front of the house." She ignored Vincelli's concentrated stare, choosing instead to focus on Martin's hands. "It was there that he discovered he was in possession of two samurai swords…" She looked across to Vincelli. "…In *red sheaths*." She returned her gaze to Martin.

"He also had with him some half used tubs of white face paint," She whispered. "And a long dark wig."

"How did you feel about what he was telling you?" He asked, halting his note taking to look at her.

"I was utterly horrified." She replied. "I told him he was unbelievable, he tried to touch me and I pulled away." She stared blankly for a moment, just shy of Martin's eyes. "I called him an animal, but then…"

"Then…what?"

"But then I began to *really* fear for my safety." She whispered. "He became desperate, he told me that Lisa had gone to see him -"

"Lisa?" He interrupted. "The girl from the carnival?"

"Yes." She nodded. "He said that she'd warned him, warned him that *they* were coming for him."

"*They?*" Martin asked. He glanced at Vincelli who shook his head and shrugged. "I thought you believed it to be Brandon?" He asked. "Is someone else involved?"

"Well let's not forget what Lisa said to me," She whispered. "She told me that *together* they are strong." She smiled at Martin. "But I just don't…" She paused. "I just don't see *Chad* as his accomplice."

"A friend perhaps?" He asked.

She shook her head slowly and remained silent.

"Ok." He said. "So, Lisa warned him that *they* were coming." He sighed heavily and scratched at his forehead. "Well we have to take these *visions* rather seriously," He whispered, holding her gaze. "Because we know with a degree of certainty, that *they*…whoever *they* are, caught up with him, and her predictions so far are holding water." He smiled at her and sensed she was relaxing in his company, despite the intense scrutiny from across the room.

"So then…" He paused and scanned through his immaculate notes. "…You began to fear for your safety. Can you tell me why? What changed at that point?"

"He did." She replied. "Like I said, he became desperate." She clung tightly once more to her pendant. "He was asking me who *they* were, he believed that I knew who Lisa had been talking about."

"You do." Martin said, pushing her just a little. "Others may not share your beliefs, Julianne," He went on. "But *you* know exactly who *they* are…don't you."

Once again she shook her head, once again she remained silent.

"What was your reply to Mark?" He asked.

"I told him about my vision." She answered. "I said that I'd seen

Brandon as clear as day when I fainted, and that he'd beckoned me to the tent." She sighed and stared dreamily at Vincelli, although she quickly looked away when she realised where her eyes had settled.

"I also told him," She added. "That Brandon, had showed me a vision of *him*…a vision that I didn't think was possible."

"How did he react?"

"Badly." She answered. "He said, 'It's him isn't it? He's back to settle the score.'"

"So he agreed?"

"He seemed to accept it was him, but then again, all the men he'd done his dirty deeds with had all lost their lives in one way or another…so he pretty much accepted there was some kind of *selection* taking place." She smiled. "He seemed more troubled by who was *helping* him."

"Yes." Martin whispered. "It is somewhat of a quandary at the moment."

"That's when he freaked out." She said. "That's when I knew I had to get out of there." She shook her head and appeared confused. "A voice began talking to me." She whispered. "Through my thoughts, as clear as day."

"A voice?"

"It was guiding me." She said. "Telling me what to do and when to do it."

"Can you explain that?" He asked.

"Well, for example;" She whispered. "I didn't consciously know where my car keys were, but this *voice* informed me with clarity, that they were on the bottom stair."

"Ok," He said, noting her words. "Go on."

"I could hear Mark shouting from the kitchen -"

"What was he shouting?"

"He was saying, 'I'm not going to die like this…I'll die when *I'm* ready.'"

Martin nodded.

"I heard him pull open the cutlery drawer," She said. "Actually, he must have dragged it off it's runners because the noise was tremendous. I heard the voice say, 'The knives are in that drawer, what are you waiting for. Go now.'"

"In your head?" Martin asked. "This voice, was it in your head? Or could you physically *hear* it?"

"Both." She said. "It was in my head, but it wasn't my voice." She laughed. "Normally when you talk to yourself in your mind, it's *your* voice you can hear. This was *not* my voice…it was *his*."

"Brandon's?"

"Yes."

"Then?"

"Well that's when I got up and ran." She said. "I ran for the hallway door, I was relieved I'd got to it before he came back in to the living room, if he'd have come back in before I got to it…I'd have been trapped…I'd have been killed."

Breaking from his note taking, Martin obliged her with the eye contact she deserved as she spoke, he nodded gently and reassured her as best he could with just a smile.

"I heard him shouting," She whispered, holding Martin's gaze. "He said, 'Aint no fucking ghost gonna kill me.'"

"Ok." He wrote it down, dividing his attention successfully between his notes and her brimming tears.

"I shouted that I was scared," She said. "I don't know why, it just came out."

"Was it for Mark's…I'll say *benefit*, that you were shouting it?" He stalled his writing as she took a moment to consider the question.

"I don't think so." She answered finally. "It was my *thoughts*."

"You were communicating with yourself?" He asked. "Replying to this *voice*?"

"I think so." She replied. "I know how it sounds."

"Julianne," He said, calmly resting his pen in the spine of his notebook. "We all have voices in our heads, it's not as crazy as you might think." He smiled. "And those voices can take on the voices of others, at a moments notice…it doesn't mean your crazy."

"I don't follow you." She answered, although clearly wanting to.

"Well," He replied, conjuring an example in his mind. "If you were to tell yourself…in your mind, *Don't be late home tonight, you know I can't sleep until I know you're home.*" He smiled at her, a little bewildered by her sudden change of expression. "Who's voice would give you that command?" He asked.

"My mum." She whispered. "Actually, she used to say that."

"Exactly." Martin replied. "We associate a relevant subject, with a relevant voice." He smiled at her. "You clearly feel protected by Brandon, so I suppose it's natural that his voice would be relevant in a situation where you perceived imminent danger."

"You're good." She said, momentarily avoiding eye contact.

"I'm human." He replied, smiling broadly. "We all think we're crazy sometimes, Julianne." He picked up his pen and readied it for use. "Don't be so hard on yourself."

"Thank you." She whispered.

"Does your mum still say that?" He asked, paying no attention to the forced coughs coming from the other side of the room.

"My Mum is dead." She replied. "She died four years ago."

"I'm…" He paused to look at her, before shooting a questionable stare at Vincelli. "I'm really so very sorry." He whispered. "I had no -"

"It's ok." She said, meeting his gaze. "I've made my peace with it now." She added. "I have my Dad, and Tyler has Mum."

At the risk of offending her with his ignorance, he floated his following question within his mind for several seconds, before deciding it was probably more offensive *not* to express an interest in the information she had clearly volunteered.

"Tyler?" He asked, apologising with his eyes. "Is he a close relative, Julianne?"

"You could say that." She replied. "He's my twin."

"You're a twin?" He asked.

"Yes." She nodded. "He died at birth, but he lives on within me." Tears escaped little by little. "He lives inside here," She tapped her hand over her heart. "He'll always be with me, that kind of connection *never* dies."

"That's *truly* inspiring, Julianne." He whispered. "Please accept my sincere apologies all the same."

"You're off the hook."

"So," He whispered. "You shouted out that you were scared, what took place then?"

"Well," She replied, consulting the bowels of her memory. "The voice told me that Mark had realised that I'd gone, and that I'd better move faster."

"Mmm - Hmm."

"I was struggling with my keys," She said. "I couldn't find the key for the car door, even though there are only five keys in the bunch." She laughed as she noticed Martin smiling.

"Then I heard him shout something like, 'Don't you fucking leave me, you're gonna keep me alive.'"

"What do you suppose he meant by that?"

"I wouldn't like to think about that," She answered, shaking her head a little. "But I managed to open the door and jump in just as he appeared in the doorway. The wind snatched the door from me and ripped it open with such force, I remember thinking it's gonna fall off…he'd have got me for sure then, if I couldn't open the door in a hurry, then I certainly wasn't going to find the ignition in a hurry, and under such pressure."

"I agree." He whispered, glancing from his notes to her.

"He began banging on my window." She whispered. "*Really* banging it. He was shouting for me to open the door, all the while I'm trying to get the damn key in the ignition."

"What was he saying at this point?"

"Nothing." She replied. "I saw this look in his eye…it was just pure, undiluted…rage."

"What was he doing?"

"He took a couple of steps back," She whispered, once again beginning to tremble. "Then he came running at kitty with such force -"

"Kitty?"

"My Kia," She answered. "I call her *Kitty*."

"Ok." He nodded.

"He came running with such force," She said. "I knew something terrible was about to happen." She raised her trembling hands to her mouth. "He kicked my window so hard…it's just a miracle it didn't smash."

Martin shook his head in disbelief. "It's ok." He whispered, leaning in to her a little.

"Then he did it again." She cried. "Only this time it smashed, but luckily I'd got the engine started by then."

"What did you do, Julianne?" He asked.

"I put it into reverse and got the fuck out of there." She replied, wiping at her tears.

Martin stroked gently at her arm, before pulling a tissue from the inner pocket of his jacket.

"Take this." He said, waving it beneath her bowed head. "Take a break."

"No," She said, taking the tissue. "I backed down the driveway, his leg was still inside my car until he pulled it free." She wiped her eyes and sighed. "Sorry."

"Don't be." He replied. "So did you stop at any point? Or did you keep going at all costs?"

"I kept going." She answered. "I wanted to come home." She looked around the living room, clearly enjoying it's familiarity and revelling within it's security. "Why was I hearing Brandon's voice?" She asked, smearing her mascara with the tissue. "When all I wanted was my *Dad*."

"What did you do?"

"I drove." She said. "Fast! Well as fast as my little car would go anyway." She looked at the picture of her Mother and Father above the fire place.

"The engine was starting to burn up," She went on. "I was pleading with her, *please don't let me down, baby…keep going.* I made it to the Washburn, and of course I was aware I was approaching the spot where Brandon had died…and Chad."

"How did that make you feel?"

"I wasn't too bothered, to be honest." She replied. "I was preoccupied with saving my *own* life at that point."

"So what happened, Julianne?" He asked. "How did you come to be parked behind the trees and stuff, right at that spot."

"The candles." She answered. "They were burning brightly, it was an *obvious* summons from Brandon…or Chad. I'm actually not sure at that point if it was Brandon or Chad, beckoning me in."

"Why do you say that?" He asked, intrigued at her sudden break from habit. "Why the sudden confusion?"

"Because…" She paused as she thought it through. "Chad was a gentle soul, he was the pacifist if you will…a diplomat." She nodded to herself. "He was more interested in prevention, rather than cure…

he wouldn't be interested in fighting, he would want to be the one guiding me to safety, he would want to stay with me while *they* - I mean…while Brandon dealt with them."

"Them?"

"Yes." She answered. "As in, whoever he was targeting at the time. In this case…Mark."

"Ok." He smiled at her. "Tell me about that."

"I was mesmerised by the candles." She said. "They were beautiful. It was only as I got much closer that I realised they were arranged in some kind of makeshift trail." She looked into Martin's eyes. "I was told to follow them," She whispered. "The voice said, 'Follow the candles, Julianne. Follow them now.'" She shrugged. "At first I was hesitant."

"Naturally."

"But," She added. "Once he told me that Mark was coming, I quickly changed my mind."

"Why?"

"He told me to conceal my car behind the tree line." She replied. "I trusted in his judgement."

"Brandon?" Martin asked. "Or Chad?"

"Neither one of them would place me in danger." She said, smiling fondly. "Brandon has been talking to me the longest, but in this instance…I feel it was Chad."

"Can I ask you something?" He tapped his pen lightly against the book. "How long has Brandon been *talking* to you?"

"Since his death," She replied. "And *ever* since."

"And what does he say?"

"He confides in me." She answered. "And I'm a *reliable* confidant."

"I understand." He whispered. "Please continue."

"They were taking me off the road," She said. "Because to stay on the Washburn Link road in *my* car, would've left me a sitting duck. He'd have caught me with ease on such a long stretch of road, then that awful truck would've claimed two vehicles."

"So you took the advice of a voice?" He asked. "I don't mean that to sound condescending," He added quickly. "But the fact remains, it was a voice that led you to the edge of a steep embankment…in total darkness."

"The *candles* led me." She said, correcting him. "There was no question of risk."

"What then?"

"Then?" She asked. "Then I drove the car behind the trees." She clasped her hands together on her lap. "The voice…" She paused to return a smile to Martin. "Sorry," She went on. "Chad's voice…"

"Ok." Martin replied, smiling still and jotting it down.

"…Told me to turn off the engine," She continued. "*And* the headlights…and even to take my foot off the brake pedal." She sat silently for a moment and considered her words. "You know something?" She asked, staring Martin in the eye. "Of all the things that my…*voices* told me, that was the one thing that proves to me, that it wasn't my thoughts taking on a voice. It was a voice taking on my thoughts."

"Explain please?" Martin whispered.

"I would've *never* have thought to take my foot of the brake pedal." She said. "The opposite would've been true. It would've been my first instinct to sit there, pressing the brake firmly." She smiled as she shook her head. "*He* told me that."

"Ok." He said, almost relieved to be approaching the conclusion. "So now you're sat within these *arranged* candles, did you alight your vehicle to extinguish them?"

"No." She replied. "I was also told not to get out of my car."

"Right, right…" He said. "The courtesy light would illuminate." He sighed. "So who extinguished the candles?" He asked.

"They blew out all by themselves." She replied.

"They were in upturned jars?"

"I don't know what to tell you." She shrugged. "They blew out the minute I was parked."

"And then what?"

"Well," She began. "I could hear an approaching engine…I knew it was something big by the sound of it. I thought it was an eighteen wheeler at first, but it was approaching way too fast…it was getting so much louder with every passing second."

"But you didn't *see* it?" He asked. "You just sat listening?"

"That's right." She said, clasping the pendant once again. "It thundered past me so fast," She whispered. "I watched the trees sway from the suction it created, it was like an express train passing through a station…you don't wanna be on the edge of the platform, right?"

Martin nodded.

"I listened as it carried on up the Washburn," She said. "And then it all fell silent as it disappeared into the night…although Chad's voice was adamant, '*Do not get out of…or attempt to move the car.*'"

"You heard that?" He asked.

"Clearly." She whispered. "I was terrified, I was crying…but I was safe…I was protected, I knew that."

"Well what we also know," Martin said. "Is that something or *someone*, convinced him to turn that truck around." He looked her deep in the eyes. "Do you know *what* that *something*, was?" He asked. "Or for that matter, *who* that *someone* was?"

"It was Brandon." She replied. "Without a shadow of a doubt." She looked again at the magazines beneath the coffee table. "You really don't seem to get it," She whispered. "He's back for blood, Detective. He's got them all…one by one, and whoever remains of his killers had better be prepared for him. Their day of reckoning is near, and he's an indestructible force to behold…believe me." She laughed. "He's like a bolt of lightening…but you can't harness lightening, it has a will all of it's own…and it *does* strike twice, but you don't need me to tell you that." She paused. "When I heard that truck approaching…I knew *he* was present…I felt him, it was unmistakable."

"Did you see anything of what happened next?" He asked.

"No." She replied. "I heard all I needed to hear."

"Like?"

"I heard it smash into that barrier." She whispered. "I heard crunching steel as it convulsed and contorted." She smiled and met Martin's curious stares. "I heard him…I heard *them*, laughing."

"You did?" He asked. "What did you hear, Julianne? Please be as concise as possible."

"I heard laughing." She whispered. "Frantic laughing, adrenaline fuelled and toxic." She rubbed at her arms as if cold. "It was mesmerising."

"Would *them*…be Brandon and Chad, by any chance?"

She nodded.

Flipping his notebook closed he raised wearily to his feet, he was unable to suppress the sigh that escaped as he did so. He noticed a picture of Julianne and Chad, it was in a small gold frame on the left hand side of the mantle piece. They were smiling and had their faces pressed together for the camera. He found himself wondering how *that* girl, so vibrant and young, could descend into the girl beside him.

"You think I'm crazy." She whispered. "I'm not crazy."

"I don't think that." He said, although somewhat disingenuously. "It's not a ghost we're hunting, Julianne." He looked down to see her kissing the pendant. "I just wish you could see that." He smiled and walked for the door, watching as Vincelli followed him.

"But the mere fact you're still *hunting*," She whispered. "Is enough."

"Why?" He asked, opening the door.

"*Because* you're *still* hunting."

"I can't promise you *wont* be required," Vincelli said, passing slowly by her. "But I don't believe we'll be seeing each other anytime soon." He walked through the door to see Martin stood waiting in the hallway.

"Thanks for your time." He shouted back to her, pointing at Martin to open the door.

"Wait!" She shouted, running out to join them in the hallway. "You didn't ask me again?"

"Ask you what?" Vincelli asked.

"I said…*ask me again*." She stood with her arms folded against herself.

"Ok." He said, deciding to play along. "How did that make you feel?"

"How did it make me feel?" She asked. "I felt there was no remaining *doubt*."

"About what?" Vincelli asked.

"That there *is* a god," She replied. "And that he presides over us." She smiled sweetly at Vincelli. "No one can speculate how he selects his angels," She added. "But select them he *does*, and in this case it was Brandon…soon to be followed by Chad, plucked from this mortal coil only to be returned from whence they sprung."

"Julianne," Martin whispered. "We understand that you're -"

"An angel of death is within our midst, Detective." She said forcefully, surprising Martin a little. "You can't handcuff a shadow," She said, laughing at them both. "And you can't detain a force of nature within four walls." She shook her head. "My dear, *Detectives*… you *still* don't understand."

"Understand what?" Martin asked. "What don't we get?"

"There is work to be done in this town," She whispered. "*You* failed. It's gods work now." She paused and glanced slowly at them both. "His *angels* are coming."

"How do you know that?" He asked. "How can you *possibly* know that, Julianne?"

"Because I *know*." She replied. "Like I said, I'm a good confidant." She smiled at Vincelli whilst gripping the pendant tightly. "They'll be back soon, Detective." She reached out her hand to him to bid him farewell, whilst clutching her pendant tightly.

"Good bye." Vincelli whispered, taking her hand and loosely shaking it.

"I'm afraid it is." She replied, maintaining unbroken eye contact for just a moment.

Both Martin and Vincelli stepped out into the bright sunshine and walked down the short drive way.

"People waste their whole lives deciding." She shouted. "Salvation or death. I wonder, into whose eyes will you stare, now that the choice has been made for you." She laughed. "Prey for salvation!" She shouted after them. "As the alternative holds little attraction."

"She's fucking insane." Vincelli whispered, listening as the door was pushed closed.

"It would appear so." Martin agreed. "At first I thought it was you, but she's been through a lot…it was bound to take its toll."

"Yeah," He answered. "In her case, it's manifested itself as fucking lunacy." He laughed. "She's like some fucking voodoo priestess or something," He added. "The way she clutches that pendant…it's like she's summoning a fucking…" He paused, although his inner voice wouldn't be silenced. …*Spirit*.

"What?" Martin asked. He stared at Vincelli over the roof of the vehicle, before Julianne caught his eye in the living room window.

"Nothing." He answered, staring back at her car. "But I've seen that car," He went on. "I've *definitely* seen that car."

"You have?"

"Yeah." He opened the door but couldn't take his eyes off that little red Kia. "*Somewhere.*"

Chapter Fourteen

<u>Wednesday 2nd June.</u>

"George, why are you still awake?" Vanessa asked, glaring sternly at the alarm clock's digital display beside her, which informed her it was twelve - forty - seven. Her voice was strained and weak, but most of all she was tired…tired of her Husbands inability to sleep.

A busy man with the weight of the world resting firmly on his broad shoulders, George Scott possessed the need, where possible at least, to please everyone. And when that wasn't possible, very little sleep would be enjoyed by either one of them. If twenty - eight years of marriage had taught her anything, it was to make up the spare bed when he started coming home later than usual.

"Because," He snapped. "I haven't fallen asleep yet!" He turned over and gazed at her, he stroked her long blonde hair, which unusually for her, was left loose rather than tied back. She was prone although her face was turned away from him.

"Funny." She whispered, still half asleep but nonetheless sensing his need to offload on her. "Then *why* haven't you fallen asleep?"

"I can't." He said. "Not even close."

She reached across to the lamp on her bedside table, and winced as she switched it on. Her eyes stung for a moment which did little to suppress her worsening mood. Dragging her slim frame to a sitting position beside him, she couldn't help but wish she'd opted for the spare room.

"Do you want a drink?" She asked. "Since we're both awake now." She popped the top two buttons on her pink pyjama top, before glancing at the bedroom window. She was disappointed to note that it was *already* open.

"No."

"Do you want to talk?" She asked.

He lay silent and stared at her.

"I hope you're not expecting anything else," She whispered. "Captain or not." She smiled although they both knew she was quite serious.

"No." He said, returning her smile. "My mind may be in overdrive, but my body is on shutdown."

Now that her eyes had adjusted quite successfully to the light, she looked at him with moderate pleasure. His silk pyjamas were crisp to the touch as she stroked her hand across his chest, and his hair, as ever was combed neatly to one side.

"Ok." She said. "Well now that I'm *fully* awake, would you like to tell me what's on your mind?"

"Ray Kennedy." He replied, staring at a crack in the ceiling above them. "He's on my mind."

"For a minute there I thought you had another woman," She said, laying down once more and cuddling up to him. "But no such luck." She added, although this time her tone conveyed no truth.

"What *about* Ray?" She asked.

"It's about four and a half years since his wife was killed." He said. "That's quite a long time under any circumstances." He added. "So why act out now?"

"I remember." She answered. "She was hit and killed by that patrol car, right?"

"Yes."

"Nancy, wasn't it?"

"Wasn't *she*." He corrected.

"You know what I meant." She resisted his invitation to flare. "I recall they'd only just moved here. She seemed nice."

"Nancy." He whispered. "Nancy, Nancy, Nancy."

"It may be four years to you, George," She said. "But to Ray, it's probably closer to ten what with the state he's obviously been in."

"I feel responsible." He said.

"We are all responsible for our *own* actions." She whispered. "Not those of others."

"We are." He agreed. "Maybe that's *why* I feel so responsible for him."

257

"What does that mean?"

"Ray accepted that it was pure chance that placed Nancy in the path of that cruiser." He sighed as he gazed skyward. "She wasn't targeted in any way, just in the wrong place at the wrong time."

"Is there a *but* ?" She asked. "Has something changed?"

"He doesn't believe it anymore." He replied. "He's fighting himself and everyone around him…it's like he knows something more of what happened that day."

"Something *more*?" She asked. "Is there something more he *should* know?"

He shook his head slowly, although Vanessa knew it wasn't denial he was expressing, it was regret.

"Do you know something?" She asked, pushing him.

"I know a lot." He replied, his voice was hoarse. "Maybe a coffee would be nice after all."

"Forget the coffee, George." She said. "What do you know?"

"That cruiser wasn't answering a call." He said. "It was speeding recklessly with no good reason." He sat up in bed and glanced around their pine furnished bedroom. "Some kids gave statements saying the car didn't have it's siren on, and that it's lights weren't flashing… as they put it." He smiled. "I dismissed their statements outright." He added. "Some witnesses, not of a tender age, would say the car had been travelling in excess of seventy miles per hour, with a little gentle persuasion they were left doubting their ability to determine it's velocity." He smiled. "Accident investigators estimated a similar speed according to Nancy's injuries." He sighed. "I argued that her injuries would've occurred similarly at fifty miles per hour, and that's what I brought them down to…since I'm a close personal friend of the lead investigator who was on the scene."

"Why?" She asked. "Why would you do that?" She sighed and sat up beside him. "I'm not judging you before you think that, I just don't understand." She ran her hand through his silver hair.

"Majority rules." He answered. "I'd only recently been posted, I couldn't be seen as the guy who ignored the testimony of three respected Officers, in favour of some kids and a couple of men, who couldn't tell me what had happened without calling me *dude* every few seconds. I had to make it go away, or at least present a strong enough case so that a board of enquiry would make it go away."

"You really shouldn't have done that." She said.

"Nothing would've brought Nancy back." He replied. "She'd still be dead."

"It needs to stay under the carpet." She whispered. "Coming clean wont bring her back, it'll destroy more lives…ours included." She kissed him gently on the cheek. "It's still no reason for Ray to kill." She added. "You're not responsible."

"And…" He whispered, pausing to look at her. "I fear, neither is Ray."

"I don't want to ask, George." She said.

"I'm no longer sure we've got the right man." He said, regardless. "My instincts are telling me he's not responsible."

"I think you're instincts are wrong." She replied. "You're letting this *other* problem cloud your judgement."

"I'm afraid not." He whispered. "I *do* believe he knows who the real murderer is, but I no longer support the theory that it's him. Of course, I've not revealed this to anyone…yet."

"Why?" She asked. "Why now?"

"The car crash on the bridge?" He asked. "Last week?"

"Yes?"

"We found a samurai sword in the back of that truck." He coughed nervously. "It had been stabbed straight through the guy's lung."

"Oh my god." She said. "But I thought –"

"Ray isn't our man." He spun himself out of bed and sat with his back to her. "The *theory* is that this was Ray's accomplice," He went on. "Or worse still, a copycat."

"I read about that in the local paper," She said. "And there was no mention of a samurai sword, it said there were lacerations about his neck, consistent with being *stabbed*. Why wasn't the sword mentioned?"

"Are you kidding?" He asked, laughing. "The panic would be immense. No one besides Vincelli saw it because it was in the rear foot well. No firemen claimed to seeing a samurai sword, once they knew he was murdered they backed away from the truck like it was still ablaze, wouldn't go near it."

"And where is it now?"

"In the evidence lock up." He replied. "In a safe place that nobody has access to." He made fists with his toes and scratched them against the carpet.

"I'm going to work." He said, raising to his feet.

"Now?" She asked. "George it's one o' clock in the morning."

"I've got do something." He whispered, unbuttoning his pyjama top. "Something Ray asked me to do." He folded the top and placed it neatly on the end of the bed.

"George," She said, walking around the bed to him. "You can't turn the clock back, you're just one man."

"So was Martin Luther King." He replied. "One man *can* make a difference, Vanessa."

"What are you going to do?" She asked. Sensing the futility of trying to stop him, she sat on his side of the bed and watched him dress.

"Do you know what Ray said to me?" He asked. "He said, that this one time he thought being a *nigger* might actually help." He laughed as she shook her head. "It's wrong, Vanessa." He whispered, pulling his customary navy blue trousers on. "It's wrong."

"It's *all* wrong." She replied. "But unless you're planning on turning back the hands of time, I fail to see what you can achieve."

"He told me to do something for him," He said, struggling for breath. "He told me to examine the recorded suicide message from that kid."

"The one who hung himself?" She asked.

"Danny." He replied. "Yes. He said I should look again."

"What for?"

"I've no fucking idea." He whispered. "Thought he was talking crazy at the time, to be honest. Now I'm not so sure."

"But what can you do?" She shouted. "You're listening to a murderer, George."

"He's not convicted yet." He replied. "His trial date is set for next month." He looked at his wife sternly. "Let's hope you're not on the jury, shall we?"

"I didn't mean -"

"I know." He interrupted. "I'm sorry, I didn't mean to…well you know." He hastily tucked in his shirt and reached for his cuff links, placing them in his pocket for the time being.

"I'm worried." She said, retreating to her side of the bed. "I'm scared for you."

"There's something wrong with this town." He said, completing his Windsor knot. "Any town that will kill a man for being different..." He paused and stood motionless for a few seconds. "...it may not even be his skin colour," He went on. "It may be that he's not from around here, maybe that's enough."

"Ray hasn't been killed." She said.

"We may not have killed his body," He answered. "But we've killed his soul." He checked his reflection in the mirror, before finally removing his jacket from the stand. His finely polished brogues would be on the rack beside the front door, along with his umbrella which accompanied him all year round.

"This year..." He said, opening the bedroom door. "Halloween goes back to the kids."

Washburn Springs Divisional Headquarters.

01 : 55.

Unease washed over Scott like high tide as he sat restlessly in his office, his jacket was thrown over the hat stand, and his tie was pulled down a little with his shirt's top button open, his feet were perched awkwardly on the desk as he fiddled idly with his cell phone. A mobile television unit was sat directly opposite his desk, which contained a moderately sized television, with a small array of audio - visual equipment on a shelf beneath it. The lights were out, although the room was illuminated adequately as Danny's image beamed out to him, it was frozen in the final few frames as he had reached across to terminate his recording.

"Nothing can stop what they'll do now." Scott whispered, electing to write it down on a sheet of headed paper before him.

"Prophetic words, Daniel." He said. "But what in God's name are you talking about?" He asked, tapping his pen on the desk. "You sound like you're referring to the twins," He said, staring into Danny's eyes. "But how *could* you be? Brandon was already dead at the time you recorded this, and Chad wasn't too far behind him."

He sighed. "So who are *they*?" He rubbed at his eyes and looked at the clock above his door. "What are you doing here, George?" He asked himself. "It's almost two in the morning." He shook his head. "You've become *that* guy." He muttered.

His concentration was momentarily broken by a disturbance at the front desk, which was directly beneath the hallway that his office occupied. He did his best to block out the commotion, but couldn't help listening as several officers negotiated with the individual, and attempted to calm him down.

"Looks like the ghouls are out tonight." He whispered to himself, pointing the remote control at the screen and rewinding it.

"Ray," He said. "What am I supposed to be getting out of this?" He listened intently as the shouting downstairs subsided, and began the cassette rolling once more.

"I've listened until I'm blue in the face," He said, turning the volume up a little and stepping out from behind his desk. With Danny's voice resonating behind him, he walked calmly and gently around his small dark office. The shouting from beneath his feet once again flared up without warning, compelling him to lower the volume and head for the door. He opened it fully and stepped out into the hallway, listening carefully as the shouting became *screaming*.

"You've made a big fucking mistake!" The voice screamed, it was trembling and out of control, high pitched and youthful but definitely male.

"He's out there!" He shouted. "You've got the wrong guy!" The screaming stopped as suddenly as it had started, but was replaced by the distinctive sound of rubber souls being driven hard into the tile floor, accompanied by muffled requests for calm.

"I've seen his fucking eyes!" He screamed again. "I've seen them - they're dead, you hear me? Dead."

"Just calm do -"

"Get your fucking hands off me!"

Once again, the screaming ceased without warning, the situation may have quietened down, but Scott's nerves hadn't. He returned cautiously to his chair having left the office door open.

If they want me, He thought. *They'll come and get me.*

He returned his gaze to Danny, although his attention remained with the precarious calm downstairs.

"I'm not afraid to die!" The voice screamed. "I'll fucking do it!"

Pausing the cassette once more, although unaware it was again in the final few frames, he jumped from his chair and ran for the door, he stood breathless in the hallway and listened with growing concern.

He's too close, He thought. *He's breached the front desk.*

"I'm not afraid to die!" He screamed again. "I'm dead anyway. I've seen him."

More alarming for Scott, was the serious lack of response from the officers attempting to appease him. He listened carefully as once again he heard rubber souls screeching on the tiles, not multiple pairs as before, but singular. And not scuffling, but *running*. He walked towards the stairs at the end of the hallway, and reached the adjoining security door just as it was flung open.

"Sir!" The woman shouted, clearly out of breath from the ongoing altercation. "We've got a serious problem at the desk." Her chest heaved up and down as she clung to the door for support.

"Well, what is it?" He asked, observing her blushes. "Lisa, what's wrong?" His concern turned rapidly to anger as he watched her hand slide down her torn uniform to her waistline, more specifically to her vacant side arm holster.

"Where is your revolver?" He asked, with no intention of awaiting her reply. "Do not tell me what I think you're about to tell me."

"He's gone crazy!" She shouted, pointing over her shoulder. "He just came in begging to be locked up!" She wiped at her tears. "He said he's gonna be murdered soon."

"Your revolver, Lisa?"

"He snatched it as we were scuffling, Sir." She cried. "He jumped over the desk and pinned me against the wall…"

"…And what?" He shouted, pressing her.

"When the others came running through to apprehend him, they struggled with him but he broke free and snatched it. He's holding it to his head, he's threatening to kill *himself*, not us."

"And that's better how?" He asked. He glanced through the toughened glass but couldn't see or hear anything down stairs. He opened it slowly and waved for Lisa to shadow him.

"Can you even imagine how this will look?" He asked quietly. "A kid kills himself in our lobby, with one of *our* revolvers."

"I'm sorry, Sir." She whispered.

"How many Officers are with him?"

"Five, Sir." She answered. "Five or six."

"Did they manage to keep hold of *their* weapons?"

"*Yes*, Sir." Her anger was crudely concealed beneath her embarrassment.

"If these fuckers wanna kill themselves," He whispered, edging slowly down the concrete staircase. "Then that's their choice. What we *don't* do, is give them our sidearm to do it *with*."

"Do you think I meant for this?" She asked.

"Later," He whispered, focused only on the steps ahead of him. "I'll probably apologise, but only if we can mediate this situation successfully."

"I tried." She whispered. "I really tried to fight him off."

"Is the perimeter covered?" He asked. "Last thing we want is someone walking in off the street and scaring him…itchy trigger finger and who knows what could happen."

"It is now," She replied. "Two were coming in as it kicked off, they're standing by."

"Ok."

"Sir, I don't think you should go out there." She whispered. She held her hands against the wall as she treaded lightly down the stairs behind him. "He's dangerous."

"I'm not going out there." He replied. "At least not yet, I want to see who it is first and then we'll take it one step it a time."

They both stood silently and hidden from view behind the primary security door, a second security door was a little further along the passage, that one led to the rear of the front desk, this one was adjacent to the lobby itself. With a large reinforced glass panel, Scott peered from behind the wall and through the glass, he was not encouraged to reveal himself further at the sight of a distraught teenager, with a Police issue revolver wedged between his teeth.

"Shoot me!" He shouted. "Save me the job!"

"No one…is gonna shoot you." A voice replied. "Just lower the weapon."

"Come on, kid." Another pleaded. "Lower the gun."

"What then?" He asked, mocking them. "I've seen this bullshit before…you'll go fucking crazy with your night sticks." He laughed. "You'll talk me down, right? Just like your conflict training taught you, and them boom! You'll have me twisted up on the fucking floor while you all high - five each other, then laugh about me over beers."

"No."

"Yes!" He shouted. "I'll get your fucking attention if it *kills* me you mother fuckers, don't pretend you care…you just don't need the resultant fallout this'll cause. I've seen those smiles *before*."

"This is all my fault," Lisa said, whimpering continuously. "I'm really sorry."

Not once losing sight of the distressed youth through the glass, Scott waved back at her, either gesturing for her silence or to retreat a little towards the stairs, she wasn't sure which.

"It's Jet." He whispered.

"Jet?"

He nodded. "James Edward Turner." He said, leaning in from view and resting against the wall. "Also known as Jet. Also known as the younger sibling of Thomas Turner…who you may or may not recall, was murdered whilst riding the Waltzers." He peered through the glass once again to ascertain Jet's positioning within the lobby, before hiding once more.

"Oh Jesus…" She whispered. "So when he said he'd seen *his* eyes…he'd literally seen his eyes."

"He's the only one to have seen him in action," He whispered. "And lived to tell the tale."

She shook her head at Scott's words whilst fastening the lower two buttons on her blouse.

"I think he was trying to kill me." She said, tucking it into her trousers. "I thought he was going to shoot me, I really did."

"Well that's all well and good." He replied sharply. "I doubt very much his intention was to kill you, he's screaming out for help… quite literally." He fastened his top button and slid his Windsor knot into place. "You say you're sorry, Lisa," He went on. "But let me tell you this…if that young man blows the back of his head off in *my* lobby, with *your* gun, we'll all be sorry." He quickly produced his silver cufflinks from his trouser pockets, and fed them quickly through his cuffs.

"I know." She whispered, avoiding his intense glare.

"I suggest you go and wait this out in my office." He said. "Are we understanding each other?" He held her stare for just a moment. "Today…any bang you hear now, *wont* be a starters pistol." He dismissed her harshly before returning his attention to the glass panel. He listened as the security door upstairs closed behind her, the magnetic click upon contact satisfied his concern that she was now safe from potential harm, with that in mind he readied himself, and reached for the handle.

"Jet," He said, whilst opening the door. "No one's gonna hurt you." He watched in horror as Jet spun around to face him. He held his hands in the air as he allowed the door to slam shut behind him. "At this stage I promise, there'll be no trouble for you…just let me help you." He was thankful that the only knee jerk reaction from Jet, had been to rear up against the wall opposite him.

Scott walked slowly into the middle of the lobby and lowered his hands to his waist, performing a graceful pirouette for Jet's benefit, as he did so.

"I'm not armed, Jet." He whispered. "Please, I implore you to trust me."

"Why?" He asked, circling away towards the main entrance. "Why should I trust you?" He wore fashionably ripped jeans and a baggy red T - shirt. He settled against the notice board and eyed Scott with suspicion, all the while maintaining a firm grip on the firearm, with both his hands and his teeth.

"Put your weapons down." Scott whispered, turning his attention to the five officers present. "Just relax," He added. "*Everybody* relax." He watched nervously as they lowered their weapons as he'd ordered, he registered a cordial response too, from Jet. His thin arms lowered slightly at the sight of them disengaging, although this only meant *his* weapon was fixed at a steeper gradient into his mouth.

"Jet," He whispered. "I don't want you pulling that trigger."

"Why?" He asked. "You don't give a fuck about me." He laughed nervously. "A couple of months back, you thought I'd killed my fucking brother. Oh, I'm sorry…I was helping you with your enquiries, right?"

"We had to find out what had happened, Jet."

"You didn't believe me, though." He answered. "I could tell by the way that fat fuck was looking at me." He laughed as he stared at the officers behind Scott. "*Detective* Vincelli!" He said. "Vincelli couldn't find his own cock."

"I know you didn't kill your brother," Scott whispered passionately.

"*You* killed my brother!" He said, fighting his tears. "I loved my brother." He stared at Scott. "You could've saved my brother…you could…you could've saved him."

"How?"

"You could've cleaned up your corrupt Police force for starters," He answered. "Or caught whoever was supplying the drugs that fucked his mind up." He laughed as tears rolled down his face.

"Nothing I can do or say, will bring your brother back." He said. "It's you I'm interested in." He paused. "I can save *you*, Jet…let me."

"You can't save me." He whispered. "But if you want to help me, then catch my brother's killer."

"We have him in custody." He answered. "Have done for weeks now."

"You think that's the guy?" He asked. "You think you have the right guy?"

"It's him."

"He's a fucking nigger!" He shouted. "I've seen this guy, remember? He's as white as rough tide with long black hair." He shook his head. "How can you lay this at the nigger's door?"

"This is getting us no –"

"And his eyes!" He shouted, his voice trembling. "Those eyes are dead! Other worldly, no emotion just…rage"

"Then why hasn't he struck since?" He asked. A feeling of moderate guilt swept through him as he held Jet's stare evenly. He hoped his eyes wouldn't convey the *secret*, currently under lock and key in the evidence stores.

When did I become a part of the propaganda machine? He wondered. *For all intents and purposes…he has struck again.*

"He will!" Jet shouted. "I don't know where but I know he's coming back within hours, and pretty soon you'll know that too… but you'll also have more bodies."

"And do you think you'll be one of them?"

"I know I will."

"How do you know that?" Scott asked, sighing despairingly.

"He's been haunting my fucking dreams," He replied. "Ever since that night…I see his face whenever the lights go out."

"I need you to listen to me." Scott whispered, holding out his arms to Jet he projected the illusion of calm. "After what you witnessed, it's only natural you're going to have nightmares. A grown man would be traumatised, let alone a seventeen year old kid."

"I'm not a kid." He replied. "I'm eighteen now."

"Ok." Scott nodded. "The *man* you saw that night, *is* in custody." He smiled, "He was a cleverly crafted illusion…*he* doesn't exist. It was a *man*, and he can't hurt you anymore."

Jet stared around the lobby at the gathered officers, they stood looking at him with Scott at the helm. He fought his tears but couldn't prevent them, as he bit down hard on the weapon and steadied his grip with his thumb on the trigger.

"His *name*," He whispered. "Is Brandon."

A chill ran through Scott's spine as he uttered those words, he realised his hands were trembling. Having decided against placing his hands in his pockets, he folded his arms.

"Brandon?" He asked, trying his best to appear nonchalant. "Are you sure you heard correctly?"

"Yes, I'm sure." He replied. "Tommy said it was Brandon, both Jake and me heard it quite clearly. Jake would tell you the same thing, except Jake is dead."

"Did Jake *know* it was Brandon?"

"Oh yeah." He replied. "I couldn't see him coz I was stuck in that fucking carriage, but I heard his reaction when he smashed the glass in the booth. He *knew* it was Brandon he was looking at."

"What did he say?"

"I watched them bury you!" He replied. "That's what he said." He laughed to himself. "No one fucked with Jake, and I mean no one."

He glanced around the room at the various faces, they were all silent as he spoke. "Whoever was in that booth," He went on. "Scared Jake on sight, the fight went from his body when he finally laid eyes on whoever was in there. He told Jake to run, run like hell in fact...and that's just what he did."

"I'm sorry, Jet."

"But something Tommy said stuck with me," He said. "Right before his breath expired, he whispered to Jake that Danny was right, I never knew what that meant."

"Danny was right?"

"Yeah." He smiled. "It's funny, but the second I mentioned the name Brandon, you folded your arms." He laughed. "Defensive aren't we?"

He didn't know how to counter Jet's testimony of events that night, he couldn't claim to dismiss his version of events because as he knew full well, Jet had watched his brother die at the hands of a man he now suspected, was still at large, and after all. *He was there*, He thought. *And I was not.*

"Suppose we have the wrong man," He whispered. "Why do you believe he wants you dead?" He asked.

"Because I can identify him," He answered. "I've seen him."

"He'd have taken your life along with your brother's." He said. "I realise that sounds harsh, but the fact remains...he let you live."

"He's gonna kill me." He whispered, staring in to Scott's eyes. "It's my time, so I'll do it my way...not his."

"No!" Scott shouted. He lunged wildly at Jet as time took on an entirely new concept, a lifetime elapsed in the moments it took to reach him, but not Jet's, his own.

Click.

The room fell silent as each man stared in disbelief at Jet, a young man still not old enough to drink legally, and yet something had convinced him to attempt to end his life. Stranger still, the revolver had misfired.

Click.
Click.
Click.

His eyes opened wide with desperation and panic as Scott wrenched the weapon from his hands. He cried openly as he knew his bid was over, falling back against the wall he slid down it like a falling picture. He sat motionless, awaiting what he assumed would surely transpire, but nobody moved, and no body spoke. Jet ran his hands through his black hair as he bowed his head between his legs.

"Why would you do that?" Scott asked, pulling the magazine from within the grip. He shook his head in amazement as he saw it was indeed fully *loaded*. He released the chamber to see the initial shot had jammed, therefore jamming all subsequent attempts.

"I'd say that's a clear message," He whispered, kneeling down next to Jet and stroking his arm. "That *god*, wants you alive."

"It's not god I'm afraid of." He replied, raising his head to look at Scott. "It's him."

"Life is precious, young man." He whispered. "Never give up on life." He stroked Jet's hair but quickly pulled his hand free, when he realised just how greasy it was. He examined the oily residue left on his palm, and smiled to Jet.

"I don't wanna die like Tommy did." He whispered. "I don't wanna die full stop, but if I gotta go I'd like it to be on my own terms."

"And it shall be." Scott replied. "But it wont be today, or tomorrow…or the day after that. You're seven…" He stopped himself. "You're *eighteen*."

"I don't know who to trust anymore." He whispered, staring past Scott at the officers behind him.

"Well you came to the right place." He replied.

"I've been brought up to hate the police." He whispered.

"Why?"

"Well maybe that's how your parents want you to feel." He answered. "But like I said, we each have a choice, everyone…your parents included."

"I wouldn't have hurt that woman." He said. "I just wanted her gun…I wouldn't have hurt her."

"I know." He said.

"So what happens now?" He asked, peering nervously around.

"Well, that depends." He said, standing up. "Where are your parents now?" He reached for Jet's hand and pulled him to his feet.

"Out of town." He replied. "They've gone away and left me on me own for a week."

Scott nodded and leaned in close to Jet's ear. "She said you wanted locking up," He whispered. "Is that still the case?"

He nodded.

"Well in that case, I can smell alcohol on your breath." He said, beckoning one of the officers over to them both. "And since you're still a minor, I don't see that I have a choice but to let you sleep it off for the night…in one of our cells." He smiled reassuringly at Jet.

"I have an obligation to protect you," He said. "And now that you're in my care…I swear to god I wont let anything happen to you."

"Thank you."

"When did you last eat?"

"Dunno," He replied. "Yesterday sometime."

"Well come on," He said, ushering Jet to the front desk. "Let's get you processed before you…*throw up* or something."

Jet smiled nervously as the other officers greeted him warmly, Scott watched as a couple of them led Jet through to the holding area and out of view.

"Nobody speaks of this." Scott said.

"Sir," They replied collectively.

"You get the picture on this?" He asked, addressing the custody officer directly.

"Yes, Sir."

"This mustn't get out." Scott whispered. "We'll *all* be sorry if it does."

"It didn't happen." He said "We'll place the kid on suicide watch." He leaned on the desk and offered Scott his fullest attention. Being a short man of stocky build, he was quickly nicknamed *The Bull*, thanks in part to his prowess with unruly prisoners, incompliant quickly became compliant. His Latino looks earned him his second nickname of *El Matador*. He accepted each with a sense of pride.

"Can you believe that?" Scott asked, handling the gun cautiously. "Talk about fate."

"It's pretty weird, Sir." He replied.

"That's not what I'd call it." He said. He glanced again at the weapon as he walked back to the security door. No less mystified now than before as to it's failure to activate, he couldn't help but wonder were he to have placed the weapon in his mouth, would it still have misfired like that, either way he didn't like his chances.

"Do *not* take your eyes off that young man," He said, typing in the access code and pulling it open. "If anything happens to him I promise you…heads will roll."

He walked slowly up the stairs and encountered the secondary security door, Lisa was stood behind it. She was leaning against the wall with her arms folded, she hadn't seen him arrive but jumped from her daydream when she heard him enter the code.

"Maybe that would explain how he got your gun." He said flatly, passing her by without a second look. "My office, right now."

She duly followed him and said nothing, listening instead to his footsteps on the tiles, she thought his shoes fitting of a ballroom dancer as opposed to ranking officer.

"You're a very lucky woman." He said, turning on the light and closing the door behind her. "Your gun misfired." He walked to his desk and placed the weapon upon it.

"I didn't hear it go off," She said. "I assumed he'd not pulled the trigger."

"Well he did," He said, slumping into his chair and staring into Danny's eyes. "He pulled the trigger four times to be precise."

"Again," She whispered. "I'm truly sorry."

"Luckily for you," He said, sliding the gun across the desk to her. "We're keeping this on a need to know basis." He folded his arms behind his head and leaned back in his chair.

"But the lobby is covered by C.C.T.V, Sir."

"But if nothing is said, no one will request it." He replied. "You're getting a sweetheart deal here, Lisa."

"So that's it?" She asked, more than a little relieved.

"You're ok aren't you?"
"Yes." She answered. "Just got a scare."
"Then that's it." He waved her out.

She walked slowly to his office door and paused once there, more than aware his eyes were now burning into her, she spun quickly around to face him.

"Sir," She whispered, a little unnerved by the look he was returning to her. "Can I ask something?"

"Make it quick." He replied.

She approached him and the television screen with renewed vigour, and leaned over his desk to get a square on view of the frozen image.

"While you were downstairs," She said. "I came in here as you asked and sat down. I didn't put the light on, I just sat down and found myself looking at his face," She pointed to the screen. "This is that kid that hung himself, right?"

"Danny." He replied, nodding.

"I assume this is his suicide tape?" She asked.

"Yes." He replied. "Do you have a point?"

"I think so." She said. "You know there's someone behind the camera, right?"

"Do you?" He countered, a little surprised by her observations.

"There's a reflection in that mirror." She said, pointing to the vanity mirror on the shelf behind Danny. "It's not clear, but someone is there."

He leaned forward and took a closer look, before scrambling frantically for the remote control. He pointed it at the screen and reversed the picture.

"Turn off the light," He ordered. "And close the door."

"With me on which side of it?"

"This side." He replied. "Hurry."

Maybe this is it, He thought. *Is this what you wanted me to see, Ray. I hope we've got something to help you...I really do.*

She joined him next to the television as he pressed play.

'Then of course there's the gang,' Danny's voice filled the room with unease and trepidation. 'And gangs like them, but it's you and me, and people just like you and me, who'll get caught in the crossfire.'

"I always found this bit a little strange," Scott whispered, staring at the screen intensely.

"Watch how the bulb flickers then blows out."

"Jesus," She whispered, watching Danny's image react slightly to the flickering, but react with fear to the eventual explosion before him.

"His eyes seem to peer *over* the camera." Scott whispered, pointing at him.

"Yes," She agreed. "But you're missing the highlight of the show, it's not his eyes you should be focusing on…it's the mirror."

"I'm looking at the mirror." He said, reversing it again.

"Watch closely." She said, as he played it over again. "There's no one in the mirror now, correct?"

"Correct." He answered. "Which would explain why it's never been noticed before." He watched closely as the light began flickering. "So it only appears in the last few frames?"

"Yes!" She said, pointing to the screen excitedly as the bulb blew out. "And do you know why?"

"Tell me."

"The mirror behind him, Sir." She whispered. "It…" She paused as a shiver coursed through her body. "…*Moves*." She shook her head and rubbed the Goosebumps from her forearms.

"That's not possible." He replied, hastily reversing the footage. "It can't move."

"The flickering light," She whispered. "And it's eventual blow out…it seems to be a diversion, something to distract whoever was there, from noticing the angle of the mirror had changed." She watched it happen again, before her very eyes.

"My god." He said, slumping back in his chair. "How is that even -" He paused the footage once again as Danny reached across to end his recording.

"Whoever he is," She said. "He's obviously checked he's not reflecting off anything prior to recording, but he didn't bank on the mirror changing angle!" She laughed. "That's amazing footage, Sir! Flickering lights! Moving objects, they all point at one thing."

"What's that?" Scott asked, clearly struggling with the sudden turn of events.

"An apparition." She said. "There's a presence in that room, mirror's don't just move…no way, *someone* moved that mirror at precisely the right time."

"An apparition?" Scott asked. "You mean like a -"

"Ghost." She whispered.

"There's no such…" His words trailed to nothing as he looked at Danny's frozen image. He began shaking as he realised that for the third time, he'd paused the picture on the exact frame as each time previous.

"You're not reaching out to end the recording," He whispered. "You're just *reaching out*." He felt a sudden rush of emotion as Danny's large blue eyes bored into his own.

"The question is," Lisa whispered. "Who is it? It's too grainy to determine."

"I know." Scott answered, nervously biting at his nails as he reclined backwards. He divided his attention between Lisa and Danny, as thoughts swamped him like a bursting river bank. "I *know*." He said again, ensuring Lisa understood exactly what he was saying.

"You know who that is?" She asked, watching as he nodded at the screen before him.

"What I don't understand," She went on. "Is why he's not scared as he's recording this? Surely, now that we know someone is behind the camera, he knew he was going to be murdered?"

"Unless," Scott said. "That *someone*, had assured him that he would not be harmed as long as he did what was asked." He mulled it over for a moment.

"I don't follow."

"No," He answered. "You're not meant to." He smiled. "It's all a fucking *diversion*."

"It is?"

"Yeah." He nodded, still transfixed on Danny's eyes. "As orchestrated by opposing parties. It's a mock suicide tape." He stood up and walked to his window. "We know with some degree of authority, that Danny had made himself two sets of enemies that night."

"Halloween?"

"Yes." He whispered, leaning against the cold concrete wall and looking down at the floodlit parking lot. "On one hand," He said. "We have the twins, but they were quickly removed from the equation…or so we're led to believe." He paused for a moment.

"On the other," He continued. "We have this gang that he speaks of, and we *know* he was scared of them…and realistically, they posed the clear threat to his safety." He gazed up at the night sky, although he couldn't decide if it was light he could see on the horizon, or the reflective glare from the television within the room.

"So do you think it's one of the gang?"

"No." He answered, looking again at the television, and gazing into *that* mirror. "I think it's the boss."

"Oh." She answered, raising her brows in surprise. "Why would he get his hands dirty on this one?" She asked. "He's got his underlings for that purpose."

"His underlings," He whispered. "As you put it, could certainly do the job…and quite possibly they *did*. But to pull this one off, it takes clout on his part…and trust on Danny's."

"I'm not -"

"You see," He said. "Danny would obviously have feared him enough to do as he was told…" He paused as he delved into the depths of his intellect and guile. "But Danny obviously *trusted* that he would keep his promise to him, once this tape was concocted."

"Promise?"

"In return for making a mock suicide tape," He whispered. "And disappearing for a while…" He manoeuvred around his desk and took to the floor. "I *promise* you, you will not be hurt."

"Do you think he would've believed that?" She asked. "I mean, this is the *boss*, as you put it." She rotated one of the chairs facing his desk, and lowered herself into it.

"If the trust was there," He replied, turning to face her. "Yes."

"You keep mentioning *trust*." She said, watching him walk slowly towards her.

"Trust is the key." He whispered, stopping before her. "Without trust we have nothing, you can't run a hot dog stand without trust, let alone a criminal organisation." He leaned down to her, aligning his eyes with hers. "He's one of us."

"I knew you were going to say that." She whispered, staring a little uncomfortably into his eyes. "There's preparation gone into this, he knew what he was doing."

"And *Danny*," He replied, moving away from her. "Believed everything he was told."

"Why wouldn't he?" She asked.

"Trust." He whispered, nodding at her. "Question is…where do we go from here?" He asked. "Who do I trust? I need this image enhancing to see who that is." He pointed to the screen but remained focused on Lisa. "Who else is involved?" He asked. "The very same individual I set to task on this, could be the individual in the mirror."

"I…might be able to help." She whispered. "If you want, this can be done externally?"

"Talk." He said, returning to her and sitting in the chair next to hers.

"My husband works in digital re mastering." She said. "It's his own business so he can undertake it personally, he cleans up old cine films and restores footage."

"Can he *enhance*?"

"Yes." She nodded. "He can improve the resolution. Like I said, he does old cine film…when he's finished with it, it's DVD quality material."

"We spoke of *trust*, Lisa." He said, patting his hand gently on her knee. "I trust *you*. Without you I wouldn't have this breakthrough." He smiled and walked again to his window. "How long will it take?"

"A couple of days." She replied. "This'll get priority."

"*Only* your husband is to do this." He said, staring once more to the distant horizon. "It's a sign of our times I'm afraid," He went on. "Trust *no one*."

Colorado General.

02 : 25.

The eleventh floor of Colorado General was deathly quiet, during daylight hours only a small team of specialists were allowed there, but at night…nobody came, and nobody left. Being on the hospital's top floor, room 109 was hand picked for a situation like Ray Kennedy, it was situated in the middle of the corridor with all adjoining rooms vacated and locked, meaning it's most infamous patient could be treated in total seclusion. A two man Police protection unit guarded Ray around the clock, although now his armed guards were posted at opposite ends of the dimly lit corridor, as opposed to in his room, where two unarmed escorts remained present at his bedside. With no more than a slice of moonlight on offer through the window, both men sat in darkness, by now utterly lost in their own thoughts as Ray slept. No longer physically restrained and enjoying his newfound freedom, he kicked off his sheets without warning, and lay there in just his shorts.

His eyes flickered open and were drawn skyward, from eleven in the evening until three in the morning, the secret was his to keep, that as long as the sky remained clear and they didn't pull down the blinds, he could know the time without asking. The moon was whole and he guessed it to be a little after two in the morning, judging by it's position within the concrete frame.

"Who's there?" Ray asked. He turned to see it was the old man's turn to be cuffed to him. "Did you just call me, Burt?" He asked

"No." He replied, yawning. "Maybe you were dreaming, Ray." He stretched his arms out wide as he woke himself up, laughing a little as he saw Ray's right hand travelling with him.

"Sorry, Ray." He said, quickly lowering his arms again. "I forget how close we are sometimes." Burt was almost sixty years old and looking forward to his gold watch. A short man as wide as he was tall, he was renowned for finding the softer side of any personality, multiples included, and settling them with his brand of humour.

"Someone just called me." Ray whispered. "I heard my name." He squirmed restlessly and appeared unsettled.

"Well I doubt very much if it was Marvellous Marvin." He replied, drawing Ray's attention to the skinny yet lanky *Boy Wonder*, as he liked to call him, who was stretched out between two chairs facing one another.

"I don't know how he does it on those chairs," Ray said. "But he's sleeping like a damn dog."

"Well as long as he doesn't start licking his balls," Burt replied, laughing. "I'm happy to leave him to it."

"I'm not asleep, *actually*." He said, his tone was very matter of fact. "I'm just resting my eyes."

"It fucking lives!" Burt shouted. "Look Ray!"

"Anyway," He countered. "It's Michael, not fucking Marvin. How many more times I gotta tell you that?"

"It's Marvin when you're with me," He said, nudging Ray. "Fuck face."

"Fuck you." Michael said, finally opening his eyes. "When you're as old and senile as you are, it's no fucking wonder you get confused." He laughed as Burt made faces at him. "All you do is talk about this gold watch," He went on. "You can't even tell the time! You haven't even got a clock at home, you're that old you still use a fucking moon dial!"

"You're a clever fuck aint you?" Burt said, bursting into a coughing fit. "I'll come over there and shove my boot up your fucking -"

"You should use your fucking head, you bald fuck." Michael countered..

"I'm not bald." He replied. "It's the light, actually."

"The fucking light?" He said. "We're in the dark! The moonlight is bouncing off your -"

"Ray!" Burt shouted, his voice muffled by his handkerchief. "Tell this fuck, I'm *not* bald."

"No." Ray replied, shaking his head at them both. "Don't place me in your shit."

Burt was by far the oldest man in the room, these days much to his displeasure, he was the oldest man in *most* rooms, a fact he'd learned to live with. Michael however was enjoying life at the other end of the scale, at just twenty - three he was the youngest escort on the team, standing at six feet - five inches, he was also the tallest, with a very unkempt mop of ginger hair, that he claimed to be proud of.

"I'd rather be bald than ginger," Burt whispered. "Take your clothes off, you look like a fucking match."

Rays laughing spurred him on further.

"You're that fucking skinny," He went on. "If you take your clothes off and stick your tongue out, you'll look like a fucking zip!"

Bicker as they may, Ray could see a mutual trust between them and genuine ease within each others company, mentor and protégé, or father and son, they worked well with each other.

"A fucking zip?" Michael asked. "I'll come over there and zip your fucking -"

"You just fucking bring it on ginger pubes." Burt shouted back, still coughing.

Oh please help me, Ray thought. *I don't know which is worse, getting punched in the face or listening to these two argue.*

Of course, he knew without hesitation which of the two he'd rather endure, he was rather fond of the two clowns which, he sensed, had been assigned to him quite deliberately, either in an effort to further subjugate his morale, or perhaps to raise it. Either way, he'd become well versed at tuning them out.

"Will you two," He whispered. "*Please…*be quiet." He lay still for a moment and was relieved to see they had obeyed, although like any ceasefire, he could see it was on the verge of collapse at a moments notice.

"Thank you." He whispered.

The first instance had now slipped his mind, he lay awake but closed his eyes, hoping this may encourage them to do likewise. After a few moments of silence, he opened his eyes just a little and squinted through his eyelids. He saw the clouds high above and enjoyed the sight of them, shifting through his field of vision and returning him to a relaxed state, until it happened again with blistering clarity… whispered into his ear like a dirty secret.

Ray.

He heard it clearly this time and sat up suddenly in his bed, listening as it resonated in his ear like a tuning fork. He was certain it was neither Burt, nor Michael.

"What's wrong?" Burt asked. "We've not said anything?"

"Shut up!" He said, holding his hands up in the air. "Someone *is* calling my name." He said, staring into the dark corners of the room. "Someone is here with us."

Burt raised to his feet and pressed lightly on Ray's shoulders. "Lay down, Ray." He said. "It's windy out there," He added. "But let's not get excited, it's just us."

He watched again as the clouds moved faster through his field of vision, what ever forces were at work high above him, he felt chillingly certain they'd beaten a path right to room 109. The howling wind rattled the door within it's frame, charging relentlessly like a beast at the gates until it finally relented and, watched by all three of them, creaked slowly open.

"It's just the wind." Burt said. "Marvin, go close the door." He pointed to it.

"Ok." He replied. Sensing this wasn't the time to argue, he dutifully did as he was told.

They can't hear me, Ray.

"So why can I?" He asked.

In just a few moments, everything they ever believed in, will change forever. Never again will they sit in a dark room without seeing my face, but for the time being…I want you.

"Don't you hurt them!" He shouted.

"Who are you talking to, Ray?" Michael asked. "You're freaking me out."

"You can't see him, Michael." Ray whispered. "At least not until he wants you to, but he's here now." He paused. "*Oh*…he's here now."

"Is this the guy you say is responsible?" He asked, sliding his chair next to Burt's.

"It's him." Ray replied. "I can feel him."

"Why's he here?" He asked, leaning in towards Burt. "Is he pissed?"

"He was murdered, Michael." He replied. "Wouldn't you be?"

"But just think of all the possibilities," Michael whispered, scanning the moonlit room nervously, yet excitedly. "If you could come back, all invisible an shit…just think what you could do." He looked at Burt. "You could watch chicks getting laid an stuff."

"You've only gotta watch a nature show," Burt said, clearly misunderstanding and shaking his head. "You're immortal, and that's the best you can come up with…you're such a fucking loser."

"I meant getting fucked!" He said. "Fucking nature show!"

"Anyway!" Burt shouted, turning his attention to Ray. "Are you going back to sleep? Or am I turning on the lights before Boy Wonder is on my knee?"

"Put the light on." Ray replied. "But I bet you it blows."

"Marvin…light." Burt ordered. "Now let's leave the crazy talk."

He hit the switch and all three of them watched as it slowly flickered into life, showering nothing but blinding light over them.

"There." Burt whispered. "Now settle down." He glanced at his watch before looking at Michael.

"You really are crazy, Ray." Michael said, pulling his seat back to it's original position by the wall, and once more spreading his ample frame across both of them.

Listen to me with your mind, Ray. And answer me likewise.

Ok. He thought, resisting the urge to speak.

Do you believe in me?

Are you gonna get me out of here? He wondered.

Do you believe in me?

I don't know anymore, Brandon. I don't trust my own thoughts these days.

You must, you're not crazy.

That's what someone crazy would tell themselves. I'm not buying it.

I can't help you unless you trust me, Ray.

Why?

In a few moments, you'll have the opportunity to leap from your window…and you must take it.
"You must think I'm fucking nuts!" He said, quickly realising his mistake. "Sorry fellas."
"Sometimes." Burt replied, reaching to the floor for his book. "Just relax."

Close your eyes, Ray. Speak only with your mind.

Ok I get it, He closed his eyes. *You just told me I'm not crazy, and yet now you're telling me to jump from an eleventh storey fucking window! Am I supposed to flap my troubles away?*

Maybe.

That's not good enough, Brandon. Maybe I wont hit the fucking pavement and decorate it with my brains…but maybe I will…and I know where the sensible money is.

You have to, Ray.

I don't have to do anything. Ever since you came along I've been getting fucked. I see you…I'm fucked. I hear you…I'm fucked. You kill every motherfucker…and oh yes…I'm fucked.

Ray -

"I'm pretty sick of being fucked!" He shouted, scaring the life out of his two escorts. "I'm so sorry, Guys." He whispered, feeling more than a little embarrassed. "I've got nothing."
"You might wanna keep it down a bit," Burt said, exchanging a curious glance with his colleague. "The marksmen outside will think we're having a fucking orgy in here."

Why are you here? He thought.

You're former friend has arranged your death, Ray. I thought you were safe from harm, I thought wrong.

Kill me? He wondered, almost out loud. *No, I'm not sure about that…he has no need, not while I'm stuck in here.*

Ray…wake up. You're gonna light some fires burning at your trial, and everyone knows there's no smoke without fire. Do you really believe he'd confess his sins to you, just for you to repeat them in your defence. You're on borrowed time. The clock was ticking when he came clean to you…now it's time.

Why should I accept what you're telling me, Brandon? He told me about you…is that true? Were you killing junkies?

Vincelli has no idea what I was…he has no idea who I was…he has no idea what I was capable of, either then or now.

Then tell me, Brandon. If you want me to trust you…tell me.

Vincelli knows nothing, Ray. We trusted Danny, we fed him the information that your friend has relayed to you, we wanted to see if he was trustworthy, the truth was far to dangerous in his hands…needless to say he was not trustworthy, but luckily he didn't know everything. Nobody could know everything, except Chad and…

…Your family?

Yes.

What were you, Brandon?

Vincelli will die, Ray. He has been marked for death. Before break of dawn this Saturday…his reign is over…then he will find out for himself just what I was…and what I still am.

I want to know, Brandon.

Six years ago, I lay dying in a dark back alley...outnumbered and overwhelmed I was incapable of defending myself as I was on the tail end of a night out with friends. I was beaten senseless and stabbed five times...for thirty dollars and a nice watch. I was set to become just another statistic, another victim of a growing drug culture...where the real victims are those who've never touched drugs in their lives, those who strive to achieve an honest living at no one's expense. I remember thinking, before I lost consciousness...that if I survived I was going to do two things. I would learn to fight, then I would find those who left me for dead, and do to them what they had done to me. Well I learned to fight, Ray.

And you got your revenge...

I woke up in hospital, somewhere between life and death on a surgeons table. The brightest light was shining down on me, as predictable as it sounds I thought it must be heaven. There were tubes attached all over my chest and drips in my arms. As they pumped blood into my veins to replace that which I'd lost, that was my re birth. They were amazed that I'd survived at all, my body had been pleading for death for five hours, but the blood...well suffice to say my body liked it. You see, it wasn't just blood...it was infected blood, infected with heroin...top grade kill you stone dead heroin, heroin extreme...or HEX as they call it. But the opposite was true for me...I'd been waiting to become an addict, waiting for that first rush, and when I got it...I was born. But you see, Ray, my survival came at a cost...then I had to have more and more.

So why were you wasting it on them? Why not keep it for yourself if you craved it so bad?

No, Ray...you don't understand. It wasn't the heroin, it was the blood. I needed the blood to function, I still need the blood to function, but not just any blood...HEX blood. Addicts became my prey...so yes I got my revenge, but it didn't taste like revenge...it tasted heavenly. I stalked them within the alleyways and shadows, always present but never seen…those alleyways became my arena…I'm undefeated in my arena, Ray. I would only pursue the dealers who dealt HEX, then I would await the customers, naturally. I would watch them take their hit, and usually they would pass out from the strength of it, but inevitably some would stumble down towards the main streets…they never made it. Once HEX began to surge within them, they were mine…they didn't know what had hit them…but I offered salvation. I still offer salvation. I am salvation.

How many have you killed, Brandon?

It was never my intention to kill them, I just fed from them…but sometimes, just sometimes, I kept drinking, and they were the unfortunate souls pronounced DOA.

What stopped them identifying you, Brandon? You can't just drink from them and walk away, if you were leaving them alive…how did you remain so anonymous?

Oh come now, Ray. You really are the most naïve man I've ever met…although that's part of your attraction. Firstly and most importantly, they were unconscious…if the HEX hadn't knocked them out, then I would. Secondly, if they had seen me…who the fuck would believe them? I mean, chances are…they wouldn't believe it themselves once they'd come down.

They're human beings, Brandon. You can't do that to human beings.

Human beings? Human beings, Ray? They're the same human beings who left me for dead in that alleyway, the same human beings who tried again last Halloween. They put you in here, Ray, yet here you lay attempting the morale high ground because you don't like my tactics. Have you the slightest idea what these individuals would do to you, just to score their next hit? They would kill you dead for the money in your pocket…of course there are those who want help, but there are those who want anarchy…they want to take everything from you…take everything from life and suffer little if any consequence. I am their consequence, Ray. I target them, I want them to die…it's their salvation.

Well that's a nice speech, but let's see if I've got this right. Are you telling me you were some sort of fucking Vampire?

I suppose in a modern sense you could say I am. You've yet to observe my skills so I wont reveal too much. But suffice to say, I don't turn into a bat...I have no aversion to garlic or daylight...I do cast a reflection in the mirror...I do not have fangs but a fashioned device, and I have not a single living relative in Transylvania. I'm just like you, Ray...to the naked eye at least, but I do possess skills that make me...well, unique.

What about Chad? Where does he fit into all of this?

His blood was pure, he shared my genes but not my curse, his only curse was looking a hell of a lot like me. And for that reason, and that reason alone...he lost his life, thanks to Danny. It was me they wanted, but for them to be certain they'd got me, they had to kill him too. This is probably somewhat of a disappointment to you, Ray. But I'm no hero, a decent member of civilised society like yourself would label me a vicious killer, this isn't good versus evil...this is their evil versus mine. With your sad life and dead wife, you've lost hope of a fairy tale ending...you're well aware that fate owes you nothing, and neither it seems...do I. If you can't trust me, then trust fate...you may well decorate that pavement with your brains, but what if? Maybe...just maybe, your journey back to civilised society will begin here...tonight...with a leap of faith. Have no doubt my friend, I am evil...and yet still I am salvation...I have never wielded a sword in my life.

Then Chad is death? Ray wondered. *But Chad was still alive when Death arrived?*

Sshh. Can you hear that, Ray?

Hear what?

He lay perfectly still, listening to what sounded like a hostess trolley being dragged along the hallway outside, it was scraping the walls intermittently, and there were voices, muffled voices.

Sounds like the maids, He thought. *Janitors…caretakers, what of it?*

On floors one to ten, you'd probably be right…but floor eleven? I don't think so, Ray. Nobody comes to floor eleven, not this section of floor eleven anyway…you know that.

Ok. He nodded his head. *So who is it?*

They've come for you now, Ray. It's time.

Come for me? What do you mean they've come for me? More than ever he resisted the urge to speak, fear and panic escalated within him as that trolley neared his door, it had squeaky wheels which echoed through the narrow passage as it approached.

Where am I going? He wondered, clenching his fists tightly.

Don't do that, Ray. I assure you that more than ever right now, they're watching your body language. Relax.

Tell me, Brandon…where am I going?

Why are you surprised? Did you really believe you'd be incarcerated within a hospital for the rest of your life? A mainstream hospital? They're taking you someplace you don't wanna go, someplace the world can't reach you…even me, but that's if you make it there.

What's happening? Tell me…please.

A hand full of top brass know tonight's the night of your transfer, no one else knows…not the press, not nobody. Your Captain is one of them… would you like to guess who the other is?

Vincelli?

You catch on fast. Your transport will be ambushed. There is a hail of high velocity rounds with your name etched in them, and you'll be dead before dawn. Once again you're left with a choice. My window, or Vincelli's hit squad. You decide.

I'll do it.

Do you believe in me now?

You get me the fuck out of here, and I'll get on my knees and fucking worship you...good enough?

Good enough. Sit tight...the cavalry is on it's way.

Ray opened his eyes and gazed around the room, he noticed quickly that he wasn't the only one in the room engaged in non verbal communication, there was an unnatural exchange of head tilts and hand gestures taking place between his escorts. He listened closely, the voices were now behind his door, and the squeaking wheels had come to a rest. Michael's attention was the first to be drawn away from the whispering beyond the door, drawn instead to the flickering light above them.
"You know what?" He said, standing up to look closer at it. "Something *is* wrong with this light."
"Please hurry." Ray whispered, as all three of them watched as the bulb began to glow. "Nancy, if you can hear me." He went on. "Please, don't let me die tonight." He kissed his wedding band for comfort. "Not yet, baby."
"Hey, old man!" Michael shouted. "Get over here and take a look at this!"
"What?" Burt asked. "You don't think I can see it from here? It's a fucking light and I'm sitting right beneath it!" He stood up regardless and walked the single stride to join him beneath it, the chain joining him and Ray grew taut. "I can hear it too!" He exclaimed, quite surprised.

Ray resisted the urge to tell them to look away, for fear of raising the alarm too soon.

Que sera sera, He thought. *Either these guys get a splinter in the eye, or I get a bullet in the skull.* He smiled, pretending to muse the question. *Do your worst kid, just get me out of here alive.* He watched as their interest in the pulsating light overhead, switched gradually to the closed door. He realised at that moment that they were playing out withdrawal tactics, to vacate the room. In an unprecedented move, Burt reeled out his handcuff key and released his own wrist from the chain, before quickly attaching what had been his end to a steel handle built into the bed. Ray knew his escorts would now either, walk out of the room, or be dragged out, replaced in all probability by a small army of riot attired transportation personnel.

"Maybe we should call one of the guys in the hall?" Michael said, his words were painfully predictable to Ray's ears.

"Radio's are broken then, Kid?" He asked.

With Burt encouraging his hapless colleague to seek help, with not so subtle eye rolls at the door, he was shocked to see him retreat back rapidly from the door as two sets of dead bolts engaged, sealing the door shut.

"What the fuck are you doing?" Burt asked. "You some kind of clown now?"

"I didn't fucking touch it?" He replied. "It just locked on it's own…you saw it too!"

"Sure," He said, shaking his head angrily. "Out the way." He pushed Michael aside and reached out to wind the bolts back, but before he could get to it the bulb finally blew, spraying fine glass fragments down on them, and returning the room to darkness.

"What the fuck is going on here?" Michael asked, bending over and waving his head at the floor. He'd failed to notice Burt scramble back towards to Ray, he sat inanimate and terrified, clinging to Ray like a child would it's mother.

"That's some fucking voodoo shit, Ray!" Michael shouted, laughing. "How did you know?" He tried to focus on them both when no reply came.

"Someone's in the room with us." Burt whispered. His features were frozen as he stared through Michael, he gazed at the upper section of the wall behind him, the only part illuminated by the moonlight.

"It's me, Burt!" Michael said, waving his arms. "It's just me." The smile disappeared quickly from his face, his words having barely left his lips when a shiver, nothing the like he'd ever felt before travelled down his spine, it tingled with an almost sexual anticipation as one by one, his muscles seized like worn pistons.

"Unlock my cuffs, Burt." Ray whispered, nudging him to break his stare into the moonlight. "Don't be afraid," He added. "Just do whatever he asks of you."

"Ok." He replied, tearing the keychain off his belt loop. "Ok."

"Ray," Michael whispered, still glued to the spot. "I gotta ask you something."

"Shoot." He replied, frantically unlocking his handcuff.

"He's right behind me, isn't he?"

"Yes." He replied. "Michael I need your clothes. Take them off, kid."

Burt stared helplessly into the black lakes of *his* eyes, even in just the pale moonlight he could instantly see these were not the eyes of any living soul. They were tortured yet innocent, and compassionate yet brutal, framed as ever by his long black hair.

"You don't want my trousers." Michael replied, looking down at the swelling puddle around his shoes. "I'm sorry, Ray."

"What the fuck is wrong with you?" Ray asked, he spoke in an angry whisper. "He's not gonna hurt you." He turned again to Burt. "Burt, I'm sorry but I'm gonna need *your* shirt." He patted him on the shoulder. "Hurry now, we don't have much time."

"You got it." He replied, kicking off his shoes. "You want my trousers too, right?"

"They'll slow me down." He replied, laughing. "If I need a parachute, I'll let you know."

He threw Burt's shirt around his shoulders and turned to Michael.

"Just look at him, Michael." He said, urging him to turn around. "There's no maggots or hollowed out eye sockets, he looks just like you and me! Except he's better looking."

He nodded with an expression of uncertainty to Ray, before turning his head with the hope that his body would follow. He wanted to see the mythical figure Ray had often talked about, but which he and everyone else had dismissed as pure fantasy. He was soon aware of a dark shadowy presence, statuesque and lean, between himself and the wall.

"Sweet Jesus." He said, quickly retreating to the bed, and Burt. "You're him." He tried to resist looking at his pale features, however well concealed within his dark mane, for fear of irritating him.

"Let's not get excited." He replied calmly. "Long hair and resurrection aside, I am *not* Jesus." He smiled, "Nor am I *sweet*."

"I know exactly who you are." Michael said, staring awestruck. "Ray talks about you like you're a fucking rock star."

"Gentlemen," He whispered, gliding effortlessly past Michael and standing in the centre of the room. "Only one man is leaving this room via the window, if you each do as I say, it needn't become three."

Ray stared at him as he stood inanimate with the moonlight flooding across him, his deathly pale features were frighteningly familiar to him, but gone was the harness he noticed, and so too the swords.

"Where are your swords?" Ray asked.

"Not necessary." He whispered. "No one in this room is going to die."

"Are you Brandon?" Michael asked, holding tightly to Burt on the bed. "Is it really you?"

"Sshh." He replied, drawing his finger across his lips before stepping closer to them both.

"I think you've seen enough." He whispered, laying his hands across their shoulders and pulling them closer to each other. Each flinching from his icy touch, they stared into the blackness of his eyes as he held them, having unwittingly been lulled into a trance like state.

"I'm pretty sick of being fucked…" He whispered, watching as their eyes closed simultaneously. He smiled gently as their bodies became limp, falling from his hands they lay seemingly asleep across the bed.

"Sweet dreams." He whispered.

Ray's attention was summoned to the window, it was shuddering violently as though under direct attack from the darkness beyond, it rattled relentlessly as the frame surrounding it, and the concrete housing it, began to crack and crumble. Ray stepped quickly away from it as it began to dislodge entirely from the wall, before tilting outwards and falling from view with an eerie silence. The wind howled menacingly, beckoning him outwards into the darkness, into the unknown beyond his four walls.

"Oh fuck." He shouted. "I don't know if I can."

Is all we see, anything but a dream within a dream, Ray? Your logical mind must decide the truth from the lies.

"What the fuck does that mean?" He shouted, attempting to near the now gaping hole in the wall.

Turn around…

Ray turned quickly around to see both Michael and Burt laying on the floor, they were in a dazed and confused state as they clambered to their feet. But more importantly, *he* was no longer present.

Move to the window, Ray. You're too close to them.

"I'm scared, Brandon." He shouted, begrudgingly doing as requested. "I'm fucking scared!"

Climb onto the window ledge, Ray, lean outwards from the ledge to buy yourself time. No one will approach you, and no one will shoot you… they'll only open fire to stop you escaping, not if you're jumping to what they consider will be your certain death..

"How do you know that?" He shouted, using one of Michael's chairs to climb onto the ledge. "They'll shoot when they come through that door!"

It's too much paper work, Ray. They'll let you jump before they'll put a bullet in you…but only if you're leaning out of the window, you must be leaning out or they will wound you to halt your escape. As a final test of your faith, you shall not hear my voice again until you jump. A dream within a dream, Ray…I'll be waiting.

"Fuck!" He shouted. "I can't do this, Brandon." He clung to the concrete frame, and as instructed moved himself to the outer section of the ledge, and looked down. Car alarms down below were bellowing in the night, people from within the hospital were screaming and running in all directions as a haunted ballad of chaos unfolded before his eyes, anarchy was erupting eleven floors down. At that moment he was aware of a deafening siren ringing through his ears, it easily overpowered all the street noise below, as it was sounding throughout the building.

"Ray!" Burt shouted. "What the fuck are you doing?"
"Get away from the window!" Michael added. "You're gonna die!"
"Brandon's waiting!" Ray shouted back to them. He watched as Michael hit the light switch, the bulb flickered into life and stung his eyes with its natural intensity.
"What the hell?" Ray whispered, clinging tightly to the metal rods within the concrete.
"There is no Brandon!" Burt shouted. "Ray, it's an earthquake!"
"An earthquake?" Ray asked, considering the chaos below.
"A big one, Ray." He shouted. "The whole fucking window went bye - bye."
"You just fucking saw him!" Ray shouted, holding the rods fiercely while the exposed cement cut into his bare feet. "He was here! You're fucking with my head!"
"No, Ray!" Burt shouted, struggling over the gale force winds ripping through the small room. "It's a fucking earthquake! Don't do this!"
"How did I get free then?" He shouted back, considering his options in a new light. "How did I get here when I was cuffed to you?"
"I can't answer that!" He shouted, dropping to his hands and knees as the room shook violently again. "Listen to the noise, Ray!"

He shouted. "It's gotta be a seven or eight pointer!" He reached out his hand to Ray, although too far back for Ray to reach, he thought it a commanding gesture for Ray to see sense and return to the relative safety of the rumbling room, as opposed to the lunacy of the ledge.

"Ray, please!" Michael shouted, still standing erect though with his arms outstretched like a surfer riding a break. "You're gonna die!" He appeared close to tears as he pleaded. "You don't deserve to go like this!" He added. "Please!"

Ray stared out into the darkness, he saw the dust was rising now and found it difficult to see anything eleven floors down, but saw that as a blessing considering his current dilemma, like a skydiver jumping from *above* the clouds, it masked reality. The building shook violently as he struggled to keep hold of the exposed steel rods within the concrete.

That's why no one has burst in, He thought. *They're riding out the quake as we are, they probably can't even hear what's happening in here!*

"I don't know what's real anymore!" He shouted, coughing as the dust entered his lungs. "I have only one option!" He added, pushing his body outwards while still clinging tightly. "If I die, I die…I wont live this life anymore." He looked desperately into the abyss he knew awaited him, it beckoned like never before.

"Give Vincelli a message from Brandon!" He shouted, releasing one of his hands but clinging tightly with the other.

"Ray!" Burt shouted, knowing full well indecision had made way for resignation. "Please!"

"Tell Vincelli, he's a dead man!" He shouted, bidding them farewell in mock salute. He looked down one final time, although he knew there was nothing to see, just enveloping dust that called like never before…freedom awaited. Releasing his grip from the steel rods he watched his world turn upside with startling velocity. *Three…two…one…* He thought. *I'm coming, baby.*

Chapter Fifteen

<u>Thursday 3rd June.</u>

"You know part of our little secret," The voice whispered. "Well… our six foot, two hundred pound secret." The voice was gentle and motherly. "It's only fair you find out the rest."

"Where am I?" Ray whispered, opening fully his eyes, to once again find himself in unfamiliar surroundings, with the only similarity being darkness, *blissful* darkness.

"Safe," She whispered. "No one can hurt you now."

"It…was…a dream." He said, listening to the driving rain hit the window behind his double bed. "I thought I…"

"It wasn't a dream, Ray." She said, touching his right arm. "I've prayed for your soul, and my prayers were answered…you found salvation." She giggled. "Or should I say, *Salvation*…found you."

"Salvation?" He asked, flinching slightly under her touch. "I gave up on salvation a long time ago." He turned to see the dimly lit figure of a woman beside him, she was wearing a dressing gown and sat in a chair beside the bed.

"I *know* you." He whispered. "Mrs Rose." He sat up in bed and stared at the wall opposite, yellow light filtered through the open blinds illuminating the patterned wallpaper, and a large painting he couldn't determine.

"Lie down," She whispered. "And please, call me Mary."

"Ok," He replied, rubbing at his head and slumping backwards. "I feel…terrible."

"You're weak." She said, touching his bare chest gently. "Soon you'll be strong, but for now just relax."

"I thought I'd died." He muttered. He turned to look at her now that his eyes had accustomed to the light, or lack thereof. She was clutching a pile of knitting on her lap as she smiled down at him. Under the yellow haze her hair appeared blonde, but his memory told him it was grey, although now a little longer than he recalled.

"He wouldn't let you die."

"How did I even get here?" He asked. "I jumped…and that's all I remember."

"A leap of faith I believe is the term." She answered. "The rest will become clear in the fullness of time."

"Ok." He replied, allowing his eyes to wander around the room. On the left hand side he could see what looked like a dresser, there was a three piece mirror on it, and a couple of framed pictures on either side. On the other side of the room and next to the door, he saw a large mahogany wardrobe. Even in the faintest of light, he could tell it was dripping fancy detail from every angle, from the brass handles to it's stiletto legs . Opposite his bed was a sideboard, he could see there were many framed pictures laid across it's length, it was under the large portrait that still eluded him, and ran almost the length of the wall, before stopping at what he could see was a large fan shaped chair, it contained what he figured was a mountain of clothes strewn over it.

"What if they come looking?" He asked.

"You're going to be perfectly safe here, safe from harm and prying eyes. This is the last place in the world they'll expect you're hiding, but it's the first place they expect you'll head for." She laughed a little.

"Why?"

"As far as they're concerned, you're obsessed with my son." She replied. "So it's therefore an irresistible draw to you…this is your *Graceland*."

"But they'll come!" He said, trying to sit up.

"They're already here!" She said, guiding him back down. "There are police cruiser's parked front and back. They arrived last night after you jumped -"

"Last night?" He asked. "I thought…"

"It's almost twenty - four hours since you jumped, Ray." She said, tapping his chest reassuringly. "One of the biggest searches in recent history has been launched, and yet you're right under their noses."

"What happens if they search the house?" He asked, glancing at the painting on the wall .

"We've been through so much," She replied. "They wont search here, it's us they're *protecting*."

"So…" He paused for just a moment, allowing the situation to sink in. "…exactly how do I get out of here?" He shook his head. "How do I escape?"

"You don't." She replied, placing her knitting on the floor. "To *escape*, implies you're running from something or someone," She stood up and closed the blinds. "You're going to walk out of here a free man."

"I don't see how that's even possible." He muttered. His eyes moved once more over the shadowy outlines of the room, it grew a little lighter by the door, as light from the hallway seeped in underneath it. He could see the walls were adorned with picture frames, but still his eyes would not reveal the detail within them. With his limited vision, he guessed that this had been neither Brandon's or Chad's room, neutrality just hadn't been their style.

No, He thought. *I'm a guest in this house, this is the guest room.*

"What time is it?" He asked.

"Almost one o' clock." She replied.

"What day?"

"Thursday." She answered. "Ray, you've been asleep for hours, not days." She stared sympathetically at him. "I understand you must have many questions," She went on. "All your questions will be answered, I just wanted to be here when you awoke, to help you adjust…and to stop you looking out of the window." She laughed.

"Yeah," He whispered, returning her stare. "That's just my luck." He laughed as the thought developed in his mind, they laughed together. "Some fugitive, right?"

"You're going to be just fine." She whispered.

"Thank you." He said, sitting up in bed. "I've spent more time on my back than a cheap hooker." He groaned as he stretched his arms out.

"Why me?" He asked, turning to look at her. "Why did Brandon choose me?"

"Your pain." She replied. "Your isolation, and detachment from life."

"What?" He asked, shaking his head.

"In the same way a child loses innocence," She whispered. "The elderly regain it. We don't have to go through life believing what society and logic dictate to us. There are powerful forces at work all around us."

"I'm not sure I buy into all that." He replied, swinging his legs out from under the covers. "I'm a straight sort of guy." He added. "If I can't see it -"

"Only pain can fire a flagging imagination," She said, leaning in close to him. "I know you are currently childless, but imagine watching your children open their presents at Christmas, the smiles on their faces and the joy in their hearts…and tell me that magic doesn't exist."

He nodded.

"You jumped from the top of a tall building," She whispered. "And not only did you survive with not a mark on you, but you flew nine miles to this address." She took his hands in hers and rubbed them. "You don't need me to answer your questions, you already know…it was you that let him in."

"Why me?" He asked bluntly.

"You have a common enemy." She answered. "It was the same man who destroyed both of your lives." She smiled. "A man with a debt to settle, this Friday night…he will settle it."

Ray sat silently for a moment, he tried desperately to focus on the portrait but still could not. He found himself gazing at all the clothing on the chair, it seemed so out of place as everything else seemed *in* it's place.

"How are they doing it?" He asked. "They *did* die, right?"

"Yes." She replied, nodding slowly. "Do you know what is often said about twins?"

"They share a bond?" He guessed. "Like some kind of a spiritual connection?"

"A psychic connection exists." She whispered. "They have a true understanding of each others thoughts and emotions, pain…love…

sadness and gladness, they feel it with one another. I wont bore you with the genetics, but suffice to say, nothing can break that bond… even death."

"So you're telling me," He said. "That a connection remains between the living twin, and the dead one?"

"They had names, Ray." She replied, although her smile was forgiving. "But yes."

"I'm sorry," He said. "I was generalising…but I didn't mean any offence."

"I know."

"So if Chad was sending a signal," He asked. "Then how did he continue to do that after his death?"

Gazing lovingly at the portrait on the wall, she raised to her feet and walked slowly towards the wardrobe.

"Chad," She said, finally. "Was never in the loop I'm afraid." She stopped beside it and turned to face Ray.

"Chad was weakened by the crash," She whispered. "He clung to life for as long as he could, but his strength was diminished and body broken." She reached for the handle. "But the fact remains unchanged…he neither sent, nor received."

"I don't understand." He replied, nervously. He watched as she opened both doors wide, pushing them back on their hinges until locking in place.

"Nor should you." She said, staring at the wardrobe and the darkness within it.

He observed with increasing unease as she stood silently, seemingly at the mercy of whatever she gazed upon, like pure blood at the alter of sacrifice.

"It's Brandon." She said, finally breaking her silence. "He is the powerful one…the satellite if you will."

"Is?" Ray asked. "*Is* the powerful one?"

"Ever since he was attacked," She continued. "He set about honing himself to physical perfection…it was impossible to touch my boy. If only they'd known then…" She reached into the blackness before her, first her hands, then her arms disappeared within. "…What they know now."

"And what's that?"

The wardrobe illuminated from within, at the flick of the switch she'd been searching for. Ray's relief was short lived as she side stepped from view, revealing in full the vast array of samurai swords and body armour. He lifted himself from the bed and walked slowly to the wardrobe, he ran his fingers down a long dark cloak that hung within.

"*He* never so much as touched a samurai sword." She whispered. "He is, quite simply…indestructible."

"Then why the armour?" He asked.

"The armour is an illusion." She replied. "Slight of hand…twist of fate."

"I don't understand," He said.

"The armour must be *seen*," She answered. "It's purely cosmetic."

"Cosmetic?" He asked, punching the chest plate lightly. "That's real armour?"

"No." She laughed. "It's requirement…is purely cosmetic."

She closed the wardrobe doors, leaving just a shard of light visible from within and took his hand.

"What are you doing?" He asked, feeling a little vulnerable in just his shorts.

"You'll see." She replied. She led him to the other side of the bed and stood him next to the dresser, before switching on a small lamp on the bedside table.

"What do you see?" She asked.

"I see…" He fell silent as he stared at the picture frames, and the photographs within them. "Oh…*sweet Jesus*." He allowed his eyes a journey through time as he gazed at the images of them, all of which he noticed had been captured on instant Polaroid type pictures, taken at varying stages of both personal, and technological development.

"There's three of them." He whispered, unaware of the movement behind him.

"Now you know." She said, placing her hand on his shoulder. "There's three of them."

"Until now," The voice whispered. "I've remained in the shadows, but when I enter that arena and step beneath the light…they will gaze open mouthed."

"It's you." Ray whispered, still staring at the pictures on the dresser. "I've been waiting for this moment." He turned slowly to see in the flesh, what appeared to be an illusion on the pictures before him. Stood casually by the large chair was the man, quite literally of his dreams. Tall and statuesque, he wore loose fitting black jeans and a white vest that showcased his muscular torso to perfection. His long black hair was tied back tightly, revealing in full his handsome features.

"Hello, Ray." He whispered. "I'm Brandon."

"Brandon?" He asked. His eyes darted from mother to son with increasing regularity. "I thought you were -"

"I *am* real." He whispered, folding his arms. "You see, I was *never* there."

"Chad and Jeff," Mary said. "*They* were in the car that night… not Brandon."

"Hold on now," Ray said, configuring a time - out gesture with his hands. "Just what the hell are you telling me here?" He walked slowly towards were Brandon was stood. "Why did *you* do this to me?"

"I did nothing." He answered, meeting Ray's angry gaze head on.

"You did nothing?" He asked, laughing. "You've turned my fucking life upside down -"

"Then by definition," He countered. "It should now be the correct way up!"

" - And now I find out you're fucking human!" He lunged at Brandon with all the strength and power he currently possessed, cocking back his right fist he sent it flying into Brandon's jaw. He watched with surprise as Brandon stumbled backwards toward the door, even more surprising to Ray was the ease with which he'd tagged him.

"I probably deserved that." He whispered, holding his jaw as he stood to face Ray once more. "Bravo." He said. "That's the spirit I've been looking for."

"You could've stopped me, right?"

"My mother could've stopped that, Ray." He answered. "It's not the power of your punch that matters…it's the power of your mind."

"I need to know." He said firmly. "One of you…is going to tell me everything."

"My husband and I," Mary said. "We were told we were having twins." She gazed proudly at her son as she sat on the end of the bed between them. "All the scans revealed *two* babies…that still mystifies me. My boys were not due for almost three weeks, when without warning I went into sudden labour." Holding Ray's attention firmly, she patted the spot next to where she was sat until he joined her there, though not without hesitation.

"So you can imagine our surprise," She continued, taking hold of Ray's right hand. "When I gave birth to three boys." She paused again as she reached out her hand to Brandon, he offered her his and sat down beside her with no further prompting.

"I love you." He whispered, kissing her gently on her cheek.

"And I love *you*." She replied, taking hold of his left hand. She sat proudly like a *Rose* between two thorns as she divided her attention between them both. "We decided together that for all intents and purposes, one of them had wished to be *invisible*, so one would remain so." She smiled. "We hid him."

"Why?" Ray asked. "Why would you do that?"

"I suppose," She answered. "It was for purely selfish reasons. I thought if they were registered as twins, then one of them would *always* be here with me." She leaned her head against Brandon's shoulder and stroked his arm. "So…*Brandon* and *Chad* were registered, the third was not, but his name was -"

"Jeff." Ray said.

"Yes."

"My god." He shook his head, but more in amazement than disapproval. "How would that even work?" He asked. "I'm not judging…I just need to know."

"It was simple." She answered. "They all had normality. They each went to school, but obviously on rotation. They all got the medical care they needed, although luckily none of them had any operations that would've left scarring."

"And this worked?"

"For a long time yes." She said. "Until Halloween last, that is."

"You see," Brandon said. "When my brothers were murdered, I was instantly consigned to a life of solitude…I have no identity now." He stood up and walked to the wardrobe.

"I'm sorry." Ray said, achieving a degree of clarity.

"My loss is my cross to bare." He whispered. He pulled open the wardrobe doors and examined the contents. Reaching to the back of a small shelf on the right hand side, he retrieved a small tub of fluorescent face paint and unscrewed the lid.

"But *your* loss…" He added, keeping his back to them both. "*Your* loss surges like electricity, it emanates from your body like the current in a cable…" He laughed. "You don't have to *touch* the cable…you need only get within a certain distance from it and the current *jumps* to a host, that's why they put those upturned bars halfway up the pylon tower." He dabbed his fingers into the tub and smeared two diagonal lines down the right side of his face. "You should have those bars around *you*," He said. "Because anyone who gets within fifty feet of you, get's electrified by your misery."

Climbing to his feet, Ray walked to the wardrobe, leaving Mary to sit and observe them both. He placed a hand on Brandon's shoulder and gazed at the weaponry.

"Is it your voice I've been hearing?" He asked softly.

"Yes."

"So…Jeff," He whispered, gazing at the multiple sets of swords. "Is the swordsman?"

"Yes." He replied, smearing another two lines down his face, only this time on the left. "He's the man of the moment," He continued. "*He* was the weapons expert, not me." He laughed as he turned to face Ray. "I was the skydiver."

"So, you can't fight?"

"Oh…I *can* fight," He said. "And a lot more besides. It could've got confusing you see…if Chad was Chad one day, and then *Brandon* the next…it would've been too tricky. So how we did it, right from the start…is Chad was *always* Chad. But Jeff and myself shared a psychic connection, I saw through his eyes and vice versa…we didn't *ever* have to update the other on what had happened that day and so on…so we shared the name Brandon, *my* name."

"So…you both learned to fight?"

"We did." He replied. "I excelled in hand to hand…he excelled in weaponry, but together we excelled in all aspects."

"And now?"

"And now?" He asked, glancing sideways at Ray. "And now, he's dead…but we still connect, death can't keep us apart…we're *special*."

"How special?"

"There's plenty of time for all that." He replied. He smeared the paint into his hands and ran his fingers through his hair.

"What are you doing?" Ray asked. "There's nothing there."

"There will be." He answered. "Just wait and see."

"Ok." He watched with growing anticipation as Brandon's excitement began to seep from his very pores, like a rock star gearing up for a sell out crowd…he was charging. He threw the tub back onto the shelf and slammed the doors closed, before spinning from Ray's view with breathtaking speed.

"What the fuck?" Ray whispered, turning to see him stood casually at the other side of the room. "How do you *do* that?"

"I'm not like anyone else." He reached down for the lamp and turned it off, returning the room to a much darker state then it previously had been. Ray stepped backwards and felt the wardrobe behind him, deciding there and then that it was probably best not to move.

"Sweet Jesus…" Ray whispered, watching as the smeared lines on Brandon's face glowed radiantly in the darkness, as he paced the room on the other side of the bed from Ray.

"If I'm to have any kind of life," He said, somewhat angrily. "Then I have to leave this place…but even then I wont be able to get a job or a place of my own, because I have no remaining identity. That means living off the grid, and flying below radar for the rest of my life…in my book, that gives us something *else* in common."

"I guess it does."

"Vincelli is a dead man, Ray." He said. "This Friday night he dies in spectacular fashion at our hands." He laughed. "They'll never see us coming!" He began gyrating his hips back and forth while smearing his hands down his bare arms, leaving a designer glow across both of them. "We *all* have another side, Ray." He whispered, reaching out his *glowing* hand to Ray. "Are you in?" He asked.

"I'm in." He answered, shaking Brandon's hand firmly. "I don't know what you want from me…but I'm in."

"I've waited for this moment," Brandon whispered. "I could've killed Vincelli at any time of the day or night -"

"Why didn't you?"

"The path of least resistance," He answered. "For many people has an unquestionable attraction, but I'm not one of them." He ran his fingers across Ray's face as Mary switched the lamp back on. "This Friday night…" He said. "I'm going to nail that bastard to a fucking cross…high and proud for all to see." He opened the door and stepped into the hallway beyond it. "Always view life as a stage," He whispered, turning to look Ray in the eye. "Your actions are vital…as it's the memory of your actions in others that will ultimately define you." He winked at him and disappeared from view.

"He's pretty intense," Mary said, ushering Ray back to bed. "He get's like that sometimes."

"No kidding," Ray agreed. "But he's very infectious…how does he do that?"

"He can certainly hold the stage, Ray." She replied. "And he'll captivate anyone who watches him." She helped him into bed.

"Is he…for *real*?"

"My boy is one of a kind," She answered. "He has much to show you…and he will in -"

"The fullness of time." Ray said. "I know."

10 : 30.

Vincelli sat in his office with a freshly made cup of coffee, his trademark overcoat was thrown across the chair opposite his desk, and the sleeves on his striped shirt were rolled up to the elbow. He considered his day ahead while gazing at the selected case files he'd laid out on the desk, beside them was the only captured footage currently in existence, of the man the press had dubbed '*The Black Widow.*'

"I'll find you, Ray Kennedy." He whispered, lighting a cigarette. "I'll track you down…I know you're not alone." He rested the cigarette in a foil ashtray, and realised his hands were trembling. Ray's escape had played heavily on his mind, but not nearly as much as *how* he'd escaped.

"You'll keep." He whispered. "First I want the *White Witch*." He laughed a little as he sucked on his cigarette.

"White witch," He said. "More like *right bitch*, if you ask me." He walked to his window and slid down the top section, he flicked ash through the open space before standing on his tip toes to allow himself an uninhibited look down. The three floors between his office and the ground allowed the gravity of the situation, or the situation of *gravity*…to hit home.

"Eleven floors," He said, feeling just a little queasy at the thought. "No *fucking* way." Quite frankly, he didn't fancy his chances of survival were he to jump from his own window. Stepping back a little he pulled the blinds down, in the hope of shading the room adequately from the already glaring sun.

"Earthquake?" He said, driving his cigarette into the foil tray. "It's the only earthquake I've ever heard of that affects one building, but leaves the next untouched."

He slid the cassette marked *Mathew Johnson E1* into the player, before dropping unceremoniously into his chair. The image began grainy, but quickly stabilised itself out to give an exceedingly clear vantage point of the furthest pump, it's foreground and the encroaching fields behind it. Having already watched the footage several times, he knew with absolute certainty, that at three - twenty - seven precisely, a quiet evening's security footage captures an outlandishly astonishing act of violence, perpetrated by the deadliest and *stealthiest* assailant he'd ever known. He increased the play speed as opposed to fast forwarding, as although he was well aware of the fact that *Mathew*, had not been at the filling station at any time prior to his death that night, it was with fresh perspective that he wished to view *other* cars, that may have used the pumps on the run up to his demise. With his feet on the desk and his chair reclined, he lit another cigarette and allowed his mind some airtime while he watched the comings and goings of pump number eight.

I wonder if twins do share a psychic a connection, He thought. *And if they did…then what's to say that bond couldn't remain active after death? I know I spoon fed the lines to Danny, but what he said about those fuckers was all him…they share a lot more than DNA, they have a phone line between them that's unbreakable even by death…and all it takes is a call…*

"Hang on," He said, suddenly lunging for the remote control. "What's that?" He reversed the footage a little, to see a small car reversing up in the darkness beside the forecourt.

"What are you doing there at…" He glanced at the time on the screen. "Eleven - Ten?"

Being a regular patron of this particular filling station himself, he knew there were air and water dispensers situated where it had stopped. The white light of the forecourt was in stark contrast to where the little car had parked, and it's own blazing headlights managed quite successfully to dazzle out any chance of him establishing the make and model, let alone it's colour.

"I'll bet that's you." He said, feeling more than a little intrigued. "Why have I never noticed you before?" He jotted down the time of the vehicle's arrival and pressed play, electing to run it at real time. He watched the car closely, whilst maintaining a constant vigil to the comings and goings of the forecourt itself.

"Well you're waiting for something," He whispered, noting an elapsed time of three minutes, yet still the occupant, or *occupants*, hadn't emerged from the car. He found himself drawn to the darkness of the fields, to the mystique they presented and to the slayer, quite possibly laying in wait just feet from where the car was currently parked.

"If you only *knew.*" He whispered. *But maybe,* He thought. *Just maybe…you do.*

If she was a twin, He thought. *Then theoretically, the psychic connection she should've shared with her sibling...is currently vacant, just waiting for someone to tune into her wavelength. Yet she claims she's hearing Brandon's voice, and not her own deceased brother. I wonder why that is...*

His thoughts were derailed as the car, without valid reason for even being present, edged forward and disappeared from view, he observed the time was almost eleven - twenty on the footage. He was certain the car hadn't entered the forecourt, even from an angle not covered, as the computerised cash register had provided them with, upon it's request, all gasoline sales amounts, and the time of dispensing, the results of which he had on his desk.

"Nothing," He said, eliminating the possibility. "So just what *where* you doing there?" He watched on, and as expected from his check of the sales list, several minutes later a car pulled up beside pump seven, and again as expected, thirty seven dollars worth of gasoline was delivered. He reached across to once again increase the play speed.

Surely if she's going to connect with anyone, He thought. *It would be her own twin...I wonder if it matters if her twin died, before he was able to communicate for himself, let alone communicate telepathically to her? I wonder if a living twin, who's lost their own twin...can railroad her...let's say 'telephone' line, for their ends? In other words, I wonder if it's possible that she's receiving voices from a living twin, who's line is now open after the death of their...twin?* He laughed a little. *This is some heavy shit...*

He sat forward abruptly and aimed the remote at the player, his excitement was at fever pitch as he watched in reverse what he almost missed completely, a small red car driving quickly through the forecourt, it's occupant neither obtaining fuel, nor utilising the facilities available.

"I've got you!" He shouted. He slowed the footage down and waited, with baited breath he struggled to contain himself as the car passed clearly through the floodlights.

"I *knew* I'd seen that car." He whispered. "Almost eleven - thirty, a little late for a nice girl like you." He couldn't prevent the smile on his face. "God's work…I think not." Feeling justly vindicated and more than a little satisfied, he let the footage play on at it's real time speed. He selected the case file marked *Nikki Farrell*, and flipped it open, all the while maintaining a visual on the screen beside him.

"Ok," He said. "Let's see if you turn up here." He looked firstly at the picture contained within, it was a combined snap shot of the sheared Mercedes, and Nikki's lifeless body. Taken from a front end perspective it revealed the shards of torn steel, and sliced cables beneath the windscreen which, bizarrely enough, had remained unscathed despite the hundreds of tons of galloping express, reaching within just inches. Seemingly staring into the camera, the image of Nikki's eyes haunted him a little, he found himself wondering if it was the car that was marked after all, or Nikki himself, or quite possibly both. Tired of returning his eyes to the screen every time the forecourt lights flickered, he decided to consult the sales report to ascertain when the next paying customer would arrive.

"Twelve - forty - eight." He said, pushing it away. "Quiet night… for now at least."

He thumbed through the pages until he found the several witness statements contained within, he quickly pulled them free before returning the file to his desk. He began to speed read through the first of nine.

"I was approaching the level crossing," He said. "When the warning lights began to flash and the warning alarm sounded. I was coming from the opposite side, and as the barriers began to lower I could the see the Mercedes slowing behind them…" He shook his head impatiently and tracked the words with his pen.

"Here we go…" He whispered. "…A small car, which had been behind the Mercedes, pulled suddenly to the other side of the road, and drove off in the opposite direction. It was with just seconds to spare, before the Volvo slammed into the rear of the Mercedes, and shunted it directly into the path of the express…" He floated the scenario in his mind for a moment, before quickly searching for further detail.

"Nothing." He muttered, rotating it within his current selection. "Maybe you…will have seen something more…Miss, Amy Lloyd."

A car on the screen attracted his already tired eyes, with a quick glance at the time he realised it was Mr Twelve - forty - eight.
"Go on." He said. "Put your fifty - six dollars worth in, and fuck off." He watched the man step from his car and walk slowly to pump number eight." As expected, the man retrieved the nozzle from it's housing, and slid it in to his vehicle before engaging the automatic delivery system. He then stretched his arms out wide and appeared to *contemplate*, his next move.
"What are you up to?" Vincelli asked, lowering the second witness statement from view. He watched on as the man walked past the pump, and out towards the fields, or in this case, the vacant *black* area of the screen. He watched closely as the man turned to see if anyone was looking, at one point even *waving* to the camera, before turning his back to it and facing the darkness head on.
"Why are you taking a piss there?" Vincelli asked, laughing at him. "There's fucking toilets -" His words trailed to nothing as *something*, sent the man recoiling back to the forecourt, urgently.
"Did you *see* something?" He asked, reversing it a little. He watched again as the man appeared to concentrate his attention into the darkness, by leaning forward and extending his neck, before turning hastily and returning to his car.
"And the rest…" Vincelli whispered. "…is history." He decided that whatever the man had seen couldn't have amounted to much, as the cashier had been repeatedly pressed for any unusual activity, or sightings, to which she had replied negatively. He let it play, once again opting for real time, and glanced at his second witness statement.
"I was standing with my boyfriend," He muttered. "We were heading over the tracks into Washburn, when the barriers began to lower. I saw a big black car stopping by the barrier as we waited for the train to pass…" Like a teacher marking an assignment, he used his pen to search for the relevant passage. "…I heard a revving sound coming from behind the black car, at which point I turned to see a smaller red car, turning to drive off in the opposite direction.

It held my attention because it was driving away quickly, but then *another* car caught my eye as it was travelling *so* fast, I noticed it's rear passenger door was open but I couldn't see why. I knew it was never going to stop in time…" He shook his head and again rotated it to the back of his pile.

"Women and cars!" He said. "Big black car…smaller red car…where's the detail?"

He glanced at his third statement, noticing immediately that the individual's occupation had been entered as *mechanic*.

"Well so far," He said. "I can place a *smaller* red car at the scene." The cigarette he'd forgotten about caught his eye in the ashtray, having burned away to nothing.

"Jason Michaels," He said. "I'm looking for the quality to come from you." He lit another one.

"I was walking home…" He tired of the routine and read quietly to himself, glancing briefly to observe the time on the footage, it was now approaching 01:00 hrs, and was *deathly* quiet. He continued through the statement with a failing attention to detail, until something jumped out from with it.

"…I recognised it as a Kia, I know this because there aint too many of them around here, it sounded to me like it needed a new rear silencer, this was the primary reason it stood out to me…" He smiled again and placed it to one side. He picked his cigarette up and gazed at it lovingly, before sucking mightily on it.

"She was there." He said, leaning back in his chair. "Coincidence?" He asked, shaking his head vigorously. "I don't believe so." Bored of seeing nothing on the screen, he increased the play speed and quickly glanced at statement number four.

"…Small…Red…Kia…" He said, holding his pen halfway down the page. "Why has no one paid any attention to this?" He asked, shuffling the statements together like a deck of cards, and placing them back within the file. "I suppose a car travelling in the opposite direction isn't too important when you consider what had just happened…but it's important to me."

The time on the footage now stood at 02: 47, and was progressing rapidly on a play speed of six times it's recorded speed. Once again, to his increasing delight, a small car with it's headlights blazing appeared in the darkened corner by the air and water dispensers. He decreased the playback rate, and reversed it once more to see when it had arrived. "Almost three in the morning," He said. "I can't believe we've never considered the possibility." As before, the small car remained immune to identification due to the glare it created on the footage, and nor did it move.

"Ok." He said, speeding up the footage. "I'll bet you're there when he arrives." He watched as the all important time approached, it was now reading as 03:21 hrs. He pressed play and leaned in closely to the screen, watching as a blue Chrysler Neon drove carefully, almost conservatively, to pump number eight.

"Clever." He whispered, smiling at Mathew's cunning. "You wanted to make sure the attendant released the fuel to you, didn't you?" He watched as Mathew climbed out of the car, he was careful not to expose his face and hid beneath the rim of his cap.

"Clever boy." He said. "I'd expect nothing less." Vincelli watched on as he inserted the nozzle, before walking off in the direction of the parked car.

"I fucking knew it!" He shouted, watching as Mathew walked around to the other side of the car, and out of view.

"Let me guess," He said. "I've got a flat tyre…and a quick bat of the eyelashes later…" He laughed. "You fell for it, hook - line - and sinker!" He concentrated on the footage, more specifically on the little car, and on Mathew, who had now reappeared on screen and was walking back to his *stolen* car

"What did she do?" He asked, almost begging Mathew's image to provide the answer. Not at all surprising to him, was the sight of the car pulling away from the area all together and disappearing completely from view. He saw the time was now almost three - twenty - six, and for the *first* time in the several times he'd studied the footage, the flickering lights above the forecourt began to catch his attention

Why do the lights surge like that? He wondered. *Kinda reminds me of the porch light outside Danny's house. Come to think of it, kinda reminds*

me of the lamp on Danny's bedside table. He paused the footage as the thought progressed. *The lights above the Waltzers, they had all blown out completely except for the strobe lights...which remained perfectly active. The white lights...why do the white lights survive? Flood and strobe lights...they resist the energies created when he...*

He pressed play on the remote control and observed the light show with growing curiosity. They began to flicker rapidly, before dimming to approximately half their wattage. With his back to the darkness of the fields, Mathew leaned on the Chrysler and stared up at the flickering lights, unaware of the shadow clad assassin stepping gracefully from the fields behind him.

It's a fucking distraction. He thought. *The flickering lights, they're a fucking distraction. The Waltzers were an obvious distraction, he wanted people to be looking elsewhere when he attacked that carriage, he wanted people to be...screaming.* He paused the footage again and stared at Mathew, he was clearly engrossed with the light show taking place before him, which Vincelli figured, would account for his sensory failure.

"You didn't hear him," He whispered. "Because he was silent, and you didn't see him...because he distracted you." He pressed play, and watched as Mathew's assailant closed the space between them, *slowly.*

"You're good." Vincelli whispered. "*Very* calculated." He felt a chill run down his spine, watching for the ninth time, as the *Black Widow* drew his weapons, and aimed them at the ground before him. He stood menacingly still for a moment, before taking a final step to achieve range, it's at this point that Mathew is seen to spin around, presumably in response to something, Vincelli figured. Then with deadly accuracy, and without hesitation, the swords slice like vicious machinery through his neck. He stopped the footage and ran his hands through his greasy dark hair.

Why does she believe she's hearing Brandon's voice? He thought. *She said she's been hearing his voice since he died that night, so either she's fucking nuts or he's still –*"

"Wait a minute now." He whispered. *When Danny made his deal with me and named them, I asked him if there was anyone else they could've been working with, if they had another extremely close friend who they would trust to be in on their little secret...he told me they had no friends that he didn't know about...except one.*

"What did you say, Danny?" He muttered, desperately trying to retrieve the words from the archive of his mind.

You were with Brandon, He thought. *You were in his garage checking out his new car, and why wouldn't you be...it was a beautiful car. You were sat in it with him, and he was about to start it when Chad walks into the garden from the patio doors, and you saw behind him... just for a fleeting moment...another one, as you put it...until he saw you and retreated quickly back into the house, and out of view.* He smiled to himself as he gazed at the drawn blinds, behind them the sunlight was strong and begging for entry. *They didn't introduce you as he was shy...and when pressed about the amazing similarity, they told you he had long dark hair, and gave the illusion of similarity...as it was down, concealing his face. Yet you never saw him again...because they told you he lived in North Carolina.*

Raising wearily from his chair he walked to the window, he sensed his small office should share what his mind was experiencing, a distinct absence of darkness. He pulled the blinds high and proud above the window, allowing an influx of light, not entirely dissimilar to fire, to pass through him.

I always believed it was you. He thought. *I also believed you were a friend of theirs...*

"But I never considered *this*." He muttered. "North Carolina is a little far to travel my friend, you'd have to sprout wings and fly!"

The reason she's hearing Brandon's voice, He thought. *Is because Brandon...is still alive. And now that he's lost his connection, he's searching for a new host...a host that he had all along in Julianne. She said that although it was never discussed, he was more than aware of her feelings for him, and that it was their mutual connection that kept them apart...she said that mutual connection was Chad, now I'm not so sure... but of the mutual connection I'm positive. He's communicating with her and somehow…she's helping him. She's always present when he hits his targets, she always seems to know when he's about to strike, and that's because she's receiving impulses from him.*

He reached across his desk, and snatched his overcoat from the chair before fumbling through the pockets for his cell phone. Locating it, he tossed his coat back onto the chair and began dialling. He listened briefly for any noise in the corridor beyond, before affixing it to his ear.

"It's me." He whispered. "By all means necessary…you acquire that girl today."

12:45.

Ray's eyes opened to the strong yet shaded light that filled the room. The memory of last night's revelations hung in his mind as he gazed with wonder at the portrait opposite his bed, it was the most beautifully vivid *secret* he'd ever laid his eyes upon. He guessed them to be in their early twenties at the time of commissioning, as clearly they had all developed individual styles and tastes, judging by their clothing. He could also see a desire within the three of them to attain some semblance of uniqueness, as the frustration between them was almost a physical being. He knew without hesitation which of the three was Brandon, his long hair was tied back tightly, yet shaved completely at the side of his head. He wore a steel chain around his neck which he pointed to with both hands, in Ray's mind, his frustration was palpable if symbolism was to be derived from his actions.

"Good morning." Mary whispered, revealing just her head from behind the door. "Or afternoon in *your* case."

"Who's the artist?" He asked, smiling at her.

"I took the picture," She replied. "On a very rare occasion when the three of them were assembled in the garden." She smiled. "It's a shame there weren't more. But in answer to your question, Brandon did the painting of it."

"Wow." He whispered, glancing again at it. "Is there anything he *can't* do?"

"Go outside." She answered. "Have a relationship, get a job, have a life of his own…and cook."

"I know." He said. "I shouldn't have said that." He watched as she pushed the door open, his eyes travelled over her as she stood inanimately within the doorway. She was wearing a figure hugging black dress, he saw the black lines running down the back of her stockings as she turned away from him.

"Follow me," She shouted back to him. "There are trousers on the dresser that should fit you."

"Coming." He shouted, hastily pulling on a pair of loose fitting black jeans. He cringed at the Day-Glo green belt attached to them, but pulled them on anyway.

"They may not be *quite* to your taste," She said. "But please, no shouting…remember who's outside."

"Ok," He whispered. Assuming the T - shirt beside the jeans was also for his use, he pulled it on and stepped gingerly into the dark hallway.

"Oh my god." Mary said, pointing to what had been Brandon's favourite T - shirt…back when he was just twelve. It depicted a member of rock *royalty*, straddling a motorbike considerably larger than his small stature, singing of *colourful* saturation. "I'll get you something today." She laughed as she took him by the hand, and led him to the end of the hallway. Since all the adjacent doors were closed, he was thankful for her guidance as she led him through a door, that in turn, led to a narrow, north bound staircase, with a door at it's summit.

"I'm going to the cemetery," She said. "But Brandon is waiting for you." She patted his hand reassuringly as she pointed up the stairs. "Everything will be answered, Ray." She added. "I know you two didn't get off to a flying start, it's only to be expected…but you need each other."

"I know." He said. "I was just shocked, I thought he was a ghost."

"As far as everyone *else* is concerned," She replied. "He is. But to you…he's so much more. He's salvation."

"I keep hearing that." He said. "Why is that?"

"The basic definition of *salvation*," She answered. "Is…to save from harm or destruction." She smiled, as once again she pointed up the stairs. "I think you understand."

"What's he doing?" He asked. "He's not sharpening his swords I hope?" He smiled.

"He's sharpening his *mind*." She closed the door gently behind him, and listened as he began his climb up the creaky wooden stairs.

Ray swallowed hard as he reached the second door, he wondered weather or not to knock, but knowing that *he* was *waiting*, inspired him to reach for the handle and open it. He pushed the door slowly and peered in, his nerves deserted him in favour of pure, undiluted amazement.

"You're...*unbelievable*." He allowed the door to creak slowly open until it reached a natural end against it's hinges. He stared in wonder, at what must have been hundreds of marbles, drifting slowly through the air inside the dimly lit room, all the way up to it's high ceiling. Feeling something of a god, he was mindful of a miniature solar system in creation before his very eyes, as he watched them rotate and even gravitate towards each other, although he was yet to set eyes on their *true* creator.

"I'm just open to the possibilities," Brandon whispered. "You should try it sometime."

"Where...are you?" He glanced around the bare room, with not so much as a closet to offer refuge, he knew he was left with just one possibility.

"Come in." He said. "Close the door behind you, and walk to the wall opposite."

Resisting all his natural urges to turn and run, he stepped inside and closed the door as instructed. There was a small window to his left although the curtains were drawn, it was contained within the sloping ceiling that enveloped it. He guessed he was in the attic as he walked slowly towards the wall opposite, mesmerised by the marbles as they glided into, and around him. He cupped one in the palm of his hand, and felt almost saddened as it dropped to the floor the second he released it.

"Why did it do that?" He asked.

"Because you suffocated it." Brandon replied. "Think of it like a fire, remove just one of the elements needed to sustain it…and it will die."

"And what element did I destroy?" He asked, treading carefully across the bare floorboards.

"You starved it of *my* energy."

"My apologies." He tried to suppress the dread welling up within him, in favour of a more positive approach. He knew from the direction of Brandon's voice, *exactly* where he was currently languishing, but the prospect of seeing him there terrified him.

"Turn around." He whispered.

With fear in his heart he turned slowly around to face the door from where he'd entered, and there was Brandon. Ray's body recoiled severely and for the second time in as many days, he contemplated a swan dive from the nearest window. Frozen to the spot, he was no longer captivated by the floating marbles, his attention was instead drawn to the space between the top of the doorframe, and the ceiling. Dressed head to toe in black, was Brandon, hanging motionless above the door. His arms were hung lifelessly next to his waist, his long hair was down around his face, although his eyes, his shiny glazed *black* eyes, gazed through and scorched a path to Ray's. Ray stumbled against the wall behind him and slid down it, unable or unwilling, he simply couldn't detach from Brandon's fearsome stare. He watched on as Brandon slowly raised his arms from his side, his palms faced outwardly as he lifted the marbles to the ceiling.

"My god." Ray whispered. He watched in awe as they all ceased rotating and began to rise, all except the one on the floor which remained idle.

"Gravity," Brandon whispered. "Like anything else, *can* be defied." He looked at the one remaining marble, it was wedged slightly between a gap in the floorboards. It rattled a little, drawing Ray's eyes to it, before breaking free.

"What are you doing to me?" Ray asked, aware of a sudden weightlessness within him. With neither effort nor resistance, he raised slowly to his feet and watched as the marble from the floor, remained level with him as it journeyed skyward. He looked down at his feet and was astounded, albeit a little scared, to see he'd left the floorboards behind, noticing as he levitated upwards, that his posture now mirrored Brandon's exactly.

"Now you see," Brandon said. "I'm like no one you've ever known."

"You're fucking amazing!" Ray shouted, laughing wildly as he reached and touched the ceiling.

"We have guests," Brandon replied, pointing to the small window. "Sshh." He faced his palms down and *pushed* the air beneath them, and began his descent downwards along with Ray, but the marbles remained firmly against the ceiling.

"How do you do that?" Ray asked, landing softly on the floor.

"I'm different, Ray." He replied. "Other than that, I don't know what to tell you."

"You caught me!" Ray said, walking to him. "I remember now… you came blasting through the dust below me, and caught me."

"Hang on a minute," He answered. "Let me get these out." He lowered his head down and gently pressed his finger into his eyes, before revealing to Ray two small *black*, lenses. "The *rest* is real," He said, opening his eyes wide. "But these are purely for effect."

"I don't care." Ray said. "I'd expect nothing less from you." He laughed and shook his hand firmly.

"We meet at last," Brandon whispered. "And not a minute too soon."

"Why did you choose me?" Ray asked, gazing around the room. "I'm nobody."

"It's a real shame you still think like that," Brandon replied. "I thought you'd had enough time to think."

"I've done my thinking." He said. "And time is *all* I've had."

"Then why do you insist on labelling yourself a *nobody?*"

"Because -"

"You wanna know something?" He asked. "The world is full of *nobodies* who think they're *somebodies.*" He laughed as he circled past Ray. "You know the types, those mindless hypocrites who hide behind their job titles…" He stood behind Ray and placed his hands on his shoulders. "…They need a fucking name badge, just to remember who they are." He leaned forward to Ray's ear. "It's all shit." He said. "Be true to yourself, my friend…don't sell out."

"I know who I am." Ray replied. "You've shown me what I need to do."

"And in equal numbers," He continued. "We have the *somebodies* who think they're *nobody*." He turned Ray around to face him. "I know which category *you* fall into." He smiled. "What the world needs now…is more *somebodies*."

"I am *somebody*."

"Then stand up and be counted." He said. "Tell the world you're here! Here I am…love me or hate me but you will fucking *respect* me!"

"It's too late for all that." He said. "You seem to be forgetting, I'm a wanted man."

"Not so." He answered. "Vincelli is a *wanted* man." He walked to the window and peered through the space in the curtains. "His time is upon him," He whispered. "And not just from me."

"Who else?" Ray asked, his curiosity spiked.

"Your captain is seeing things a little more clearly." He replied. "We deliberately left a sword when we caught up with our *final* conspirator. It wasn't a simple case of the sword proving *your* innocence…it was a display of the ease with which they can be attained, and left somewhere…but it got the cogs turning in your favour." He smiled. "Life awaits you."

"I have a question." Ray said. "The guards in my room, they saw you, right?"

"They saw *Jeff*." He answered. "Or *Death* as you know him."

"But they physically *saw* him?"

"Of course they did." He replied. "But do they remember it?"

"Apparently not." He said. "They were talking about an earthquake." He shook his head a little as he recalled the events. "You *did* pull that window out?"

"No." He waved his finger between them both. "The *earthquake* did that."

"So, there *was* an earthquake?"

"Yes." He whispered. "But did I *induce* the earthquake?"

"Did you?"

"I'm afraid so." He replied. "Flickering or exploding lights weren't gonna do the job, for you I needed something more."

"I can't even think of the questions I gotta ask you *now*." Ray said. He lowered himself to his knees and brushed his hand across the dusty floor. "How the fuck do you do that?"

"It wasn't your average earthquake." He whispered. "It came as a result of what I did to the guards."

"I know it sounds stupid," Ray said. "But did you *erase* their memories or something?"

"They say fact is stranger than fiction," He said. "And in this case I'd have to agree." He walked to the centre of the room and gazed up at the marbles, his long hair seemed to extend down his back as he cocked his neck backwards.

"Tell me." Ray said, watching as the marbles began to orbit the light fixture.

"When I showed you the day Nancy had died, I took you on a journey within your *own* memory." He said. "If you recall I was merely showing you that which you already knew." He held his arms out and turned slowly around all the while gazing upwards. "But as real as it seemed, you had to return to the present as you were merely inhabiting a corner of your own *spent* existence."

"Ok." He replied. He watched as the marbles began rotating under Brandon's command, twirling in unison with his body as he pirouetted in the centre of the room.

"With them," He said. "It was slightly different."

"How?" Ray asked.

"I took them back in time." He replied. "They hadn't forgotten… it simply hadn't happened."

"You mean you…" He paused. "…You…What?"

"I took them back." He said again. "I didn't just reverse, or wipe their memory…I turned the hands of time, but only for them, you remained on a parallel time line, which is why you remembered me being there." He turned to face Ray, glancing just once to the ceiling above. "You'll have to forgive me," He said, laughing. "I've got a lot of balls in the air."

"Explain." Ray ordered.

"The last thing they recall," He answered. "Is you, shouting out that you were sick of being fucked."

"And then what?"

"And then," He answered. "The earthquake struck!"

"No." Ray said. "I know you can do some shit, but time travel… you must think I'm crazy."

"How can you *possibly* doubt me?" He asked. "Look at what you already *know*." He shook his head in disappointment. "Why do you think the light came on?" He asked. "You saw that strip light shatter yourself, I suppose the handyman came in and replaced it while you were looking down? It came on…because it was never broken in their eyes, it was never broken because…I turned back the hands of time."

"I just don't believe -"

"It's all an illusion, Ray." He said. "*Everything* that you can imagine, can be manipulated or defied."

"And the earthquake?"

"Time lines are like fault lines," He replied. "Disturbing them has results."

"Then why all this?" Ray asked. "Why go to all this trouble?" He stood up and walked to the window, desperately wanting to, but resisting the urge to open the curtains. "It's all for nothing."

"Nothing?" Brandon asked. "All for *nothing*?" He laughed, although clearly un amused. "You really haven't learned a damn thing have you?" He asked, pushing Ray against the wall. "Nothing is without reason, and nothing is without consequence."

"You could've sent me back!" Ray shouted, wiping away his tears. "You could've -"

"Why?" Brandon asked. "Why the fuck should I have sent you back? You act like a fucking moron! You didn't deserve that privilege and you still don't. You've learned nothing!"

"Just tell me why!" He said, again dropping to his knees. "Why put me through all this?"

"*I*, as you put it," He replied, squatting down beside him. "Put you through *nothing*." His anger softened. "Cause and effect." He whispered. "The chaos theory if you will."

"What?"

"The flutter of butterfly wings on one continent," He replied. "Can result in a typhoon on another…they call it the *chaos theory*."

"I don't understand."

"One seemingly innocuous event," He said. "In your case, a packet of cigarettes...resulted in the total and *complete* destruction, of the rest of your life." He stroked Ray's head. "In my case, a harmless night out...*forever* changed the course of my life with disastrous consequences." He smiled kindly. "*Nothing*, is for nothing."

"But why kill them all?" He asked. "Why not just go back and undo it?"

"Honestly?" He asked. "If you were given the opportunity to hurt those who'd hurt you, would you take it? Or would you erase it and all hold hands?" He winked at Ray. "It's extremely satisfying, I'm sorry to say."

"You like killing?"

"I like *revenge*." He answered. "And why shouldn't I?" He stood up and paced the room angrily. "For what they did to me, to *us*... they deserve *Death*...not *Salvation*."

"They created a monster." Ray whispered. "You can't seriously -"

"*They* created *nothing*." He shouted. "They wouldn't understand creation if it bit them on their fucking cocks!" He stalked Ray wildly. "*I* created what I am! I'm the innovator here not them, I'm the master of my own voyage." He laughed. "People, *most* people... simply don't understand creation, for them it ends with childbirth." He leapt to the floor and circled Ray like a panther. "Why should the miracle of creation end there, there's so much to be explored and discovered...music to be listened to, artist's to be discovered, pictures to be painted and trails to be blazed." He reached out and raised Ray's face until level with his own. "I'm a trailblazer, Ray." He whispered. "Duplication is *boring*...innovation is *exciting*."

"So how does *he*, come back?" Ray asked. "How do you summon him?"

"Time reversal." He replied. "I reverse *my own* time line...I take myself to a specific point on the evening of Halloween, when Jeff and I were in this very room."

"Before he left with Chad?"

"Yes."

"You mean...he returns as a living human being?"

"No." He answered. "He's a human being at the point I return to, but when *we* make the transition back to *my* present...he's an empty vessel."

"He's dead?"

"Yes." He whispered. "Operating merely on *pulses*."

"So…you reverse time to the point where -"

"Yes." He answered. "Like with the guards, I reverse the time line to the point where the *event*…the life changing *event*…hasn't even happened."

"Which is all well and good," Ray said. "But you're telling me… that when you return to *your* present…"

"He's dead."

"Do they both return?"

"No." He replied. "I can only sustain Jeff."

"Why?"

"Because it was Jeff and I that shared the link." He whispered. "Jeff was my other side, the other side of *me.*" He stood up and gazed at the rotating marbles. "I am the butterfly wings," He whispered. "Jeff is the typhoon."

"Oddly enough," Ray said. "I think I understand."

"But I can't direct him." He said. "I can't spend the whole fight instructing him, so I have someone else do that for me."

"What?" He asked, raising to his feet. "Who?"

"A friend." He replied. "She is the go - between."

"I don't under -"

"Watch your head." He clicked his fingers and brought the marbles crashing down to the floor. He laughed at the sight of Ray ducking and diving to avoid them, it was a source of much needed amusement for both of them. "My workout is over." He said.

"Thanks for the warning." Ray said, rubbing his head. "Now who's this -"

"Her name is Julianne." He said. "I don't believe you've met her, but she's -"

"Chad's girlfriend."

"She is a very special young lady." He whispered. "On my instructions…she marks the intended *victim*."

"On your instructions?"

"I'm *dead*, remember?" He said. "So it's not like I can swing by and do it myself."

"How does she do it?"

"Merely a touch." He whispered. "She only has to make physical contact, whilst holding her pendant...the hate in her heart does the rest."

"And *she* controls him?"

"She *directs* him." He replied. "I'm able to communicate with him *via* Julianne, but she is his *master*...she pulls his strings."

"So that's how *Death*...targets his victims."

"Yes." He whispered, leading him to the window. "I do the rest."

"Does she have a psychic *connection* with him?"

"No." He answered. "She has a psychic connection to *me*, and is able to see what I see...as he did, and feel what I feel...as he did. She's as good as there, which is why she's able to successfully direct him...with *pulses*."

"And Vincelli?" He asked.

"We'll both have him." He replied. "He's going to be difficult to reach...but we've saved him for last for that very reason." He laughed. "Now that they know we bring the pain, *anyone* foolish enough to stand between him and us...deserves to die. And die they shall."

"Are you expecting resistance?" He asked, peering through the space between the curtains. "Do you think they'll still challenge you?"

"I think they'll shit their pants, Ray." He laughed. "They have no idea what we're going to bring down on them."

"And me?" He asked. "What do you want from me?"

"I want your heart and soul." He said, placing an arm around Ray's shoulder. "I want you to look within yourself, and show me what you're really made of."

"Are you taking me with you?"

"No." He shook his head. "The passenger seat is already taken, I'm not even *telling* you."

"Why?" He asked. "I thought that was the whole idea?"

"It's probably for the best..." He whispered. "That you don't get caught in the *crossfire*."

Friday 4th June.

FOUR HOURS TO LAUNCH

Swinging his car in a full circle on the uneven gravel parking area, Vincelli glanced in his rear view mirror as he hit the brakes, before reversing up to the steel blue door to the left of the large loading bay shutter. He smiled as he watched the steel door being pushed open from within the building, although it quickly faded as he realised that *that* was *all* they were doing. With his eyes fixed angrily on the door *via* his mirror, he grabbed his cell from the passenger seat and dialled.

"*Who* just opened the door?" He asked, his hostility was more than evident. He nodded as he listened. "Get him back down here," He said. "Right now." He ended the call and sat silently. With barely the time it took to place the phone in his pocket, he saw the door fly open and an openly apologetic man attired in a dark suit, approaching his car.

"I'm sorry," He said, opening the car door for him. "It's my first day."

"It's *everyone's* first day." He answered. "We've been closed for six months."

"I'm sorry, Sir." He said. "Some of the security men told me to come and open the door, I didn't know who you were."

"I was beginning to think some…*retraining* was needed." He stepped from his car and walked past the man towards the steel door. Standing at the rear of the newly converted warehouse, he observed it's fascia with a sense of pride.

"Looks like shit," He said, turning to the man. "But then the side you never see, always does." He laughed. "As long as the main entrance is all glittery and inviting, that's all that matters." He stepped through the door before turning to block the man's entry. "Always be aware of the side that people *don't* want you to see," He said. "Because you can guarantee it's dark…and *slightly* dangerous." He stared angrily into his eyes. "Don't blame others for your own mistakes, young man."

"I'm sorry." He said.

"You show me the respect I deserve in future." He turned and walked inside, leaving the man to close what was actually the fire escape.

"Ok." He whispered. He walked slowly behind Vincelli and followed him nervously up the rear stairs. He glanced down at the polished shoes his mum had bought for him, all the while wishing he'd not worn white socks. He reached the kitchen area, that was intended to be his domain as of ten o' clock that evening, to find Vincelli stood wielding a large kitchen knife.

"What's your name?" He asked, walking over to him.

"Peter." He answered, rearing back through the door he'd just opened.

"How old are you?"

"Twenty - two."

"And you're employed as?" He tossed the knife in the air and caught it quickly, blade in hand.

"I'm training today as a kitchen porter." He glanced nervously at Vincelli, watching as he thrust the handle in his direction.

"Good." He whispered. "I'm sure you don't need training with this, do you?"

"No." He answered, taking it from him.

"I'm starving." He said. "There's some nice looking crusty bread on that table," He pointed to the work surface beneath the shiny steel cupboards. "Find something nice to go on it." He walked out of the room, leaving Peter to search for a suitable topping.

Vincelli pushed open a security door and entered the highly illuminated night club, he stood and surveyed the newly refurbished premises with a sense of growing pride. Surrounded by four imitation marble pillars, and forming an obvious focal point within the club was the dance floor: it had a large skylight above it, which opened like a car's sunroof at the flick of a switch from within the DJ's podium, which itself was situated at the helm of the dance floor and up a small flight of stairs. He walked slowly towards the dance floor, before turning around to look at the wall opposite him. He smiled at the large wooden cross suspended against it, and the projection unit mounted beneath it.

"Wonderful." He whispered. "Just wonderful." He walked across the dance floor until he reached a security door, it was marked *private*, and had an electronic key pad beside it. He typed in the four digit code and pushed it open before walking into the corridor, and turning for a last look at the deserted night club. He closed the door and walked down towards the office at the end, it was his office, although the name on the door read simply *Manager's Office*. He tapped gently on the door and waited as two sets of dead bolts were released. He pushed the door open and stepped inside, he turned quickly on himself and slid each lock back into place, before glancing quickly at the clock on the wall, it was six o' clock.

"I was wrong," He said, smiling. "Apparently we *will* be seeing more of each other." He walked to the corner of the windowless office, ignoring the two well stacked men present as he went. He dropped into a leather couch against the wall and focused his attention on Julianne, as she stood suspended and handcuffed to bolts driven into the wall. Her bloodied face was battered and bruised, and her mouth was covered with duct tape, that was in fact wrapped completely, several times around the back of her head. He ran his eyes over her body, and was mildly aroused at the sight of her breasts through her T - Shirt, that had been sliced, or *ripped* open. Her skirt was pushed up, revealing her slender yet *bruised* legs, which were bound at her ankles.

"Go on." He said, glancing at one of the men, before tilting his head to Julianne. "I wanna watch."

"Fine by me." He said, pulling himself off the desk. He walked casually up to Julianne, and was clearly drawing pleasure from her muffled cries as he slid his hand down his pants and masturbated, while caressing her breast with his other.

"That's nice," He whispered, turning to Vincelli and his colleague who were openly egging him on. "What else have you got for me?" He asked, sliding his hand down her exposed stomach to her upturned skirt. "It's been a while for you, hasn't it?" He lowered his hand further and was excited at her struggling. "Mark may not have had the balls to fuck you…" He said, firmly rubbing his hand up and down between her legs. "…Even that night when he fucking drugged you!" He laughed as her eyes recognised what he was saying. "You didn't know that, did you?" He asked. "You thought it was because you *bumped* your head." He laughed wildly as she tried to scream. "He was planning to rape your *sweet* ass that night."

"But he developed feelings for you!" Vincelli said. "Don't worry, that wont be happening here tonight." He laughed, they all laughed. "Don't fucking tickle her, Carl." He said. "Fuck her!"

Julianne's cries grew louder as he unbuttoned his jeans, and allowed them to fall to his feet. With one hand pressing firmly over the already present duct tape, he tore frantically at her underwear before it too fell to her feet with some further persuasion. He forced her legs open with ease, before pressing himself firmly against her body.

"You fucking bitch." He said. "It's been a while since you've had it! You fucking *love* it."

Vincelli stared into her eyes as her body was shunted with increasing force against the wall. He looked at the man next to him, who in turn was gazing at the spectacle before them.

"That's enough." Vincelli said, raising to his feet.

"What?" Carl asked, stopping but not *ending*. "You just said -"

"I know what I said." Vincelli replied, pulling him away from Julianne. "This isn't for your pleasure," He continued. "It's for her *suffering*." He pulled the duct tape from her mouth and leaned into her closely. "Are *you* ready to tell me what I want to know?" He asked. "Because if your not, I'm going to set the pair of them on you!" He observed the inverted cross hanging from her neck, and remembered how she caressed it.

"I will." She cried. "Please...*please*...you're policemen." She stuttered hysterically as she tried to speak. "Help me...pl - please... he - help me."

"That's sweet." He said. "I'll help you, but you have to *help* me... help you."

"I'll tell you." She whispered. "I'll...I'll...tell you."

"Good girl." He said, attempting to cover her up with her torn T-shirt. "They *are* nice." He said, pushing down her skirt. "You'll have to tell me *everything*, or else they're coming out to play. *Understand?*"

"Y...yes." She said. "Pl...please...don't let them hurt me anymore."

"I thought you were different." She said, watching as the third man approached her.

"Different?" He asked, removing his jacket. "You thought Mark was different! If I were you, I'd stop trusting my judgement." He laughed at her.

"You're not like them, Martin." She said. "You see…seemed… kind."

"It's the oldest act in the book, Julianne." He replied. "Good cop…bad cop…all that shit."

"When did you become a part of all this?" She asked. "You've only recently joined in."

"Let's stop with the stalling." He said. "Coz honestly…we don't have the time."

"I *know* you've not been in on this long." She whispered. "Or else…*He'd* want you."

"Which brings me to my question." He said. "Is *Brandon Rose*… still alive?" The question floated between them for a moment, before she watched his eyes move to her skirt.

"Yes." She whispered. "I feel his presence…*still*."

"Is *Brandon*…the swordsman?"

"Yes." She replied. "It's…It's…him."

"How does he do it?" He asked. "Come and go with such speed and agility?"

"It's the drug." She whispered, following his eyes. "He has to have *HEX*."

"Now you don't strike me as the type of girl," He said. "Who'd even know about *HEX*, so that's one truth point for you." He smiled broadly at her. "Why?"

"It gives him…" She paused. "Powers."

"Like?"

"Flight." She said. "He becomes *superhuman*."

"What?" He asked, turning to look at Vincelli. "Superhuman… how?"

"Well flight alone is pretty fucking *super* in my book." She shouted, regretting it instantly.

"That wasn't wise." He whispered, running his hand slowly up her inside leg. "Is this how we're going to play?"

"I'm sorry!" She begged. "Don't...*please*...don't."

"Superhuman...how?" He asked, removing his hand.

"The *HEX*...combined with the blood of it's host -"

"Hold on." He said, placing his finger firmly across her lips. "You said, he has to have *HEX*." He removed his finger and stared into her eyes. "Blood?"

"It's not just the Heroin," She whispered. "It's the blood. He needs the *HEX*...but only once it's been injected into their system. Once their heart's begin circulating the drug, it's then that he strikes. It's then that he becomes..."

"Becomes what?"

"A...*Vampire*." She whispered. "By *design*."

"A...*Vampire*?" He asked. "Are you serious?" He hadn't heard Vincelli coming, but turned to see him stood beside him, gazing at Julianne, and the inverted cross around her neck. He reached for it and caressed it between his own fingers, all the while reading her *reaction* to him touching it.

"You're not being *completely* truthful." Vincelli said, tearing it from her neck.

"No!" She shouted. "Give it -"

"Shut the fuck up." Martin said, clamping his hand firmly across her mouth.

"It seems to me," Vincelli whispered. "That you're more scared of us touching *this*, than of us touching *anything* else." He nodded to Martin.

"I think you're right." Martin replied, once again running his hand up her inside leg. They all watched on as she struggled and writhed, she tried and failed to scream through Martin's hand, but not once did she loose sight of the pendant.

"You *are* right." Martin whispered, reaching the top of her inner thigh. "I don't think you mind *this*...at all."

"Tell me about the pendant, Julianne." Vincelli said. "This will continue until you do."

"Is that a yes?" Martin asked, releasing his grip a little.

"Yes." She cried. "Please...*stop*."

"Ok." Once again, he removed his hand. "Tell us."

"Brandon...is...*not* the swordsman." She whispered. "It's his Brother."

"Chad?" Martin asked, feeling more than a little confused. "Do you mean Chad?"

"Or the *other* one?" Vincelli asked. "I *know* there were three of them…" He paused. "…And evidently, so do you."

"I don't know -"

"You just told us that Brandon, is still alive!" He countered. "Now, my mathematics has never been great…but if two were buried, and one remains…"

"Ok." She cried, gazing up her bleeding wrists. "Ok."

"Ok." Vincelli whispered. "Now let's forget Brandon for just a moment, I want to know who's helping him kill. I *know* there's more than one out there. You just told me that Brandon…is a vampire, now whether he sleeps upside down in a cave or *not*, the fact remains, that Tommy died at the hands of someone *not* wielding swords, and he was *bitten*." He used his hands like scales before him, as he weighed up the situation. "So in my book," He said. "*Brandon* killed Tommy." He dangled the pendant before his eyes. "What I want to know." He said. "Is who the *swordsman* is."

I can't tell them the truth, She thought. *They'll kill me here and now if they find out…*

"The pendant summons *Death*," She whispered. "Or *Jeff*, as he was otherwise known."

"So you knew all along?" Vincelli asked. "That they were *triplets*, and not twins."

"It was hard not too." She said. "I'm connected to Brandon… *spiritually*."

"If that's the case," He whispered. "Then where's *loverboy*, right now?"

"He communicates with *me*," She replied. "Not the other way around."

"Like a friend who only wants to talk about themselves?" He asked, laughing.

"No."

"So how exactly does the pendant work?" He asked.

"*Whoever* has the pendant," She whispered. "Can control who he kills."

"And you did that?" He asked, tucking the pendant neatly in his trouser pocket. "How?"

"By touching the intended target." She replied. "Brandon would relay to me who I had to touch, then *Death* would be able to find them."

"How did you touch Nikki Farrell?" He asked. "I know your car was behind the Mercedes."

"I didn't." She answered. "*Death* didn't kill him." She gazed around the room, trying her best to avoid eye contact with all three of them. "It was Brandon who killed him."

"So why where you there?"

"Brandon had instructed me to mark him," She whispered. "But I messed it up…I failed to make contact, but then he saw an opening and took it."

"I see." He whispered. "And Mathew Johnson?" He asked. "How did that work?"

"He was easy." She replied, laughing against her best intentions. "All I did was call him over, I told him I couldn't start the car…he leaned in and started it."

"And you touched him?"

"Yes." She nodded. "I reached for his hand as he turned the key."

"Ok." Vincelli said, turning his back on her. "We've established that…*Death*, didn't kill Tommy. How about Jake?" He spun around to face her once more. "In your *own* words, you were too scared to meet them…so how did you mark him?"

"Earlier in the evening." She answered. "I was instructed to mark him, virtually as soon as we arrived there…I saw him…I touched him."

"Is that why you didn't want to meet them?" He asked. "By the *Waltzers*?"

"No." She shook her head. "I didn't want to meet them, because I knew that *Death* was coming for Jake."

"And you were scared?"

"Yes." She replied. "But you're going to find out *all* about that."

"Bravo!" He said, clapping his hands. "You've got guts." He smiled at her.

"What about Mark, Julianne?" Martin asked. "We spoke so much about it, I wonder is there anything you could add? For the purposes of our…*investigation*, of course."

"Like you said, I believed he was *different*." She replied. "I needed Mark."

"You loved him?"

"I hadn't been told to mark him." She said flatly. "I don't think Brandon wished to compromise my emotions." She sighed. "I think he knew I had feelings for him…I believe he waited for Mark to reveal himself to me, to take the sting out of it I guess."

"And finally…" Vincelli shouted. "There's the little matter of… *me*?" He pulled his cigarettes from his coat pocket. "You've marked me."

"*You* have the pendant." She whispered. "Your mark is broken."

"Do you expect me to believe that?"

"It's the truth." She replied. "It's null and void."

"I have one final question." He said, lighting his cigarette. "You say that Brandon, *has* to have *HEX*?"

"It's a draw to him." She said. "It's almost primal."

"I see." He smiled. "Are you a user, Julianne?"

"No…"

"You *will* be." He whispered. "Let's see how *primal* his instincts really are."

ONE HOUR TO LAUNCH.

With the radio playing gently, Scott sat silently in his car and gazed out at the failing light, it seemed to diminish with each passing minute, along with his hopes. His expression was saddened as he observed the steel shutters, they had been affixed to each possible entry point, front and back, at 21 Donalds way, Ray's house. No one believed *Ray* would show his face, but unsurprisingly his address had become somewhat of a Mecca for the morbid folk, and a target of hate for the *good* and *righteous*. Cufflinks already in hand, he rolled up his sleeves and consequently, noticed it had just turned nine o' clock.

"Where are you, Ray." He whispered, imagining his presence. "Contact me, *please*." He found himself drawn back to a time when the steel shutters were *not* present, when the glass was visible and the garden neat. It had been bright that day, he recalled. The sunshine had been strong *despite* the chill in the December air. He hadn't been present to witness first hand, but he knew with certainty that Nancy's blood had smeared the glass panel of the front door, and more poignantly, her blood had smeared his *conscience*.

"And now Julianne." He whispered. "Reported missing... this morning." Sighing heavily, he threw his cufflinks onto the passenger seat and gripped the wheel tightly, whilst maintaining an uninterrupted line of sight, on Ray's house.

"Don't give up, Ray." He said. "Wherever you are...don't do anything *stupid*."

His concentration was broken by his cell phone, it's screen illuminated brightly from within the cradle it was perched. The number was not currently stored, nor was it one he recognised. He reached slowly across to accept the call, but was mildly pleased as it was cut off, and forwarded instead to his mail box. He relaxed deeply into his seat, but couldn't seem to shake the foreboding sense of urgency that began to well up within him. He knew without a shadow of doubt that his phone would almost certainly ring again, he counted the seconds mentally until he watched the screen illuminate once more, and wasted no time in hitting accept.

"Hello?"

"*Sir?*" The ladies voice asked in return. "Is that you?"

"Yes." He replied. He listened to her panic stricken voice with growing concern, as it came through a speaker mounted against his courtesy light. "Lisa?"

"I've got the tape." She said. "I'm here at the studio with my husband, he's just developed it moments ago." She began crying.

"Who is it?" He asked, already trembling.

"It's Vincelli." She replied, attempting to stem her hysterics. "I'm scared."

"Stay on the line." He whispered. He ran his fingers through his hair whilst contemplating her words.

How do I find him, He thought. *I can't launch a manhunt...for all I know he's got however many uniform's and detective's working with him...I can't show him my hand or else he'll vanish...gone forever...just like Danny…just like the twins…just like Ray…just like…Julianne. Oh Jesus…He's got her, I just know it. No fucking wonder he insisted on interviewing her at home…he didn't want on record whatever it was she knew, and…he wanted the schematic of her house. Does that mean that…Martin…*

His thoughts crashed to a halt as what he initially *thought*, was lightening, appeared high in the blackened sky above. He concentrated his attention firmly on it, and noticed it was in fact several lasers, ripping through the darkness and reaching high enough to disturb *god*. They rotated slowly in a circular motion, accelerating gradually until spinning so fast that a solid green circle was formed. He stared in disbelief as another two lasers, *red* in colour, began criss - crossing within the existing circle, until they too accelerated to form a solid *cross*, within the existing circle.

'Well folks…' The radio announced. 'It's finally here…it's almost launch time here at *The Crossfire*, and with just thirty minutes to go the queue's already hit the parking lot. Remember now, it's a fancy dress launch party so if you've not donned your scariest costume, you wont be admitted this evening. There's no need to wait until October thirty - first, it's Halloween tonight here at *The Crossfire*. I'm Jesse Myers, and I'll be laying on the tunes 'til four in the morning, but don't worry if you can't make it as we're broadcasting live *right here*, all evening.

Wait a minute, He thought. *Danny said something about people getting caught in the crossfire…It's you and me, and people just like you and me, who'll get caught in the crossfire. You told him to say that…you've been dangling this under our noses all along.*
You're calling him out aren't you? You want Ray to come to you, you're inviting him through the door…but you're also inviting…

"Lisa." He said, watching the *target* high above. "Look out of the nearest window."
"What?" She asked, clearly perplexed by his sudden request. "You want me to do what?"

"Go to the window nearest where you currently are," He said. "And look *out* of it."

"Ok." She whispered.

"*Hurry.*"

He started the engine as he listened to her moving across the room, he hoped she would immediately see the *target* for herself. Or in her case…the *warning*. It was obvious to him that she was reluctant to seek a clue, it was also obvious that she was visiting several windows.

"There's a laser!" She said finally, and clearly short on breath. "I think it's that new club…it's been advertised on the radio all week."

"You listen very carefully to me." He whispered. "If you can see those lasers in your rear view mirror…then you haven't driven far enough."

"I don't under -"

"Get away from those lasers!" He shouted. "Do you hear me?"

"What's happening?" She shouted back. "I'm fucking scared!"

"It's Vincelli!" He said. "That's his club…it's him…he's the boss."

"How do you know he's there?"

"He's there." He said. "That's a target he's displaying…he's calling him out."

"Ray?"

"No." He replied. "The Black Widow."

"…Sir?"

"Get *far* from those lasers." He said. "Good ship *Payback* is once again on the horizon."

THIRTY MINUTES TO LAUNCH.

Wearing jeans and a white vest, Ray stood nervously in the doorway to the bare attic, he gazed at Brandon as he stood perfectly still beneath the dim yet distinct halo of light that surrounded him. His hair was tied back tightly and as always, his leather trousers and tightly fitting black sleeved T - shirt clung to his muscular physique as though wet. With his body armour and harness *already* secured tightly to his torso, he rotated himself slowly to face Ray.

"It's almost *launch* time." He whispered, opening his eyes to reveal the black *lenses*.

"I hate those." Ray said. "They look…*scary*."

"Indeed they do." He replied. "At least, that's the idea." He held his hands up for Ray's inspection, wiggling his fingers he summoned his attention to the black nail varnish he'd applied. "And this…" He said. "Well…I thought it looked cool."

"I'm scared, Brandon." He muttered. "I'm scared for you."

"Don't be." He replied. "Be scared for *them*…they're in for a world of pain tonight." He smiled. "Be scared for those who *witness* me…" He added. "…They'll never forget *this* show."

"*Please*," He begged. "Tell me where…I *have* to help."

"Close the door." He whispered, summoning Ray to join him beneath the light. "All the answers in the world reside in a man's heart." He said, watching as Ray closed the door and stepped tentatively towards him. "If you don't know where we're going yet, I assure you, you soon *will*."

Leaving Ray stood beneath the light, Brandon walked slowly and *silently* across the floorboards towards the door. Facing the wall as he did so, he flicked the switch and engulfed the room in total darkness.

"What are you doing?" Ray asked. He could only guess as to Brandon's whereabouts within the room, as he expertly embraced the darkness as only *he* could.

"Shadow's walk with me," He whispered. "They protect and guide me, until I *want* to be seen that is." Without warning his face appeared suddenly to Ray's surprise, it glowed with a green tint while his hair now illuminated brightly with a red glow, he smiled as he remembered Brandon's penchant for fluorescent camouflage.

"*Now* you see me…" He whispered, gliding effortlessly around the room. "…And now you *don't*." He vanished from view in the blink of an eye, leaving Ray to once more contemplate his location.

"Ok." Ray said. "You've got style, kid." His balance faltered as the floorboards beneath his feet began to rumble, not violently like the hospital had, just gently enough to reposition furniture…had there been any, and knock pictures from the walls…had there been any.

He was relieved as once again, *florescent* Brandon, appeared before him. He remained visible as he walked back to the door, Ray's eyes followed him and he watched as Brandon flicked the switch once more.

"It's all an illusion, Ray." He said, smiling broadly at him. "Slight of hand…"

"What's the illusion?" He asked, returning his smile. "I'm not sure I understand."

Ray turned to see Brandon's mirror image stood silently, and menacingly before his eyes. His long black hair hung like the Reapers veil over his *deathly* pale and expressionless features, as his eyes moved from the familiarity of Brandon, to the stranger before him.

"It's you." Ray muttered, "You're back…you've come…*back*."

"He can't communicate with you." Brandon said. "Remember, he's the other side of *me*."

"What does that mean?"

"It means," He whispered. "He can communicate with me, but only via *her*." He walked to his brother and looked him up and down, before parting the hair from his face and taking a closer look at him.

"Why *is* he so pale?"

"This is exactly how he looked that night." Brandon answered. "This was his costume."

"Is he ok?" Ray asked. "Why hasn't he said anything?" He watched curiously as Brandon *inspected* his brother, all the while mystified at *Death's* failure to register a single emotion.

"He's awaiting the *pulse*."

"From…Julianne?"

"Yes." He answered, waving his hand before the eyes of *Death*. "Something's wrong, he's not responding." He grabbed his shoulders and shook him violently. "Julianne knows when I displace…she feels it as I do." He stood motionless and stared into *Death's* eyes. "She should be instructing him now." He whispered. "Something is *very* wrong here."

"What?"

"Her *line* is down," He whispered. "I can't connect to her…

they've got her."

"Brandon!" Ray shouted. "I don't understand what you're saying!"

"Right now..." He said. "She's either unconscious or *dead*." He paced wildly across the room as *he* stood and stared. "Without her, *Death* is useless."

Ray watched helplessly as Brandon opened the door, and charged down the stairs before disappearing completely from view. He turned to face *Death* and was mindful of a mannequin in a shop window, as he stared blankly back at Ray through his thick hair.

"You promised me..." He whispered. Fearsome features belied his fragile words. "...You promised I wouldn't be..."

"You're speaking!" Ray said, although clearly unsure *who* was speaking. "Is that..."

"Help me." He whispered. "I need you...I need you."

"Brandon!" Ray shouted, backing away from him. "He's talking!" He pressed himself against the wall, maintaining what he considered to be a safe distance from *Death*.

"Kill them all." He said, locking eyes with Ray. "Leave *no* one... kill them all."

"Where?" Ray asked. "Tell me where."

"He's not the one talking." Brandon said. "That's Julianne." Clutching against himself the *real* killing kit, he handed to Ray a matching pair of samurai swords, each in a glorious black lacquered sheath and stretching some three feet in length, while he placed another equally identical pair on the floor beside him.

"I've got to strap him up." He said. "He needs to step *into* this harness, so I'm gonna need you to lift his leg a little so I can get him into it."

"She needs you." Ray muttered, placing them gently on the floor. "She needs *us*."

"She needs *us*." Brandon said, looking to *death* whilst waving the harness at Ray. "Help me with this."

"Ok." Ray answered, kneeling before *Death*. "I'll lift...you slide that under." He gently raised his right foot, just enough for Brandon to slide one half of the harness beneath him.

"Now the other one." Brandon said, working hastily. "Lift."

"He's looking at me." Ray whispered, gazing up at his pallid complexion while lifting his left foot a little. "He's looking down at me, Brandon."

"It's fine." He replied, sliding the other half of the harness beneath him. He pulled the harness up tightly until it secured beneath his groin, before feeding his arms through the body of it and locking it at his waist. He pulled tightly on the tensioning straps until firmly locked on.

"We're set."

"Set for what?" Ray asked. "He's useless to you!" He shouted, grabbing at *Death's* hand and shaking it about. "You need me!"

"I *need* Julianne!" He said. "I have to reach her or else it's all in jeopardy."

"Tell me where!" He shouted firmly. "You may not have needed me before, but you sure need me now." He grabbed Brandon's shoulders and held on to him. "It's not a crime to accept help," He said. "You have to tell me where it's going down…I'll follow you."

"You're right." He whispered, somewhat reluctantly. "The *Crossfire*." He said. "It's launch night tonight and he'll be there, it's his establishment."

"The Crossfire?" He asked, recalling his dream. *One of us must die*, He thought. *But who will get caught…in the Crossfire.*

"Don't leave the house," He said, pointing to the small window. "Until *they* leave."

"What?" Ray asked. "How do you know they're even gonna leave?"

"They'll leave." He replied, laughing. "Trust me…everything they have will be heading *my* way." He strapped the two black swords he'd given to Ray firmly into *Death's* harness, while he set about securing the other two to his own waist.

"Why are you carrying?" Ray asked, watching him complete his final preparations.

"Because," He answered, tightening them to his belt. "It all adds to the illusion."

"Why haven't you strapped them to your back?" He glanced at Brandon's battle ready counterpart. "They're better there, surely?"

"They are." He agreed. "And when we arrive at the Crossfire, I will strap them to my back as *he* does…but *he* will be secured to my back during flight."

"Ok." Ray said. "So how do I know where to find this place?"

"Look to the sky," He whispered. "*For your invitation*."

"I'll take your word for it." He replied. "So what now?"

"Help me get him downstairs," He replied. "Then…*we* launch."

FIFTEEN MINUTES TO LAUNCH.

As Scott brought his car to a *shrieking* halt at the rear of the Divisional Headquarters building, he gazed skyward to see the laser beams were now perfectly stationary, the *target* hung perfectly still as though hooked to a star. He switched off the engine and alighted quickly, before slamming the door shut and running down the ramp towards the cell area. He pressed the bell frantically and literally *felt* the seconds pass, until the call was connected.

"Hello." The woman's voice answered, finally.

"Who's that?" He asked, staring directly into the accompanying camera.

"Theresa." She replied.

"Are you sure about that?" He asked, detecting uncertainty in her voice.

"Yes." She answered, detecting sarcasm in his. "What can we do for you, Sir?"

"You can buzz me through to the airlock."

"We can't buzz you through." She replied. "Hang on a minute, Sir."

"I don't have a minute." He replied, tapping his wrist watch in full view of the camera. He stood patiently and listened as the distinct rattle of keys approached from inside the building. He peered through a small pane of glass within the large shutter, to see *The Bull*, approaching him, albeit a little apprehensively.

"Step clear, Sir." He shouted. He peered through the glass and up the vacant ramp, before radioing back to his colleague. "Clear?" He asked.

"All clear."

"My apologies, Sir!" He shouted, unlocking the final shutter that separated them, and dragging it along it's tracks to allow him entry. "Friday nights can get a bit...*out there*."

"None necessary." Scott whispered, watching as he slammed it firmly shut.

"To what do we owe this honour?" He asked, locking it down.

"I'm taking Jet." He replied. "It's time for him to hit the bricks... as it were."

"That's fine by me." He tapped on the main entrance door. "He's only here on your say."

"How is he?"

"He's still in a pretty bad way." He replied. "He's worried us to the point that we've put him on a ten minute watch."

"I see." He whispered, staring at *The Bull*.

He could even have you, He thought. *How can I possibly know how far this goes, people are easily swayed in the pursuit of the mighty buck... friendships...relationships and partnerships are all expendable under it's weight. It seems everyone is willing to chase easy money, but god forbid they should actually earn it...when they'll happily kill for it.*

They both stood silently and watched on, as a small viewing hatch was opened on the other side of the small, reinforced glass panel. A woman of considerable dimensions stood gazing at them both somewhat curiously, before finally turning the key and ushering them inside. She gazed nervously at Scott, observing that although he was dressed very much *down* compared to his usual standards, he was as sharp as ever.

"I'm sorry, Sir." She said. "I was a little surprised to see it was you."

"It's fine," He said. "I'm here to take Jet."

"Thank god." She said, locking the door behind them. "I know you've done him a turn, Sir...but fact is, that kid needs some professional help." She led Scott towards the row of holding cells, leaving *The Bull* to sit down at the desk, and reacquaint himself with his crossword.

"He's in this one." She said, opening the viewing hatch on cell number *three*.

"Ok." He replied, gazing curiously around his newly discovered surroundings. "Open it up please, Theresa." He stood clear as she turned the key and pulled the door open. "You can leave us." He whispered, fixing his eyes on the clearly distressed young man.

"You sure?"

"Yes." He whispered. "Collect his belongings, we'll be leaving immediately."

"Why are you here?" He asked, sitting up on his cot. "I'm *not* leaving."

"Listen carefully," He whispered, watching Theresa leave them. "I helped *you*...now I need you to help *me*."

"What the fuck are you talking about?" He asked, vaulting to his *bare* feet. "You haven't helped me none!" He shouted.

"*We*..." He paused to halt Theresa's return to them. "It's ok." He said, extending his palm in her direction. "It's ok." He said again. "His things, please." He watched her leave for the second time in as many minutes. "*We*...have work to do." He whispered. "You and me." He stepped into the cell and patted Jet on his back. "I need you to identify him."

"You must be fucking insane." He said, avoiding Scott's touch with the panache of a gifted boxer. "I'm not going anywhere that *he's* going."

"You're coming with me, Jet." He said. It was clear to them both he was no longer *asking*.

Chapter Sixteen

LAUNCH.

As *Death* stood motionless in the complete seclusion, and darkness, of the *Rose's* garden, it was clear to Ray as he stood within the framework of the open patio doors, that as long as Brandon was able to rouse Julianne, *Death* was set to destroy *anyone* who would dare oppose him. The moonlight struck his pale features like a spot light, and although expressionless so far, he was a fearsome sight to behold as he awaited the *pulse*, even more so now that Brandon had draped a hooded black cloak over him. He knew without hesitation that they would fear *him*, it was Brandon however, that he feared *for*. Without warning, the sky exploded. He looked up as fireworks blasted high and proud into the clear night sky, but as loud as *they* were, they failed to quell the pounding drums echoing through the breeze as the club's sound system went *supersonic*.

"It's time." Brandon whispered, approaching *Death* from the shadows. "Hook us up." He backed himself into his brother's body and allowed Ray to secure all four locking pins on the harness.

"What's it like?" Ray asked. "Taking off…what's it like?"

"It's like a skydive," He answered. "In *Reverse*." He smiled at Ray as he reached out his hand. "Do *not* leave this house…until *they* do."

"I wont." He answered, shaking his hand firmly. "But once *they* do…I follow that?" He pointed to the laser. "And if that goes out…I'll follow the noise."

"I'm gonna need you, Ray." He said, nodding his head and smiling gently. "Be there."

"I will." He stepped back a little as Brandon looked up, he knew the darkness was calling him forth, and summoning him to action.

"*Adios!*" He said, crossing his arms across his chest, and gripping the harness tightly. His feet raised from the ground, as did *Death's*, slowly at first and just by inches, enabling Brandon a moment to close his eyes, and bow his head, before accelerating skyward, and *freefalling* to the great beyond.

Levelling himself out at around five hundred feet, Brandon spread his arms outwards and adopted his freefall position. With *The Crossfire* firmly in his sights, and the laser already reflecting within his black lenses, he steadily gained forward momentum, while *Death's* hooded cloak caught the wind and flapped like crows wings. Brandon smiled excitedly as he looked down at the large parking lot, it was surrounded by trees on every side and would, he figured, provide ample storage for his *broken* brother. He saw masses of revellers queuing beside the fascia of the building, just waiting for their turn to enter the arena. With fireworks still being launched from the roof of the venue, he felt secure in the knowledge that tonight at least, there was adequate distractions already assisting him. He swung his body to an upright position and lowered into the tree line quickly, he dropped to within just inches of the muddy ground, apparently *hovering*, as he had done during launch, before bowing gently to the forces of gravity and dropping to earth.

"I'm coming." He said. "I'm coming to get you." He reached behind to release all four of the harness's strong points, before sliding out of the harness completely. He peered through the shrubbery to glimpse the main entrance, noticing as he did so, that there were six burly men sporting *old school* tuxedo's, manning the large entry point. He noticed that it seemed to be the sole responsibility for one of them, to walk up and down what remained of the queue, and extract his clientele like rotten teeth, before subjecting them to a random security screening, by way of a hand held metal detector.

"I hope you don't pick me." He said, watching as the man plucked a young woman from her friends. "I'll have to revert to plan B, if you *do*."

"Leave…no…one…" *Death* whispered. "Kill…them…*all*."

"Exactly." Brandon replied, pulling his swords from around his waist. "I'll have to kill them all." He pulled the lethal blades from within their sheaths, and inserted them into two concealed slits at the top of his rear armour plate, before sliding them carefully down his back, with just the handles remaining visible, although perfectly flush with the nape of his neck. As the cold steel became warm against his skin, he stood motionless, mirroring *death*, and contemplated his strategy.

"I *need* you." He whispered. "I can't do this without you." He carefully removed the hooded cloak from *Death's* shoulders, and slid it around his own. He pulled the hood over his head, successfully concealing the swords beneath it.

"I'm *Death* now." He whispered. "While you await the *pulse…* that is." With his black cloak pulled tightly around him, he stepped through the tree line and walked with purpose to the main entrance. He was relieved to see the queue had subsided, although several revellers were still congregated *behind*, the all important red ropes. There were two main doors, both were large and made entirely of glass, with brass handles that met each other when closed. He looked at the door staff as he approached them, in turn they looked at him, carefully running their eyes up and down his cloaked body. He reached them and stood before them, awaiting their approval for admittance. His heart synched with the beat pounding from within the venue as he feared they would, inevitably, ask him to remove his hood for a thorough inspection.

"Do you want to come in or not?" One of them asked, swinging the door open before him.

"I certainly *do*." He replied, stepping past two of the largest *penguins* he'd ever seen.

"Enjoy your evening," He said, ushering him inside to the noise. "And welcome to *The Crossfire*." He stood at around six feet, with spiked blonde hair, and an unusually fresh face for someone in his occupation. "They've laid on some great entertainment tonight," He shouted. "You wont forget tonight in a hurry."

"I don't doubt it…" He whispered. "Not for a single second."

"Have a good evening." He said, directing Brandon towards the next set of doors. They were thick wooden doors which, he figured, would see him directly into the club. Beside them was a man of similar proportions to the one he'd just encountered, with a shaved head and unflattering personality. He opened one of the doors as he too surveyed Brandon with growing interest, his cocky attitude was increasing in clarity, as was his menacing features, as Brandon neared him.

"What have you come as?" He asked, smirking.

"The *Reaper*." He shouted. "Or *Death*." Already his face had begun to glow, as the fluorescent lights behind his final obstacle hit him.

"Enjoy!" He shouted, tilting his head towards the open door.

Walking slowly into the heaving club itself, Brandon was immediately aware of the powerful rigs above him, his black *lenses* did nothing to blunt the severity of the laser and strobe lighting, as they flickered and flashed in synch with the explosive bass pounding *through* his body. He looked firstly at the DJ, his booth was raised before him, and the *already* crowded dance floor was beyond that. There was a large bar area to his right, it was lined with both mirrors and green neon lights, as the many jostling bodies desperately attempted to gain the attention of it's five tenders. He walked towards the wall furthest from him, it was within a darkened section of the club, it contained a small bar and kitchen area, dining booths, and arranged couches. The large cross suspended on the wall caught his attention, it appeared to be ablaze, until closer inspection revealed a projection unit, *beaming* the flames across it.

"Where are you?" He whispered. He turned to see many eyes on him, passing over him, admiring him, *wanting* him. He smiled at a group of girls by the bar, they waved back like schoolgirls with a crush. He walked towards them as he gazed around for outlets, or *staff only* areas.

"What are you?" A *pretty* witch shouted, leaning in to him as he passed.

"You look so cool!" Another gushed. "How does your face glow like that?"

"Where are you?" He whispered, ignoring their comments. "Tell me."

"Ignore us then!" The witch shouted, snatching his hood down as he passed her.

"Don't touch me!" He shouted back, quickly pulling it back into place. He stared angrily at her as the four of them laughed, however she did not.

"I'm sorry." She said, pulling her blonde fringe from her eyes. She froze under his intense scrutiny, as his *black* eyes bored into her with devastating effect.

"He looks like that Black Widow." One of the others said, laughing still.

"It's those eyes!" Her friend chimed in. "Didn't they describe him as having *black eyes*?"

"Yeah!"

"But they caught that *black* guy?"

"He escaped, *remember*?"

They giggled annoyingly as Brandon held the blonde's attention to himself, he knew she'd seen the handles beneath his hood, he knew she *knew* who he was.

"Sshh!" He held his finger across his lips, before transferring it to hers and smiling.

"I wont tell…" Her words trailed off as she nodded helplessly, completely under his influence as her friends watched on, all under *influences* of their own. Leaving her behind, he walked across the dance floor to the other side of the of the large relaxing area, and saw a door marked '*private*.'

"You're in there." He whispered. "I'm coming, Julianne."

"Just relax, Jet." Scott whispered, driving hurriedly into the club's parking lot. "Nothing is going to happen to you." He manoeuvred his Lincoln as close to the tree line as possible, keeping the club's main entrance on his left, and the tree line on Jet's right.

"Now," He whispered, switching off the engine and headlights. "It's my belief that the *real*…Black Widow, and the wrongly accused one, are *both* going to turn up here tonight."

"Why?" He asked. "Why tonight…why here?"

"Your brother worked for a powerful man," He replied, removing his seatbelt. "And that man is the main priority of *both* of them."

"But you've got the *wrong* one in custody?"

"We *had*...the wrong one in custody." He sighed and glanced at the door security. "He escaped custody, Jet." He continued. "I gave the order that you were *not* to be told."

"So...he's out here...*somewhere?*"

"He is."

"So..." He paused for a moment. "What convinced you that you had the wrong one?"

"I know who *The Boss*...is."

"Who?" He asked, staring harshly at Scott.

"He's one of mine." He whispered. "He's the man that gave *your* brother the instructions that would...*eventually*...lead to his death. That man is here tonight, he owns that club."

"I fucking told you!" He shouted. "Corrupt bastards the fucking lot of you!" He fought back tears as Scott's revelation hit home.

"I'm sorry." Scott said. "I know that's a bitter pill to swallow."

"A bitter pill?" He asked. "You were supposed to protect us!" He shook his head angrily.

"I'm working on it, Jet." He said. "I'm gonna get the Black Widow."

"You *can't*." He said, his tone ached of desperation. "He'll flat out...*destroy* you."

Gazing nervously over his shoulder, Brandon observed the two *bouncers* who were stood at opposite sides of the dance floor, although up to now, they appeared to be conversing with each other by way of hand gestures. He rammed the door open, smashing the entire locking mechanism free of it's wooden housing. He slid quickly inside, peering back just briefly to see they were still stood in place, before closing the door behind him. He walked quickly down the narrow passage to the manager's office at the end, and once again discovered the door to be locked. Rearing up a little, he thrust his right foot into it and watched as it swung open under his immense force. Removing his cloak, he watched it fall to the ground as he listened for movement within the room.

"Oh fuck!" He whispered, seeing Julianne was suspended against the wall, battered and bruised, she was barely conscious as her head lolled back and forth.

"I'm gonna get you out of here." He said, rushing to her and attempting to shroud her exposed torso with his own.

"Don't…" She whispered, weakly. "Don't get too close…" She tried to focus on him, but simply couldn't adjust her blurred vision.

"I've got to…" He said. "I've got to get you down." He reached up for the handcuffs, his warm breath found hers as he closed the space between them.

"No…" She said. "No, you're…much…too…*close*."

"What are you -" His words seized as he realised what she had meant. "Oh *no*." He whispered, listening to her heart as it resonated within him.

"No…" She said. "You…*mustn't*…they'll…kill…you."

"I can't." He whispered. He leaned into her and ran his face along her slender neck, his eyes closed as his *bliss* surged to every extremity he possessed. "I wont." He pulled away a little but her *magnetism* dragged him back to her, inextricably…he was drawn, undeniably… he was *hungry*.

"I'm so…*sorry*." He whispered, licking slowly along her neck. "I need to taste you, I have to have you in my veins." He reached into his trouser pocket, and produced his fashioned *device*.

"No!" She cried, seeing the black of his eyes. "No! No! No! They'll kill you!"

"I want you." He whispered. "I want you inside me." His eyes half mooned dreamily, clearly *already* intoxicated as he sampled her *bouquet*, like a connoisseur of the finest wines. Inserting what was in effect a modified brace, he licked his lips seductively as his two, razor sharp, hypodermic *fangs*, readied themselves for incision.

"Normally," He whispered, holding her jaw and turning her head away from him. "I'd take the wrist." He breathed heavily on her neck as he moved in towards her, feeling her resistance fade he relaxed his grip on her jaw, of this she *didn't* take advantage, in fact had her hands been free, she knew she would embrace him now, and *never* let go.

"I can't stop myself…" He said. "…I've held back for *too* long." He opened his mouth wide, and closed his eyes tight, as his *fangs* sank into the soft flesh of her neck. She recoiled from the pain, but fell weak from his touch, she groaned as his touch erased her suffering, replaced instead by his *bliss*.

Blood trickled down from his lips as he sucked, extracting blood from her body to his. He heard the outer door marked *'private,'* being flung against the wall, but no longer cared. He heard a rush of bodies as they streamlined down the narrow hallway, but just couldn't stop feeding on her. He was aware of the door marked *'Managers Office,'* being thrown open under an influx of three men, Vincelli, Martin and Carl. They each were dressed in sharp grey suits.

"No!" Julianne cried. "Brandon, you're going to die." She felt him fall away from her body, and turned her head to watch him stumble, before falling to the ground.

"Well." Vincelli said. "I really didn't think this would be quite so easy." He drew the 9m semi - automatic, which he had concealed neatly within his trousers, as did Martin.

"Goodnight, Brandon Rose." He whispered, enjoying Brandon's vulnerability as he reached up his hand to him. He aimed the weapon directly against his forehead, and pulled the trigger. Julianne screamed in terror as Brandon's whole body hit the wall, his head snapping backwards as though hit in the face with a sledgehammer. Exploding through a grisly exit wound, blood, skull fragments and brain tissue spattered against the plain white wall beside Julianne's body, as he came to a permanent rest beside her.

"No!" She screamed, attempting to look down at him, but unable to forget the *two* pistols once again taking aim on him. His body jolted from the velocity of the bullets entering him, as his legs and shoulder blades were systematically targeted.

"Leave him!" She screamed, thrashing wildly against the wall. "Leave him alone!" Her cries filled the small room as the shooting finally stopped, as both Vincelli and Martin looked at him proudly. Carl sat across the room on the couch, clearly attempting to avert his gaze from Brandon's, who appeared to stare back through his black lenses, motionless and without pulse. He lay against the wall, silently, as blood ran down his pale face from all angles.

"And there we have it." Vincelli whispered, addressing Julianne. "You see, there is *no* magic…only the illusion of magic." He laughed. "And this one," He gazed down at Brandon. "He's one of the best illusionist's I've ever known, I'll credit him with that."

"You didn't have to kill -"

"But we did!" He shouted, silencing Julianne instantly. "Like I said…he *was* good. He had you completely submerged in his lies."

"No." She whispered. "He's special…he's not like anyone else."

"The swordsman!" He shouted, again looking down on Brandon's lifeless body, and to the swords he never got to draw. "All this shit about him…or *you*…summoning his dead brother, to return from the grave and cut them all down one by one." He shook his head and patted Julianne on the side of her face.

"Don't…" She turned her head away from him.

"Did you really think I was gonna believe that?" He asked, punching her squarely across her jaw. "You fucking look at me!" He shouted. "Don't you fucking dare, turn your head on me!"

"Just do it." She whispered, begrudgingly obeying and turning to face him. "Do it!"

"You had us going," Martin whispered, concealing his gun in the rim of his trousers. "That was a great story…the pendant…the swordsman…the flying…*Bravo*." He clapped his hands together, turning and encouraging his colleagues to do the same.

"Fact is, Julianne." Vincelli said. "It's just him…and he's just human." He held her eye contact for as long as it took for her to understand. "He's dead." He whispered, drawing her attention to the lifeless body beside her. "We killed him…and you helped us."

"No…" She screamed. "No…he's not gone…*please…Brandon… don't be gone.*"

She watched as Vincelli kneeled down before him, grabbing a handful of his once beautiful flowing mane, and snapping his head back in his hands to stare into his *black* eyes.

"You see this?" He asked, looking up at Julianne. "Watch this." He carefully dabbed his forefinger into Brandon's right eye, fully aware he had Julianne's attention, before extracting it slowly, with a small black lens on the tip.

"What are you doing?" She asked. "What's that?"

"This…" He said, standing up beside her. "Is part of his *illusion*." He held it closer for her inspection. "His…*black*…demonic…eyes," He went on. "Are nothing more than fucking contact lenses."

"No." She muttered, staring in disbelief. "No…no…that's not…"

"…Possible?" He asked. "Oh…it's possible." He stepped away from her, allowing Martin to take his place.

"Game over." Martin whispered. "This is where it ends." He stroked her face gently.

"But…he was…*drinking*…my…"

"So he liked blood!" Martin exclaimed with a grin. "It doesn't make him a fucking *vampire*. There's no such thing…as *vampires*."

"An angel of death…" Vincelli said, smiling at Brandon's demise. "Where is the *angel of death*, now?" He spat on Brandon's body. "All I see is a fucking pussy." He laughed.

"And he's not talking about the ginger one between your legs." Martin muttered proudly.

"Right," Vincelli shouted, clicking his fingers. "Let's go." He summoned his two colleagues to join him on the other side of the broken door. "We'll deal with you later." He said, waving at her. "We're gonna let you spend some quality time together first though, let's see if you *still* feel his presence." He laughed, the three of them laughed.

"So *that's* why you had a security shutter installed?" Martin asked, watching as Vincelli reached up above the door, and grasped the roll down shutter.

"Yeah." He replied, pulling it down to the ground. "My mousetrap was *quite* successful." He pulled up a small square of carpet, revealing a metal plate within the ground. In it was a retractable hook, mounted on steel plates that elevated when pulled until flush with the surrounding concrete. He pulled the hook level with the shutter, and reached for the padlock laying in the space beside it.

"I knew he'd bust the door." He said, locking it into the hook. "But no one will get past this."

"And that one?" Martin asked, pointing to the outer door that led back into the club.

"The same deal." Vincelli answered, snapping it closed. "We'll lock it…then celebrate."

"You fucking evil bastards!" Julianne screamed, which, despite the noise from the other side of the door, they heard. "He's coming!" She added. "*Death* is coming for you."

Scott sat silently, as did Jet, as they both watched a steady procession of taxi cabs pull up beside the main entrance, before the occupants alighted and, one by one, disappeared into the building. A group of four girls had caught his eye, not least for the flesh on display as they sat on the kerb, but for the fact that they'd *exited* the venue just an hour after the doors had opened. He found himself wondering if they operated some kind of *stamping* system, where by patrons could be *stamped* with a florescent logo, enabling them to come and go if they pleased. Although *that* was merely the sub - plot, his real attraction was why one of them crying, apparently pleading with her friends as she dialled on her cell phone. Putting it down to *man* trouble, his curiosity passed as he rolled his seat back a little to avoid detection, as on more than one occasion the door staff had gazed across at his vehicle.

"Just keep yourself out of sight." He whispered. "Try not to let them see you."

"This doesn't look right," Jet replied, lowering the back of his seat. "I'd sooner them see us, than think I'm sucking your dick."

Scott laughed a little as he gazed easily into his side mirror, noticing as he did so, a car's headlights dying just around the corner from them on the small slip road leading in. Intrigued, he kept looking in that direction, until the figure of a man emerged, crouched down, and running for cover in the trees beside them.

"What?" He asked, switching his attention to his vehicle's rear window.

"What?" Jet asked, following his eyes to the back window. "What's wrong?"

"Stay still." He whispered, pressing Jet back into his seat. "Don't make a fucking sound."

"What's happening?" He whispered, nervously.

Scott watched in disbelief, acutely aware of the adrenaline surging through his veins, as he saw Ray, running along the tree line like a cat.

"He's coming right to us!" He whispered. "He's coming right along your side." He spoke with fear in his voice, not fearful of Ray, but fearful of *losing* Ray.

"Who?" Jet asked. "Not the…"

"No." Scott answered quickly. "Not him…the *other* one." He watched as Ray approached stealthily, or at least what *Ray* considered to be stealthily.

"The *innocent* one?" Jet asked, lowering himself down as much as he could.

"Yes." He pushed himself on top of Jet, pinning him to his seat, whilst he peered as best he could through *Jet's* side mirror. "Stay there." He whispered. Watching as Ray neared their vehicle, he placed his trembling hand on the door release. He made sure his feet were not snagged to anything as he readied himself, although he couldn't help laughing to himself, *mentally*, as Ray had chosen to opt for a ten foot car, instead of the vast tree line, for cover.

They both lay perfectly still, almost to scared to breathe, as Ray ran to the Lincoln's rear passenger door, and squatted still as he peered through the windows to the main entrance, missing completely, the two terrified occupants as they lay in the darkness.

"Come on, Ray." He whispered. "One step closer…" He waited for his moment, and with split second accuracy propelled the door wide open, catching Ray square on the temple as he moved closer. Scott Grabbed Ray's arm as he fell away from the car, and was effectively hauled like a water skier, as he glided out across Jet's body to the ground.

"Don't move!" He whispered forcefully, while laying on top of him. "Don't move, Ray."

"This isn't fuckin happening!" Ray shouted. "You can't do this."

"Shut the fuck up!" Scott replied. "Get in the fucking car…and don't make a sound."

"What?" Ray asked, clearly confused as he caught sight of Jet, peering nervously at him.

"I *know* it's not you." Scott said, scrambling to his feet while holding the waistline of Ray's jeans. "It's all over," He whispered. "I know the truth…I'm doing this for you dumb ass."

"How did you know?" He asked, wiping the dirt from his T - shirt.

"I watched the tape." He answered, ushering Ray to the car. "I saw Vincelli in the mirror, but the question is…how did *you* see him?"

"I didn't." He answered, crouching down beside the car. "Brandon told me there was something I'd missed, something that a *good* detective would never have missed." He shrugged. "I didn't understand at first," He continued. "I'm not even a detective. But I see now what he was saying, either Vincelli wasn't a good detective…"

"Or," Scott interrupted. "He hadn't *missed* it at all."

"No!" Jet cried, retreating in terror to the other side of the car. "It's fucking him!" He screamed. He started the engine as he frantically wound up the seat up a little.

"Don't start that fucking car!" Scott shouted, reaching across and grabbing the ignition keys. "It's not fucking him!" He said, attempting to calm Jet down from the wide eyed panic that had gripped him. "He's the fucking *innocent* one!"

"Not him!" He shouted, crying hysterically as *carnival* evening came flooding back.

"Then who?" He asked. "It's only us here!" He watched as Jet's finger raised to the tree line, his eyes followed it with sheer undiluted terror.

"He's been here all along." He whispered. "Right beside us."

Both Ray and Scott turned to peer into the tree line behind them, the lighting was shallow as it had clearly been intended to illuminate the parking spaces, not the dense tree line framing them. Ray stepped a little closer and pulled a branch to one side, revealing *Death*.

"Shit!" He shouted, reeling backwards with fear, but quietly and quickly reprimanding himself.

"Sweet fucking Jesus!" Scott said, falling down beside the car, completely and *utterly* frozen. "He's fucking…*real*."

"He can't do anything!" Ray said, attempting to calm them. "He's awaiting what's called '*the pulse*,'" He went on. "Until he receives that…he's harmless."

"Harmless!" Scott shouted. "Are you fucking kidding me?" He opened the glove box and retrieved his gun, before disengaging the safety switch. "He's a fucking serial killer, Ray!" Standing to his feet he took aim.

"No!" Ray shouted, blocking his path, and attracting the attention of the door staff. "This must happen!" He said. "When that pulse hits him…nothing will stop him." He reached for Scott's gun and clasped it tightly. "If you're holding this gun when he awakes, he'll slice you in half." They stood silently, neither relinquishing their side of the weapon.

"He's a killer, Ray." He whispered. "He's a killer." He glanced over Ray's shoulder at him. "Why's he stood there like that?" He asked. "What's going on?"

"He's *waiting*." He replied. "Brandon's in the building…he's trying to get Julianne -"

"She's in there?" He asked, tilting his head at the club, but staring *Death* in the eye.

"Yeah." Ray answered. "Brandon's trying to get her back."

"I knew Vincelli had her," He whispered. "I just didn't think he'd have her *here*."

"It's her." Ray whispered, raising his thumb behind him. "She's controlling him."

"Ray," He whispered. "I know you didn't kill those people…but right now, I *still* believe you're fucking crazy."

'Available units…' The radio hissed, the dispatcher's tone had struck all three of them as urgent. '…proceed presently to The Crossfire nightclub, one - seven - three, Miners industrial. Potential sighting of Ray Kennedy, aka Black Widow…seen within the premises by a girl currently *outside* the premises, three companions present. Please be advised…extremely dangerous…approach with weapons drawn.'

"It's her!" Scott said, drawing Ray's attention to the four girls he'd seen earlier. "The blonde girl in the witch's costume."

"How do you know?" He asked, gazing across to her. "Could be anyone of them?"

"No," He answered flatly. "It's her."

"Put the gun down." Ray whispered. "Just give it to me, *please*."

"He just moved!" Jet shouted. "He just raised his head…I saw him!" He pointed to the pale face within the tree line, shrouded by not just branches and shrubbery, but also his long dark hair, which hung still like thick velvet curtains, *black out* curtains. Ray turned quickly to see he *was* in fact moving, his eyes were on them, that much he *knew* for sure.

"Who are you?" Scott asked, gun in hand. "Tell me who you are!" He backed off around the hood of his car, before opening the driver's side door, and pulling Jet to safety.

"Get out of here, Jet." He shouted. "Your work is done." He watched as Jet vaulted from the car and fled at speed. "Don't go in there!" Scott shouted, realising he'd retreated to the *safety* of the club. They watched as he was grabbed with force by the door staff, who in turn returned him to the pavement as only *bouncers* know how. He could be heard screaming at them, and pleading *with* them, as they stood and laughed.

"Fuck off!" Drifted casually across the parking lot, passing *hysterical* girl, ignoring *influenced* girls beside her, until reaching *fearful* man.

"What's your name?" He asked, attempting to aim his gun with trembling hands,

"My name is *Death*." He replied, smiling menacingly at Ray.

"Put the gun down!" Ray shouted, backing away from *Death* as he stepped from the trees.

"Captain!" He shouted again. "Drop the weapon!" He ran around the car but failed to reach him in time, he got a shot off at *Death* before he could wrestle the weapon from his hands, it struck him in the chest.

Death stumbled back a little as the bullet entered him, he looked down at his wound which was bleeding a *little*, but not in a manner consistent with a gunshot wound. He turned his attention to Scott, who had once again frozen to the spot in a state of sheer panic. *Death* walked slowly around the car and stood before him, and rightly he trembled at the fearsome killing machine that was now stalking him, he collapsed to the ground, clutching Ray's legs as he went.

"Please…" Ray whispered. "I know *Brandon*…I'm on your side."

"I know who you are." He said, glaring down at Scott. "It's time." He turned to face the door staff, some of whom had ventured closer, but with his *equalisers* strapped to his back and on full display, only a *little* closer. He smiled at them as he rotated his body to face them head on, although he remained perfectly still.

"That's the Black Widow." One of them shouted, running back to the doors. "That aint no fucking costume, that's *really* him."

"How do you know?" Another asked, also running.

"That's a cop!" He answered. "He just shot him and he kept fucking going."

"I've heard about him!" He panted heavily. "They're saying he's a fucking ghost!"

"You coming in?" He shouted. "Girls…in or out?" He waited. "Fuck 'em. Lock it down."

"Please!" Ray shouted, addressing the whole parking lot. "Do not stand in his way, do *not* under any circumstances attempt to stop him." He looked around desperately, Scott was still on the floor, but he was moving, much to Ray's relief.

"It ends tonight." *Death* whispered. He walked purposefully towards the main entrance, charging from the screams that echoed through the breeze. *Hysterical* girl ran wildly, at one point falling as her heels snapped beneath her. *Influenced* girls sobered with a moments notice as he closed in on them, his vision now tunnelled to the main entrance, bur regardless, they ran for their lives. Striding menacingly towards the glass doors, he reached across his shoulders and drew his *equalisers*, holding them at his sides as his pace quickened with each step, they *sparked* occasionally on the concrete beneath them. He smiled through his hair as the door staff frantically barricaded themselves within the building, in a desperate attempt to protect their clientele. They could be seen hastily directing some revellers back into the club, while others remained *front line*, manually holding down their fortress. *Death* walked through the red ropes, reaching the glass doors to a rapturous reception of *screams* and *terror*. He gazed through the doors, the four burly *bouncers* on the other side of them daren't score eye contact as he scanned *beyond* their human barricade, before looking at them individually, one by one, he passed his evil eyes over them. They were afraid, they were very afraid.

He stepped back a few paces, not once looking away from them, but enjoying the chaos developing before him, the screams were…*beautiful*. He flicked his hair from his face as he reinserted his *equalisers* into his harness, before charging straight for the doors, and exploding through the reinforced glass like a missile. With glass spraying in every direction, he rolled straight over the cowering *barricade,* and landed like lead beyond them. A state of confusion ensued as they all turned around, wondering how he'd done it, and where he'd landed.

"He's fucking there!" One of them shouted, ushering customers outside as they all began to bottle neck in the hallway. "Everybody get out!" He shouted. "Get out as fast as you can!"

Opting to leave the *equalisers* in his harness, *Death* marched headlong into the fleeing crowd, like an otter in a flowing stream, he forced his way against the tide. Many of the crowd were clearly not even aware *why* they were being evacuated, as to them, he was just another reveller in fancy dress as he forced his way through them. Without warning, strong arms gripped him tightly from behind and forced a *bear hug* upon him. Stopping dead in his tracks, he looked at the black sleeves of the man's dinner jacket, and the white cuffs beneath it. He gripped the man's arm against his shoulder, and smiled menacingly as he dropped his weight to one leg, and shot his other leg between the man's whilst dragging him completely over his shoulder. As the *bouncer* fell heavily to the floor, he stared up as *Death* loomed over him, raising his foot he stamped it down heavily onto his chest, and drew his *equalisers*. Without hesitation, he stabbed each of them in a *one - two* motion into his legs, he screamed in agony as *Death* pulled them free and pointed them at the approaching evacuees, they stopped dead in their tracks as they realised the town's very own *executioner* was before them. They turned rapidly as confusion once more turned to terror. He pointed his swords to them as he glanced over his shoulder, securing his personal circle. No one was following the *hero's* example.

"Tell us what you want!" One of his colleagues begged. "Why are you here?"

"To kill them *all.*" He whispered, glancing at Ray behind them.

"His name may not be down…" He continued. "But I assure you… he's coming in."

"Let him go by!" Another shouted, pulling Ray past the gathered security. "Go on now."

"Anybody touches him…they *die*."

With lightening speed he crossed his swords before him, they sparked together as contact was made, before he stared ahead at the retreating revellers, they were now being herded *back* through the thick wooden doors.

"Follow me." He said, ensuring Ray was behind him. "I hope you've got a strong constitution." He smirked, watching as Ray's mahogany complexion became pallid. He walked towards them with speed as he rotated the *equalisers* beside him, those unlucky enough to be at the rear of the fleeing crowd, either collapsed with fear, or outright ran for their lives, whether it be away from, or around the approaching assassin. The thick wooden doors were slammed shut as he neared, but without so much as breaking stride, he kicked one of them so forcefully, it didn't just open, it detached from it's hinges and assumed flight, albeit for a millisecond. Ray cowered behind him, unsure of what he should actually be doing…the theory was the easy part, he just hadn't taken into account the resourcefulness of the human nature, and the rage it was now being subjected too.

As *Death* stepped into *his* arena, the flashing lights and booming trance like music hit his senses like a rock, successfully blinding him from the approaching knife. Whilst his eyes adjusted, it was stabbed firmly into the centre of his chest, he reeled backwards, not from pain but *surprise*. Assigned to these doors, was *cocky* bouncer. Having removed his dinner jacket and bow tie already, he now wore just his white shirt which he'd loosened at the top.

"You motherfucker!" He screamed. "I'll kill you myself!" With the lights reflecting of his glistening head, he charged forward and inserted the knife twice more, before being stabbed through his stomach with both swords, to the hilt. He fell limp as the blades, most of which were visible through his back, dripped blood and matter much to the horror of the *still* fleeing revellers, and Ray.

"Enforcer number one." *Death* whispered. Pulling the swords free of his flesh, he watched him fall down to the ground.

"He's part of the gang?" Ray asked, looking down at his convulsing body, and tortured expression. "How did you know that?"

"Inner circle." He whispered. "The guy's at the door, they're just window dressing, these are the trusted…loyal…*employees*. They're not just watching the club, they're watching him." He smirked. "He's in here…I can smell his fear."

Death walked slowly into the light show that awaited him. The strobe lights flashed with an almost *intoxicating* manner of their own, as the lasers ripped through the club finding every dark corner sooner or later. He stared beyond the dance floor into a darkened area, to see all of the club's patrons who *hadn't* got out of the front door when they had the opportunity, huddled in a corner, either having been herded there by *someone*, or having every means of possible escape cut off. The club fell silent except for the perpetual *screaming*, as the music finally stopped.

"Did you do that?" Ray asked, with the beat still ringing in his ears.

"No." He laughed at Ray's *innocence*. "The record finished."

"Yeah." He replied. "Of *course* it did."

Having been concealed behind one of the marble pillars, a thick set man of gigantic proportions loomed rapidly into the frame, and with *brass* knuckles attached to each hand, his intentions were clear. Still attired in full penguin regalia, he charged wildly towards *Death*, and with battle scars running across his *weathered* face, an equally fearsome complexion greeted his current adversary.

"Old school." *Death* whispered. "Bring it on." Lowering his swords he feigned hesitation.

"Kill me!" The man roared, raising his fists for a killer one - two. "Fucking kill *me*!"

"I will…" He whispered, glaring into his eyes. "…Come to me."

"I'll fucking have you motherfucker!" He screamed. "You're gonna die tonight!"

"Keep running," *Death* whispered. "You'll be the easiest yet." With lightening speed, he arced his swords high in the air and dropped them savagely across the man's face.

"Add those to your collection." He whispered, watching as the fight drained from him.

The man raised his hands to the slabs of loose flesh that had *once* been his face, and shrieked in horror as his vision blurred, shut down and flooded - by a river of red.

"What have you done to me?" He shouted, retreating in terror. "Who are you?"

"The media call me the Black Widow." He replied. "But, my name is *Death*."

Stumbling back against the wall, Ray watched on as *Death* thrust a sword directly through the man's throat. He felt the urge to vomit like never before, as the man gagged and struggled for breath. Bleeding like a slaughtered animal he dropped to his knees, still clutching the sword's laced handle as he went.

"Oh my god." Ray whispered, watching as *he* snatched the handle from the man's grip, before placing a boot on his forehead, and sliding him off it. As the man fell to the floor, he hovered over him and was clearly deriving pleasure from his suffering, his pain, and the screams.

"No body said we were the good guy's, Ray." He said, turning to face him. "We're evil."

"Why did you do that?" He asked, covering his mouth. "You slaughtered him."

"Enforcer number two." He replied. "That's the guy that took Mark to your house."

"To plant the swords?" He asked, attempting to ignore his sudden sense of justice.

"No." He answered. "To water your plants."

"Why are these people still here?"

"They're stuck." *Death* replied. "The whole point of this is to demonstrate *real* power."

On the carpet ahead of him, he saw the remains of what had been a steel roll down shutter, it had been obliterated, reduced to mere scrap metal, he was mindful of a lion in a rabbit hutch.

"You cant' have a demonstration…" He continued. "…Without

an audience, or in this case…a *captive* audience." He laughed. "They will witness true power tonight."

"What are you going to do?" Ray asked nervously, glancing again at the blood soaked *enforcer* on the carpet before him.

"Welcome to the show." He said, marching forward once more. He stepped beneath the lights and one by one they surged brightly, before exploding and shattering fragments down on him. Picking glass from his hair as he went, Ray ran dutifully behind him, he was in fact too *scared* to lose sight of him, since every law enforcement agency in the land, most of which would be blazing a trail in his direction, still thought *he* was the Black Widow. More disturbingly to Ray, he knew they would *all*, if Scott failed him, shoot him on sight.

The trapped revellers screamed in torment as *Death* neared, stalking them like a wild animal, with only the strobe lights remaining operational and flashing his arrival intermittently. Ray stuck to him like glue, watching in every direction as *Death* stood motionless, apparently staring *up*.

"Quiet!" Ray shouted. "Stop screaming!" He ran along the outer line of the crowd whilst attempting to calm them. "Why haven't you left?" He asked.

"He wont let us!" A vampire girl screamed, clutching tightly to her *mummified* boyfriend.

She pointed to the fire escape behind them. "The doors are sealed."

"Then run to the main doors!" He shouted. "They're all smashed up!"

"You're fucking kidding!" A man shouted from behind her. It surprised Ray that he hadn't noticed the man sooner, since he had to have been well all over six feet tall, with a green face and imitation bolts stuck in his neck.

"Why?" Ray asked, understanding their fear, but not their refusal to move. "You must!"

"We're not running past him!" He shouted. "We're safer as a crowd, he'll kill anyone that breaks away from the herd…he's a fucking monster."

Ray turned to gaze at the dance floor behind him, he couldn't see too much as the fleeing DJ had left the smoke machine running. He struggled to see past the dense smoke effects which, when coupled with the dazzling strobe lights, played tricks on his eyes anyway.

"There's nobody there!" He said, turning back to *green* man. "You have to run...*please*."

"He's in there!" *Mummified* man shouted, pulling bandages from his face. "Somewhere."

It simply must be Brandon. He thought. *It has to be him...he's revealed himself.*

"Look," He shouted, gazing again at the dance floor, and the encroaching smoke. "He's not gonna hurt you." He turned back to *Vampire* girl. "I swear he wont!"

"We...watched...him!" She cried, burying her head into *Mummified* man's chest.

"What?" Ray asked, switching his attention to him. "What did you see?"

"He tore this man apart!" He replied. "Some guy in a suit... might've been a bouncer, I'm not sure." He stared across to the dance floor. "He struck from above and tore him apart, and I do mean *apart*." He shook his head desperately. "If that wasn't enough, he then tore the guy's pants from his body and sliced his fucking cock off. I've never seen anything like it, his rage was just off the fucking scale."

"He sliced his..." He paused. "Are you *sure*?" He asked.

"We all saw it!" *Vampire* girl screamed. "He sliced his cock off with those swords!"

"We just heard him screaming," *Mummified* man shouted. "And then he took him..."

"Where?"

"He took him...*up*." He gripped *Vampire* girl tightly. "Somewhere."

"Up?"

"Smoke rises, right?" He asked, nodding.

"Yes?"

"*Something* is in that smoke." He pointed to the engulfed area high *above* the dance floor.

Ray turned to see *Death was* stood perfectly still, in pretty much the same place he'd last seen him. He walked slowly over to him whilst concentrating on the area *above* the dance floor.

"I think I know where *Brandon* is." He said.

"I do too." He whispered, still gazing up at the wall. "He's watching us."

"These people are scared, why are you holding them hostage?"

"I'm waiting…" He paused. "…Or should I say, *we're* waiting… for the police."

"Are you fucking nuts?" He asked. "They're gonna kill me *dead*!"

"If anything happens to the one man who *believes* you -"

"Scott?"

"Then you're right back in the frame." He nodded. "So if we're to guarantee your freedom, we need witnesses. And lots of them." He returned his attention to the darkened wall before him, and gazed up.

"The police have arrived." He whispered. "It's gone *too* quiet."

Ray looked across the dance floor to the exit, although the smoke and strobe lights hindered his vision, they accentuated the laser target finders attached to the S.W.A.T. teams' firearms, with brutal clarity.

"The police?" Ray asked. "Now what?"

"We begin."

"Begin?"

"Let's not lose sight of the *real* reason, we're all gathered here."

"Vincelli."

"Correct."

"Where is he?" Ray asked. "I've not even seen him yet."

"I have."

"Where?"

"Show him!" He shouted.

They *all* watched as the projection unit flickered into life and engulfed the cross with *flames. Death* smiled as Ray reeled back towards the crowd, and one by one they began screaming once more.

"Detective Vincelli!" *Death* shouted. "It's been a while." He pointed his swords to the cross, to the *crucifix*, and winked. Stripped of all clothing, he hung on for his life in just his pants, his wrists and ankles were bound tightly to the beams. Any failure to support his *own* weight, would result in the rope around his neck *assuming* the strain for him.

"All that good living," He shouted, referring to the substantial overhang in his midsection.

"It just might cost you your life *after all*." He laughed. "You fat fuck!" He stepped a little closer to him, all the while aware of those *laser beams* assuming different angles behind the dance floor. He laughed wildly as he looked at the duct tape around his mouth, *again* it was wrapped several times around the back of his head.

"Has the cat got your tongue?" He asked, looking up to him, though not *worshipping* him.

"I bet you'd love to answer me," He shouted. "But you can't speak, never mind *speak*, you can't even *swallow* right now can you?" He laughed. "I know what's currently in your mouth…don't I? He paced up and down beside him, wielding his swords closer and closer to Vincelli's bare flesh. "It's no secret," He shouted, pointing back at Ray. "He thinks you're a cock sucker!" Using his powerful right hand, he thrust his sword into Vincelli's leg, before twisting it slowly. Vincelli *attempted* to scream.

"*I bet that HURT!*" He shouted, pulling it free. "Be careful you don't swallow, just keep doing what you're best at…*sucking*." Laughing menacingly, he dragged Ray from the crowd and forced him to confront Vincelli, man to man and eye to eye.

"Ladies and Gentlemen of the Jury!" He shouted, pointing his swords to Vincelli. "*That* man is charged with Murder, drug running, blackmailing, kidnap and inciting rape." He smiled. "And!" He shouted. "The *worst* pants I have ever seen!"

"Please…" Ray whispered. "Stop this…*please*."

"How do we find him?" He asked, ignoring Ray's pleas for clemency. "*Guilty*, or *Guilty?*"

"Guilty!" A girls voice cried.

"Who would *say* that?" Ray muttered angrily. "Who said that?" He shouted into the crowd.

"I said it!" A girl answered, pushing her way to the front. "It's *dying* time in the crossfire."

"Julianne!" Ray said, running to her. "Please!" He shouted, although failing to secure her attention even a little. "Stop him!" He wanted to hold her, or even just touch her, but stopped short since they weren't really even acquainted.

"Stop him?" She asked, passing him like the wind. "He's a force of nature, Ray." She whispered, gliding towards *Death* whilst holding her arms crossed against her chest. "You can't tell an avalanche to just stop and turn back."

"You can stop *him*!" He shouted. "Please Julianne, this is *not* right. I'm begging you to *please* call him off. You're better than this."

She stepped slowly to the vision before her, her work, her conjuring. She was irresistibly drawn to him as he stood with absolute power, presiding quite literally over a man's life or death. She knew in her heart what his speciality was.

"*My* angel." She whispered, pulling the hair from his face and kissing him gently. "Thank you, I've been waiting for this moment." She slid down his powerful body like a lap dancing pole, landing gracefully at his feet as she stared up to Vincelli.

"I summon *Death*, you fool, no pendant can match our connection." She said. "I bet you *really* wish you'd killed me when you had the chance." She gazed lovingly up at *Death's* face whilst holding on to his leg. "I control the relentless killing machine, who's mercy you now find yourself at. *Death* or *Salvation*? The choice is made."

"Julianne!" Ray shouted. "Don't do this!" He wanted to stand before her and beg, but in doing so meant standing before *Death*, and most likely he thought, facing it.

"It's too late in the game." She said. "The time to be merciful came and went a long time ago."

"Let them do their jobs!" He shouted, drawing her attention to the many *lasers* currently taking aim at *Death*. "Vincelli is finished," He went on. "It's *already* over."

"I can't suffer anymore!" She cried. "I want it to end."

"It's over!" He shouted. "You just can't see it for yourself…we've come full circle."

"We haven't." She whispered. "Not *yet*."

She gazed at the marksmen dotted in various locations behind the dance floor.

"I think that's for the best." She said finally. "They *should* do their jobs." She raised slowly to her feet and faced *Death* for one final time. "We deserve happiness." She whispered, placing her arms loosely around his shoulders whilst gazing at the marksmen beyond. "Until we meet again, My *love*…my *Brandon*." She kissed him gently on his cold lips and caressed his face. She listened as the club's many amplifiers became live, not with the sound of music, but *breathing*.

"Julianne!" They boomed. "You're deviating."

"I'm sorry!" She shouted, hastily removing the *equalisers* from *his* grip. "It's over!"

"What's going on?" Ray asked, raising slowly to his feet. "Put them down before you -"

"Everybody deserves a second chance!" She whispered, shielding her glistening eyes from the lasers as they picked her out in the darkness. "Most will take full advantage of any second chance they're given," She turned to face Vincelli. "*Others* are destined to make the same choices over and over. *Salvation* or *Death?*" She laughed through her tears as *Death* lowered to his knees behind her, in effect, standing down.

"Julianne!" Ray shouted, watching as the red lasers became *dots* on the back of her head, clustering together like fireflies in the darkness. "No!" He shouted. "They're gonna kill you!"

"Julianne!" The amplifiers boomed. "What are you doing?"

"Brandon!" Ray shouted, turning to face the smoke. "Stop her!"

"He can't." She whispered, turning to face Ray as she stood before Vincelli. "He can't!"

"Why?" He asked.

"Because," She smiled. "He *doesn't* exist." Her tear soaked face glistened under the strobe effects from the dance floor. "Why do you think he's remained inside the smoke?"

"I don't understand!" He said, watching as her eyes travelled down his body, to his hands.

"Nor should you." She whispered. "Look in your hands."

"My hands?" He asked, gazing down slowly. "What are you talking -" His voice froze, as did his body, and he hadn't realised it until that point, but there was a *microphone* in his right hand.

"Good bye, Ray." She whispered. "Good bye *Brandon*." She thrust the sword directly into Vincelli's throat, he gasped in pain as his eyes rolled skyward, and seconds seemed like hours as the air behind her was sliced apart, by approaching *Death*.

I want true retribution. She thought. *I want to return to innocence. I want to exchange the vows I never made, have the children I never had, and live the life I never had…my heart is an ocean of untold love stories. There is only one true solution, there is no way back from tonight.*

She shuddered as the high velocity rounds sliced through her, like a warm knife through butter, as did *Death*. They fell together, sliced down in a hail of bullets, landing beside one another beneath the *bleeding* crucifix above them. Her once sparkling eyes died like a candle in a thunder storm, and mirrored *Death's*…as they gazed to each other.

Chapter Seventeen

<u>Six months later.</u>

Ray sat alone in the graveyard, in the years he'd been coming to visit Nancy's grave, not once had he noticed the garden bench against the tree line to the right of her plot. It was cold, freezing in fact, but the golden December sun shone down on him, encouraging him to loosen his thick black winter coat, and remove his woolly hat to greet the sun face first. He gazed to the sky as he relaxed on the bench, once more enjoying his own company, but by no means content in his solitude.

"I'm glad it's all over." He whispered, choking back his tears. "I'm crying…but I'm not sad, I'm *finally* happy." He gazed at her grave and raised to his feet. "I wish I had my dog back," He muttered, standing beside her grave. "I wish I had *you* back for that matter, but that ship has sailed." He placed his cold hands on her black marble headstone, and closed his eyes.

There's nothing left to face, He thought. *I know the truth now, you're gone and I have to accept it…never again will I see your beautiful face, never will I kiss your lips and hold you tight…never will I get to say goodbye to you…my love, my Nancy. I just wish you could truly know how much I loved you, how much I cared for and needed you. Maybe the pain would be easier to bare if only I'd had the chance to say goodbye, to be with you as the lights went out and take away your suffering, to make sure you at least knew your life had mattered, and that you had made a difference, to everybody you touched, and me. You were special, and to live inside someone's heart after your death, is not to truly die, your memory lives on…and guides me through every single day of my life. Goodbye my darling wife, wherever you are…I hope you're well.*

"I understand it now." He cried. "I didn't truly appreciate what it was I had, until someone took it all away from me." He wiped the tears from his face with numb hands, and dropped to his knees. "You take so much for granted, it's easy to lose sight of the things that *really* matter. Life matters! Love matters! Relationships matter! But people's opinion of you *does not* matter…as long as you can look yourself in the mirror, and know in your heart, that you're a good person who cares for others…fuck 'em." He laughed a little to himself as he stroked her gold lettering.

"I met a young man," He whispered. "He taught me so much in the short time I knew him." He paused. "Truth be told, to this day I'm not really sure he even existed as he came and went like the breeze." He looked to the sky. "But I know in my heart he *did* exist, as he is the one who smashed through the skylight above the dance floor, and disappeared quite literally in a plume of smoke. He wasn't what you'd call an angel, or maybe…he was." He gazed at the clouds as they shielded the sun from him, in they moved from every angle and turned the sky to black, he quickly buttoned up his coat and retrieved his woolly hat from the pocket.

"But," He went on, pulling his hat tightly across his head. "Fact is…he showed me how to live, he showed me how to lift my head up and face the day." He peered around the graveyard and felt satisfied he was alone. He took out his wallet and flipped it open, in the clear plastic window was a picture taken long ago, of him and Nancy with their heads bowed together and smiling *seriously* for the camera in Ray's hand.

"I think you should have this now." He whispered, removing it from his wallet. "It's time for me to clean up my act, and that means clearing out my closet." He smiled as he removed a coin and held it out for *her* inspection.

"But before I decide," He muttered. "Let's let fate decide, because I kinda like this picture." He flipped the coin high in the air and watched it accelerate away from him, before gravity reversed it's momentum and dropped it back down towards his hand. It didn't land. He stared up to see a hand outstretched above his head, and the silhouette of a somehow familiar figure towering above him, with the sky as his background.

"Never let fate decide." He whispered, closing his hand tightly over the coin. "Fate is little more than a train of consequence on a journey to the unknown…be the master of your own *voyage*."

Ray gazed in wonderment at the figure before him. He fell back against the soft earth of Nancy's grave as he tried to see the man's face, although it wasn't easy since he wore a Stetson - which was pulled down to his eyes, and a storm coat pulled above his mouth, but the flowing black hair beneath the hats rim was a clear giveaway.

"Brandon?" He asked, already knowing the answer. "Tell me it's you!"

"Hello, Ray." He replied, nodding. "I heard what you said…I was moved."

"It's true." He whispered, climbing to his feet. "You taught me how to live again."

"Not that." He whispered. He gazed up to the forming clouds high above them and held himself in a hug, revealing to Ray his black nail polish. "I'm referring to your…*parting words*," He said. "They were…*beautiful*. It seems lessons have been learned."

"I have you to thank for that." He agreed. "I owe you much."

"You owe me nothing." He answered flatly. "You've sacrificed so much *already*."

"Then," Ray said, smiling. "You owe *me* much."

"Ask away." He whispered, gazing down at the object of Ray's constant affection.

"Why did Julianne say you didn't exist?"

He laughed at the question. "I'm dead, remember?" He whispered. "I couldn't let them see *me*, all they had to see was *Jeff*, and of course, you. Seeing me would've destroyed the whole illusion. They killed… the Black Widow, case closed."

"But who do they think he is?"

"They don't know." He smiled. "They have his body, but have *not* the answers."

"Why?" He asked. "He was laying right there, beside -"

"They concluded," He said sharply. "That *he* was an individual, with an obsession for the *Rose* twin's. That he was killing in their name and…" He paused. "…Bore a striking, almost uncanny resemblance to them both, which is why some witnesses believed there was in fact, three of us."

"And?"

"Case closed."

"Case closed?" He asked. "But it went wrong?"

"Well…that's a matter for debate." He whispered. "I set the stage for you, and you gave me *exactly* what I asked for." He pressed his palm against Ray's chest. "You gave me *heart and soul*…you gave me compassion."

"I thought I'd -"

"*Let me down?*"

"Yes." He whispered. "I thought I'd failed you."

"You're a gentle, kind and honourable man." He said. "There are others like you, but sadly, they hide in the shadows. You see, many people are just too afraid to be different, they're too afraid to be individual's as they fear ridicule, so they go with the flow, even though the *flow*, is swimming *against* the tide."

"And you?"

"Me?" He asked, clearly enjoying the December breeze. "I'm *still* running in the shadows, *still* blazing trails, and *still* avoiding the windows." He laughed.

"Where do we go from here?" Ray asked. "Will I see you again?"

"No." He replied, sensing Ray's sadness he continued. "You wont be *looking* for me."

"I'll *always* be looking for you." He said, staring at the photograph in his hand.

"No, Ray." He whispered. "You wont *remember* me."

"How can you say that?" He asked. "I owe my life to you, so… thank you." He reached out his hand to Brandon and fought the tears he knew were coming, luckily it had begun to rain.

"Everybody," He whispered, taking Ray's hand gently in his own. "Deserves a second chance." He squeezed tightly as he drew Ray in to his body. "Most people will take full advantage of any second chance they're given...whilst *others*, are destined to make the same choices over and over...and over...and over...and over..." His voice became quite hypnotic as Ray found himself once more, under the spell of *Brandon Rose*.

"What's..." He struggled to speak as *sleep* overpowered him like never before. "I feel..."

Brandon took hold of Ray's other hand and pressed his thumbs firmly into his wrists, he felt their pulses fuse almost immediately as Ray's body slumped against his own.

"It's not our actions that define us," He whispered. "But the memory of our actions in others." He smiled as he supported Ray's *sleeping* body against his own. "All that I am I gladly sacrifice"

"Where..." He muttered, slipping further away. "Where are... you?" His eyes jolted open under the crushing pain engulfing his chest, breath was a memory as he choked for air, and stared into the brilliant *whites* of Brandon's eyes.

"I wont be a minute..." Brandon whispered. "I...wont... be...a...minute..." His voice drew across the ages, resonating deeper and deeper as it echoed within Ray's cave like mind. "I............ wont............be............a............minute."

"Where..." He spluttered. "Am...I?" His eyes closed as his world faded, quite literally...to black.

"It's not where I'm going." He whispered, releasing Ray to gravity. "It's where you're going." He stood and watched as Ray fell helplessly to earth, arms outstretched he landed directly before Nancy's headstone, sleeping on her grave as the rain hurtled earthbound, and his life ebbed to nothing.

"**I WONT BE A MINUTE!**" Tick - Tock - Tick - Tock - Tick - Tock - Tick - Tock.

The words exploded like a starter's pistol against his ear, but the passing of subsequent seconds eluded him as he jolted to life with the sun shining on his face. His heart was jumping through his chest as he opened his eyes, fear and irrational panic gripped him severely as a slamming sound scared him *lucid*. He was home, although things were somehow different as he raised his hands to block out the filtered light, streaming through the blinds, passing through the impossibly *homely* living room, to find him dead on.

"What?" He asked, shifting violently in his recliner to see the dining suite to his left. "How's this happening?" He shouted. "What am I *learning* now?" He jumped to his feet and ran again to the window, instinctively he reached out to separate the blinds for an unhindered glance through the window.

"Not again!" He shouted. "It's never going to end!"

Tick - Tock - Tick - Tock - Tick - Tock - Tick - Tock - Tick - Tock - Tick - Tock - Tick

He clasped his hands tightly against his ears, to block out the hammer blows he believed were reigning down on his skull, and was momentarily distracted from the fact, that they had moved against his touch.

"I moved them!" He said, gripping them again. "I fucking moved them!" His excitement was short lived as *someone* caught his eye, *someone* was standing across the street, apparently directing him, rousing him into action…*slowly*. It was Brandon, his long hair was flowing beautifully, reflecting the radiant sunshine of December's *Indian* summer. He was shouting, but like a muted television set, he shouted *silently*, whilst banging his forefinger against the face of his watch…*slowly*.

Tick - Tock - Tick - Tock - Tick - Tock - Tick - Tock - Tick - Tock - Tick - Tock - Tick

He was clearly enraged and desperate as he pointed towards the end of Ray's road, his actions were drawn out and lethargic as he mouthed silently…*Run*. His long black coat whipped up occasionally in the breeze, as he drew Ray's attention once again to his watch.

"Nancy!" Ray shouted, listening as her parting words echoed through the timeless corridor that had become his life. He vaulted through the glass panelled front door, leaving it to swing wide and hit the wall. Ignoring Brandon completely, he charged down his road hell bent and eyes ablaze with rage. He quickly reached the junction at the bottom and turned left with astonishing pace, and there she was, a little further down and yet to take the step that would, if history was to be repeated, end her life. How beautiful she looked in her pink floral cardigan, and her favourite pair of jeans that showed off her slim, never ending legs. As he chased her desperately his tears travelled backwards and across his face, from the stream of wind he created for himself.

"Nancy!" He screamed, although drowned out by an otherworldly gust of wind. He charged relentlessly down the main road, passing three young boys as they rode their B.M.X's and gazed upon him excitedly. He caught a glimpse of her beautiful face as she stopped momentarily, before turning to step into the road.

"Don't!" He shouted. "Stay there…Stay there!" Again, his best efforts were drowned out, although this time not by a gust of wind, *otherworldly* or *otherwise*, but by the roaring of an engine, the engine propelling the mammoth cruiser about to smash the very life from her eyes. It was louder now, ringing in his ears like a jet engine reaching rotation, but there were no sirens, and a distinct absence of the mythical *blue Ford Taurus* he'd heard so much about. Her lips were pursed together as she stepped out, about to release the final breath she would ever have as the noise closed in on her. Time stopped as he realised he was too late to stop *her*, his heart ached as he watched her freeze in the snarling cruiser's path, so much so he hadn't realised, his hands were finally on her. But the noise, had arrived. Snatching her to safety, he reeled her in like a fish on a hook and shielded her from the chaos he now knew was about to unfold, as it was no longer one engine, it was two.

He gazed in horror, as an equally thunderous black Dodge Charger met it head on in an explosion of twisted metal, and shattered lives. And if it was at all possible for the smoke filled wind to whisper, whisper it did, from *Brandon's* lips…to Ray's ears.

Time can not be collected in a jar, nor can it be locked in a vault, or stored in an account, yet so many talk of 'saving time.' Time is not for saving, it is for spending, but spend it wisely my friend, as a day in your life is a dollar in your pocket: Once spent, you'll never see it again. Remain eternal in the memory of others, embrace creation and blaze trails. Live in the now and release the past…to gravity.

Brandon Rose.

My Name Is Death

With many thanks and great appreciation, Julia Collins for unwavering belief in this project. You have been there for me during many highs and many lows and for this I am forever in your debt - you are a true friend. Terry Hall, for keeping me smiling during those times when it didn't seem possible. Hayley Sale, for your hours dedicated and tireless contribution - you have been an asset to this project, my deepest thanks. Jim Hamley, thank you for being original - you are an inspiration to many. Thanks also to Alan Rice, for putting up with my shit for longer than I (or you) care to remember. And finally to the people over the years who've provided invaluable wisdom relating to the human condition, inspiration takes many forms and sadly not all are positive, but I thank you too.

About the Author

Alan was born into a working class family in Liverpool. He originally had the idea for this book fifteen years ago but put it to one side to continue his journey through life and develop the idea further. Alan has captured many elements of the human condition and fused them with both joy and rage. The result of which is his breathtaking first novel. It makes you laugh, cry and realise life is for living. Being a creative person it was always his dream to bring his idea to any like minded individuals and to those who share his passion for creation.

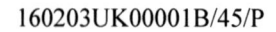